COMPROMISING THE BILLIONAIRE

The Winters Saga
Book Nine

IVY LAYNE

GINGER QUILL PRESS, LLC

Compromising the Billionaire

Find out more about the author and upcoming books online at www.ivylayne.com

Contents

Also by Ivy Layne

Don't Miss Out on New Releases, Exclusive Giveaways, and More!!

Join Ivy's Readers Group @ ivylayne.com/readers

THE HEARTS OF SAWYERS BEND

Stolen Heart

Sweet Heart

Scheming Heart

Rebel Heart

Wicked Heart

THE UNTANGLED SERIES

Unraveled

Undone

Uncovered

The Winters Saga

The Billionaire's Secret Heart (Novella)

The Billionaire's Secret Love (Novella)

The Billionaire's Pet

The Billionaire's Promise

The Rebel Billionaire

The Billionaire's Secret Kiss (Novella)

The Billionaire's Angel

Engaging the Billionaire

Compromising the Billionaire

The Counterfeit Billionaire

The Billionaire Club

The Wedding Rescue

The Courtship Maneuver

The Temptation Trap

Chapter One

Aiden

"You wanted to see me, sir?"

She hovered in the doorway, balanced on her toes as if preparing to flee. In her crisp navy suit and tightly pinned chignon, Violet Hartwell was the picture of a corporate professional.

I gestured to the chair on the other side of my desk and said, "Yes, Ms. Hartwell, please sit down."

I waited until she took the seat in front of me, smoothing her skirt demurely and crossing her feet at the ankle. She met my eyes with one bold look before dropping them to the surface of my desk.

Interesting.

She was daring enough to apply for a job at Winters Incorporated using a fake name. Daring enough to sneak around poking in my files. But not daring enough to look me in the eyes.

That was probably for the best. I had a plan and her eyes were a distraction. I wasn't going to get sidetracked trying to decide exactly what shade they were. Somewhere between the deep blue of a summer sky and the lavender of dusk.

Not important. She was here so I could figure out what she was doing in my company, not think about her eyes.

"Ms. Hartwell, you've been with us for what—two months now?" I asked, shuffling through the papers on my desk as if reviewing her résumé. I wasn't. The papers had nothing to do with Violet, but she didn't know that.

"Yes, sir," she said, politely and carefully.

"And you're enjoying your work with Winters, Inc. so far?"

"Yes, sir," she said again, meeting my eyes with a quick, wary glance.

She was nervous.

She should be.

"Your supervisor says you're sharp, detail oriented, and able to juggle multiple projects easily."

That hadn't been all he'd said. According to Carlisle, Violet Hartwell was ice-cold, with laser focus. A perfect machine, contained and efficient. Polite, but not friendly. Distant. Reserved. He hadn't been happy to hear I planned to steal her from his division.

"That's very flattering, sir," she said, her eyes scanning the surface of my desk.

What was she looking for? She was hyper-alert, those dusky lavender eyes taking in every detail, from the way I'd arranged my pencils to the labels on the manila folders beside my monitor.

Ever since a second review of her paperwork had pinged Security's attention, I'd had my eye on her. I was almost positive she wasn't working for a rival company. If one of my rivals sent in a spy, they would have made damn sure the ID would hold up.

Security had been watching, monitoring her trips to the file room, taking note of her attempts to hack into my email. She was better than I would have expected from an amateur, but my security team was the best.

I could have fired her. That was the easiest solution to the problem of Violet Hartwell, or whatever her name was.

I should have fired her. I had too much going on, to deal with her myself.

I'd decided to have Security deliver the news and escort her from the building. Then, either by happy accident or some plan on her part, we'd shared an elevator for six floors.

I can't remember the last time I was so acutely aware of a woman.

A strand of her icy blonde hair had escaped its twist to curl around her ear. She'd snuck sideways glances at me from those captivating eyes as she pretended to review one of the files she carried, putting so much effort into ignoring me that I couldn't look away.

I couldn't tear my eyes from the curve of her ass in her sedate navy suit, the length of her legs ending in a pair of dangerously high heels. The suit was boxy, more professional than feminine, but it couldn't hide the generous breasts beneath her primly buttoned blouse.

She'd smelled of flowers. Sweet peas, like the kind that grew on the arbor in the back gardens of Winters House. Sweet peas that brought back cool spring mornings, the simple joy of playing in the woods with my brothers and cousins as a child. It knocked me off balance to have the nostalgic scent wreathed around the target of an internal investigation.

In an instant, she'd shifted from nuisance to puzzle, and I wanted the answer. Who was this woman with the bombshell body beneath the professional façade? Why was she at Winters, Inc.? And why was she so interested in me?

I watched her sitting on the other side of my desk and waited to see if she would fill the silence between us. Most people did, unable to help themselves, babbling on and on just to fill the empty space with words. I can't tell you how much I've learned just by keeping my mouth shut at the right time.

Violet was immune to my ploy. Her hands rested in her lap, fingers laced together, a neutral expression on her face. She would have been all cool composure if not for the avid curiosity in her eyes as she studied the surface of my desk. She wanted to know what I was doing. That's why she was here. And that's why she was going to give me exactly what I wanted.

"Violet, have you heard I've been looking for a new administrative assistant?"

"No, sir, I hadn't heard. Don't you already have a staff of four?" The first thread of trepidation wound through her voice.

"I do," I agreed. "But I find that even four of them can't keep up, and I've been interested in adding a fifth. I asked my department heads to keep an eye out for a suitable candidate and Carlisle recommended you."

I hid my surge of triumph as her eyes went wide with shock. She hadn't seen that coming. But you know what they say—keep your friends close, and your enemies closer.

Violet Hartwell wanted information about me. I was going to give it to her, and then I was going to watch every single thing she did until I figured out her game.

She thought she could get the best of me.

Soon enough she'd learn how wrong she was.

"I appreciate being considered," she said, smoothly, "but I don't think I'm qualified. I'm a project manager and—"

"Carlisle seemed confident that your skills would transition perfectly to fit my needs. Are you saying you're not interested? It's quite a promotion."

Not so much a promotion as a trap.

To a legitimate employee, working in my inner circle would be a dream come true. I'm Aiden Winters, CEO of Winters Incorporated. Most top-tier business school graduates would commit murder for the chance to take one of those desks outside my office.

For just a second, before her cool façade slipped back into place, Violet looked like she was ready to bolt. I couldn't help but enjoy the irony. She couldn't say no because turning down the opportunity of a lifetime would draw far too much attention and attention was the last thing she wanted.

From what my investigations had uncovered, Violet wanted to be left alone to quietly do her job and snoop around on me in her spare time. A promotion to my personal team would make that impossible.

Her eyes flared wider, their gorgeous purple shade vibrant against her creamy skin. When they narrowed, I knew that she knew. Carlisle had only good things to say about Violet, that was true, but she'd done nothing that would justify such a major promotion.

There was only one reason I would offer it to her: *If I was on to her game.*

She'd just figured that out.

Her eyes met mine, and behind that neutral expression, I saw the burn of defiance. I'd wondered if she'd quit rather than face exposure. I was about to get my answer, and I had a feeling it would be the one I was waiting for.

"I...I'd be honored, S-sir," she said, with just that slightest hitch before her words fell into place. It shouldn't make my cock twitch every time she called me 'sir', but it did. So cool. So contained.

There was a world of meaning in the way she said 'sir'. I wanted to hear it again, over and over. And now I would.

I was the spider to her fly. I'd have plenty of time to learn everything I wanted to know about Violet Hartwell.

I stood and held out my hand, forcing Violet to stand as well. Her slim fingers slid across my palm, her grip surprisingly firm, her skin soft and warm. As she leaned forward a wave of sweet pea-scented air drifted to me. I caught a glimpse of the shadow of her cleavage before she straightened.

Yes.

I was going to learn everything I wanted to know about Violet Hartwell.

Everything.

"You have a 3 o'clock meeting with Human Resources to discuss your new position, salary, increased benefits, and the rest. I'll expect you to start here tomorrow morning."

"But my projects—"

I cut her off with a wave of my hand. "Carlisle has everything under control. Tomorrow, Ms. Hartwell."

She gave a brisk nod and turned for the door, her chin jutting up just a little, that hint of defiance leaking out. With her back to me, I didn't try to hide my in-depth study of the way her ass swayed when she walked. If she looked this good in that modest suit, I couldn't wait to see what she looked like naked. If things went the way I planned, sooner or later I would.

I was so distracted by Violet's ass I didn't notice my cousin Gage until he stepped into the room and pinned me with a hard look. Shutting the door behind him, he crossed the room and dropped into the chair Violet had so recently vacated.

"What the fuck, Aid? You were staring at her ass like you were going to leap over your desk and jump her. Isn't she an employee? She's in Carlisle's division, right? Did she come on when we acquired the company we folded in or is she new?"

I sat and leaned back in my chair, crossing my arms over my chest, not even trying to hide my grin of satisfaction.

"She's new. She came on about five weeks after we acquired CD4 Analytics. She had experience in data mining and project management, and Carlisle said she's been an ideal employee."

"But?" Gage probed.

"But her paperwork doesn't wash. We didn't pick it up when we hired her or she never would have gotten the job, but the security review caught something off with her last name. We've been watching her. She's been looking at files that have nothing to do with her division. Trying to hack email."

"Do you know who sent her in?" Gage asked.

"I think she's working for herself."

"What does she want?"

"That's the interesting thing," I said. "So far she seems to want me. She's poking into my emails. My files. I decided the best way to deal with her was to give her exactly what she wants."

Gage leaned forward. "I don't like this, Aiden. If she lied on her application, fire her. If she's digging around where she shouldn't be, fire her. Don't bring her into your inner circle."

"I have a plan," I said, trying to deflect.

Gage ignored me. "I saw the way you were looking at her. I've never known you to get involved with an employee. It's asking for trouble, and you know it. We have a zero-tolerance policy for harassment here. You know that, you set the fucking policy."

"I set the fucking policy because we are not that kind of company. But Violet Hartwell is not a regular employee. She's a spy, here under false pretenses, and whatever she wants, it has to do with me. You should have seen her face when I offered her the job. I thought she was going to bolt from the room. She was happy, buried in Carlisle's division digging away for whatever it is she wants to find. Now she has to deal with me."

"I don't like this," Gage said again. "Why don't you just put the Sinclairs on her, find out what she's up to, and then fire her. I can't emphasize enough the part about firing her."

"Oh, I put the Sinclairs on her. Cooper hasn't uncovered her real name yet, but the condo she's living in is owned by a shell company, and the real owner is unknown. We'll find out."

"You're not firing her because you want to investigate her? Or because you want to fuck her?" Gage asked, studying me with curiosity.

I couldn't blame him. I was all business. Outside of my family, this company was my life. I would destroy anyone who threatened it. But Gage knew me better than anyone, and he'd already figured me out.

"Both," I admitted. "She's not off the table because she's not a real employee. At best she's a spy. At worst she's a criminal. Either way, she's fair game."

"You have women lined up to date you. Why don't you go fuck one of them?"

"I have," I said. "I'm bored."

Gage gave me the smug smile of a man who went home every night to the warm bed of the woman he loved. Gage and Sophie were newly married, and so far it looked like the honeymoon would never end. They lived with me in Winters House, our family home. The place was huge, and still I managed to walk in on them at least once a day. They couldn't keep their hands off each other.

On top of that, I'd been watching my cousin Annalise falling head over heels for her first love, had watched every other member of my sprawling family pair up, and if I was being totally honest, all that love and devotion had left me feeling restless.

I was happy for them. No, I wasn't happy. I was fucking ecstatic. Our family had been through more than its share of rough times. All the money and power in the world can't fight death. It can't undo murder.

We'd lost Gage's parents when we were children, and then my own when we were teenagers.

The Winters family had been plagued by scandal and loss and grief for too many years. The only thing that made it better was seeing the people I loved find their own happiness, one by one.

Gage was right, I never had any trouble finding a date. I was adept at fending off the fortune hunters, and when I wanted a woman, I had one. Lately, the idea of taking out one of my regular companions had lost its luster.

Maybe it was all that true love in the air, but I wanted something different. Not what my family had. Not what Gage had.

Winters, Inc. was wife, mistress, and child all in one. After my family, the company had been my sole focus since my father had died. I had no plans to change that. I didn't want to fall in love. I didn't need a relationship. I just wanted something...different.

"What do you mean, you're bored?" Gage asked. I should have known he wasn't going to let me off the hook.

I shrugged a shoulder and tried not to think of that peek of Violet's cleavage. Getting her into bed would be tricky. She was smart, and she was on her guard. She hadn't given me a single sign that she was attracted to me, but that shell of hers was so well practiced, I already knew I'd have to work for it.

Good.

I liked a challenge.

Knowing Gage wouldn't give up, I went on, "I'm intrigued, okay? She's not a corporate spy, but she's up to something. She's looking for information on me, but when I offered her the chance to work by my side, she balked. I want to know why. If I can talk her into bed while I'm figuring it out, all the better."

Gage let out a sigh of defeat. "She's your type, that's for sure."

"I don't have a type," I said.

"Really? So she's not a carbon copy of Elizabeth?"

No one in my family had liked my first wife. If I tried to look at Violet objectively, I could see why Gage would say that. She had the same cool composure as Elizabeth, the same icy blonde hair, even the same elegant sense of style.

But Elizabeth had been cold to her core, something I wished I'd found out before I married her. Violet was an entirely different creature. I'd seen that hint of defiance, the way she'd raised her chin when she strode out of my office.

She was scared and against the ropes, but she wouldn't give in.

Elizabeth was a stone sculpture, hard and frigid all the way through.

Not Violet.

I'd glimpsed the woman hiding behind the mask.

There was passion beneath that perfect exterior.

I was going to expose it.

And I wasn't going to justify myself to anyone.

"She's not Elizabeth, Gage," I said with finality. "I've got this under control."

"That's what you say now." He stood. "I'm keeping an eye out for complaints to HR. If this ends up in a lawsuit, I'm letting you swing."

"It won't," I promised. "I'm giving her exactly what she wants. Me."

Chapter Two

Violet

Crap.

Crap, crap, crap.

I strode out of Aiden Winters's office, ignoring the curious glances of his executive assistants, and pressed the button for the elevator with a steady hand. No one watching would suspect that I was a breath away from completely freaking out. I stepped into the empty elevator and held the half smile on my lips until the door slid shut.

Then I collapsed into the corner, pressing my hot cheek to the cool metal wall, and tried not to hyperventilate.

He knew. There wasn't a question in my mind. Aiden Winters knew I was there under false pretenses. He knew I was up to something. He probably knew my name wasn't Violet Hartwell.

And he hadn't fired me. Instead, he'd moved me to a position where he could keep an eye on me.

Crap.

As the elevator slid down, floor by floor, I wracked my brain for any reason Aiden might have for giving me such a coveted job. None of them were good.

He wanted to catch me in the act.

He wanted to figure out why I was there.

The elevator doors slid open and I fixed my customary, cool half smile on my face. Just because I was on the edge of a panic attack didn't mean anyone else had to know. I made it down the hall and around the corner to my tiny office without anyone stopping me. I usually worked with my door open, but today I closed it firmly before dropping into my desk chair.

The only sensible choice was to quit.

I should pack up my desk, go home, and never come back. My plan had been a little crazy to begin with. This was so totally unlike me, I could hardly believe what I'd done when I'd applied for the job. And when Carlisle had hired me, I'd accepted before I could think better of it.

I'd just been so angry. Aiden Winters, and Winters Incorporated, had stolen Chase's company. And they were going to give it back. I just had to figure out how to force Aiden's hand. Somewhere around here there had to be something, some evidence of his misdeeds, proof of the kind of man he really was.

And when I had it, I'd use that proof to force Aiden to give Chase his company back.

I squeezed my eyes shut tight and rolled my head back. When I opened them, I was staring at the ceiling, squinting a little at the fluorescent light above and wondering how the hell I ever thought my plan was going to work. Had I imagined Aiden Winters would leave his diary laying out on his desk, open to a page about other companies he'd stolen or a confession that he'd cheated on his taxes?

No, I wasn't that naïve. But I'd figured that once I got into his email I'd find something. No one was completely innocent. People were rarely what they seemed to be. If I'd had any illusions about the world of business, I'd lost them after my first job. Still, I hadn't thought it would be this hard to dig up a little dirt on Aiden Winters.

I was running out of time. Chase would be home from his consulting job in a matter of weeks, and if he found out what I was up to...I wasn't going to think about that.

If I were smart, I'd cut my losses and get the heck out of here. I'd been holding my own in Carlisle's department, my inadequate skills in project management and data mining bolstered by the time I'd spent working for Chase before Winters, Inc. had cheated him out of his company.

This was not my dream job. I was a bookkeeper, and I liked it. I missed my smooth, clean columns of numbers, familiar software. I missed sorting receipts and tracking down errant payments and bills. I didn't want to be a project manager, and I absolutely didn't want to be Aiden Winters's executive assistant.

I should quit. Go home and start putting out résumés for a real job. One I was qualified for. A job that didn't have the potential to land me in jail if I got caught breaking into confidential files or hacking email.

A brisk knock sounded on my door and I let out a barely audible *eep* before pulling myself together and turning my chair to see my supervisor, Carlisle, in the open doorway.

"So, how did it go?" he asked.

"Mr. Winters offered me a position as his fifth executive assistant," I said, smoothing my skirt over my knees. "He said you recommended me."

"I did, though I have to admit I was hoping he'd pick someone else. You've been an asset to this department. We'll be sorry to lose you."

"Thank you. It's going to be an adjustment."

Carlisle gave a slow nod, and I didn't miss the speculation in his eyes. I couldn't tell him that I didn't want to take the job, and he was too polite to point out that I wasn't qualified for it in the first place.

I was sure he wanted to ask what was going on, but my stiff, formal demeanor held him back. I wasn't friendly or easy-going. Not in general, and especially not in the office.

Friendliness was not a quality prized in our household when I was growing up. Composure was our highest ideal. Never reveal emotion. Never let anyone know what you're thinking. Hide your flaws and show only perfection.

Carlisle was a nice guy from what I'd seen, and I wanted to confide in him. Not about my true reason for taking the job. I wasn't an idiot. I wanted to tell him that I was intimidated by Aiden Winters and afraid I wouldn't be up for the task, and that I'd really rather stay exactly where I was.

Except I couldn't say any of that.

First of all, because that kind of confession was so far from my normal behavior I suspected if I opened my mouth to speak no sound would come out.

And second, because if I did manage to confide in my supervisor, and if he did feel sorry for me and intercede on my behalf, Aiden would tell him I was an imposter and kick me out on my ass.

I was on my own, and if I had any hope of succeeding at my task I had to keep cool and stay focused.

So Aiden wanted to keep an eye on me?

Let him.

I'd figure out a way to work around him.

No man with that much power, that much money,

could truly be a good person. I'd met enough men like him to know the truth. He could be compromised. I just had to keep looking for a way in.

I let a detached, polite smile curve my mouth. "I have an appointment with HR in two hours, but before I leave I'll make sure I put together a summary of my current projects so whoever steps in will be up to date."

Carlisle's eyes flicked away for a long moment before they met mine. "That would be helpful. I'm assuming he wants you to start tomorrow."

"He does," I confirmed.

"Violet," Carlisle said. I raised my eyebrows and looked up at him expectantly. He opened his mouth to speak, then snapped it shut. When he opened it again, he only said, "Stay on your toes with Winters. This is...unusual. You've been a hard worker and like I said, I'm sorry to lose you. Just stay alert, that's all."

"Is there something I should know?" I asked. I didn't like his hesitation or his concern.

Carlisle let out a huff of air and shook his head. "Not exactly, it's just that Winters's assistants are known for being cutthroat. Territorial. I know you can take care of yourself, but just keep an eye out, okay?"

"Of course," I said, coolly, my heart sinking.

Great.

Perfect.

So now I didn't just have to deal with Aiden Winters, I'd also have to fend off his rabid pack of executive assistants.

"Good luck, Violet," Carlisle said, before smacking his hand against my doorframe twice and shutting the door behind him.

Good luck.

I had a feeling I was going to need it.

The meeting with HR took over an hour. I signed papers and nodded along as I was updated on the changes to my salary, benefits, and title. By the time I got back to my desk, a headache was brewing behind my eyes. I ignored it and settled in to finish updating my project notes.

Again, I thought wistfully of my old job in the accounting department at CD4 Analytics, before Aiden Winters had cheated Chase out of his company and kicked him to the curb. Every single employee had been fired. Aiden had wanted Chase's technology and his contracts. The rest—the people, the years Chase had spent building CD4—none of that had mattered to Aiden Winters.

I'd loved that job, but it was gone, and if I walked out of this office and looked for another one like it, I'd lose my chance to get Chase his company back. I owed him too much to give up now.

It was well past dinner when I finished wrapping up the details of my project management work. Before I left for the day, I decided to take another trip through Aiden's emails. Maybe I'd get lucky and find something.

After an hour of scanning through endless communications about acquisitions, employee issues, budgets, and spreadsheets, my head was killing me, and I was no closer to finding dirt on Aiden Winters than I had been my first day on the job.

I knew his business emails were succinct, direct, and always on-topic. He didn't share off-color jokes or make inappropriate comments. He didn't forward questionable emails and when he received an email with any of the above, his reply promptly shut it down and brought the discussion back on track.

Only in his messages to his family did his professional composure fall away. There he never hesitated to joke, tease, or bust someone's chops. It was clear that he loved his family, and despite the long hours he worked, they seemed close. If I'd hoped his banter with any of them would give me the smoking gun I needed, so far I'd been disappointed.

My stomach twisting with hunger, I retrieved the empty box I'd grabbed from the copy room and packed the meager personal contents of my desk. My favorite red stapler I brought with me to every job. My coffee mug. The cactus Chase had given me for my birthday the year before, saying it reminded him of me: prickly on the outside, protecting my soft insides.

Most people who knew me would laugh at that description. Not the prickly part. They'd tell you I was anything but soft. I'd been called a lot of names—ice queen, frigid, you can probably guess the rest. Never soft.

Only Chase really knew me and that was fine. I wasn't looking to make friends. Especially not here. Not at this job.

I slung my purse over my shoulder, hefted the half-full box in my arms. The rest of the floor was deserted when I made my way to the elevator. I pressed the button, expecting a short wait. I stood there, staring up at the number ten illuminated above my head. The executive floor.

Maybe I should take the stairs.

I considered hiking my way down seven floors in these heels, carrying a box. It had been a long day. My head was killing me, I was dying for food, and the last thing I wanted was to negotiate seven flights of stairs in four-inch heels. I just wanted to go home, have a glass of wine with my leftover spaghetti, and binge watch some TV.

Before I had a chance to make a decision about the

stairs, the whir of the elevator sounded through the closed doors. The light above moved from ten to nine to eight. Seven had barely illuminated when the doors slid open to reveal Aiden Winters, his arms crossed over his chest, leaning against the back wall. He didn't look surprised to see me.

Chapter Three

Violet

Double crap.

I hadn't liked dealing with Aiden before, with my shields up. I definitely didn't want anything to do with him now when I was tired and hungry and exhausted. Pretending I was none of those things, I stepped into the elevator and lifted my chin in his direction.

"Mr. Winters," I said, and looked to the number panel beside the door. P1 was lit. My parking spot was two floors below. I started to shift the box in my arms so I could hit the button when Aiden stepped in front of me and hit it for me. Of course, he knew where I parked. He probably knew my bra size.

At that thought, I swallowed. Hard. Based on the way his eyes had lingered on my breasts when he'd shaken my hand earlier, I had a feeling if he tried to guess my bra size he wouldn't be far off.

"Looking forward to starting your new position tomorrow?" Aiden asked, back to leaning against the wall of the elevator, his brown eyes locked on my face. There was something lurking there, and I suspected it was a laugh. He had me cornered, and he knew it.

"Of course," I said, raising my eyes to his. "I appreciate the opportunity."

"Oh, I'm sure you do," he said, not even trying to hide the amusement in his voice.

This was bad. I looked away, fixing my gaze on the closed door of the elevator, wishing it would move faster. How could we not be at P1 already?

The elevator stopped on two and the doors opened to admit two marketing executives I knew by face, but not name. They nodded to Aiden and me as they filed in. Aiden took the opportunity to step closer, giving them the side of the elevator he'd vacated. He stood beside me, the light wool of his suit coat brushing my arm.

There were layers of fabric between us, but I could feel the heat of his body. A warm, woodsy scent surrounded me. Not cologne. More like soap and man. He shouldn't smell this good. I tried to ignore the way my heart thumped harder as I breathed him in.

I did not need this.

I did not need to be aware of Aiden Winters as a man. I had enough trouble as it was. Not that I would do anything about it.

Obviously.

That would be beyond foolish. While my plan was admittedly not the best idea I'd ever had, I wasn't a fool.

I mean, I could see that Aiden was attractive. Objectively speaking, he was beautiful. Handsome. Smoking hot. Dark hair with hints of auburn. Warm, bittersweet chocolate eyes fringed by thick lashes. Strong cheekbones and luscious lips.

He was tall, I guessed 6'3" or 6'4", with broad shoulders

and a powerful build. I knew he worked late almost every night and was in early, but somewhere in his busy day, he had to find time to work out because there wasn't a hint of anything soft about him. No padding under his chin or roundness to his belly. He was all lean strength and tightly coiled energy.

At 5'8" I was a little taller than average and still he loomed over me, even in my heels. Just standing beside him, I felt surrounded. The elevator came to a stop at P1 and the two marketing executives stepped off.

Aiden did not.

I gave no hint of the spike of panic in my chest or the way my empty stomach clenched tight. Why was he still in the elevator? All the executives parked on P1. What did he want from me?

Ugh, stupid question. He probably planned to stare me down until I collapsed in a quivering mass of guilt and nerves and confessed everything.

Good luck, Mr. Winters. Scarier men than him had tried to stare me down and failed.

I fell back on the cool smile I'd perfected when I was under pressure and said, "Did you lose your car, Mr. Winters?"

"You can call me Aiden, Violet," he said, turning a little to face me, his posture inviting me to do the same.

I ignored the offer of intimacy, noticing that he hadn't asked permission to use my first name. Earlier he'd referred to me as Ms. Hartwell.

He was trying to unsettle me.

It was working.

"No thank you, Mr. Winters. I prefer formality in an office setting."

I heard a low sound in his throat and couldn't stop my

eyes from flashing up to his. I almost took a step back at the heat I saw simmering there.

I wanted out of this elevator and away from Aiden Winters.

Suddenly, I wasn't sure I could do this. Maybe there was another way we could get Chase his company back. We could sue, or...but we'd been through that already. I never would have jumped into a ridiculous scheme like this one if we hadn't already exhausted all of our other options.

I just needed a little more time.

I wasn't going to run scared until I'd gotten what I needed.

The doors opened on P3 and I stepped out, more than ready to leave Aiden Winters behind for the day. He followed, keeping pace beside me as I walked down the long row to my car.

"Are you stalking me, Mr. Winters? I know you didn't park here."

"Not stalking you, Violet," he said, that laugh still lurking beneath his words. "Just walking you to your car."

"Is that a service you offer all of your executive assistants?" I asked, tartly.

"On occasion, if necessary."

"I was told the parking garage was secure. No dark corners here," I said, raising my head to take in the abundance of LED lights in the ceiling. Much like the rest of the Winters, Inc. building, the parking garage was immaculate and brightly lit. It was probably safer than the gated parking behind the condo I lived in.

"Oh, it's secure," Aiden affirmed. "Still, I like to be thorough."

There was no hiding the suggestive meaning in his words. I fought a shiver as my brain flashed through all the ways Aiden Winters could be thorough. I don't think I'd ever been so grateful to see my car.

Surprise stole his laughter when we stopped behind my electric blue Volkswagen Beetle. I had daisies appliquéd on the back window and a pink-haired troll doll hung from the rearview mirror. The car was cute, spunky, and seriously fun to drive.

I'd made a dent in my savings account buying it a few years before. Most people would think it wasn't me, but I knew different. Maybe my Beetle didn't match my outside, but it went with my inside just fine.

I ignored Aiden's considering gaze and unlocked the doors, carefully fitting the cardboard box in the back beside my purse before opening the driver's door and preparing to get in. Sending Aiden a dismissive glance over my shoulder I said, "We're at my car. You can go now."

"I'll see you tomorrow, Violet. Don't be late."

My hands were steady as I slid the key into the ignition, but my heart was pounding so hard I was sure he could hear it. He stepped back from my parking space and dropped his hands into his suit pockets, waiting, watching, as I put the car in gear and pulled out. I felt his eyes on me as I drove away.

Thirty minutes later I'd changed into yoga pants and a T-shirt and was waiting in front of the microwave for my frozen dinner, a glass of wine in hand. I'd pulled the pins from my hair and washed my face.

Professional Violet was gone, left in the closet and bedroom along with my suit and hairpins and makeup.

Alone in the condo, there was no one to see. I didn't have to be perfect. For a little while, at least, I could just be me—messy and emotional and scared to death. In the morning, I was going to get up, put on my armor and carry that box up to the tenth floor where I was going to take my position as Aiden Winters's newest executive assistant.

I couldn't afford to be messy, emotional, or scared.

Not until this was over.

After a night of fitful sleep, I opened my eyes to the blare of my alarm and a suffocating sense of dread. It wasn't too late to quit. I didn't even have to quit, I could simply not go back. I could just stay here, holed up in the condo until I found a new job, one far away from Winters, Inc.

I could forget about CD4 Analytics and justice for Chase.

Except that I couldn't. Chase had always looked out for me. He always had my back. He'd worked so hard building that company. I had to try to fix this.

There was no way Aiden Winters was innocent. I just had to keep looking and I would find what I needed.

Resolved, I dragged myself out of bed and into the shower. The scent of sweet peas, flowery and clean, woke up my brain and I went about the business of erasing the Violet who left her hair loose and wore yoga pants and bought a bright blue Volkswagen Beetle.

I pulled my hair back into a tight chignon and dressed in my plainest, most severely professional black suit, embellished simply by pearls at my ears and around my neck. Only my dangerously high heels gave a nod to any sense of feminine fashion.

I got off the elevator on the tenth floor to see the first desk, the one normally occupied by the most junior of Aiden's assistants, unoccupied. The other four executive assistants were already there, their desks arranged in a quadrangle, facing each other.

That they intended to exclude me couldn't have been

more obvious, but just in case I missed the message, all four of them studiously ignored my entrance.

Fine. I wasn't here to make friends.

More than that, I could see where they'd be irritated. I didn't have an MBA. I hadn't fought tooth and nail for the opportunity to work side-by-side with Aiden Winters. I'd been plucked from project management in a new division for no reason anyone but Aiden and I could fathom.

I might have understood their attitude, but I wasn't going to put up with it.

Setting my box of things on the empty desk, I turned to face the others and said, "I'm Violet Hartwell. I'm assuming Mr. Winters told you I'd be joining you?"

The one closest to me, a dark-haired man in his mid-20s with a rumpled shirt and a cup of coffee at his elbow gave me a sideways look and said, "Sure. I'm Thomas." Pointing at the other executive assistants in turn, he said, "that's Marisela, Henry, and Peter."

The other three gave me cool nods but stayed silent. Thomas went on, "Until you're assigned specific work, you can answer phones and do the filing. Notes on phone protocol are in the top drawer of your desk. Coffee, copier, and fax are in there." Thomas gestured to an open door on the far side of the room. "The rest of us have full plates, so don't expect us to hold your hand."

"Understood," I said. Turning my back to them, I unpacked my things. I desperately wanted to put my coffee mug to use, but I had a feeling that phone was going to start ringing any minute, and I had no idea what *phone protocol* involved. I pulled the file from the top drawer and began to read.

I'd handled at least a dozen calls, most of them correctly, and finished reading the protocol file before I gave in to the need for caffeine. Standing from the desk, I picked up my mug and said to the room, "I'm getting coffee. Cover the phones for a few minutes."

I knew better than to wait for agreement. I doubted any of them would ignore Aiden's phone while I was away from my desk, but asking permission to get coffee would be a mistake.

They already hated me. If they thought they could bully me, my life would be a misery.

The coffee machine was sleek, high-end, and I was pretty sure it could make any coffee drink on earth. Unfortunately, I had no idea how to make that happen. I stood in front of the touchpad and screen, squinting as if that would make the button's purpose clear.

Normally I'd ask a coworker for help, but not today. Not when my coworkers looked like they'd be just as happy to poison me as help me make a cup of coffee. I pressed a few experimental buttons, one that looked like a mug of coffee and another that looked like it would add cream, and listened to the voices filtering in from the outer office.

"I can't believe we have to put up with her," a female voice said. Marisela.

"I pulled up her résumé. She's got no business sitting at that desk," a male voice put in. Not Thomas.

"She must be fucking him. How else would she have gotten the job? He doesn't even need another assistant." Marisela again.

"Her?" That was Thomas. "The ice queen? No way. I'd be surprised if she fucked anyone, much less the boss."

The other assistant, the one who hadn't spoken yet said, "You guys know Winters doesn't do that. I've got no clue why he would have hired her, but there's no way he's sleeping with her."

"Probably not," Marisela agreed. "Anyway, she'd have to melt enough to pry her legs apart. She won't last long."

"And hey," said the one who'd stood up for Aiden, "now we have someone to stick with the phones, and the files, and whatever other grunt work we don't want to do."

At that insight, the conversation ended. They probably thought sticking me with the phones and the filing was a punishment. If I'd actually wanted the job, it would have been. As things were, I was more than happy to be out of the loop. That just gave me more time to dig around on the computer and in the file room. If they were going to freeze me out, I'd have a better chance to continue my investigations.

I left the small break room with a cup of black coffee. Not quite what I'd been going for, but it was caffeine and it smelled like heaven. My four coworkers studiously ignored me, and I returned the favor.

The ice queen comments used to sting. I was over it. When I was alone, or with Chase, I could relax. Laugh. Sometimes I was almost fun.

Around other people I froze up, my shyness translating into a chilly formality I could never quite break down. I'd had friends in college, girlfriends, even dated some. It had been easier back then, finally away from home and surrounded by other kids trying their wings for the first time.

Maybe if things had gone differently at that first job, maybe if everything that came after, with my boss and my parents had worked out, maybe then I'd be different. Maybe I'd be better at joking around and laughing. Maybe I'd be able to loosen up. Make mistakes.

But things hadn't gone differently. I'd spent my entire life trying to make my parents happy—trying to be perfect—

and the first time I made a mistake my life had fallen apart. When the dust settled, all I had left was Chase. He was the only one I could trust.

I wouldn't take that risk again. Not with my heart. Not even with friendship. The only person I trusted was Chase. Everyone else was on the other side of a thick wall and I had no interest in letting them in.

If that made me a frigid bitch of an ice queen, then fine.

I could live with that.

I didn't need friends.

I just needed to bring down Aiden Winters.

Chapter Four

Violet

If I thought working for Aiden Winters would be exciting, I would have been wrong. In the two weeks since I'd been promoted to Aiden's newest and most unnecessary executive assistant I hadn't done much of interest.

To tell the truth, it was boring. I was used to being busy, even more so in my job as a project manager since half the time I was scrambling to keep up while not wanting to let anyone know I didn't know what I was doing. In contrast, answering Aiden's phone and filing had me half-asleep.

Not so for the other four assistants, who, as Thomas had said, had their hands full working with Aiden on various projects, drafting proposals, and a variety of other tasks that put them right in the heart of Winters, Inc's global business. I could understand now why people fought for the opportunity to sit in one of those desks. Aiden worked them hard, but they were gaining experience and making connections they wouldn't have without his mentoring.

All four of them continued to alternately ignore and irritate me. The one who'd stuck up for Aiden that first day, Henry, mostly left me alone, but Marisela and Peter loved playing little pranks. Silly, childish tricks I would have thought too immature for two business school graduates with executive aspirations.

Maybe a part of us never grows up, because they seemed to gain great amusement from stealing my stapler, switching the sugar for salt in the break room, disconnecting my phone, and other annoyances they thought would drive me off.

I didn't respond to their provocations. Ever. I could fight back, and if it went on much longer, I would. I was willing to put up with it for the time being, because as long as those two were occupied with their pranks, they weren't interested in what I was doing at my workstation when I wasn't answering the phone and filing.

Not that what I was doing was fascinating. Aiden's email was boring. None of the business messages seemed at all shady, and his personal communications were all about rebuilding a house on their estate in Buckhead and preparations for his cousin's wedding.

There were a few emails between Aiden and Cooper Sinclair of Sinclair Security that alluded to a search for someone I thought might be family. I couldn't tell—those emails were worded in the shorthand friends share when they already know what they're talking about—but nothing about them seemed particularly sinister or criminal.

Aiden was trying to find someone who'd gone missing. It was curious, but I didn't think there was anything there I could use to get Chase back his company.

Even worse, this enforced proximity to Aiden Winters was making me doubt my whole plan. I was starting to think it might be possible that he was actually a decent person. Despite the way he'd stolen Chase's company, I couldn't see any evidence that he was the cutthroat corporate shark I'd imagined him to be.

Well, maybe the shark part. I heard him through the door in meetings, his voice raised, slicing through the opposition like a razor-edged sword. He worked insane hours. He was driven and ambitious, and he expected everyone who worked for him to be the same.

But so far I couldn't find any evidence of him being underhanded. He didn't take credit for others's work. He always took the time to compliment his team when they did a good job, even thanked them for their dedication. The one time his younger sister Charlie had stopped by he'd greeted her with a smile of such tender affection it made me catch my breath.

I struggled to align these two visions of Aiden. The corporate shark who'd stolen Chase's company and the hard-working, devoted head of his family. Could the man who joked with his little sister be the same man who'd tricked Chase out of CD4 Analytics? With every day that passed, I was finding it harder to believe the truth.

One evening, after the other four assistants had left for the day, I sat at my desk, a fresh cup of coffee at my elbow, scanning through contracts on Aiden's server. I was trying to find the original agreement for the purchase of CD4 Analytics, but so far it had proven elusive. Aiden had been closeted in his office for hours on a conference call with Las Vegas, something about a real estate investment, and he'd been so quiet I'd forgotten he was there.

I managed not to jump out of my skin when the door behind me opened. Casually, I closed the document I'd been skimming and swiveled my chair around. Aiden's brown eyes were distracted and his hair was tousled as if he'd been running his fingers through it. He looked rumpled and tired and all too human.

Aiden took in the empty desks before his eyes locked on me. "You the only one here?"

"It's seven o'clock, Mr. Winters. I'm just finishing up myself. Is there something I can do for you?"

Say no, say no, I thought as hard as I could.

"I could use your help with something, if you can stay," he said.

My heart sank. So far I'd avoided working one-on-one with Aiden, but it looked like my reprieve was over.

"Of course. What do you need?"

"For you to order dinner to start with. Pick one of the takeout menus in your desk, and call in the order. My favorites are highlighted on each menu, I don't care which restaurant. Whatever sounds good to you. Let the front desk know, and they'll go pick it up. In the meantime, I want you to compare these two contracts and highlight any differences in the second."

He dropped two packets of paper on my desk. "When the food gets here, bring it in, along with those contracts."

"I'm not in legal," I started to say, but Aiden shook his head, dismissing my objection.

"I don't need someone from legal. I just need a sharp eye to double check."

He disappeared back into his office. I did as ordered, but I wasn't sure I could call it an *order*. I usually thought on my feet better than that.

I should have told him I had plans.

A date.

Anything.

Anything except for sitting there and staring at him when he asked me to work late. He'd just looked so...oddly vulnerable. With his jacket off and his sleeves rolled up, his auburn curls in disarray and his eyes tired, I'd had the crazy urge to force him to take a break, to relax and get some rest.

The only person I ever took care of was Chase. Everyone else could fend for themselves. The last person I ever expected to want to take care of was Aiden Winters. But clearly, he needed it. He worked too much.

I knew he had family to go home to. Maybe not a wife and kids of his own, but his cousin Gage lived in their family home, along with Gage's younger sister Annalise, who office gossip said had only recently returned home.

I could see working late when there was nothing but an empty house waiting for you. I'd done that myself often enough when Chase was away. Aiden didn't need to drive himself so hard, but he couldn't seem to stop.

Not your problem, I told myself. *You're not here to take care of him, you idiot. You're here to find compromising information to force him to give up Chase's company.*

Aiden Winters is the enemy.

It shouldn't be so hard to remember that. Most of the time it wasn't. Only when he caught me off guard.

I'd ordered dinner from one of my favorite restaurants, getting us both the spicy Ramen Aiden had highlighted. That place made old-school Ramen by hand, the broth rich and meaty, the noodles soft and filling, the meat spicy enough to make your eyes water.

It was as much comfort food as chicken and dumplings. I couldn't stop myself from ordering something for Aiden that might help him relax.

I'd worried he might try to trip me up once he had me alone. I stayed on guard as we ate and reviewed the contracts he'd given me, but Aiden gave not the slightest hint he knew I was anything other than a regular employee.

He thanked me for getting dinner, for paying such close attention to the contracts and catching a few errors he'd missed himself.

He'd been friendly, but professional, and entirely appropriate. I didn't know quite what to make of that. The next day he acted as if I didn't exist.

After that, I tried to avoid working late if he was in the office, even though it was easier to snoop when everyone else was gone. It's not like I was finding anything anyway. While we were caught in this holding pattern it was hard to convince myself to give up, but as each day passed I knew my plan was less and less likely to pay off.

I still hadn't been able to find the paperwork related to Aiden's purchase of Chase's company and the fact that it was missing was starting to bother me. Was it possible there was more to this than I knew? More than Chase knew? The only way to figure that out was to ask Aiden, and it was too late for the direct approach.

A week after that late dinner in Aiden's office, I was still treading water, still searching and getting nowhere, when Aiden opened his office door to find me alone at my desk. As usual, the other four had gone to lunch without me. Every day they made a big production of agreeing on a restaurant and time as if deliberately not including me would hurt my feelings or scare me off.

Since I had no interest in eating lunch with them anyway, I ignored them. Mostly. It was hard to be the subject of such unrelenting dislike, but I tried to remind myself that it didn't matter. They weren't my friends, and I wasn't going to be here long. If they wanted to act like they were still in elementary school, that was their problem. I wouldn't let it be mine.

"Everyone at lunch?" Aiden asked.

"Yes, sir," I said. A glint flashed in his eyes when I called him 'sir' and the side of his lips quirked up.

"I ordered lunch in," he said, "the same thing we had last week. When it gets here, put the phone on voicemail, and bring it into my office. You're eating with me, and then I want your help with the next revision on those contracts."

"Yes, sir," I said, trying not to notice the way the quirk of his lips bloomed into a grin. I couldn't ignore the blush that grin brought to my cheeks. I swiveled my seat back to face my computer, but I heard a choked laugh as Aiden went back to his office.

The Ramen arrived fifteen minutes later. Dreading the meal ahead, I carried the food to Aiden's door and rapped twice.

"Come in, Violet," he said, still sounding amused. I was on edge, my throat tight, my stomach in a knot. I could handle playing the professional with scary Aiden, but playful, amused Aiden was a different story.

That grin knocked me off balance.

I took a deep breath and squared my shoulders, striding into the room as if I didn't have a single worry. Aiden pushed his chair back and gestured to the seat beside him.

Crap. Why did he want me to sit next to him? It was just as easy to sit on the other side of his desk with all that heavy, thick wood between us.

Masking my nerves with efficiency, I crossed the room to the seat he'd indicated and began unpacking the cartons and covered bowls in the bag of takeout. I'd had takeout from this place enough on my own to know what to do and I busied myself combining broth and noodles with meat and seasonings until we both had a complete meal sitting in front of us.

After that, I was forced to take a seat beside Aiden. This

close I could smell him, that woodsy, warm scent I thought was half soap and half him. I leaned forward and dipped my face over the plastic bowl of noodles, inhaling the salty rich broth, trying to banish Aiden from my senses.

It didn't work. Now I was smelling noodles and soup, but it didn't erase the man beside me. I didn't think anything could do that.

Surprising me, he dug into his lunch and gestured for me to do the same. It felt like a stay of execution. Maybe this would be like the other night. We'd eat. We'd work. He wouldn't grin at me like that again.

As we ate he filled me in on the progress of the contracts. He was doing some business with a friend out in Las Vegas who owned a casino, and as soon as they got these contracts wrapped up, they'd move on to the next phase of the project, a mixed-use development that combined retail and condos.

Real estate wasn't my thing and contracts bored me to tears—I was a numbers girl—but I couldn't help but get a little excited about the project as Aiden described it.

Not for the first time I had the feeling that Aiden didn't work this hard for the power or the money, or not only for those things. He had a genuine enthusiasm for his work. He loved this company, not just as a means to an end. It was disarming, and it didn't fit the rest of the picture.

We'd long since finished our lunch and were going over the contracts, line by line, re-examining changes and double checking the numbers, when the door to Aiden's office swung open.

The outer office was still empty, and with no one to stop her, Aiden's visitor strolled right in.

Chapter Five

Violet

She was tall and slender, with a sweep of champagne blonde hair as sleek and shiny as glass. Her gray eyes were granite, hard and impenetrable, until they narrowed on me in cold disapproval.

She came to a stop in front of Aiden's desk, propped her hands on her hips, and said, "Aiden, we need to talk."

This woman was trouble. I didn't have to feel Aiden go stiff beside me to know she was up to no good. Not that I could talk, but still. Anyone who had Aiden Winters bracing was bad news.

She knew exactly how beautiful she was with her sharp cheekbones and red, red lips. Standing before Aiden's desk with her hips canted slightly, her elegant charcoal sheath dress showed her long legs to their best advantage.

Sending me a flinty look she said, "You can leave."

Aiden's hand closed over my leg as he gave an almost imperceptible shake of his head.

Crap.

I would have loved nothing more than to escape.

Okay, my good sense was telling me to escape, but I was just a little curious. No, I was a lot curious. This woman was not here on business. That dress was not office appropriate. Just a little too short, with a little too much cleavage. And I already knew Aiden wouldn't have tolerated an employee with the nerve to speak to him so rudely.

Ignoring her comment he said, "Elizabeth, this is Violet Hartwell. Violet, this is Elizabeth."

With an impatient huff, she added, "Elizabeth Winters. His wife."

With Aiden's hand on my leg, I couldn't hide my jerk of surprise. His fingers tightened, sending an unexpected bolt of heat between my legs.

"Ex-wife," he clarified. "Elizabeth, I can't force you to give up my name, unfortunately, but we've been divorced for four years. You haven't been my wife for a long time."

Apparently, Elizabeth had decided to ignore me. The flinty look left her eyes and her lips turned up in what I guessed she thought was a sweet smile. It didn't look sweet to me, it looked predatory. I found myself leaning into Aiden, my shoulder brushing his.

"Wishful thinking, darling. We made a mistake—"

"We made a lot of mistakes, Elizabeth," Aiden interrupted. "I'd like to avoid making any more."

"That's why I'm here. Your little sister and her—husband—" At the word husband, Elizabeth rolled her eyes, "have been spreading rumors that you and I are at odds, and it really has to stop. I'm still not sure why you allowed her to marry him. Though I suppose you couldn't stop her. Charlotte has always been uncontrollable."

I'd never seen Aiden's brown eyes go cold so fast.

In a voice like ice, he said, "She prefers to be called

Charlie, and I couldn't be happier about her marriage to Lucas. Among his other noteworthy qualities, he loves her to distraction. As I learned the hard way, that's the most important factor in a successful marriage."

Elizabeth tossed her hair back over her shoulder and let out an amused laugh. "Aiden," she chided, "you and I both know love has nothing to do with marriage. Not in our circles. I've long since forgiven you for deciding to go your own way, but don't you think it's time we talked?"

She shot a sidelong glance at me, wordlessly commanding me to leave. With Aiden's hand still gripping my thigh, I wasn't going anywhere.

I wasn't sure I wanted to. Had I thought Aiden a shark? If I had it was only because I hadn't met this woman yet. How had he been married to her? She didn't look like there was an ounce of softness to her, from her angular body to her sharp smile. He worked too hard, had too much responsibility on his shoulders to come home to a woman like this.

"Elizabeth, I can't imagine what you think we have to talk about. Charlie said that you told her we were getting back together. I have no clue where you got that idea, but hell could freeze over and I still wouldn't want to be in the same room as you."

Ouch. Even Elizabeth flinched at that. She took a step forward and opened her mouth to say something. Before she could get a word out, Aiden surged to his feet, pulling me up beside him.

He moved so fast I wobbled a little on my heels. Aiden wound his arm around my waist to steady me, pulling me tight to his side.

Inappropriately tight. Coworkers did not plaster themselves against one another like this. What was he doing?

Even if I'd wanted to step away, knew I should step away, Aiden's arm was like iron around me. And I didn't want to leave him. Whatever point he was trying to make with this harpy, I'd rather help than get in his way.

"I thought you could take me to the Foundation event tomorrow night," she said, smoothly, as if Aiden hadn't just told her how much he disliked her.

This woman had some serious balls.

"Is it possible that you don't have an escort? I can't see you leaving something like that to the last minute," Aiden said, wryly.

Elizabeth waved one red-tipped hand in the air, dismissing her would-be date. "He can make other arrangements. I've been thinking about it, and after hearing some rumors at lunch the other day I thought it would be more sensible for us to go together."

"No fucking way," Aiden said, flatly.

"There's no need to be rude," Elizabeth said, one thin eyebrow raised. She was both repellent and fascinating. She considered his use of the word *fuck* to be rude but not the part where he told her he wouldn't want to be in the same room with her even if hell froze over. See, I would have taken it the other way around. I wasn't big on swearing myself, but the second was a far bigger insult.

Then again, Elizabeth Winters seemed impervious to insult.

Elizabeth was gathering herself to retort when Aiden went on, "I'm not available, Elizabeth. I'm involved."

"With whom?" she demanded. "I would know if you were dating someone. There's nothing that goes on in the city that I don't know about. At least nothing that matters."

I never saw it coming. If I had, I would have gotten the heck out of there the second Elizabeth walked in.

I think.

Aiden's arm tightened around my waist, turning me, angling me to face him. He shot Elizabeth a triumphant look and said, "I'm involved with Violet. I would have thought that was obvious."

Before I could say a word, Aiden's head dipped. His mouth slanted over mine. At the touch of his lips, I went stiff with shock. In my heels, I was only a few inches shorter than him and our bodies fit together like puzzle pieces, my hips pressing to his, my breasts pillowed against his chest.

This close, I could feel the heat of his body through his dress shirt and my blouse, the steely strength of his legs against my own.

His kiss started out possessive, a statement of ownership more than anything else. I barely had the chance to taste his breath, to feel his fingers splayed out across my back before he angled his head and took the kiss deeper, his lips claiming mine, urging them apart for his tongue.

He licked across my lower lip and it fell open, letting him in. The stiffness drained out of me and I felt my body molding to his, my head tilting up, everything in me opening, meeting him halfway.

He tasted of salt and heat, his lips firm but soft, not bruising, but sampling. Savoring. One hand slid down my back, his fingers curving around my hip, pulling me harder against him.

Somewhere beyond the buzz of arousal filling my brain, I heard Aiden's name repeated over and over, and a bang, like something being thrown or a door slamming.

I didn't care what it was.

Two seconds after Aiden's lips touched mine, my brain stopped working and my body had taken over.

The bar of his erection pressed into my stomach, thick

and hard despite the clothes between us. I rolled my hips into him, letting my legs part when he pushed his thigh between them, reaching up and sinking my fingers into his hair. Thick and soft, like silk, I twined my fingers in the strands and pulled his mouth harder against mine.

He let out a groan.

Or I did.

I don't know. I didn't know anything except that this kiss was everything I never knew I'd needed, and I never wanted it to end.

Big hands closed over my hips, lifting me, setting me on the desk. Papers slid, cascading to the floor. We let them go, Aiden nudging my legs apart to stand between them, his fingers deftly sliding the button of my jacket open.

My blouse was a flat grey silk, buttoned to my chin. Prim. Dull. And so thin the heat of his hand might as well have been touching my bare skin. My nipple pebbled against his palm as he squeezed, hefting the weight of my breast, and groaned into my mouth.

The shrill peal of the phone sliced through the fog of arousal clouding my mind.

The phone was ringing.

Why was the phone ringing?

Why was there a phone when Aiden was kissing me?

Every muscle in my body locked tight.

Why the hell was Aiden Winters kissing me?

And why was I kissing him back?

I jerked away, breaking his hold, and slid off the desk, almost losing my balance. Aiden let me go, his fingers trailing down my arm as if he was reluctant to move away. I couldn't look him in the eye. If his phone was ringing, that meant someone had taken it off voicemail.

The outer office wasn't empty anymore, and I was in here kissing the boss.

My knees went weak and I sank into my chair. What the hell was I doing kissing my boss? Never mind the whole mess of why I was here in the first place. I knew better.

I knew better, and I wasn't that kind of girl. I didn't go around kissing people, much less at work. After the fiasco at my first job, I never got involved with anyone at work.

Ever.

No exceptions.

But Aiden Winters kisses me and I melt?

What was wrong with me?

"Violet? You okay?" Aiden asked, his voice low and a little rough.

Slowly, I shook my head, rubbing the back of my hand against my lips. "Why did you do that?" I asked, and even to me, my voice sounded plaintive and a little lost.

Aiden didn't answer my question. He reached out a hand and closed it around my upper arm, urging me to my feet.

So quietly I could barely hear him, he said, "You're a puzzle, Violet. I like puzzles."

I wasn't sure if it was a promise or threat. Since it was all I could do to stand without my knees knocking together, I decided to worry about that later.

Aiden reached out to smooth my hair back, rubbing his thumb across my lower lip before tugging my blouse back into place, straightening my jacket, and smoothing my skirt over my hips. In that same barely audible tone he said, "There. Your lips are a little red, but otherwise, no one will know."

At least one of us was thinking. My mind was on fleeing, not straightening my blouse. The last thing I needed was to stumble out of the boss's office with my hair a mess and my clothes askew. No one would call me an ice queen then. No, they'd go straight to office slut.

Taking a step back, Aiden folded his arms across his chest and scanned me from head to toe. He reached out and tucked a strand of hair behind my ear before he said, "You'll come with me to the Foundation event tomorrow night. I'll pick you up at seven thirty."

"I can't...we can't. I don't...why would you even..."

Aiden interrupted my sputtering. "Be ready at seven-thirty tomorrow night or don't bother coming to work on Monday. Understood?"

Unable to think of anything else to say, I gave a short nod, turned on my heel, and left Aiden's office. It wasn't hard to ignore the curious stares of my coworkers as I strode past my desk and headed for the bathroom.

I needed a minute to get my head together. An hour would be better, but a minute was all I had. I locked myself into a bathroom stall, sat on the closed lid, and dropped my head into my hands. The heat of my flushed cheeks burned my palms. I could feel the swelling of my lips.

When was the last time I'd been kissed?

Like that?

Never.

I'd never been kissed like that. I thought kisses like that belonged in movies.

I was the ice queen. I was the frigid bitch no one could melt enough to fuck.

One touch of Aiden's lips and my body turned to liquid heat. My panties were damp, my breasts swollen, nipples scraping against the lace of my bra.

If we'd been alone? If it hadn't been the middle of the day and we hadn't been in Aiden's office?

I'd like to say I would have stopped him. Stopped myself. But that would be a lie.

I was in big trouble.

And, apparently, I had a date with Aiden Winters.

Chapter Six

Violet

I couldn't see my bed. It was under there somewhere, buried beneath piles of dresses. Shoes scattered the floor, almost giving me a black eye when I tangled my toes in the straps of a pair of gladiator sandals and pitched face first into my bedside table.

Fortunately, a long forgotten bridesmaid dress broke my fall. I don't know what that was doing out of the closet. I was desperate for something to wear to the Winters Foundation event, but mint green chiffon was not going to make the cut. It had been bad enough wearing that thing the first time.

Staring at the mess in my bedroom, I determined two things. One, for a girl who didn't get out much I had way too many dresses. And two, I really needed to clean out my closet. Oh, and three, I still had no idea what I was wearing to the party. Or why I was going.

Aiden had given me the perfect out. Be my date, or you're fired. Couldn't be much simpler than that. All I had to do was say *No* and this whole disastrous plan of mine fell apart.

Wasn't it time?

I'd been there almost three months and I hadn't found a single thing I could use against Aiden. Either his skeletons were at the very back of the closet, or he didn't have any.

I was beginning to think it was the latter. I knew all about the Winters family. Everyone knew about the Winters family. It wasn't just that they were ridiculously wealthy and powerful. It wasn't only that they ran Winters, Inc., a company that had subsidiaries in every corner of the globe and made more money than most countries' GDPs.

Beyond all of that, they were famous for scandal and murder. Aiden's aunt and uncle had died in a mysterious murder-suicide when he was a child, and his parents had been killed in a seemingly identical crime years later. I didn't remember the first, but when his parents died they were all over the tabloids.

None of the Winters children could set foot outside their gated estate without facing a swarm of reporters. In the years since, the media had hounded all of them, eager for any hint of scandal they could spin into drama.

Knowing that, it was hard to imagine they could keep any secrets, much less that Aiden was hiding the kind of secret I could use as leverage against him. For two weeks I'd been right outside his office, privy to every detail of his business, and I hadn't seen or heard a single thing that led me to believe he was the kind of man who would steal a company.

But, I knew what I knew. I'd been there, seen the buyer he'd sent by proxy, met with him alongside Chase. If only we'd reviewed the contracts line by line the way Aiden did his own. If only we'd realized our corporate lawyers were susceptible to bribery. We had a lot of *if only's*.

Chase had given up and walked away. I wasn't willing to do that. Not yet.

Aiden said I was a puzzle, but he was a mystery I had to solve. I knew he was guilty. Hadn't I spent two months working in a department that had been created from the ashes of Chase's company? The proof was right there. I was a fool to doubt it. And an even bigger fool to feel a tingle of excitement at the idea of going to a party with Aiden Winters.

This was going to end in disaster, and I couldn't bring myself to walk away.

I left the mess in my bedroom and headed for the kitchen. I needed a glass of wine before I thought about cleaning up. I was going to have to find time to go shopping because nothing I had was suitable for a formal event. I refused to consider any of my three bridesmaids dresses. I didn't do ruffles. I was pushing the cork back in the bottle when the doorbell rang.

Weird. Chase sometimes had friends drop by at odd hours, but since he'd been gone on this consulting job they hadn't bothered. A quick check on the security camera showed a uniformed courier standing outside my door holding a large rectangular box. I pressed the button on the intercom and said, "Yes?"

"I have a delivery for Violet Hartwell."

"A delivery? Who is it from? I didn't order anything."

"It's from Aiden Winters."

Of course, it was.

I unlocked the door and swung it open, taking the oversized, unwieldy box from the courier's arms. "Hold on just a second," I said, intending to get my purse and scrounge up a few dollars for a tip.

Freed of the box, the courier stepped back, gave me a friendly wave, and said "It's already been taken care of. Have a nice night."

He disappeared down the hall, leaving me balancing the heavy box on one arm as I struggled to flip the lock closed on the front door. By the time I reached the kitchen table, I was about to drop it. I recognized the name on the lid as a high-end boutique I'd never stepped inside, even the smallest accessory far outside my budget.

My hands shook a little as I pulled up on the sides of the glossy, white box. I shouldn't open it. I shouldn't accept whatever was inside. I couldn't stop myself from lifting the lid and carefully peeling back the white tissue paper.

I sucked in a breath at the sight of the dress inside the box. Strapless tulle, the color of midnight, set off by a burst of gold at the waist that sent streamers across the bodice and down through the full skirt, ending in gold stars. The navy would perfectly complement my pale skin and odd bluish-purple eyes. The gold was only a few shades darker than my hair. The dress might have been made for me, though I never would have chosen something so feminine and fanciful myself.

If I'd bought a dress, it would have been black and probably boring. Carefully, I lifted the gown from the box and checked the tag. A long sigh escaped me. I'd never thought I'd wear Valentino. For just a second I felt like Cinderella. Except Aiden wasn't the prince, he was the evil stepmother. Or the wicked witch.

Never mind, he was the bad guy, that's all I needed to know.

I remembered that I was lying to him and sneaking around inside his company to try to find information I could use against him.

Fine, then we were both the bad guy, and this was no fairytale.

At least I got the dress. Pulling it completely free of the

box, I discovered a matching pair of midnight blue and gold spike heels. I love shoes. I mean, I *really* love shoes. I kept my work clothes simple, professional, and mostly dull. But not my shoes.

Shoes were my weakness and my indulgence. Heels, sandals, more heels. I owned one pair of sneakers, a single set of flip-flops, and countless pairs of stilettos, wedges, pumps, kitten heels, cone heels, ankle boots. None of them anywhere close to as expensive as the heels Aiden had bought for me. I slipped one on my bare foot and sighed again as it fit perfectly.

I didn't have to try on the dress to know it would fit as well. I did anyway, and as I pulled up the zipper, the bodice closed around me as if it had been hand sewn for me alone. For just a minute I thought about sending it all back, telling Aiden it was over.

I knew I wouldn't. I wanted to wear this dress. I wanted to go out with Aiden.

I was a complete, total idiot.

Putting that thought out of my mind, I removed the dress and shoes, carefully putting them away for the next day. Then, I made myself deal with the pile of discarded dresses on my bed, responsibly pulling out a few I could donate, including the mint green chiffon bridesmaid dress. Maybe someone could make some use of it because it wouldn't be me.

When I was done, I curled up in bed with my tablet and pulled up videos of formal hairstyles. If I was going to go to the ball with Prince Charming, I was going to do it right.

Aiden didn't mention the delivery at work on Friday. In fact, I barely saw him all day. He left for a meeting before noon and didn't return until three-thirty, when he stopped by my desk, stared down at me and said, "Why don't you leave early, Ms. Hartwell."

"Yes, sir," I said, and started the process of shutting down my computer and gathering my things. I heard the resentful whispers from behind me. I ignored them. I was getting very good at ignoring my coworkers.

Just that morning I'd driven Peter and Marisela crazy by drinking my salted coffee as if there were nothing wrong with it. The more serene my expression, the louder I could hear Marisela's teeth grinding together. I'd almost lost my composure and burst into laughter at her frustration, but that would have ruined my fun.

I was ready well before seven-thirty, my hair pinned up into an elaborate twist of curls and braids, formal enough for the event, but fanciful enough to suit the dress. I buried my nerves in preparation, taking more time with my makeup than I had since my first dance in college.

I wouldn't know a soul there aside from Aiden, and I didn't want anyone to question my right to be on his arm. He went out with the most beautiful women in Atlanta. In the country, really. I couldn't match up to them—I wasn't an actress or a model—but I was going to give this everything I had.

I opened the door at Aiden's knock. His expression when he saw me was more than gratifying. I took a tiny step back at the heat in his eyes as he took in the swell of my breasts, tightly contained by the strapless bodice, my bared shoulders, the curve of my waist and the flare of the filmy skirt.

"You're stunning," he said, simply. "I knew you would be."

"Thank you for the dress." My cheeks warmed under his stare.

"You're welcome. Shall we?" Aiden offered his arm, and I took it, pushing away all my doubts. It was too late to get out now. I might as well do my best to have fun.

All I could do was hope that if my charade came to an end, it wouldn't be tonight.

CHAPTER SEVEN

VIOLET

Aiden led me to a limousine waiting in front of my building. I don't know why I was surprised. He held the door and helped me inside, lifting my skirt so it wouldn't trail in the street as I settled myself against the smooth leather upholstery. Aiden got in on the other side, sitting next to me, a little too close for comfort.

I was in way over my head. He knew what he was doing every step of the way, and I was running to keep up. Proving me right, he opened a cabinet opposite our seat and pulled out a chilled bottle of champagne, already opened.

Wasn't this romantic...

Did he think this was a date?

A real date?

I accepted the champagne and took a long sip, not sure if the idea thrilled or terrified me. Maybe a little of both. I did not want him to kiss me again. I didn't. Okay, maybe just a little. Once. I wouldn't mind if he kissed me one more time.

I didn't want to play a game any more than I had to. Taking another sip of champagne, I swallowed and asked bluntly, "Why am I here? A hundred women would jump if you needed a last-minute date for a party. Why me? And why that scene in your office yesterday?"

I expected him to laugh and blow off my question. Instead, he said, "I don't want a hundred women. I want you."

"You can't."

"I do," he said, simply. "And to answer your other question, that scene in my office was my ex-wife doing what she does best. Tormenting me. She fought me on the divorce tooth and nail, and I only managed to get rid of her with a huge payoff. I'm assuming she's run out of money and before she goes and hunts up another sucker, she's making a run at her original piggy bank."

"Cynical," I said.

Aiden sipped his champagne and shook his head. "Accurate."

"If she's that awful, why did you marry her in the first place?"

"Valid question." Aiden's eyes met mine. I couldn't look away as he studied me for an endless minute.

I don't know what he was looking for, what he hoped to learn, but he must have arrived at some conclusion. "I married her because I thought I was supposed to. I was twenty-four, trying to run the company, trying to be head of the family, and out of my depth with both of them. I missed my parents and I thought Charlie needed a mother. She was fifteen, her only female cousin was gone, and my brilliant solution was to marry Elizabeth, who did a very good job of playing the sweetly devoted girlfriend right up until we said our marriage vows."

"I'm sorry," I said. "Sometimes it's too easy to make bad

decisions for the right reasons. Why did you decide to divorce her?"

"You met her yesterday, right?"

A laugh bubbled up, and I covered it with another sip of champagne. "Well, yes, and she did seem fairly horrible."

"Honestly, I probably would have put up with it for longer. She went out of her way to make my life comfortable, as far as I know she never cheated on me, and she was —" he paused, considering, "adequate in bed."

"Did you cheat on her?" I asked, suddenly needing to know. He wasn't painting a picture of marital bliss.

"No. I was tempted a few times, but I never did. I believe in keeping vows."

"So what was it? What happened to make you decide you didn't want to be married anymore? She doesn't seem to understand that you don't want her, and you've made it clear you can't stand the sight of her, so I don't get it. What did she do?"

Aiden looked at me again with that solemn, penetrating gaze that made me feel like he could see all the way to my soul. Finally, he said, "I heard her call Charlie fat. I know it seems like a small thing, but Charlie and I are close. She was only ten when our parents died. I did my best but I was no stand-in for them. I confronted Elizabeth about it and she went off in a litany of Charlie's faults. I talked to Charlie, and I found out that Elizabeth had been cutting her down for years. Charlie kept it to herself because she didn't want to cause problems in my marriage. That killed me, the idea that my baby sister was being systematically demoralized by my wife and I didn't even know. I was supposed to be looking out for her. Our home was supposed to be a safe place, and I'd made it the opposite."

"You didn't know they didn't get along?" I asked. I

didn't have any trouble imagining the woman I'd met in Aiden's office being a raging bitch to his little sister. She was the kind of competitive female who wouldn't be able to stand her husband adoring another woman, even if that woman was his younger sibling.

Aiden shrugged one shoulder and looked away. "I knew they weren't close, weren't friends, but I didn't realize how cruel Elizabeth could be. No one deserves that, but especially not Charlie."

He sat up and poured us each another glass of champagne. I looked at it doubtfully. I wasn't sure I needed another glass. I wasn't a big drinker and too much alcohol seemed like a bad plan. I took it anyway.

Aiden went on, "I can see why she thinks we might get back together. Charlie's out of the house, happily married, and we got along well enough when we were married. I worked all the time, and she spent my money."

"The ideal marriage," I murmured.

"For Elizabeth, I think it was. She wanted social standing and a bottomless wallet."

"And what did you want?" I asked before my brain fully formed the question.

"I thought I wanted a wife. I was young, focused on work and what was left of my family. I convinced myself that if I just got married, everything would fall into place. It took me six years to realize that I didn't want a wife. I wanted a marriage like the one my parents had. Not the same thing."

I stared at Aiden, my eyes wide with shock. "You stayed married to her for six years? *Six years?*"

The side of Aiden's mouth quirked and he said, "I worked a lot."

I took a sip of champagne and muttered, "I bet."

I couldn't quite imagine Aiden married to Elizabeth. They would have looked good together, no question there. She was cold but beautiful and I hadn't met many men as handsome as Aiden. But I was coming to see that the core of him was warmth. He cared about people. He loved his family. From what I'd seen and heard, Elizabeth only loved herself.

The limo cruised to a stop outside the Intercontinental Hotel in Buckhead. The door opened, but Aiden came around to help me out.

He's not Prince Charming, I reminded myself, *and you're not Cinderella.*

Though I was starting to think Elizabeth was definitely the evil stepmother. It sounded like Aiden's little sister would agree.

He led me in, filling me in on the event we were attending, a fundraiser held by the Winters Foundation in support of literacy programs. We'd barely cleared the doorway to the ballroom when a stunning woman in a red ball gown glided up and stopped in front of Aiden, reaching up to press a kiss to his cheek.

"Abigail," he said, warmly, "everything is beautiful. It looks like you have another success on your hands."

"I hope so."

A striking man with dark hair and silvery eyes came up behind her and wound his arm around her waist. "She works so hard putting these things together and then when they finally happen, the nerves hit."

She poked him in the side and whispered, "Don't tease."

He ducked his head to kiss her cheek and whispered back, "I love to tease." Those silver eyes landed on me and he raised an eyebrow. "I don't know you," he said. Abigail poked him in the side again.

"Jacob, Abigail, this is Violet Hartwell. Violet, this is my brother, Jacob, and his fiancée, Abigail. Abigail works for the Winters Foundation in event planning, and, as you can see, we're very lucky to have her."

"It's nice to meet you both," I said, the resemblance between Aiden and Jacob clearer now that I knew they were brothers.

I'd heard whispers about Jacob around the office. People said he was scary, a shark in a business suit who made Aiden look warm and cuddly. Seeing him whisper in his fiancée's ear, the blush that rose on her cheeks, I had a hard time imagining the stories were true.

"I'm going to get Violet a drink," Aiden said, "we'll catch up with you later."

I let Aiden lead me across the room to the bar, nodding when he asked, "Champagne?"

Why not?

This was a one-time thing. I was going to drink, have fun, and enjoy ogling Aiden. His brother was attractive, but Aiden was easily the most devastating man in the room. He wore his tuxedo like he'd been born in it, and his neatly arranged hair left me wanting to mess it up, to sink my fingers in the silky strands and pull his mouth down to mine.

Uh-oh.

No, Violet.

No kissing Aiden.

That was also a one-time thing, and that time was over. I tried to tell myself that getting closer to Aiden, being his date for the night, might shake loose the kind of information I was looking for. People were drinking and gossip would run rampant. Maybe someone would say something I could use.

I could barely convince myself that was my motive for being here. I didn't know what I was doing anymore, and when Aiden pressed the champagne glass into my hand I took a long, indelicate sip.

"Hey, slow down there. We haven't even had dinner yet," he said.

"It's fine," I reassured him, even as I felt bubbles of champagne tickling my brain. "I never get drunk."

"There's a first time for everything," he said under his breath.

"I won't embarrass you," I promised.

"It never occurred to me that you would," he said, smiling down at me, the combination of affection and desire in his eyes making me a little dizzy.

No kissing, I reminded myself.

I felt the burn of eyes on my skin and glanced across the room to see Aiden's cousin Gage glaring at me. I met his blue eyes and didn't look away. I expected him to move toward us, to break my gaze, something, but he just stood there and stared, looking furious. Aiden noticed his cousin at the same time a sweet looking blonde beside Gage scowled up at him, then glanced curiously across the room at me.

I looked away from Gage to see an annoyed expression on Aiden's face. What was that about?

"Your cousin doesn't seem to like me."

Aiden didn't hide his irritation from Gage. Sliding his arm around my shoulder, he turned me in the opposite direction from his cousin, toward the open terrace doors. "Ignore Gage. He's in a mood."

Gage's office was on the opposite side of the executive floor from Aiden's, and they often worked side-by-side, so

I'd seen him here and there. He always ignored me, so it was a surprise to be the subject of his focus.

"Does his mood have anything to do with me?"

"Maybe," Aiden said.

Maybe meant yes. I ran through all the possible responses I could think of and decided saying nothing was my smartest move. Aiden knew I wasn't who I said I was. We seemed to be ignoring that, but he hadn't forgotten.

We were in a stalemate, each waiting for the other to make a mistake. But if Aiden knew, it wasn't a stretch to imagine Gage did as well. Clearly, whatever game Aiden was playing with me, Gage disapproved.

I didn't have it in me to care. One way or another, my time at Winters, Inc. was coming to a close. Chase would be back in two weeks and I had to wrap up this ridiculous plan of mine before he came home. I didn't want him to find out what I was up to. Not unless I found the information I needed. As each day went by and I came up empty it seemed less and less likely that would happen.

In two weeks all of this would be behind me. Until then, Gage Winters could deal with it.

I was so distracted by Gage's attention I didn't see Elizabeth until she stepped right in front of us, halting our slow progress towards the terrace doors. She wore a platinum sheathe that skimmed her slender figure and almost perfectly matched her cold gray eyes. With her hair in an elaborate knot, I realized with a wave of discomfort that she and I looked alike.

Light blonde hair, pale skin, tall, frosty demeanor—the more I thought about it, the more I realized Aiden definitely had a type. Granted, her eyes were gray to my lavender blue, and she was more slender. She was also a raging bitch to the core, while I wore my bitch on the surface, and only when necessary. Still, unease filtered through me as I saw Aiden's eyes bounce between us.

Before he could speak I said, "Can we help you?" in the same tone someone like Elizabeth might use when talking to the help. She flinched just a little, and Aiden's arm slid around my waist, his fingers warm through the light tulle of my dress.

"I see you're insisting on going through with this charade," she hissed under her breath. "I know the two of you aren't dating. Aiden has never mixed business and pleasure. Just tell me what you want me to do, and I'll do it, darling—"

I have no idea what came over me, but Aiden deserved better than to be this woman's cash cow. He'd given her six years. That was more than enough.

I leaned into Aiden's side and looked up, sending him a melting glance before narrowing my eyes on Elizabeth and saying, "He's not your darling. And he's not interested. Coming to the office was bad enough, but this is just desperate. Pay attention, Elizabeth. People are talking. I suggest you look for greener pastures before you use up the rest of your social currency chasing after someone who doesn't want you."

Elizabeth sputtered, her chilly gaze suddenly hot with embarrassment. Aiden bent his head and said in a low voice, "If I were you, I'd listen to the lady, Elizabeth. I'm finished being polite. Approach me again, for any reason, and you will find yourself unwelcome anywhere you want to be. Is that clear?"

Elizabeth's mouth snapped shut and she gave a single nod. I lifted my chin to smile up at Aiden as he swept me around her and out through the terrace doors.

Chapter Eight

Aiden

Fucking hell, she was magnificent. I never thought I'd find a woman who could out-frost Elizabeth, but Violet had cut her to pieces with a few elegantly phrased words. The impotent fury, the helpless embarrassment on Elizabeth's face—I'd be savoring that memory for a while.

Gage was right; on the surface, Elizabeth and Violet were cut from the same cloth. I wouldn't deny that with both I'd been attracted to their cool elegance. But at twenty-four I'd been too immature to realize that there was nothing beneath the surface with Elizabeth.

Elizabeth was the imitation.

Violet was the real thing.

I'd had my mouth on hers. One kiss and all that ice had melted into heat. Just for me.

Violet had it all.

The frost and the fire. Intelligence and a sense of humor. I'd barely cracked the surface with her, but I'd seen enough to know I needed more. Cooper had almost finished his investigation and I knew all I needed to know about Miss Violet Westbrook.

Westbrook, not Hartwell. Hartwell was her mother's maiden name.

I knew that she was a bookkeeper and not a project manager. I knew her last job had been for CD4 Analytics before Winters, Inc. acquired it. The only thing I didn't know was why she'd gotten a job essentially working for her old company under an assumed name. And in the wrong department. She was, by all accounts, an excellent bookkeeper.

I could have sent Cooper digging further, but I wanted the rest from her.

I wanted Violet to trust me enough to tell me the truth on her own. I could have come clean and ended this farce, but I had a feeling if I did that, she'd run. I watched her drain her third glass of champagne and considered letting her get a little bit drunk and seeing if I could pry her secrets from her.

I considered it, and then tossed the idea out the window. I didn't want to get her drunk and trick her into telling me the truth.

I wanted her to trust me.

I needed her to want me.

I was getting somewhere with her. The way she'd looked up at me before she'd cut Elizabeth to pieces, the press of her hand to my chest, the possessive affection in her eyes—Violet wasn't that good of an actress.

She hadn't needed to protect me from Elizabeth. I'd been taking care of myself for a very long time. I could deal with my ex-wife. Whether she'd be willing to admit it or not, Violet had stepped in because she liked me.

It wasn't enough, but it was a start.

We wandered toward the dining room and found our seats at a table just in front of the podium. This was the boring part of these events. A speech, polite applause, and a mediocre meal. Abigail had tried to step up the quality of the food but it was never as good as what Abel served us at Winters House. I seated Violet and took my place beside her, leaning in to brush a hand over her smooth shoulders and inhale her warm, sweet scent.

The dress I'd chosen suited her to perfection. She probably would have picked something more sedate, less fairy princess and more queen of the realm. But I'd seen the daisies on the back of her car, hadn't missed that she'd chosen bright blue and not gray or black. A Beetle instead of a sedan.

The deep blue of her dress brought out the lavender in her eyes, and the gold starburst was the perfect mix of elegance and whimsy. Exactly like Violet herself.

Abruptly, I wished we were anywhere but the ballroom of the Intercontinental. I didn't want to share her with three hundred other people. I wanted her to myself. And as much as I loved that dress, as stunning as she was wearing it, I wanted to pull down the zipper and free those lush breasts, to taste all that creamy skin, to find out if she smelled of sweet peas everywhere.

It was my good luck we were at the table. If we'd been standing up there was no way I could have hidden my erection. I had to kiss her again. I would. As soon as it was humanly possible to get her alone and away from this crowd, I was putting my mouth on hers.

I couldn't remember the last time I'd had to resort to my hand over a flesh and blood woman, but I'd lost interest in anything female that wasn't Violet since the first time we'd shared an elevator.

I'd stroked my cock more than once since that day, thinking of her, but since we'd kissed...let's just say I was wearing myself raw with fantasies of what might have happened if we'd been anywhere but my office.

I had to keep myself in check. She hadn't talked much about her personal life but, my gut told me Violet was fairly inexperienced. She had an air of innocence, even when she was rolling her hips into mine and moaning into my mouth —there was surprise mixed in with all that passion. A hint of shock, as if she wasn't quite sure what was happening, why she was so overwhelmed.

It was tempting to push her, as much to keep her off balance as to satisfy my own desires. I slid my hand under the tablecloth to her lap and tangled my fingers with hers. The man next to her was closing in on eighty and had occupied them both with a long, detailed explanation of his hobby. Birdwatching. I rubbed my thumb over the side of her hand and watched a faint blush rise in her cheeks.

Innocent.

The couple to my right took a seat. I knew them socially. The wife was a talker, and I listened with half an ear as she rambled on about their recent vacation. This dinner was going to last an eternity. Hidden by the tablecloth, Violet's right leg nudged mine, her foot rubbing the inside of my calf. I shifted in my seat, trying to make room for my swollen cock.

What was it about this woman? We were holding hands for fuck's sake. It wasn't like she was on her knees under the table.

Don't imagine Violet on her knees under the table, you asshole.

Don't imagine Violet on her knees at all.

I must have been insane to think this was a good idea.

I'd wanted Violet out of the office and on my arm, but not in the middle of a crowd.

Abigail took her place behind the podium and introduced the speaker, a literacy advocate who ran one of the programs the Winters Foundation supported. I believed in literacy. I was 100% supportive of the Winters Foundation. I was the one who wrote the checks to fund the damn thing. I should have been paying attention, and I didn't hear a word either of them said.

The only thing I paid attention to was Violet's hand in mine, and I was unreasonably annoyed when I had to drop it to cut into my steak. I didn't want food. I wanted to stand up, throw Violet over my shoulder, and carry her off. Somewhere. Anywhere. My imagination hadn't gotten that far.

Back to Winters House? Winters House which was crowded with family? Not just Gage and Sophie, who lived there full-time, but my cousin Annalise and her fiancé Riley were there, using the rooms that had been hers as a child while they waited for their house to be rebuilt after a fire.

Winters House was over seventeen thousand square feet, plenty of room for everyone and way too crowded to bring a woman I wanted to make love to for days.

That was all fantasy. I'd get Violet in bed eventually, but it wouldn't be tonight. It was too soon, and we had too many lies between us.

I glanced to my left and saw Violet's eyes were glazed over. The octogenarian beside her was still talking about birdwatching. He hadn't noticed that Violet's murmurs of interest had grown flat. The woman beside me had finally turned her attention elsewhere and I leaned into Violet to whisper, "There's dancing after dinner."

She tipped her head towards mine and whispered back, "I haven't danced in years. I'm not sure I remember how."

"It's like riding a bicycle," I promised. "Just put yourself in my hands, and let me take care of you."

Her eyes dropped to my mouth and lingered, sending another rush of blood to my cock. Seriously, this woman was going to kill me. She accepted a glass of champagne from a waiter, and looked away, taking a long sip. That delicate pink flush was back in her cheeks. Yeah, she was thinking exactly what I was thinking. Another long sip of champagne told me she wasn't nearly as comfortable with those thoughts as I was.

Finally, the interminable meal ended. In an act of sheer will, I got my cock under control enough to stand up and lead Violet to the dance floor. Abigail typically planned for formal dancing at the start, followed by more popular, faster music as the evening wore on and people had a chance to loosen up.

That suited me just fine. I had no interest in dancing to the latest pop songs, but pulling Violet into my arms for a foxtrot or waltz? I could do that all night. Every single one of the Winters children had been forced into years of dance class at the country club. We'd hated it at the time, particularly the boys, but I had to admit the lessons had paid off. Women loved a man who could dance.

Violet may have been a little rusty, but she let me lead and halfway into the first song we moved together as if we'd been dancing for a lifetime. In her heels, she was only a few inches shorter than me. Her body fit perfectly to mine. The music came to a stop, and so did we.

"Another dance?" I asked as the opening bars of the next song began.

Violet's eyes were soft and dark, almost purple when she said, "Please."

"Anything you want," I promised. I led her into a waltz

and she followed easily, surprising me. When I turned her in a spin she flowed back into my arms, not resisting as I took the opportunity to draw her closer. The waltz was a perfectly appropriate dance when the partners kept their distance, but when you pulled a woman in close it became something completely different.

That waltz was followed by another. By the end Violet's eyes were dark as night, her cheeks flushed. I was getting closer and closer to the edge, almost at the point where throwing her over my shoulder seemed like a reasonable way to end the evening. The band changed tempo and started up a Glenn Miller classic.

"Can you?" I asked. The foxtrot and waltz were one thing, but swing dancing—real swing dancing—was different. I'd learned. We all had. I wasn't expecting Violet to raise an eyebrow and challenge, "Of course, but can you?"

I didn't bother to answer but pulled her into the fast-paced dance. A wide, unaffected smile split her face and she moved in my arms as if she'd been waiting her entire life for this one dance. I spun her, dipped her, and held her against me until we were both breathless and laughing.

I noticed out of the corner of my eye Jacob and Abigail on the dance floor, holding their own. Gage had coaxed Sophie into the dance, and she bit her lip in concentration as she tried to keep up.

The music faded away and Violet said, "Champagne. I hate to say it, but I'm thirsty."

We made our way off the dance floor, heading for the open doors of the terrace. Passing a waiter carrying a tray, I took two glasses of champagne and handed one to Violet.

"Dance class?" I asked.

Violet laughed, her eyes sparkling as she took a deep

drink of the champagne. I wasn't going to tell her to stop. I'd get her home safely, and I liked her with her guard down.

"Five years," she said. "You, too?"

"My mother's command. All of us went. Even Charlie, though I practically had to drag her in."

"Us too. I never minded, but Ch-, my brother, hated it. He only went for a year before he quit."

"But you liked it?" I probed, letting the brief mention of her brother go without comment. If I probed, she'd clam up. This was the first time she'd talked about herself. I wanted to hear more.

"I did. I loved it—the music, learning the steps."

"And the boys?" I teased.

I still remembered the girls from dance class, their starched dresses and shiny shoes. The flirtatious smiles. Those first few years of dance class none of us thought much of the girls. We were all still thinking about video games and secret clubhouses. I'd hated dance class right up until my hormones kicked in, and it became an exquisite torture.

I was moving Violet back as we talked, guiding her along the edge of the terrace where tall potted plants in the corner created a private nook. On the way, I snagged another two glasses of champagne and exchanged our empties.

"You know how it was," she said. "Lined up on each side of the room. The boys with their sweaty hands. Waiting for the instructor to pair us up. I was shy, and the boys made me nervous."

"And now? Do boys still make you nervous?"

She stared up at me, her lips parted, breath held, as if frozen on a precipice. I waited for her to choose, my own breath tight in my chest. After an endless moment, she looked away, took the champagne glass from my hand, and lifted it to her lips. In one long sip, she drained it and set it on the railing of the terrace.

Those deep lavender eyes met mine. "Only you. Only you make me nervous."

Her confession was the most honest thing she'd ever said to me. I closed my hands over her shoulders and ran them down her arms, her skin warm and impossibly soft. She leaned into me and raised her mouth to mine.

Every moment of the evening, of the last few weeks, had been leading to this. I drew her hands up, leaving them to rest on my shoulders, and cupped her face in my palms, feeling her frantic pulse beat under my fingertips.

It started in a whisper of touch, my lips brushing hers, her breath mingling with mine, tasting of champagne. Her lips opened, inviting, and I didn't hesitate. Her hands moved up, fingers burying themselves in my hair, pulling me against her as the kiss turned abruptly hungry.

Carnal.

Her mouth under mine was hot and eager, her tongue sliding against my own, her lips falling apart as I slanted my mouth into hers over and over again, drinking in her barely audible moans.

I turned her, pressing her back to the wall, crowding her, needing to feel her against me, to keep her still. To keep her exactly where I wanted her as I kissed her again and again.

I was barely aware we had company, too caught up in Violet to care about anyone else until she went stiff in my arms and let out a sound of distress. Angling my body to shield her from whatever had caused her to tense, I turned to see Gage standing behind me, his arms crossed over his chest, his face like thunder.

Glaring back at him, I stepped fully in front of Violet, pulling my phone from my pocket and sending a quick text to my driver. There was no way we were going back into the ballroom after that kiss.

First, I had to get rid of Gage.

"What?" I asked, impatient. For all the times I'd walked in on Gage and Sophie in all manner of compromising positions, everywhere but in their own rooms, you'd think he could keep his fucking nose out of my business. A kiss in the corner wasn't a big deal. It wasn't like I had anything to hide.

"Can we talk?" Gage asked stiffly, looking past me to Violet, his blue eyes hard with dislike.

Chapter Nine

Aiden

"No, we can't," I said. I glanced over my shoulder to see Violet smoothing her hair back, her lips a little pink, her eyes cool and remote. Fuck. She'd been liquid fire in my arms less than a minute ago and now the ice queen was back.

I loved the ice queen. When Violet went all frosty and formal she was hot as hell, but I'd liked where we were, wrapped in each other, her fingers in my hair, her lips under mine.

I stepped forward, preparing to lead Violet past Gage. He shifted to block me.

"What the fuck are you doing?" he asked, under his breath.

Behind me, Violet stiffened. Fucking fuck. All I wanted was one fucking night with Violet. We all knew the game we were playing, and we all knew it had to end at some point. I couldn't imagine Violet planned to keep up her secret identity forever, especially since she knew that I knew. She didn't know how much I knew, but she knew enough. And not being a fool, she could guess that Gage was in on it.

"This isn't the time," I said. "I'll talk to you tomorrow."

Violet shifted to the side, maybe thinking to escape. I wound my arm through hers to hold her still and said to Gage, "We're leaving. We can talk tomorrow. If you think you're going to stop us, or make a scene, know that I will fucking level you. I don't want to ruin Abigail's event with a brawl, and I know neither of us wants to make the papers tomorrow, so keep your mouth shut, step aside, and let us leave."

"I hope you have a plan," Gage muttered as he moved out of our way.

"I always do," I answered as I led Violet down the terrace and back into the ballroom.

The dancing was in full swing, and between the noise and the dimmed lighting, we managed to escape attention. Violet let me guide her down the hall towards the elevators in silence.

Eventually, she said, "You're taking me home?"

"Not exactly," I said, "just away from here."

I caught a flash of uncertainty in her eyes, but she only nodded in answer. At the elevators, Violet caught sight of a discreet sign and pulled her arm from mine.

"I have to powder my nose. I'll be right back."

She wasn't wearing powder, but I let her go without objection. If Gage had spooked her and she thought to take off she'd be disappointed to find out there was nowhere to go.

While I waited I checked my phone and saw an answering text from my driver. He was out front and had prepared the back of the limo with a freshly opened bottle of champagne and two glasses.

We want to go for a ride, I texted.

Destination?

Not at the moment, I answered.

You got it, Boss.

Violet reappeared and came straight to my side. Something tight in my chest eased as I realized she hadn't been looking for escape. Any stray tendrils of hair had been smoothed back into place. Her makeup was flawless, the gloss reapplied to her lips. The ice queen in full form.

I loved that she didn't let Gage intimidate her. Whatever was going on under the surface, Violet had a spine of steel. No one would get past her guard unless she let them.

No one except for me.

The elevator doors opened and we entered. I had the momentary thought of pressing her into the corner and messing up everything she'd just straightened. I held myself in check. In moments we'd be safely hidden away in the limo. We would leave as Aiden Winters and his Ice Queen. I'd melt her soon enough.

Violet made herself comfortable in the back of the limo, her eyes flaring the tiniest bit when she spotted the open bottle of champagne in the bar. She raised one delicate blonde eyebrow and waited.

I poured us both a glass of champagne and handed her one. "I thought we'd go for a ride."

"A ride where?"

"Just a ride," I said and watched her take a sip of the champagne. She took a long, slow look around the inside of the limo, her eyes settling on the partition separating us from my driver.

Answering her un-asked question I said, "It's soundproof. Completely private."

"How can you be sure?"

"Trust me." I wasn't going to tell her how I knew it was soundproof. There were details about my life Violet didn't need to hear. Other women were the past. Violet was the only one who mattered now. Echoing her promise from earlier in the night I said, "I won't embarrass you."

She took a sip of the champagne and said, "This is all terribly decadent. The champagne. The limo. You bought me Valentino."

"I saw it and thought of you," I said.

She rolled her eyes, the champagne working its way through her shields. "When did you see it? When did you have time to troll the women's formals department?"

I wasn't about to tell her I'd had my personal shopper send me pictures of the selection of gowns in her size and from those I'd chosen the one she wore.

"I have my ways," I said.

"I bet you do," she said, rolling her eyes again. "I bet you have all sorts of ways." She let out an abrupt laugh that turned into a snort, and clapped her hand over her mouth, giggling.

Violet was adorably tipsy. I'd seen her ice queen, and her passion, but I'd never seen her cute. I wanted to pull her into my lap and kiss the giggles from her lips. And I would, in a minute. First I had to know why she was laughing.

"What's so funny?"

"It's just that—" she struggled to get out the words, her shoulders shaking in amusement. "Gage is imagining that I'm some kind of seductress out to take advantage of poor defenseless Aiden, but you've got moves for days and I wouldn't know how to seduce anyone, much less a man like you."

"I don't know," I said, entranced by the sparkle in her eyes, by the way she was laughing at herself and not the least bit worried about Gage. "You're doing a pretty good job right now."

Violet tossed back the rest of her champagne and handed me her empty glass. She shook her head, negating my words. "Please," she said with derision, still laughing a little. "You're just playing with me. I have no idea what I'm doing with you. And you're going to be disappointed. I've never even—"

She cut off abruptly, her eyes flying wide with horror. I had to know what she'd been about to say.

"You're not a virgin," I stated, positive of that fact. She was close to thirty. There was no way she'd never had sex. I watched the laughter drain from her. She let out a sigh, her teeth sinking into her lower lip as she appeared to consider something.

"No, I've had sex, I'm just not good at it," she said, bluntly. As if wishing she could take the words back, she closed her mouth tightly and gestured to her empty champagne glass.

I held it up and said, "Not until you tell me what that means."

"Champagne first."

I might have argued, but I sensed that another glass of champagne was the only thing that would pry an explanation out of her. We'd only kissed twice, but after the way she lit up for me, there was no way this woman was bad at sex. Inexperienced maybe. I'd buy that. But what she didn't know I could teach her. She had all the instincts she'd need.

I handed her back her champagne glass, now full, and watched with greedy eyes as she lifted it to her lips and sipped. She'd seated herself on the longest side bench of the limo, maybe thinking to put some distance between us.

I was done with distance.

I slid closer as she drank.

"So?" I asked.

Violet shrugged one bare shoulder and looked away. "I shouldn't have said that. It's just that I freeze up, or get shy. I don't know what I'm supposed to do, and then it's over. That's all. It's not a big deal." Embarrassment heated her cheeks and she drained her champagne glass. Plucking it from her fingers, I put it aside. I didn't offer to refill it, and she didn't ask.

"So you've never had an orgasm?"

Violet's eyes looked everywhere but at mine. She hitched her shoulder up in an attempt at a shrug and mumbled something under her breath.

"What was that?" I asked, softly.

She shook her head and I leaned forward, sliding my arm around her back and pulling her across the seat into my arms.

Brushing her ear with my lips I whispered, "Tell me."

I grazed my fingertips along her jaw, tracing her lower lip and stroking down the curve of her neck. She let out a breath and shivered.

"Tell you what?" she asked, the question vague. Distracted.

I nipped the lobe of her ear lightly, loving the way she jumped in response, arching her back and pressing her breasts into my side.

"Have you ever had an orgasm?" I pressed. My hand dropped to trace her bodice, stroking across the upper swell of her breasts, so tightly contained in her ball gown.

Violet swallowed hard and shook her head. Her words were little more than a whisper when she said, "Only by myself."

Pressing a kiss to the edge of her jaw, just below her ear,

I savored the thrum of her pulse against my lips. "Do you want to have one with me?"

In a voice heavy with arousal, she answered only, "Aiden."

I didn't know if it was permission or a plea, but the sound of my name from her lips sent a rush of blood straight to my cock, I'd never been this hard. I'd never wanted a woman this much.

I tipped her head back and ran my tongue up the cord of her neck, tasting her skin, the heat of her. She drew in a sharp breath and murmured, "Aiden, please."

Permission and a plea.

It was all I needed.

Pulling her beneath me on the wide bench seat, I took her mouth with mine. Hesitation and embarrassment fled as she opened for me, her tongue seeking, twining and stroking, her lips, her mouth, her body—all hungry. Eager. I kissed her until my breath strangled in my chest, my cock a pulsing bar. I held onto my control by my fingernails.

I'd asked her to trust me. I wouldn't fuck that up, but I had to have more.

I found the zipper running down the side of her bodice and slowly, deliberately pulled it down. All it took was one hitching breath from Violet and her breasts rose, pushing at the filmy tulle of her gown. Bracing myself on one arm, I peeled the fabric away and drank in the sight of her.

I'd had a lot of fantasies about Violet's breasts. I'd caught only the most miserly glimpses. A hint of cleavage, a curve beneath her blouse. We'd only kissed the one time in my office, and I'd barely touched her before we were interrupted. And now here she was, on display for me, and she was fucking gorgeous.

Full and round, capped with tight, petal pink nipples,

her skin so pale I could see the blue veins running beneath, softer than silk. Her heart pounded beneath my fingers as I cupped her left breast and dipped my head. Her sweet pea scent was warmer here, flowers and the scent of Violet. Intoxicating. I ran the pad of my thumb over the top of her nipple and the tremor that ran through her almost had me coming in my pants.

I couldn't wait. I stroked her nipple before I closed my lips around it, pulling hard. She gasped out my name in shocked surprise, going stiff for just a second before her head fell back and she arched, pressing her breasts into me, giving me more. Inviting me to take.

I went a little wild, stroking her breasts, sucking, licking, closing my teeth over her nipples in gentle bites that had her whimpering and writhing against me. I'd like to say I'd planned it, but I was as lost as Violet. I pulled her leg over mine, opening her, and drew my hand from her breast to slide it under her skirt. The rasp of lace met my fingertips, wet and hot.

Fucking hell. In my wildest, most debauched fantasies of fucking Violet nothing was as hot as her breast under my lips and my fingers grazing the slick heat of her pussy. The wisp of lace between her legs was in my way.

A sharp jerk tore the fabric, and I had free rein to touch. To tease. I wanted her wild, as wild as I was. Desperate and needy and hungry.

Her clit was swollen with arousal, begging for attention. I wanted it in my mouth. I wanted to push her skirts up, spread her legs wide, and feast on her. Even half mindless with need I knew that was the wrong move. If she'd never come before, she'd never had a mouth between her legs.

If I pushed her too hard, she'd freeze up on me, and if

she pushed me away before I made her come, it might kill me.

I needed to see that, to see her unravel for me. I needed to feel it. To hear it. To smell it. I needed her pleasure to be mine, for me alone.

I dipped my fingers into her pussy, gathering the slick moisture and rubbed them in a slow circle around her clit. Her breath caught in her chest and she made a sound somewhere between pleasure and alarm.

Lifting my head from her breast, I moved to take her mouth with mine. I wasn't going to let her get shy. I wasn't going to let her wonder what she was supposed to be doing. I wanted her half-crazed. I wanted her to let go, to let me take care of her. To let me give her what she needed.

Her hand came up, her fingers fisting in my hair as she held my mouth to hers, throwing herself into the kiss. Her knees drew up and fell open as she unconsciously offered herself to me. I dipped a finger inside, my head spinning at the feel of her heat clasping me. She was so fucking tight. Tight and hot and rocking up into my finger, her body moving on instinct.

I kissed her harder and drove a second finger inside her, reaching deep, fucking her with my fingers, pressing my palm against her swollen clit. Her hips jerked into my hand, hard and fast, and she broke into pieces beneath me, the sharp rush of pleasure cracking her open, drawing out cry after cry as she shuddered through her peak.

I didn't come with her, but it was a close thing. I hadn't come without touching my cock since I was a teenager, but the sight of Violet overcome, her frantic moans, the greedy clench of her pussy on my fingers, was almost too much.

I'd dreamed about fucking Violet.

A lot.

I had a long list of places and ways I planned to fuck her, but not in this limo.

Not the first time we were together.

Ordering my cock to chill the fuck out, I feathered a kiss across her lips and straightened her bodice, not zipping it closed but preserving her modesty. When she came down, I didn't want her to feel exposed. Vulnerable.

I didn't know why it mattered so fucking much, but I needed her to feel safe with me. I needed her to know I would take care of her.

It was fucked up considering everything between us. Her lies and mine.

But this—what happened when we touched each other, the way she'd come apart in my arms—this was a deeper truth.

This was something real, and I wouldn't let her regret it.

Chapter Ten

Violet

I dressed for work on Monday in one of my nicer suits, a lightweight plum wool with a fitted skirt and matching jacket. The jacket had a long, lean cut with an inverted collar. The style was modern and spare, but the skirt had a flare just above the knee that gave it a hint of the feminine.

After the disaster of my first position, I stuck with severe and professional as my style watchwords for work. But I didn't want to be wearing a boxy black blazer the first time I saw Aiden after he'd given me the most spectacular orgasm of my life.

Silly, dressing for Aiden. There were so many reasons dressing for Aiden was a bad idea. He was my boss. Our whole relationship was based on a lie. My lie. I'd only met him because I was trying to uncover his secrets and force him to do what I wanted.

He was Aiden Winters. So far out of my league I needed a telescope to see him, and even if my dishonesty weren't between us, he'd never get serious with me.

There were so many reasons I shouldn't dress for him. Shouldn't want to be alone with him. Shouldn't hope for a repeat of Friday night.

I might have spent a little extra time on my hair and makeup, though I was probably the only one who'd notice. If I'd wanted Aiden's attention, I was disappointed. I walked in Monday morning, fifteen minutes early, to find the executive floor in a state of complete upheaval. Phones rang and went unanswered. Marisela, Thomas, Peter, and Henry alternately barked on the phone, rushed around with stacks of paper, and pounded away at their keyboards.

Aiden's door stood open, his office empty. I was greeted by a note on my desk in his sharp, bold handwriting listing urgent tasks. I gathered from my orders and what I heard from the conversations in the room, that a carefully negotiated deal was on the verge of falling through. Aiden and Gage had gained new information about the company they were acquiring, information that significantly changed the foundation of the agreements.

Bitterness flashed through me as I absorbed the tension, the excitement in the air. I remembered this from the days when Chase was negotiating the sale of CD4 Analytics. The adrenaline, the rush. And look how that had turned out.

Were Aiden and Gage preparing to screw someone else out of everything they had? Was the owner sitting in Gage's office thinking his life was about to change when in reality he'd find himself shut out of the business he'd worked so hard to build?

Let it go, Violet.

I hadn't been able to find a shred of proof that Aiden had been behind what happened to Chase.

Nothing.

I had to admit that it was possible I might have my facts wrong, that somehow Chase and I had misunderstood.

Which probably made me the biggest sucker in Atlanta. I couldn't imagine how we could have misunderstood. Contracts were signed, money was transferred, and the next thing we knew Chase was locked out of his building. A few days later the building was sold and CD4 Analytics had been folded into Winters, Inc.

It happened that fast.

When Chase reviewed the contracts his lawyer discovered small, key points had been altered between his final review and his signing. Somehow he'd been distracted and the documents switched, but they were legal and he couldn't prove he hadn't known what he'd signed. In the end, Chase was shut out and Aiden had control of his company.

I wanted Aiden to be innocent.

I did.

Every time I looked at things from a different angle they always came out the same. Chase had been kicked out of his company and Aiden had taken his place.

The worst part was that they weren't even using half of the technology they bought. Getting rid of Chase hadn't made sense considering the most valuable part of the company wasn't ready for end-users yet. Chase was still fine-tuning it and without him, they couldn't make it work.

I'd been working in the department Winters, Inc. had created out of CD4, and I'd heard enough gossip to know the best parts of the company they'd stolen were dead in the water. It didn't make sense.

The more I knew Aiden the less I would have expected

him to make a mistake like that. It would have made far more sense to keep Chase on than it had to get rid of him. Aiden was too sharp, too practical for a mistake like that.

And there I was, making excuses for him again. It turned my stomach to work on another acquisition for Winters, Inc. I was tempted to toss my purse, my mug, my stapler, and my cactus in the box still beneath my desk and walk out forever.

Not yet.

I'd give myself until the end of the week to find something, I could use to get Chase's company back. If I hadn't found anything by the end of day on Friday, I was cutting my losses and leaving.

A little voice in my head asked if I was staying for Chase or staying to see Aiden just a little longer. I shut it down. My date with Aiden had been a moment out of time. A dream. Now it was over, and it was never going to happen again. Ever.

If I wanted to stay for the rest of the week, if I wanted a little more time to finish out this plan, I had to do my job. Ignoring my desperate need for coffee, I pulled my chair up to my desk and started with the first item on Aiden's list.

Given that I was the most junior and least qualified of his executive assistants, my list was the most basic. Pulling data, assembling a few spreadsheets I guessed Aiden and Gage would use to negotiate a change in pricing.

Just as I was about to deliver everything he'd asked for, an email popped into my box with files attached and the note; *Four copies, collated and stapled, marked for signing. NOW*.

It was from Aiden's email address. I pulled up the documents and saw they were revisions to the contracts being negotiated in Gage's office. I sent them all to the printer and headed for the copy room so I could get started putting little yellow tabs next to all the lines that required a signature.

The copy room was empty and strangely quiet. It only took me a minute to realize the printer/copier was completely powered down. I'd never seen it turned off. Hopefully, I pressed the power button on the side. Nothing happened. It was plugged in, but it wasn't getting any juice. A quick look around told me that the coffee maker was similarly dark. A blown fuse? This was the last thing I needed.

I poked my head out of the coffee room and caught Marisela's eye. "How long has the copier been down?" I asked briskly.

She shrugged one shoulder and turned her eyes back to her monitor. "I didn't know it was. Look, I have too much to do to babysit you. If you can't get it working, call maintenance."

I tried unplugging it and plugging it back in, flipping a switch on the wall, and poking at some of the buttons. Useless. I was good with computers, great with spreadsheets, and I was a half decent programmer. Nowhere near as good as Chase, not really good enough to pursue it as a job, but I was decent. However, I knew nothing about hardware. I expected to plug things in, press the power button, and have them turn on. When that didn't happen, I was lost.

I picked up the phone in the break room and called down to maintenance, impressing upon the woman who answered that if the copier didn't get fixed, Aiden and Gage were going to be very unhappy. She promised someone would be up in a matter of minutes.

I paced the tiny copy room, my nerves piling higher

with every second that passed. I couldn't forget Aiden's 'NOW'. He did not sound like he was in a patient mood.

All my confusion and bitterness aside, I didn't want to mess up his negotiation. Maybe I should. Maybe I should be looking for ways to sabotage him, but I couldn't, wouldn't, cross that line. All I wanted was to find a way to force him to give Chase's company back. I didn't want to hurt him.

It really was only a few minutes until someone strolled into the copy room, took a quick look, and disappeared, saying something about a breaker. He'd barely turned the corner when the copier and coffee maker came to life. I heard him in the outer office saying something about a space heater in a long-suffering voice of complaint, and Henry answering that he had cold feet. Who has cold feet in June?

I didn't care. Now that the printer was working I could resend my documents, get them ready for signing and hand them over to Aiden and Gage. One of the many benefits of working for a company like Winters, Inc. was the equipment. They spared no expense and the machine in the copy room printed, collated, and stapled four copies of the contracts in only a few minutes. It took me longer to go through and mark the locations for initials and signatures than it did for the machine to prepare the documents.

I knew these papers could only represent a small portion of the deal they were negotiating. There weren't enough documents here for this to be the whole thing, but it must be an important part if they were making changes. I couldn't bring myself to extend my curiosity.

Just being on the edges of an acquisition made me anxious. Again, I thought about throwing in the towel and cutting my losses early.

What was the point of staying until Friday? Did I really think I was going to find the smoking gun I was looking for?

I strode across the central hallway and around the corner to Gage's section of the executive floor. His office doors were closed, his two assistants working furiously at their desks. The closest one looked up as I approached and said, "Oh, thank God. We're having problems with our printer over here."

"I'm sorry it took so long," I said, holding out the documents to her. "We had a flipped breaker in our copy room and I had to call maintenance."

She held up a finger instead of taking the documents. "You're here now. Just knock on the door and hand them in."

I rapped on the closed double doors to Gage's office with a light knock. I could hear tense voices on the other side and the shuffle of someone standing and walking to the door. It swung open to reveal Gage, his blue eyes tense, his jaw set. I handed him the contracts and went to step away.

"Wait," he said, tersely. His eyes scanned the top page, then the second, then the third, as he rapidly flipped through the contract. When he was done, he went back to the third page and ran his finger across the line holding a sequence of numbers.

His eyes rose from the papers, hot with rage. In a low, controlled voice he said, "I told Aiden you'd try something like this. He swore you wouldn't."

"I don't know what you're talking about," I said, keeping my chin up and my voice cool. Gage was furious, but I refused to let him rattle me. I'd done exactly what Aiden had asked. No more and no less.

"Then what the fuck is this?" He demanded showing me the line of numbers in the contract. They didn't mean anything to me.

"I have no idea. I didn't review the contract, I only printed it up. If there's an error, it's not on my end."

"Don't fuck with me, Violet whoever you are. I saw the contract before Aiden sent it to you. I know you changed the numbers. This deal is on the edge as it is. Maybe you thought you could take advantage. Maybe you're working for them. I don't really give a fuck. You're fired."

Chapter Eleven

Violet

"You're fired."

I refused to flinch at those two words. Oh, the irony. I'd lied on my application, I'd hacked Aiden's emails, I'd been digging through the confidential files, and now I was being fired for something I hadn't even done. I was almost tempted to laugh, but I wasn't giving an inch.

Gage wanted a reaction. He wouldn't get one from me.

He stepped fully out of the doorway, closing the door behind him. To the assistant I'd spoken with, he said, "Call security."

She picked up the phone and quietly summoned two security officers to the executive floor.

"Nothing to say?" he pushed.

I kept my mouth shut. I hadn't done anything wrong, but it was useless to defend myself. Life had taught me that begging for mercy just made you look guilty. Hadn't I been about to quit ten times that day already? Now the decision had been made for me.

I had no interest in standing outside Gage's office under

his angry stare. "I'll go back to my desk and get my things together."

"You're just fucking ice-cold aren't you?" Gage stepped closer, trying to intimidate me.

He could try. But he was right, I was ice-cold and there was nothing he could say that would shake me. I turned to walk away. His hand shot out and closed around my wrist, fingers biting into my skin. "You're not going anywhere without a security escort."

"Fine," I conceded. "Let go of me."

The door behind Gage opened and Aiden stepped through, closing it behind him. His eyes landed on Gage's fingers wrapped around my wrist.

"What the fuck?"

Between gritted teeth, Gage said, "She changed the numbers in the contract."

Aiden's dark eyes flashed to me.

I shook my head. "I did not. I opened the files only to print them. I changed nothing. I did exactly what you asked me to do, and no more. I don't know what happened, but it wasn't me."

Aiden studied my face, staring into my eyes, taking in the resolute set of my chin. Looking at his cousin, he said "Let go of her goddamn wrist. Now."

Reluctantly, Gage loosened his fingers. I had the urge to snatch my wrist back, but I wouldn't show that much weakness. Slowly, I let my arm fall to my side.

"Did anyone have access to the documents after you opened them on your terminal?" Aiden asked slowly.

Understanding hit me in a thunderbolt. I knew the others hated me, but messing with company contracts? That was a huge escalation from stapler stealing and switching salt for sugar.

"When I went to get the contracts off the copier, it was dead. We had a breaker flip and I had to call maintenance. I called from the copy room and waited there. I was away from my terminal for close to ten minutes."

"And were the files open while you were gone?" Gage asked, grudgingly.

"Yes," I admitted, feeling like an idiot. It had never occurred to me that the other four would go that far, but it should have. "I'm sorry. I didn't think—"

"Look at me," Aiden demanded. My eyes rose to his before I could think about refusing his order. "Swear you had nothing to do with this."

In a clear, steady voice, I said, "I swear I did absolutely nothing to sabotage your deal or this contract."

Looking past us, Aiden spoke to Gage's lead assistant. "Can you access the copier by my office?"

She nodded, careful not to look in my direction. "Yes, sir."

"I'll send you these contracts," Gage said brusquely. "Mark where we need signatures and bring them in as soon as you have them."

"Yes, sir," she agreed.

Aiden hadn't taken his eyes off of me. Two security officers exited the elevators and walked toward us, eyeing me carefully. Were they expecting me to run? Aiden let out an irritated growl.

"I don't have time for this today, Violet. I don't know what your game is, but I'm tired of playing it."

"I'll clean out my desk," I said quietly.

It was for the best. Maybe the others had tried to sabotage me, but I was taking it as a sign from the universe. My ill-conceived plan to save my brother's company was dead in the water. I should get out of here while I still could.

"Go back to your desk and stay there. I don't want you to leave that seat until you talk to me."

"I fired her," Gage said. Aiden shot him a glare.

"She's unfired. She's my assistant, not yours. You don't get to fire her." To me, he said, "If you leave before I'm ready to boot you out, I will hunt you down and drag you back. Do you understand me?"

It took everything I had not to crumple under the force of his anger. I kept my chin up and my voice level when I said, "I understand."

Aiden gestured for the two security officers to come closer. To the first, he said, "Escort Ms. Hartwell back to her desk and remain on the floor. No one from the executive team leaves until cleared. No one."

The officer nodded briskly and took a step to place himself behind me. "Yes, sir."

To the other, Aiden said, "Check the cameras on the outer office. I want to know if anyone approached Ms. Hartwell's terminal while she was in the copy room. Pull the keystrokes."

"Yes sir. I'll check into it immediately."

Aiden nodded at him in agreement and he turned to leave. Looking between myself and Gage, Aiden shook his head. "We don't have time to deal with this mess until these contracts are signed. After that..."

He trailed off. Just as well. I wasn't sure I wanted to know what came *after*. I still thought getting fired sounded pretty good.

Pulling my dignity around me in a shield, I nodded once and turned on my heel, keeping pace with my security escort. Just before we reached my desk I asked, "Am I allowed to get a cup of coffee?"

With a hint of a smile, the security officer said, "We'll

both get one. I have a feeling it's going to be a long afternoon."

I picked up my mug from my desk and looked up to see Marisela and Thomas gawking at my escort. I ignored them both but didn't miss Marisela's smirk and Thomas's smug smile as they watched us disappear into the copy room.

I wasn't really surprised. Gage had confronted me so aggressively, it'd taken me a minute to catch up, but there wasn't any doubt who was responsible. Peter didn't have the balls to mess with one of Aiden's contracts. Henry was too loyal. But Marisela was both cocky and petty. My money was on her. Thomas would have egged her on, but I was betting he wouldn't risk his job just to get back at me.

I made myself an extra strong latte—I'd finally figured out the coffee machine—and parked myself at my desk. Fortunately for all of us, I didn't have anything left on my list from Aiden, and I spent the rest of the day on my normal duties: Answering emails, the phone, and other busywork no one else wanted to do.

At one o'clock the security officer standing guard over the five of us took lunch orders. They weren't kidding around about not letting us leave. By the middle of the afternoon, Marisela was starting to look a little uneasy. I was only worried that the contract negotiations would extend into the evening.

I wanted to go home, pour a nice glass of wine, and hit the couch. I only had a week and a half until Chase came home, and I'd have to share the TV. I had to catch up on my shows before then. I reminded myself that I could always get my own place, but since I was about to become unemployed, again, it seemed more practical to keep imposing on Chase's hospitality.

Someday I'd pay him back for everything he'd done for me. Someday.

At six o'clock, Marisela tried to leave. The security officer who'd been watching us politely stopped her. When she blustered at him, he ignored her. She went back to her desk and sulked.

Just before seven Aiden and Gage strode in, flanked by two more security officers. They headed straight for Marisela. She did her best to look innocent, but she couldn't quite pull it off. Aiden stood before her desk, looking down at her with a mixture of pity and disgust.

"I'm going to assume it was a spur of the moment idea. If you'd taken the time to think it through, you would have remembered the cameras and the keystroke tracking software. Sloppy. I'm disappointed on a number of levels, Marisela. You had promise, but you let yourself get emotional and you made a stupid mistake. You also endangered a key negotiation. The company comes first. Always. Clearly, you're fired. I don't recommend using me as a reference."

Marisela started to babble, an angry, tearful mix of accusations against me and claims of injustice. Security closed in, impervious to her entreaties. Aiden turned to leave, stopping by my desk on his way out.

"I meant what I said. You don't walk away until I send you away. Got it?"

"Yes, sir," I said.

No one moved until Marisela, her security escort, Aiden, and Gage had all left. Thomas, Peter, and Henry gathered their things and scurried out without a word. Hard to say how much of a role they'd played in altering the contract and trying to get me fired, but I had a feeling their stupid pranks would stop.

I didn't really care. I had much bigger problems than salt in the sugar bowl.

Up until now, I'd always thought leaving was my prerogative.

I had no doubt Aiden meant what he said. If I walked away before he was ready to let me go, he'd find me. So far, he'd kept me close despite knowing I couldn't be trusted.

Now, when he had the perfect excuse to get rid of me, he demanded I stay. My plan to save Chase's company had fallen apart. Instead of catching Aiden Winters, he'd caught me. Until he decided to let me go, I was trapped.

Chapter Twelve

Aiden

The week started as badly as the previous one had ended well. Our supposedly cut and dried acquisition of a shipping company had gone tits up first thing Monday morning. The mess with the contract, Marisela, and Violet sure as hell hadn't helped.

On top of that, Gage and I were barely speaking. We'd finally had it out this morning over breakfast.

Gage had started in on me as soon as I sat at the table. "You have to fire her. She's a liability and keeping an eye on her is a waste of company resources."

"Stay out of it," I said, ignoring him to put hot sauce on my scrambled eggs.

"The hell I will," he'd responded.

The frustration beneath his words told me Gage wasn't prepared to let it go. Fine. We might as well settle this. "I'll fire her soon. I promise. But you're going to have to drop the attitude. I'll get Violet out of the company, but I'm keeping her in my life. I don't want to worry you're going to be an asshole every time you see her."

"You've got to be fucking kidding me," Gage said. He

was usually good at controlling his temper, but something about Violet got under his skin. I had a feeling I knew what it was.

"You're wrong about her, you know," I said, calmly, before taking a bite of eggs. The hot sauce seared through my sinuses and my eyes watered. Better than a hit of caffeine for waking my brain up in the morning.

"I'm wrong that she took a job with us under a false name and has spent her entire time with the company trying to dig up dirt on you?" Gage challenged.

"No, you're right about that. I think I've figured out what she's been up to. But that's not what I meant."

"Then what?" Gage stabbed at his eggs, sending them sliding across the plate. He was seriously pissed.

I took pity on him and said, "She's nothing like Elizabeth."

Gage rolled his eyes, abruptly reminding me of himself as a teenager. Some things didn't change.

"She isn't," I insisted. "They look alike, I'll give you that."

"Violet has a better body," Gage commented, "I never noticed until she wore that dress, but she's got a nice—"

I stabbed my fork in the air in his direction. "Shut the fuck up. You keep your eyes off her. She's mine."

"For fuck's sake," Gage said, "Are you serious? First of all, I'm crazy about my wife, but I'm not blind. And Sophie is the one who pointed out Violet's, uh, assets."

I shook my head, trying to imagine my sweet, quiet cousin in law commenting on another woman's rack. The picture wouldn't gel. But Gage was right, he was crazy in love with Sophie. I still didn't like hearing him talk that way about Violet.

"This isn't about her body," I said. "And she's nothing like Elizabeth where it matters."

"I doubt that," Gage muttered.

"You're being an asshole," I said, and told him how Violet had chased Elizabeth off at the ball, putting her in her place with a few well-chosen words.

"She's just scaring off the competition."

"Violet isn't a gold digger," I said.

"You don't know that," Gage said, shaking his head at my obstinance.

"I do."

I didn't. Not conclusively. But my gut told me that whatever Violet wanted with me, it wasn't access to my wallet. She was up to something, and it had to do with our acquisition of CD4 Analytics, but I was almost positive the personal side of our relationship had not been a part of her plans.

Too bad. I'd meant what I'd said.

I wasn't letting her go until I was ready.

And I wasn't ready yet.

"Look," I said. "Just back the fuck off. I know what I'm doing. I'll have her out of the company within a week or two. Until then, leave her alone."

"Fine," Gage said, setting his fork and knife neatly on his plate. "Just let me know when this blows up in your face so I can help you clean up the mess."

"Thanks for the vote of confidence," I said to his retreating back. The only response was a raised middle finger as he disappeared through the doorway.

I hadn't managed to have a real conversation with Violet all week. I was too busy, working too late to try to see her after hours. I was exhausted and frustrated. By mid-day, the shipping acquisition finally tied up, I decided the hell with it and sent Violet an email.

I need you to work late. Order dinner, your choice.
A

Not my smoothest move, but the last few days had been endless and I'd worked through my reserves. I needed to see Violet. Alone. I walked past her desk every day and the sight of her serene features, the sound of her cool, composed voice, soothed me.

If I loved the way she'd handled Elizabeth, that was nothing next to the way she'd dealt with Gage. If I hadn't been so stressed I would have found it funny—all the things she was guilty of and he'd fired her over the one thing she didn't do.

Fuck that. She was my assistant. If anyone fired her it would be me. That day was coming. I couldn't justify keeping her in the company for much longer. She hadn't done anything unforgivable. Yet.

I wasn't worried about her reading my emails. I'd already taken steps to cloak anything confidential. The same for the files. She was far better than an amateur hacker, but she wasn't a match for my security team.

We were stringing her along, keeping her contained, but with every day that passed, I could justify it less. Violet had to go. I only had to figure out how to do it without losing her completely.

It was nearing six when I looked up from my desk to see Violet hovering in the doorway, an uncharacteristically hesitant expression on her face.

A little more eager than I intended I said, "Dinner here?"

"Soon," she said. "I ordered Italian."

"Great," I said, glancing down at the paperwork I was reviewing. I was tempted to shove it out of the way and replace it with Violet.

"I shouldn't be here," she said. "You never ask any of the others to work late."

"I think we both know you're not like the others," I said. It was the second time I'd openly alluded to her deception. Her only acknowledgment was a brief nod.

"You should have let Gage fire me," she said.

"Why? What are you planning to do to me?" I asked before I could think better of it.

Violet's shoulders slumped forward barely an inch, but from her, it was an admission of defeat. Taking a deep breath, she straightened, her eyes softening as they took me in.

"You work too much," she said. "You're tired. You should go home and get some sleep. You're the first person here and the last one to leave. This place won't fall apart without you. You know that, right?"

"So Gage tells me," I said, dryly. "I don't want to talk about my work habits. I just want you to have dinner with me."

"Why?" she asked, softly.

"I told you. You're a puzzle and I'm not through figuring you out."

"You know this is a terrible idea," she said. "You should fire me. Or, I should quit."

"Just have dinner with me," I said, "and we'll worry about the rest of it later."

The gods of timing were on my side. I heard the elevator ding and the doors slide open. Violet looked over her shoulder and straightened. She stepped back out of my office doorway, turning to say, "Thank you, Chris. I would have come down to get it."

"It's no problem, Ms. Hartwell, I was coming this way anyway."

I was smiling to myself when she walked back in my office carrying a brown paper sack that smelled enticingly of garlic and tomatoes. She started to set the bag on my desk and I stopped her.

"Not here. Let's eat on the couch."

Violet looked at me doubtfully but did as I asked, taking the paper bag to the coffee table in front of my black leather couch and unpacking it. I went to the wet bar across from the couch and pulled a bottle of red wine from the storage rack. The wet bar was a throwback to my father's time. Gage and I weren't big drinkers, and neither of us drank during the workday. I'd snuck this bottle in with Violet in mind.

"What are you smiling about?" she asked, sounding vaguely disgruntled. She should since she was the one amusing me.

"You."

"What about me?" she demanded, flipping open a styrofoam container of garlic knots. The buttery, garlicky scent hit me, and my mouth watered. Lunch had been a quick sandwich hours before.

"Chris called you 'Ms. Hartwell' and brought dinner up to the office. Who else around here gets called by their last name?"

"Other than you and Gage?" Violet asked. "I don't know, I haven't been here that long. Everyone calls Gage's head assistant Ms. Emerson."

"She's been here since my grandfather's day," I said. "You're a new hire, on the young side, and you not only have them calling you Ms. Hartwell, you've got Chris so wrapped around your finger he brought you your dinner. You're a very appealing combination of standoffish and charming."

The pink in her cheeks only proved my point.

"I'm not charming," she said, shaking her head. "Chris spent the afternoon here on Monday guarding all of us. He's a nice guy."

"No, he's not," I said, this time full out laughing. "Chris is a former Navy SEAL on loan to Winters, Inc. from Sinclair Security. I put him on all of you Monday afternoon because the guys he's been working with were on another project, but he's here training them. He's a hard ass son of a bitch, and not easily taken in. But you, he likes."

Violet shrugged one shoulder. "I think he just appreciated that I wasn't a pain in the ass about the whole thing."

"As opposed to Marisela?" I asked. Marisela's treachery had been disappointing. She had potential, but if she was going to let a little thing like competition lead her into bad decision-making, we were better off without her.

Violet shook her head and didn't comment. She eyed the deep leather couch and the low coffee table before taking a seat on the carpet and curling her legs beneath her. She pulled her container of linguine closer and picked up a plastic fork. Setting a glass of red wine in front of her, I sat on the couch, my own food in one hand and a fork in the other.

"You don't have to sit on the floor," I said, trying not to stare at the length of thigh exposed by her skirt.

"I'm fine," she said. "If I sit up there, I'll spill this all over myself."

I wasn't going to complain, considering the view. "That wasn't the first time Marisela played a trick on you, was it?"

Violet kept her eyes on her pasta, slowly twirling her fork in the strands and lifting it to her mouth. She chewed slowly, thinking. "It's not a big deal."

"Maybe not, but I want to know."

"They have a right not to like me," Violet said, slowly. "What Marisela did with the contracts was way over the top. She shouldn't have taken out her dislike of me on the company. But the rest of it—" She shook her head in dismissal. "You and I both know why you gave me this job. But they don't. All they see is that I'm new and unqualified. They worked their asses off to get where they are. I'd be frustrated too."

"Was it just Marisela, or is it all of them?" I asked, trying to keep my question casual.

I'd suspected my executive team would give her a hard time when I'd put her in the job. Back then, the idea hadn't bothered me.

It did now.

Chapter Thirteen

Aiden

Violet forked up more pasta and shook her head again. "It doesn't matter, Aiden."

"It matters if they're petty and emotional enough to waste time hazing another employee when they should be focused on their jobs."

"Marisela egged them on," she said, grudgingly. "It's been fine since she's been gone."

"You'll tell me if that changes," I said.

"It doesn't matter," she repeated.

"Because you're not staying?" I prompted. Violet lifted her eyes to mine and for a moment I imagined they looked a little bruised. Just a shade hesitant.

A second later the periwinkle turned cool, and she said, "Exactly."

"And did you find what you're looking for?"

Her impenetrable eyes locked on mine, she shook her head.

"Are you still looking?" I held my breath as if everything hinged on Violet's answer.

Her lips pressed tightly together, she shook her head

again. Her expression, her posture, everything about her was controlled, but her voice was thin and lost when she said, "I don't think there's anything to find. This was all a mistake."

"All of it?" I pressed. I wouldn't let her dismiss me so easily. Coming to work for the company under false pretenses had definitely been a mistake. But the rest, what was between us, that was something entirely different.

Violet dropped her eyes and turned her attention to her dinner. For someone who'd taken a job under a fake name with a secret agenda, she seemed to have an aversion to lying.

Interesting.

Everything about Violet was interesting.

I let it go. I had a plan and pushing Violet too hard about her reasons for being here was not part of it.

She finished her linguine and pushed the container away, rising up enough to sit on the couch, her wine glass in her hand. It didn't escape my attention that she'd chosen a spot as far from me as she could get.

Violet was determined to resist me.

I was equally determined to convince her not to.

Finished with my own meal, I traded the empty container for a smaller one. I opened it to reveal a single, oversized cannoli, not missing the flash of interest in Violet's eyes as she took in the dessert.

"You only ordered one?" I asked.

"It was noted on the menu that it was your favorite," she explained.

"And you didn't want one? You don't like dessert?" I saw the way she looked at the cannoli. Violet liked dessert.

"I do," she admitted. "I just don't usually eat it."

"Why not?"

"I also like fitting into my clothes."

"Take a bite," I offered, holding up the cannoli. The couch was deep and long. Sitting on opposite sides, she was too far away. I moved, closing the distance between us.

The scent of flaky pastry and creamy, sweet filling reached her nose and her lips parted. I'd been dreaming about those lips.

I ran the end of the pastry along her lip. Her eyes on mine, the periwinkle darkened to a dusky lavender. She stared at me, unblinking, and took a slow bite.

As the sugar exploded on her tongue, her eyelids drooped, her gold lashes fanned out against her cheeks. A tiny noise, almost a moan, escaped her and my cock, already half hard from watching her mouth, turned to stone.

Fucking fuck. Feeding this woman dessert would rate as one of the most erotic experiences of my life. Until I managed to feed her dessert naked. I almost moaned myself at the thought.

Mesmerized by the bliss on her face, her closed eyes, the smear of sweet ricotta on her lower lip, I nudged her mouth with the cannoli, suddenly desperate for her to take another bite.

Her eyelids fluttered as she did, this moan a little lower and louder. I'd planned to wait, to seduce her with wine and words before I touched her, but I was coming undone. I set the cannoli back in the container and pulled her wine glass from her fingers.

Taking her face in my hands, I drew her forward, licking that full lower lip, tasting sugar and Violet. She swallowed and her lips parted to speak. The barest sound escaped before I closed my mouth over hers.

Violet let out a whimper. I braced for her to pull away.

Her hands went to my shoulders, then slid up, her

fingers diving into my hair, closing and pulling me closer. Despite its size and relative privacy, I'd never had a woman on my office couch.

I kept my life compartmentalized. Family was for home, work was for the office, and my personal life had little to do with either. Since the moment Violet had entered my life, everything had been upside down. I didn't fucking care.

I'd been thinking about this all week. Having Violet alone again, laying her back, seeing her platinum and gold hair and creamy skin against the black leather as I touched her and tasted her. I eased her down, covering her body with mine completely, in a way I hadn't been able to in the limo.

My office couch was almost as wide and deep as a twin bed. I hadn't bought it with sex in mind, instead thinking of long nights in the office when I might need a quick nap. My forethought was paying off.

I settled over her, kissing her, deep, wet, lush kisses punctuated by sweet moans. Violet's hands were fisted in my hair, her legs spread to make room for me between them, her dull navy skirt hiked up almost to her waist. The heat of her core rocked into my hard cock, only a few layers of wool and cotton and lace between us. I thought about getting all that fabric out of the way and just sinking inside her, filling her with me and fucking her hard, making her come on my cock over and over.

I let out a groan at the thought and kissed her harder.

I wasn't fucking her on the couch in my office. That was not the plan, no matter how good it would feel. No matter how badly I wanted it. Resisting the urge to slide my hand between her legs and rip away her underwear as I had in the limo, I slowly, deliberately, unbuttoned her blazer, then her white cotton blouse.

Beneath the crisp fabric, my fingers found warm silky skin and soft lace.

I pulled my mouth from hers for just a moment. Long enough to appreciate the sight of her full breasts restrained by delicate white lace, her pink nipples hard and straining against the almost sheer fabric.

Lowering my head, I closed my lips over the tip of one breast, cupping her in my hand, squeezing and plumping her flesh, feeding her to me, sucking hard on her nipple through the lace. The sound of her moan, her breath catching in her chest pushed me to the edge.

Fingers fumbling with desire, I pulled the cups of her bra down, filling my hands with her breasts, pressing them together, my mouth moving from one nipple to the other, feasting on her.

The scent of sweet peas wreathed her damp skin, going straight to my head and I almost forgot why I had her here. I was lost in her lush body, and her moans, and the rock of her hips against me. She wanted more and she was too overwhelmed to know how to ask.

Reluctant, I pulled my mouth away and slid down the couch, turning her so she half reclined in the corner, her upper body supported by the cushions, her legs splayed wide.

Dropping to my knees, I reached up to hook my fingers in her white lace panties. I was going to have to take her lingerie shopping because this pair had to go. It was in my way. The fragile lace didn't put up much resistance as I tore the side and pushed it down the other leg.

Finally.

Fucking finally, I had what I wanted.

Violet's sweet, wet pussy only inches from my mouth.

At the sound of tearing fabric, Violet's head cleared enough for her to realize where she was, and where I was.

As I'd guessed she would, as soon as she understood what I was about to do, her body went stiff. Her hands went to my head, ready to push me away. I didn't give her the chance. I'd tease her later. I didn't have time now. Her clit was swollen, peeking out from beneath its hood, begging for my attention.

I closed my lips around it and sucked.

She tasted of salt and woman. At the hard pull of my mouth, she half-shrieked, half-moaned, the stiffness draining from her body. Her fingers sank into my hair, not pushing me away, not pulling me deeper, just holding on. Anchoring herself as the unexpected pleasure pulled her under.

I feasted on her, as I had at her breasts, but more. I wanted her taste on my tongue forever. I sucked and kissed and licked. I drove my tongue into the heart of her, scalded by her heat, filling her with one finger, then two.

I fucked her with my hand and my mouth, sucking her clit hard and deep until she went stiff again, every muscle pulled tight as I drove her to the peak and pushed her over.

Once wasn't enough. She shuddered through her orgasm, her body shaking with fine trembles as she whispered my name in halting sounds and tried to pull herself back together. I rested my cheek on her thigh and watched.

The jerking rise and fall of her ribs, the way her rough breaths shook her round breasts. The goosebumps that rose on her skin, the flex of her gently rounded stomach, the ease that took her as the orgasm faded.

She was just coming back around when my wet fingers stroked down her pussy in a light, teasing touch. If she hadn't been so aroused, so sensitive, she would have barely felt it. As it was, she shivered and whispered, "Aiden, what are you—you can't—"

"Shhh," I said, my face so close the rush of air blew across her clit, and she shivered again.

"I haven't—for you and—I can't again. I've never—"

"You can," I promised. "And you're going to."

I lifted my head from her thigh, catching her eyes with mine. Disbelief and arousal and a hint of greedy desire swirled in her twilight gaze. I stroked my fingers lightly down her pussy again and she strained into them.

I couldn't tear my eyes from hers as I dipped my fingers inside until they were slick and slid them up to circle her clit. She gasped and rocked up into the teasing pressure.

"How? How can you—?" she begged, her breath ragged.

One long lick that ended with my tongue pressed hard into her clit and she fell silent. I teased her entrance with my fingertips, almost losing it as she rocked into them, drawing me inside.

Fuck.

I was going to fucking come in my boxers like a teenager.

Getting my mouth on Violet was better than the best wet dream I'd ever imagined back then. And she thought she was bad at sex? I'd never had a woman I wanted as much as I wanted Violet. I wanted to make her come all day. I wanted to come with her, fucking her so hard and deep she'd feel me for weeks.

Not yet. Not fucking yet. I poured all of that need and desire into eating her pussy, reveling in every gasp and moan. Her head rolled back into the leather, eyes squeezed shut. Working her with my fingers and my mouth, I pushed her higher, harder, until she shattered, her legs closing around me, fingers knotted in my hair.

She was fierce in her pleasure, like a goddess demanding worship, and I gave it willingly. I gave it fucking happily. I'd worship her pussy all day and all night if she let me.

Every muscle in her body went limp as bliss faded into contentment. Drying my slick mouth against her leg, I moved up the couch and resettled her, pulling her into my arms, cradling her head against my shoulder. Her hand rested on my chest, fingers absently stroking as she breathed slowly, in and out, every so often letting out a deep sigh.

Her hand moved down, lower, and lower. When her fingers grazed my belt buckle, I caught them, drawing them back up to my chest. She shifted. I tightened my arm, holding her in place.

"Not now," I said. "Not this time."

"You don't want me to—?" Her question faded away in uncertainty.

I hated seeing Violet uncertain. Even when she had no idea what the fuck she was doing, she always held together her façade of unerring confidence. I wouldn't be the one to pull it apart.

Pressing a kiss to the top of her head I said, "I do. I really fucking do. But not now. This was for you. And for me. You have no idea how long I've been thinking about getting my mouth between your legs."

Her body hitched, and I wasn't sure if I'd shocked her or she was choking back a laugh. Maybe both.

"When I get you naked and alone, when I have you all to myself in a nice big bed, I want you to do everything you want to me," I promised. "But we're going to need more room, more time, and more privacy than we have right here."

Violet melted into me, letting out another of those deep

sighs. She toyed with the buttons of my shirt, the silk of my tie, winding the fabric around her fingers and tugging it straight, over and over.

Her hair had come loose, and I worked my fingers through the long strands, stroking and petting, not ready to let her go. I was half-asleep, and Violet's eyelids had long since slid closed, when the faint murmur of voices filtered through my office door.

The office door I'd closed, but not locked.

Fuck.

Just as I was convincing myself it was only a security check, I heard Gage's voice, followed by Sophie's softer tones.

Fucking, fucking, fuck.

Violet heard them a second after I did. I don't think I've ever seen anyone move that fast. She sat bolt upright, eyes flying wide in shocked panic. They flashed across the room at the door, then scanned wildly for some escape. She was off the couch and scrambling for her shoes a second later.

"Bathroom," I said, nodding in the direction of my private washroom. With a jolt, she was gone, her bared breasts half covered by her jacket, shoes in her hand. Her torn underwear taunted me from the carpet and I shoved them in my pocket, standing as if I was in no rush and packing up the containers from dinner. Only the faintest of rustling sounds reached me from behind the closed bathroom door.

I was behind my desk, tie straightened, pulling on my suit jacket, when the door to my office swung open.

"You almost done?" Gage asked.

"Just about. What are you two doing here?" I knew Gage had been home because he wore a T-shirt and jeans instead of a suit.

"We're on our way out to dinner, but I realized I forgot my wallet in my desk. I took it out to look for a business card and then shoved it in a drawer and forgot about it."

"It's a little late for dinner," I commented.

Sophie, tucked into Gage's side, bit her lower lip and stared at the carpet with an expression so guilty I had to stop myself from laughing. I'd walked in on them often enough to guess why they were running late.

In a grave voice, I said, "I see."

She bit her lip harder and Gage gave her a tight squeeze. "We'll walk you out."

Fuck. I couldn't think of a good reason to say no. I'd been putting my jacket on, so they knew I'd been about to leave, and Violet was trapped unless I could get Gage and Sophie out of my office.

"Sure," I agreed as if I didn't have a woman stashed in my washroom. "Go ahead and grab your wallet, I just need to take a last look at these papers and then I'll be ready. One minute."

Gage gave me a suspicious look, but let Sophie pull him from my office. The moment they were gone I crossed the room and rapped softly at the washroom door. Violet had managed to restore herself to order. Under her breath she said, "My purse is in my desk drawer. Keep an eye out while I get it and I'll go down the stairs."

I didn't like the idea of Violet creeping away like we had something to hide, but I said, "I've got you."

She had her purse in her hands and was disappearing through the stairwell door before Gage and Sophie got back to the elevators. We'd beat her down to the garage, but that wouldn't matter since her car was two levels below the executive spaces. She might technically have been part of the executive team, but that didn't rate a parking space near the CEO and owner.

I caught the scent of sweet peas and Violet and leaned against the opposite wall of the elevator from Gage and Sophie. Gage eyed my rumpled shirt and messy hair and said, "You look like you slept at your desk."

I wasn't going to admit I didn't have bed head—I had sex hair. "I'm tired."

With the gentle look that was vintage Sophie, Gage's wife said, "You need to get more sleep. You can't run on all cylinders all the time. Eventually, the stress will catch up to you."

"She's not wrong," Gage said.

"Of course, I'm not," Sophie agreed, "I'm a nurse. I know what I'm talking about."

"I know you do," I said. "And you're right. This weekend should be relaxing once I get business out of the way."

Gage gave me another of those suspicious looks. "And you're going by yourself, right?"

Shooting him a grin I said, "No, I'm not."

Chapter Fourteen
Violet

There was no way I was going into work. I couldn't do it. I got up when my alarm went off and dragged myself into the shower, still half asleep. I'd tossed and turned for half the night trying to decide what to do.

I'd thought what happened in the limo was the most mind-blowing experience of my life, but that was nothing next to what had happened on Aiden's couch.

I'd read about oral sex in books. I'd had two boyfriends I'd done it with—me giving, never receiving. They'd both said returning the favor was gross and a little weird. It was clear Aiden didn't share their opinion.

My body tingled in memory. Enthusiasm didn't quite cover it. Aiden had put his mouth on me like it was the only thing he'd ever wanted, like kissing me there, licking me there was more important to him than anything on this earth.

And he'd made me orgasm twice. Twice. I didn't think that was possible. Another thing I'd read about and written off as exaggeration.

I was vaguely sore between my legs and had beard burn on my breasts. I wanted to go back to the night before when we were alone, and this time I wanted to do everything. I wanted to strip off my clothes and then his. Wanted to touch him. I wanted to feel him inside me, get my hands and my mouth on that hard cock I'd only felt through his clothes.

Another mystery. What kind of guy didn't want to get his back? He'd made me come three times and hadn't even let me touch him.

Aiden Winters was so far beyond my understanding of men, I didn't even know where to start trying to figure him out. I reminded myself that there was no point in trying to figure Aiden out. All of this was temporary.

No, not temporary.

It was over.

I couldn't walk into that office and face him. There was no way I was going back there.

It wasn't just what had happened in his office. And the limo. It was more than that. Somewhere in between Aiden feeding me cannoli and racing down the stairs, my heels so loud against the concrete I was sure I'd be caught, sure at every landing the door would pop open and Gage would be there with his accusing glare—somewhere in there I'd realized that I couldn't do it anymore.

I'd started this stupid plan thinking I'd be at Winters, Inc. a few days, I'd find some dirt on Aiden Winters, I'd threaten to expose it if he didn't give Chase his company back, and that would be that.

In retrospect, I'd been an idiot. Anger didn't bring out my best reasoning skills. When I was furious, bone-deep enraged, I acted like a moron. My temper lost me my first job. My temper got me kicked out of my parents' house.

And my temper had convinced me I could best Aiden Winters.

The truth was, there wasn't any dirt to find. Aiden Winters was a good man. Not an angel or he wouldn't have scammed Chase out of his company, but everything else I'd seen had convinced me he was essentially a good person. He loved his family. He looked out for his employees. He ran a charitable foundation for heaven's sake.

My heart twisted in my chest at the weak words. Aiden was more than a good man. He was sweet and thoughtful. He was bossy as hell and brilliant. He carried so much on his shoulders—his family, the company—and he never faltered.

He took care of everyone in his life and no one was taking care of him.

Not your job, I told myself, firmly. *So very much not your job.*

It wasn't. This was over. Not just because I'd realized there wasn't any dirt to find on Aiden. No, it was over because, as I'd raced down the stairwell to hide from Gage, I'd realized that if I found any dirt, it would break my heart.

That was really the end.

I couldn't talk myself into looking for something I didn't want to find. I'd failed my brother, and I'd made an utter fool of myself.

Things couldn't go any further with Aiden. The whole idea was absurd. Even if you put aside the fact that we'd met because I'd lied, and worse had been trying to manipulate him to my own ends, he was still way out of my league. My life was nowhere close to the world Aiden Winters lived in.

If I hadn't scammed my way into his company, we never would have met. That's the way it should have been. I knew how Gage felt about me, and I'd seen Jacob's reserved reaction to meeting me. I wouldn't come between Aiden and his family, even if he wanted me to.

Standing in the kitchen, staring at the coffee maker and wrapped up in a thick terrycloth robe, I made a decision. Before I could change my mind, I picked up my phone and pulled up my email. It didn't take long to type up my resignation.

Yes, I'm a coward.

A better woman than me would have quit over the phone, especially after everything that had happened the night before. A braver woman would quit in person. That was the right thing to do, and I cringed at the thought.

Aiden had said I couldn't leave until he was ready to get rid of me. I didn't have to ask if he was ready. If nothing else, I owed him three orgasms. Aiden wasn't the kind of man who'd let that go unanswered.

My thumb hovered over the *Send* button as I thought about what might happen when Aiden read my email. Maybe I should go out of town for the weekend. Maybe I should move to Alaska. I thought about the Winters's connection to Sinclair Security and I realized Alaska wasn't nearly far enough. He'd threatened to hunt me down if I ran.

There was a very good chance that when I quit, Aiden would shrug his shoulders and move on. He was drowning in gorgeous women. He didn't need me.

But if he didn't...

If he didn't shrug and move on, there was nowhere I could hide that he wouldn't find me. I squeezed my eyes shut and lowered my thumb to hit send.

The phone rang in my hand. Between the sudden vibration and the eruption of sound, I screeched and dropped the phone. Staring in horror, I read Aiden's name on the display.

Moving in slow motion, I leaned down and picked the phone up off the kitchen floor. The call went to voicemail, but before I had the chance to be relieved, it began to ring again.

Nauseous, I tapped the green answer button and lifted the phone to my ear.

"Have you left yet?" Aiden said quickly. He sounded like he was moving. From a distance, as if he'd moved the phone away from his mouth, I heard him say, "Yep, love you too. See you Sunday."

"Violet. Are you there?"

"Uh, Yeah, I'm here. I mean, yes. Yes, and I need to talk to you—"

"We can talk on the plane. I'll be there in twenty-five minutes. We're going away for the weekend. Meetings in Vegas today, maybe tomorrow if we don't get things wrapped up. We fly back on Sunday. Pack for business and casual."

"Excuse me?" That was all I could get out.

"I know you heard me, Violet. You have twenty-five minutes."

"You can't just order me to go away with you for the weekend," I said, feeling my spine go poker straight.

"As your boss, yes I can. But if it would make you feel better—Violet. Sweetheart. Darling. Would you please pack so we can go to Vegas for the weekend?"

My knees went a little weak and I sagged against the counter.

Sweetheart? Darling? What was going on?

I dropped my head, my wet hair falling in my face, and said in a low voice, "Aiden, hasn't this gone far enough?"

Calmly, Aiden said, "I'll decide when it's gone far enough. Pack your things. It's a four-and-a-half-hour flight, so you can dress comfortably for the plane and change right before we land. I'm leaving now. Twenty-five minutes."

He hung up.

I stared at the home screen on my phone in disbelief. Maybe I could reason with him when he got here. Or, a sneaky little thought crept in, I could pack and go to Las Vegas with him for the weekend. I could balance the scales before I quit and I never saw him again.

I knew what Vegas meant.

Vegas meant a bed.

Sex.

I had a quick, vivid flash of the night before, his mouth, his fingers, the thick bar of his erection through his suit pants.

On a scale of innocent to completely evil, how bad would it be to drag this thing out for three more days?

Aiden wasn't a fool. The Sinclairs had probably found out every detail of my life five minutes after Aiden realized my last name wasn't Hartwell. It wasn't much of a deception when the target knew the truth.

Chase wouldn't be back for another week. He'd never have to know I went away for the weekend with the man who stole his company.

I put my phone on the counter and scrubbed my palms over my face. What was I thinking? I should go get dressed and be prepared to tell Aiden I wasn't going with him. That was the right thing to do. It was the only thing to do. Anything else would be completely insane.

Taking the job at Winters, Inc. hadn't been my brightest move, but I was usually fairly smart. Smart enough to know that my brother would be incredibly pissed off if he found out I'd had anything to do with Aiden Winters, much less had an affair with him.

This whole thing had spun out of my control so quickly I didn't know how to stop it.

No, I knew how to stop it. Aiden wasn't a monster. If I looked him in the eyes and told him I truly wasn't interested, he'd back off. And that was my problem. I was a terrible liar, and Aiden could see right through me.

He knew I was interested.

I was so interested I hadn't been able to sleep the night before thinking about how interested I was.

Interested in getting his clothes off.

Interested in seeing how good sex would be considering the three orgasms he'd already given me.

The person making this complicated wasn't Aiden Winters, it was me.

I was a liar and I couldn't bring myself to do the right thing even when I knew what it was.

At that thought, a harsh laugh brought tears to my eyes. Wasn't that what my parents had said right before they kicked me out? I was a liar who didn't know right from wrong.

But this wasn't about my parents. It was about me.

It was about wanting a taste of something I wasn't supposed to have, something that was out of my reach.

One weekend.

Three days.

I could have three days with Aiden. Three days in a hotel room away from his family, away from Winters, Inc. A moment out of time just for us before I had to make myself walk away. There was no possibility this could go further, but I could have these three days before I had to say goodbye.

Chapter Fifteen

Violet

I was racing to my bedroom before I could think better of it. Twenty minutes left. I could do this. I hit my hair with the dryer for a few minutes, then combed it and twisted it into a loose bun. If I left it like that it would dry in smooth shiny waves by the time we arrived in Las Vegas. I could keep it in the bun for the meetings and then wear it down later.

I did my makeup quickly, going for subtle, dropping everything in my travel bag as I went. Clothes were a little harder. My work clothes were conservative. Dowdy. That was on purpose, but I didn't want to look dowdy today. I dug into the back of my closet and pulled out an ice-blue linen suit.

It was perfectly appropriate for business, and the shade of blue looked great with my hair and brought out the blue in my eyes. The skirt wasn't short or tight, but it was fitted through the hips and had a flare right above the knee that was flirty and feminine.

As far as suits went, this was as pretty as I got. I packed it in a hanging bag with a cream shell to go beneath and tucked a pair of thigh high stockings in the toe of my favorite spike slingbacks.

Taking Aiden's advice, I dressed casually for the plane in jeans and a cardigan. There was no way I'd fall asleep, but maybe I could close my eyes for a few minutes.

Staring at my open underwear drawer, I had a desperate and futile wish for lingerie. Most of my underwear tended toward the practical. I had a few matching lace sets, and Aiden had destroyed the panties on two of them. I couldn't bring myself to regret that.

I'd sacrifice all the panties in the world if Aiden wanted to tear them off me.

I shoved the best of what I had left in my suitcase, added two cocktail dresses, shoes to match, and a few more low-key options for daytime. I was zipping the suitcase closed when the doorbell rang.

"One second," I called out as I grabbed my phone from the counter and unplugged the nearby charger, dumping both into my purse. I swung open the door, purse in hand, garment bag over my arm, my suitcase beside me.

Aiden gave me a long, measuring look before his face broke into a devastating smile and he said, "That's my girl. I knew you'd be ready."

Giving him my best ice queen look, I handed over the garment bag and stepped into the hall, pulling the keys out of my purse as I waited for him to retrieve my suitcase and shut the door. With a wry smile, Aiden took my luggage and waited while I locked up the condo.

Aiden was quiet on the ride to the airport. I decided he was saving any argument until we were in the air and I couldn't change my mind. I forgot to be nervous as he followed me up the stairs into the private plane. It hadn't occurred to me we'd be flying in his jet.

I'd forgotten he had a jet, because, well, who had a jet? People like Aiden Winters. The inside looked more like a living room than an airplane. An attendant told us we were about ready and asked us to take one of the oversized leather seats and fasten our safety belts.

I was snapping mine when Aiden asked, "Tired?"

"A little, yes," I admitted, though you could drag me over hot coals before I'd admit the reason. "Why?"

Aiden lifted a finger and traced a half circle beneath my right eye. Oh, yeah. I'd tried to cover the circles with makeup, but Aiden saw right through it. Of course, he did.

The plane gave a jerk as it began to move. We taxied to the runway, and the attendant popped her head in to let us know we were third in line. She gave a discrete glance at our fastened seatbelts and retreated.

"I know why I didn't sleep well," he said in a low, teasing voice, "but that shouldn't have been a problem for you."

I cursed my fair skin as the heat of a blush hit my cheeks. Tartly, I said, "Yes, well, I would have been more relaxed if I hadn't had to sneak out of the building like a criminal."

Aiden winced. "I apologize for that. It won't happen again."

"No, it won't," I agreed, and though I sounded composed as I said it, the words made me a little sick.

It wouldn't happen again because I wouldn't be working for Aiden after this weekend. I'd already decided I couldn't cash my last paycheck. Bad enough that I'd lied to get the job and spent half my time there trying to find dirt on Aiden. Getting paid for sleeping with the boss was a whole new level of wrong. Even if we hadn't technically slept together yet.

The plane eased forward and stopped. I leaned my head back against my seat and tried to close my eyes. I hadn't thought to bring anything to do on the plane during my hasty packing job. More movement, another brief wait, and the attendant appeared one last time to let us know we should prepare for takeoff.

I closed my fingers over the armrests and braced. I didn't enjoy flying. It wasn't so much the up in the air part as the takeoff and landing. Aiden nudged my arm and wrapped his fingers around mine. I looked up in surprise, squeezing tight and he said, "You don't like flying?"

"I don't like takeoff," I clarified. "Or landing."

"It'll be okay. I promise."

I clamped my fingers on his with bruising pressure as the plane picked up speed and smoothly lifted into the air. I kept my eyes squeezed tightly shut until I felt the plane level off. Once we were above the clouds I forgot we were suspended in a metal tube thousands of feet in the air, and I relaxed.

Aiden lifted our joined hands to his mouth and kissed my knuckles. Separating our fingers, he stroked his over my jaw and leaned in, pressing his lips to mine in a soft, slow kiss. I was a little dizzy when he lifted his head and said, "There's a bedroom in the back. Why don't you go lay down and take a nap? I'll wake you up in time to change before we need to buckle up for landing."

"There's a bedroom on the plane?" I asked, appalled at how naïve I sounded. Aiden's answering grin told me he didn't mind.

"Go," he said, "before I decide to join you instead of prepping for this meeting."

I unfastened my seatbelt and stood, taking a moment to get my balance before I looked to the back of the plane.

Sure enough, there was a dark walnut door in the center of the rear wall. I made my way there and opened it to find a queen-size bed and a flat-screen TV. A small closet on the wall beside the door held my garment bag.

Fatigue dragged at me as I stared at the bed, the dark gray coverlet folded neatly down beneath two fluffy white pillows. Before I could second-guess myself, I toed off my shoes and climbed under the sheets. I lay there thinking that I'd never be able to sleep, wondering if Aiden would change his mind and walk through the door, telling myself I should have stayed home before my eyes fell shut and I was out.

The next thing I knew, Aiden was sitting beside me, brushing my hair off my face. My eyes opened and he said, "We have about fifteen minutes before landing if you'd like to get changed."

"Okay," I whispered. A soft smile curved his lips. Aiden didn't smile enough. When he did his dark eyes lit with warmth. I lifted a finger and traced the fine lines beneath those dark lashes.

"What?" he asked.

Still half asleep, I said, "I like it when you smile."

His lips pressed to my temple and he said, "Wake up, sweetheart, before I call Dylan and bag the meeting completely."

He was gone, the door clicking shut behind him. Sleep fell away and my brain came back online. I sat up, half of my hair tumbling out of my bun. Shoot. My hairbrush was in my suitcase. At least it was mostly dry. I scavenged for the hairpins that had fallen out while I'd slept.

Turning my head upside down, I roughly finger combed it, stood back up, shook it out again, and twisted it into a low bun at the nape of my neck. It was the best I could do for the moment.

A few minutes later my suit was on and I was stepping into my sling backs, carrying my neatly folded jeans and cardigan. I packed them and my discarded sneakers in the garment bag and left it hanging in the closet.

I took my seat beside Aiden and busied myself with the safety belt. With a glance at my suit, he said, "You've never worn that before."

"Not to work, no."

"Why not?"

I didn't know how to answer that. I settled for, "The color feels a little...frivolous."

"It's not," Aiden disagreed. "You look beautiful."

There was nothing to say but, "Thank you."

I thought I looked nice, but the heat, the intent in Aiden's eyes made me think I might look just a little bit better than *nice*.

A dark SUV was waiting for us at the airport. The driver stowed our luggage in the back as Aiden opened my door for me. Once he was seated, he checked his watch and made a quick phone call. "Just got in the car. Are you ready for me or should I check in first?" A pause. "Sounds good. See you soon."

With the time change, it was barely noon, still early in the workday. I thought it was time to ask, "What exactly are we doing here?"

"We're meeting with Dylan Kane, the owner of the Delecta casino. Do you remember me telling you about our project? The mixed-use with a casino, retail, and residential?"

"I remember, but I didn't know it included a casino. That seems kind of random for Winters, Inc."

"It is, a little," Aiden said. "We're friends, Dylan, me, and Jacob. Jacob's real estate company is actually the third arm in the investment. He couldn't make it to this meeting, but he went over most of his issues a few weeks ago when he was here. I probably could have handled my part over the phone, but everyone keeps telling me I need to take more time off work so..."

"And when did you decide to schedule this meeting?" I asked, suspicious.

"Last Saturday," he said with a straight face.

Last Saturday. The day after the ball and the limo. I didn't know what to make of that, so I kept my mouth shut. Instead of saying something stupid, I looked out the window and took in the sight of the desert and the mountains surrounding the city.

"Have you ever been to Vegas before?" Aiden asked.

"No," I said, dragging my eyes from the vista. There was something about the way the mountains rose from the flat desert, as if they'd broken their way through, stabbing up to the sky in an abrupt incline. There didn't appear to be foothills or a gradual rise. It was just desert and then—boom—mountains. "I've only been out west twice. Once to San Francisco in college, and to Phoenix in high school when my father had a business trip during spring break. I forgot how dramatic the desert is."

"So did I," Aiden said, but he wasn't looking out the window. His eyes were on me.

Chapter Sixteen

Violet

Aiden had been here before, because he led me through the casino to the elevators in the back, tugging on my hand a few times as I got distracted by the flash of lights and ringing bells. I'd never been inside a casino before. Not a real one. I went on a cruise with my parents once and had snuck into the casino on the boat, but it had been nothing like this. This was pure elegance, sleek and decadent on a grand scale.

Aiden hit the number of the floor and the elevator rose smoothly. We walked out into a lobby that could have belonged in any high-rise office building. Approaching the attractive blond sitting behind the front desk he said, "Aiden Winters for Dylan Kane."

She gave a sharp nod and rose to her feet. "Yes, sir, if you'll follow me? You can leave your bags here. I'll see to them."

I don't know what I expected of Dylan Kane. I thought he'd be older, for one thing. He looked like he was about Aiden's age and he carried the same aura of absolute authority. Confidence. And handsome. Not as handsome as

Aiden, but with his dark hair, tanned skin and eyes the same fresh, crisp green as a Granny Smith apple, he was striking.

He and Aiden shook hands and patted each other on the back of the shoulder in that weird half hug thing men did with their friends before Aiden introduced me. Dylan shook my hand firmly, looking me in the eye, not bothering to hide his curiosity.

Not once did his gaze stray to my breasts or my legs. Young, powerful, and not a creeper. This guy must be beating them off with a stick. Then I noticed the wedding ring on his left hand and had to wonder what kind of woman he'd married.

Dylan gestured for us to sit. "Are you free for dinner? Leigha made reservations and Axel and Emma are coming too."

"Sam and Chloe?" Aiden asked. Dylan shook his head.

"Out of town. So, do you need anything to eat, drink? I know it's past lunch time for you."

"Lunch would be great," Aiden said. "I didn't eat on the plane, and Violet took a nap. She could probably use some coffee and I think we're both hungry." He looked at me and I nodded.

"I'd love coffee," I said with fervor, making both men laugh. "Someone called me before I had time to get breakfast or caffeine, and told me I had twenty-five minutes to get packed for the weekend."

"I'm surprised he's not dead," Dylan said with a laugh.

"So am I," I said, smiling back at him.

Aiden made a disgruntled sound in the back of his throat. "If I gave you too much advance notice, you would have found a way to get out of it."

Dylan's eyes bounced between us, intrigued, and I

raised an eyebrow in assent. "Probably. I was about to email my resignation when you called."

Dylan laughed, thinking I was kidding. Knowing that I wasn't, Aiden said, "Don't even think about it."

Dylan was charming and funny, and it was interesting to see Aiden with a friend. We were here for business, but he was more relaxed with Dylan than he was in the office. It helped that they'd hammered out most of the details of their agreement and were past the negotiation stage. I took notes when Aiden needed me to, and tried to pay attention, but I was bored by mid-afternoon, buzzing a little after multiple lattes, and restless from sitting.

Dylan's assistant had checked us in at some point during the meeting, and as we rose to leave, she handed us key cards and told us a room number. I wasn't ready to be alone in a hotel room with Aiden. Not when we were expected to go out to dinner in a few hours. He must have felt the same way because he pocketed the key cards and suggested, "Do you want to see a little of Vegas?"

"Sure," I said. "I'm not much of a gambler."

"Neither am I," Aiden said, "unless it's poker. I like to put my money where I can control the outcome."

"Then what is there to do?" I asked.

What I knew about Las Vegas could fit on the back of a postage stamp, and it was summed up with one word. Gambling.

"I was thinking we'd go shopping," Aiden said.

I wasn't going to argue with shopping. The black SUV was waiting for us when we walked out of the hotel. Aiden helped me into the back and we were off.

I was no stranger to high-end window shopping. Buckhead had almost every premier store you could imagine. Dior. Fendi. Gucci. Armani. Tiffany. I didn't actually buy things in those stores, but I'd walked past them enough that seeing them here in Las Vegas didn't faze me.

Not until Aiden came to a stop in front of Agent Provocateur. My eyes went wide, and I said the first thing that popped into my mind.

"You can't tear underwear from this store. Do you have any idea how much it costs?"

Aiden's dark eyes slid to me, and he said under his breath, "I think admitting that I do know how much it costs is a bad idea."

"Probably," I mumbled. "I don't think—"

Aiden overrode my objections, hooking his arm through mine and pulling me into the store. I'd never seen anything like it. The inside was sumptuous and seductive, all velvet curtains and thick carpet, silk and lace everywhere. A saleswoman approached in a tight pink dress, her garters showing clearly beneath the short hem.

"Can I help you?" she asked, her eyes glued to Aiden, quickly taking in his custom tailored suit, the Patek Philippe watch on his wrist. She could smell money, and she looked eager to help him spend it.

I was the subject of her appraising glance a moment later. Her shiny red lips curved in a slow smile. "I have just the thing for you."

Taking my hand, she led me to the back of the shop, past lingerie like I'd never seen before, straps and buckles and black lace. Bustiers, corsets, barely-there bras and crotchless underwear. Garters and silk in all colors of the rainbow.

I looked back over my shoulder to see Aiden stalking behind us, his eyes taking in all the store had to offer.

The saleswoman stopped at a floor-length silk negligée in deep, smoky lavender. The high neckline, suspended from two delicate silk straps, would leave nothing on display below my collarbones. The back, on the other hand, dipped so low it would expose half of my rear end.

The silk was so fine, so delicate, it would hide almost nothing of the skin it covered. Every contour of my breasts, the peak of my nipples—the silk would mold itself to my body, showing everything it pretended to hide.

I caught sight of the price tag. Over five hundred dollars. I started to object when Aiden said, "Put it in the dressing room."

The saleswoman nodded. "Certainly, sir. I have a few other things in mind?"

"Let's see," Aiden invited. What followed was a deluge of lace and silk. I refused to look at the price tags.

At one point, as he contemplated a bra and thong set of the palest pink lace, I hissed, "You cannot spend over four hundred dollars on underwear, Aiden."

"I can spend my money on whatever I want, sweetheart."

The look in his eyes as they moved from the transparent lace to me was so hot I almost bit my tongue before I said, "Well then, you can't tear them off."

"Maybe we should just skip the underwear altogether," he said, so quietly I barely heard him.

I didn't dignify that comment with a response.

He didn't try to join me in the dressing room. I wasn't sure if I was relieved or disappointed.

I was relieved.

I was.

I was not the kind of woman who fooled around in the dressing room of a lingerie shop. At least, I never had been before. Aiden did peek, once. I'd barely pulled a short lace slip over my head when he rapped his knuckles on the dark wood trim around the dressing room doorway.

The lace slip was semi-transparent but dark enough that it wasn't completely revealing. With butterflies in my stomach, I reached out and inched the heavy velvet curtain open just enough for him to stick his head in.

He took a long, slow look from the tips of my toes to the top of my head. At first, I kept my eyes firmly glued to the crystal chandelier dangling from the ceiling. It was one thing to let Aiden look and another to watch while he did it.

I risked a quick glance and the tight set of his jaw, the look in his eyes, had my lower belly clenching.

My nipples hardened under the soft lace. Aiden's eyes heated as he watched.

In a choked voice he said, "Are those thigh-high stockings?"

I glanced down at the stockings I'd pulled on when I'd dressed on the plane. I always wore thigh highs, the kind with lace at the top and sticky rubber on the inside to hold them up. I couldn't stand garter belts, and I didn't like the way pantyhose felt around my waist. I didn't usually think of them as particularly sexy—they were just part of my work wardrobe. No one ever saw them but me.

"Yes," I said, "why, do you like them?" I don't know where I found it in me to tease him. The flare of his eyes at my words sent a rush of heat between my legs.

"I like them." Squeezing his eyes shut tight for a long moment he said, "Try everything on and, if it fits, we'll get it. I'm staying out here before I do something I'll regret."

I tried everything on and, as ordered, divided the haul between two hooks on the wall of the dressing room—things that fit and things that didn't. From the items that fit I chose the two least expensive. Once again dressed in my suit, I pulled back the heavy velvet curtain and handed Aiden the two hangers. He took one look and shook his head.

"I know more than that fit." Scanning the dressing room, he said, "Which ones?"

"Aiden, you can't. It's not appropriate. This isn't—I can't—"

Why was this obvious only to me?

He shouldn't be buying me anything. Taking me away for the weekend on the pretense of business was bad enough, but spending this kind of money buying me lingerie was just... Inappropriate didn't begin to cover it.

I wasn't his girlfriend. I wasn't his mistress. I didn't want to force the issue, especially not there, in the dressing room, surrounded by silk and lace, my head clouded with thoughts of sex and Aiden.

I tried again. "Aiden, this is fun, but it's just for this weekend. You know that. I can't let you waste your money on all of this—"

I waved my hand at the thousands of dollars of lingerie hanging on the wall behind me. I opened my mouth to speak, and Aiden pressed his finger to my bottom lip in a shushing gesture that immediately pushed me from helpless confusion to ice queen.

Before I thought better of it, I pulled my head back and nipped the tip of his finger.

Hard.

Aiden groaned low in his throat and took my chin in his hand. His touch was light, gentle. I could have stepped away. I don't know why I didn't.

His warm brown eyes studied mine and, beneath the heat of lust, there was more. Emotions I couldn't decipher. He pressed his lips to mine once before moving them to my ear. "You make your choices, and I'll make mine. I'm buying everything that fits. If you don't want it, you don't have to keep it. My buying it doesn't obligate you to anything. We're starting with this weekend. Then we'll see."

The touch of his warm lips to my cheek contrasted with his practical words, mesmerizing me. If he'd given me some vague condescending reassurance, I would have smacked him down. But this? Before I could think of what to say, he pointed at the two hooks on the wall and repeated, "Which one?"

Deciding I wouldn't sacrifice my dignity over an argument I couldn't win, I pointed at the hook on the left, holding the lavender gown the saleswoman had chosen when we arrived, the dark lace slip Aiden had watched me try on, four sets of bras and panties, a bustier and matching thong in petal pink, and a slip and matching robe in a deep plum.

I refused to consider the total of the price tags. I didn't want to know. If Aiden wanted to waste his money, that was his problem. I had too many of my own already.

Chapter Seventeen

Violet

I left Aiden to pay and strolled to the shoe store a few doors down. The last thing I needed was another pair of shoes, but that didn't mean I couldn't look.

Aiden joined me at the window, carrying the pink and black bags from Agent Provocateur, and said, "Do you want to go in?"

"No," I said. "I'm over my budget on shoes for the month as it is." He started to speak and I held up my hand. "Don't even think about it. All of that is one thing," I said, waving my hand at the bags he held. "Shoes are different."

"How are shoes different?" he asked, taking my hand as we strolled back toward where we left the SUV and driver.

"If you have to ask, I don't think I can explain it," I said. I wasn't sure I understood myself. I could argue that the lingerie was for him. I'm pretty sure that was a lie, but it sounded like the truth. Still, he'd get something out of the lingerie.

Shoes, though...shoes would be for me. They were my special indulgence, my favorite splurge. Every pair in that shop window had been so far beyond my normal budget I never would have bought any of them on my own.

If Aiden got them for me... It just felt too intimate. A man might buy lingerie for a fling, but he bought shoes for a girlfriend. I didn't need to get confused about Aiden. I knew where we stood.

He let it go, and as we made our way back to the Delecta we kept the conversation light, talking about the details of the project he and Jacob would build with Dylan.

I barely remember dinner.

Dylan's wife Leigha was nice, and not at all what I'd expected. I'd been looking for a tall blonde showgirl and instead got a very curvy, very sweet brunette. They were no longer newlyweds, but Dylan couldn't keep his eyes, or his hands, off his wife.

One of the Sinclairs, Axel, lived in Vegas, and he brought his wife Emma, a redhead with a bombshell body who was just as nice as Leigha. The food was amazing, the company fun, and I was too distracted to enjoy any of it.

I couldn't stop thinking about what would happen after dinner. About the big, wide bed in the hotel suite. About all the things I wanted to do in that bed.

And I did want it. I would never have gotten on that plane with Aiden if I hadn't wanted to go to bed with him, hadn't been absolutely sure about it.

I was still absolutely sure I wanted to have sex with Aiden Winters.

I did.

I really, really did.

And I was a total mess over it. My skin was too tight, every nerve in my body on edge. If one more emotion decided to swirl inside me, I'd split open. My body wanted him.

My nipples had been hard, my breasts swollen, ever since I pulled on the sheer lace bra Aiden had purchased. Beneath the matching thong, I was damp. Needy. His hands, his mouth, hadn't been enough. I wanted all of him.

My body was not confused.

My brain was all over the place.

I was not going to know what I was doing. I had no game, no tricks, and I'd never in my life attempted to seduce a man. I'd had two long-term boyfriends and we'd had plenty of sex, but it was ordinary.

Turn off the TV, turn off the light, roll towards each other under the covers, insert tab A into slot B, and repeat. That was pretty much it. It hadn't been bad, it was just...ordinary.

Aiden was anything but ordinary.

The ice queen got me through almost every situation in life that scared me. When I got nervous, I got frosty, and everyone backed off. Once people knew they couldn't get to you, they stopped trying. But the ice queen act couldn't help me here.

I didn't want to freeze Aiden out. I wanted to give him everything I had—all my passion, all my need. I wasn't sure I knew how, or if it would be enough. The thought of disappointing him had me half sick with dread. The thought of trying not to left me dizzy with anticipation.

At one point during dinner, Aiden moved my wine glass out of reach, but I don't remember drinking too much. I didn't get drunk, or even tipsy. He slid his hand over my knee as I was geeking out with Leigha over accounting, and I completely lost my train of thought, my cheeks burning red when Leigha said, "Violet? Are you okay?"

Aiden's fingers squeezed. I cleared my throat. "I'm

good. Just,—" I resisted the urge to look at Aiden and took a sip of water. "Tell me more about your master's program."

Leigha was an accountant. I'd completed the first year of a master's degree in accountancy and had been meaning to go back and finish it. I told myself I was still trying to save up the money. I'd started through an employer sponsored program and when I'd lost that job the tuition money had dried up.

I liked bookkeeping and I was good at it, but my long-term plan had been to finish my master's and look for more complex work in the accounting field than I was qualified for as a bookkeeper. It didn't occur to me until we were halfway through the conversation that as far as Aiden knew, I was a project manager.

Then again, if Sinclair Security was as good as their reputation, Aiden already knew I wasn't a project manager. He probably knew how many credits I'd had toward my master's degree when I dropped out.

It was one more reminder that I shouldn't be here. I shouldn't be with Aiden. When I got home, I was going to quit, drop this ridiculous quest to get Chase's company back, and figure out what to do with the rest of my life.

After I got through tonight.

I barely spoke on the elevator ride back to our suite. My throat was tight, my heart thudding under my ribs. Aiden stood a foot away, not touching me, his eyes on my face.

"You didn't eat much dinner," he commented, carefully.

Lifting my chin, I met the reflection of his eyes in the polished doors of the elevator. "It was delicious, but I wasn't that hungry."

Aiden answered with a considering, "Mmmm."

I was wound too tight to ask what that meant. We walked into the hotel suite to see an iced bottle of champagne and two glasses sitting on the dining room table. The suite was enormous. Sitting room, dining room, wet bar, and two bedrooms, everything the height of luxury.

I was pretty sure Dylan could have just put us in a room with a bed for all the use we were going to get out of the rest of it.

I was here to have sex with Aiden. Now that we were here, I just wanted to get it over with before I lost my nerve completely.

I looked from the champagne to Aiden, expecting him to open the bottle and pour me a glass. Instead, he took out his phone and tapped the screen. A minute later I heard a *bloop* from the small black speaker in the wet bar and the familiar tones of an old Harry Connick, Jr. song filled the room.

Aiden turned and reached for my hand. Then he did the last thing I expected. He danced with me. He didn't kiss me, or reach for my zipper, or lead me into the bedroom.

He held me close, and we danced.

In heels, I was exactly the right height to dance with Aiden, the top of my head just even with his cheekbone. His lips were at my temple, one arm around my back, the other holding my hand.

One song flowed into the next and gradually, inch by inch, my tension eased away. I could have danced with Aiden all night. His breath against my skin, his fingers warm through the thin silk of my dress.

He still wore his suit coat, and the fabric was too thick. An itch started under my skin. I wanted him closer. Wanted to get rid of everything between us and feel him. My hands were moving before I'd thought it through, sliding up over his shoulders, beneath his jacket, pushing it down his arms.

Aiden caught it before it fell to the floor, tossing it over a chair and pulling me back into the dance, closer this time, feathering his lips across my hair. He lifted his hand from my back and stroked it over the long blonde waves I'd freed from their daytime bun.

"I've never seen your hair like this," he said. "I like it."

I couldn't seem to get a word out. I pressed my forehead into his neck. He smelled so good, woodsy and male. I wanted to taste that scent, to taste his skin. My head was spinning, and my steps faltered.

Aiden stopped and lifted his palms to my face, cupping my chin, raising my lips to his. He nipped at my lower lip and sucked it, tracing his tongue over it before pressing his mouth to mine, urging me to open to him.

His tongue brushed mine, and all I knew was want. His kiss was hot and wet, slow and deep. He threaded his fingers into the hair at the nape of my neck, holding me in place as he kissed me until I was dizzy with it.

My hands raced over him, tugging at his tie, pulling at the buttons of his shirt. I didn't care about finesse or seduction. I just wanted to touch him. I had to touch him. His shirt caught on his hands and I yanked in frustration.

Aiden broke the kiss just long enough to remove his cufflinks and toss the shirt to the floor. My hands were on his belt, and then he was kissing me again, his mouth skimming over my jaw, landing on my neck just below my ear. He sucked hard on the tender skin and a violent shudder wracked my body.

Heat pooled between my legs. The soft lace of my bra scratched my nipples. I wanted it all off. Hooking my thumbs in Aiden's pants, I shoved them down, taking his underwear along with them. He stepped back just enough to kick off his clothes and my eyes went wide.

He should have looked ridiculous standing there in only

a pair of dress socks. My mouth went dry. Ridiculous was the last thing I would call Aiden Winters. I'd never seen him naked, not even close, and my imagination hadn't done him justice.

Golden skin stretched over broad shoulders and tight muscles. Powerful thighs, taut abs delineated by ridged muscle, and between his legs—my eyes settled on his cock and I couldn't pull them away.

I thought I'd gauged his size through his suit pants. I'd been wrong. He was hard and thick. I wasn't sure I'd be able to get my fingers around that cock, much less fit it inside me. I wanted to try. I reached out a hand, almost touching when Aiden's fingers caught mine and pulled them away.

"Not yet," he said. "The look on your face is the hottest fucking thing I've ever seen, and if you touch me right now I'm going to disappoint us both."

I dragged my eyes from his erection, too aroused, too enraptured by the sight of his naked body to be embarrassed. Sparks of gold flashed in the brown of his eyes, and they burned. He reached behind me and tugged down the zipper of my dress. With a dip of my shoulder, I let it fall.

Aiden stared, absorbing me in my sheer pink demi-cup bra, panties that hid nothing, and tall, spiked black heels. I lifted a foot to step out of my shoes. Aiden scooped me into his arms, growling, "Leave them on," as he strode to his room, stopping only to kick open the door.

He set me on the bed, gently, leaning down to pull off his socks and grab something from the bedside table.

"Take off your bra," he ordered.

It didn't occur to me to do anything else. I reached behind me and unfastened it, letting one strap, then the other, fall down my arms. The delicate lace slid down with every breath, moving in tiny degrees until it caught on my hard nipples and hung.

Aiden's jaw was tight, flags of red on his cheekbones, but he didn't move. He just watched as I shifted the tiniest bit and the bra fell away. I tugged it from my arms and tossed it over the side of the bed, laying back to brace myself on my elbows, my back arched, breasts high on my chest.

Aiden leaned down and tugged my panties over my hips, taking care not to tear them. I bit my lower lip to hold in a laugh. Seeing it, Aiden said in a murmur, "I'm framing these."

I reached for his arm. He held back just long enough to roll on a condom before he covered me with his body, settling in between my thighs and taking my mouth with his.

Long, slow, drugging kisses. He wrapped one arm around my back, pressing my breasts into his chest as his mouth moved over mine, drifted down to nip and suck at that so sensitive patch of skin below my ear.

He pressed his hard cock between my legs, sliding it against my pussy, spreading my slick heat until we were both wet with my need for him, grinding together, the fat head of his cock rubbing over my clit, back and forth. I wrapped my legs around his hips, holding him tight, sliding closer and closer to the edge, and he wasn't even inside me.

The first orgasm hit me in a fast, hard wave that left me gasping as he ground his cock into my clit and let my pussy pulse against him. I was so caught up in the pleasure, drowning in it, that I didn't tense as he pushed the head of his cock inside me.

All I could do was fight for breath and roll my head back into the bed. If I hadn't just come, it might have hurt. It had been a long time, and I'd never seen a cock like Aiden's, much less had one inside me.

My body pulsing with pleasure, languid with orgasm, I spread my legs further and rocked up into him, taking more, the painful stretch of it sharpening the last waves of my climax.

He pushed, and I rocked until he'd fit every inch of that glorious cock inside me.

Aiden pressed his forehead to mine, his breath coming in harsh pants. I clamped my knees to his sides, tilting my hips so the base of his cock ground into my clit. Aiden groaned.

"Vi, baby, I wanted to make this good for you, but I can't —fuck, Vi."

He was shaking from the sheer effort of holding back, and I was done with it. Sinking my fingers into his hair, I drew his head down and bit into his earlobe for just a second before I whispered, "Fuck me, Aiden. Hard."

Something inside him snapped. He pulled his hips back and slammed them into me, the thick base of his cock grinding into my clit, sending shards of bliss through every inch of my body.

I held on, my mouth against his neck, my legs around his waist, as he fucked me in fast, brutal strokes, just the way I'd asked him to.

I couldn't get my breath before I came again, shivering, gasping, my pussy clenching on his cock as my body refused to let him go. I clawed at his shoulders, shaking from the force of it.

He said my name. Just *Violet* as he went stiff and shuddered against me.

Aiden rolled to his back, taking me with him. I melted on top of him, every bone in my body limp and satisfied. My head rested on his shoulder and I nudged it closer, reaching my tongue to taste the hollow of his collarbone. Salty and Aiden, he tasted as good as I thought he would.

Our hearts pounded against one another as we lay there, his fingers stroking up and down my spine in a long, slow caress. I was half-asleep when he eased me to the side and got up. I thought about moving, heard water run, then shut off. He came back and lifted me, tossing back the covers, easing us both beneath.

I never thought about it, just rolled into him, sliding my leg over his hip until it tangled with his, throwing my arm over his chest, and resting my head on his shoulder. We drifted like that. I think I slept a little. When I opened my eyes again, his fingers were moving absently in tiny circles on my arm.

My hand drifted down his side, over his hip, between his legs, to find him half hard. His skin was like velvet where it covered his full sack, and silky smooth where it stretched over his rapidly hardening cock. I played my hand over his length, squeezing and stroking, enjoying the weight of him, the feel of him, soft and smooth, steely and hot.

My thumb rubbed a bead of pre-come down over that tender spot on the underside of the head and he shivered.

I pulled myself from beneath his arm and slid down the bed. He said, "Violet," but I ignored him.

I wanted this, and he was going to give it to me.

Resting my cheek between his hips, I opened my mouth and licked at the next bead of pre-come that rose. Aiden shivered again, and his hand closed over my shoulder. Not pulling me back, just holding on.

He was too big for me to take all of him, but I used my mouth and my tongue, licking and sucking, tasting every inch of that beautiful cock until his hands hooked under my arms and he dragged me up his body.

His kiss was ragged. Desperate. Uncontrolled. He pulled me up the bed, up and over his body until I was straddling him before he filled his hands with my hips and brought me to his mouth.

I'd barely braced my hands on the headboard before my eyes rolled up from the sensation of his lips sucking on my clit, tugging and pulling, devouring me, fucking his tongue inside me, taking me with a reckless hunger that had me shaking in orgasm twice before he flipped me to my back, rolled on a condom, and drove himself inside me.

He pulled my hands over my head and held them there, burying himself deep between my legs over and over, his mouth on my neck, teeth grazing my skin, biting and sucking, claiming me with his body as he pushed me to another peak, spilling himself into the condom as the pulse of my body pulled him over the edge.

This time I was out before he left the bed, my body limp, eyes drifting shut. I woke in the night curled into him, my leg over his, his arm tight around my shoulders. I wiggled closer to his heat, moaning a little with the pure pleasure of being so close to Aiden. He pulled the blanket up higher and brushed his lips across the crown of my head.

I heard him say "Sleep, Vi," before I drifted off again.

Chapter Eighteen

Aiden

I felt Violet wake up before she moved. One moment she was curled against me like a warm kitten, her legs intertwined with mine, her arm thrown across my chest, the soft weight of her breasts on my skin. The next she went stiff, her breath catching in her lungs.

I imagined her eyes flying wide with panic. I kept my own closed.

I could have stopped her. If I'd rolled into her, pulled her to me, kissed her, I might have kept her in bed. But, I was playing a long game and this was about more than sex.

I listened to her slip from the bed, her feet padding on the carpet as she crept from the bedroom, probably in search of her suitcase.

When did I decide I was playing a long game?

Before or after I'd had her in bed?

I could be the arrogant asshole most people thought I was and say it was after I'd fucked her, but I'd be lying.

At first, when we'd uncovered her scheme, I'd only been playing with her. She was smart, and hot, and I was bored.

I'd been entertained by the idea of seeing if I could talk her into bed while I figured out what she was up to.

Everything had changed, and I had no idea when it happened. In bits and pieces. The frost in her eyes when she put Elizabeth in her place. Her defiance and dignity when Gage had tried to fire her. Her ice queen and her innocence. All of it had chipped away at me until I'd known I was keeping her before we got on the plane.

And now that I'd had her?

The soft click of a door closing filtered through the hotel suite, followed by the hiss of the shower. I already knew she'd try to put distance between us after the night before.

I'd let her, to a point.

If she thought she was going to take control, she was very wrong.

Now that I'd had Violet in my bed, she wasn't getting away.

I've slept with a lot of women. I'm not bragging, it's just reality. I've always had safe sex, and I've never led a woman into thinking I was offering more than I was prepared to give. I didn't need to lie or trick them. It was a side effect of being Aiden Winters.

The bonus was that plenty of women were more than happy to spread their legs for power and money combined with decent looks. And the downside? I was sick and tired of the kind of women who wanted to fuck power and money.

The world was filled with Elizabeths.

I wanted Violet.

She didn't want me to spend money on her. She wasn't angling to be my girlfriend. But when I kissed her, she turned to fire in my arms.

I'd never had sex like that before. Not once. I'd never

wanted to claim a woman like that. I'd been rough with her. I hadn't meant to. I'd had some kind of idea I'd be gentle, seduce her with smooth words and soft touches.

I'd done all right when we were dancing—until I kissed her. Just thinking about her hands pulling on my buttons, dragging off my clothes, and my cock was half hard.

I hadn't had to seduce Violet. She knew what she wanted, and she'd wanted me. Not my wallet. Not my company. Me.

She thought this was just for the weekend, had told Dylan she'd been about to resign. He thought she was kidding, but I knew she wasn't.

Violet thought we understood each other, but she was wrong. She needed me. She just didn't know it yet.

I emerged from my room freshly showered to find the other bedroom door closed, her shower still running. It only took me a minute to order up a full breakfast. Violet was still in her room when it arrived.

I poured myself a cup of coffee and settled in to wait her out. She couldn't stay in there all day. She had too much dignity to hide from me.

The door finally swung open to reveal a Violet I'd never seen before. Her eyes were cool, but this was my ice queen doing weekend casual. Like me, she had bare feet and wore jeans. Her long hair fell around her face in shining sheets. I liked it even more than I had the night before. In the daylight streaming through the windows, it gleamed silvery-gold. At the edge of the boat neck collar of her T-shirt I caught a glimpse of pale pink lace.

She was wearing the underwear I'd bought her. I was absurdly pleased. Even more so when her hair slid back off her shoulder to reveal a bite mark on her neck. I should have been remorseful. I'd been too aggressive with her, should never have marred that perfect, creamy skin.

I didn't care.

I wanted to mark her.

I wanted every fucking person who saw her to know she belonged to me.

"You ordered breakfast?" she asked, eyeing the carafe of coffee and my half-empty cup, the trays of dishes covering half of the dining room table.

"I got a little of everything. I didn't know what you'd want."

Pulling out the chair catty-corner to mine, Violet sat, tucking one bare foot under her leg. I poured her a cup of coffee as she lifted the lids on the plates.

"Do you mind if I eat the omelet?"

"It's all yours." I said. Wanting to poke at her a little, I said, "Did you sleep well?"

Violet's eyes flashed up to meet mine before she looked back at her plate, a flush rising on her cheeks. Refusing to let it get the better of her, she lifted her chin and held her hand out for the cup of coffee.

"I slept fine. You?"

"Great. Right until I woke up alone," I said, giving her a pointed look. If she thought we were going to pretend nothing had happened, she was going to have to think again.

Violet didn't apologize or try to justify sneaking out, only took a long sip of her coffee, watching me over the rim of the china cup.

That was fine. I had no interest in talking about it. Our bodies had communicated perfectly. We didn't need words. I was fucking thrilled to have breakfast with my ice queen because I knew the second I got my mouth on hers, she'd catch fire again.

No, I wanted to talk about something else, something she'd said the night before to Leigha that I was betting Violet hoped I hadn't heard.

"Are you going back to school to finish your master's degree?" I asked casually, refilling my coffee and pulling the plate of French toast in front of me.

Violet let out a quick breath of surprise before she covered it and said carefully, "I don't know."

"You don't know?" I challenged.

I loved her ice queen act, but I was tired of her hiding things from me. She raised her eyes to mine, that dusky lavender wary. Thoughtful. I stayed silent and watched her as she studied me.

Finally, she let out the breath she'd been holding and said, "I've been meaning to. I just—" She popped a bite of omelet in her mouth to stall.

"Is it the money?" I asked, enjoying the way her eyes narrowed in annoyance before she shook her head.

"It was, for a while. And then it was...other things."

"Other things?" I prodded.

Something about her discomfort with the subject unsettled me. Violet did not strike me as the kind of woman who left things unfinished, especially something as important as her master's degree. She wouldn't have pursued graduate school unless she'd wanted to go, so why had she quit one year in?

"It's hard to explain," she said, cutting into her omelet with the side of her fork, separating a precise piece before she stabbed it with the tines and popped it between her lips.

"Does it have to do with the reason you took a job at Winters, Inc.?"

"No," she said, so quickly I had no doubt she was telling

the truth. "No. It's—" Violet sighed and shook her head. "I don't like to talk about it."

Tough luck. I'd known there was something off when she'd mentioned it at dinner. I'd find out one way or another, but I wanted to hear it from her.

Something had happened to derail Violet's life, and I needed to know what it was. Logic told me any damage had long since been done, but Violet was mine. If someone or something had hurt her, I needed to know about it.

I set down my fork and reached for her hand, taking it in mine, rubbing my thumb across her knuckles. "Vi, I want to know you."

Her hand went still. She remained like that, frozen, for a long moment. So long, I started to wish I hadn't pushed. When she moved it was to draw back, pulling her fingers from my grip and bracing her heel on the edge of her chair. She wrapped one arm around her raised knee and picked up her coffee cup.

Her defenses in place, she said, "I wanted to go to graduate school right after college. But my parents didn't want to pay for it. They'd been unhappy that I majored in accounting. I was supposed to major in something more ladylike. Art history, or English literature. I was supposed to be in college to find a husband."

"You're kidding," I said. I knew the women in my mother's generation faced these kinds of archaic expectations, but these days?

Violet shrugged one shoulder. "My parents are old-fashioned. They'd already disowned my older brother for being a little wild. They were very strict with me. Anyway, I wasn't comfortable with the idea of taking out loans to cover the cost, so I thought I would work for a few years and save up the money. I probably wouldn't be able to put together enough to fully cover tuition, but I could at least get a start."

"That's practical," I said.

"That's what I thought. And then my father offered me a third option. One of his good friends had an opening in their accounting department for a junior bookkeeper. The company had a tuition match program and after I'd been there for a year they would pay most of the costs of graduate school. It seemed like the perfect solution."

"You took the job?" I asked, wondering why her father, who didn't seem to want her to work, would have hooked her up with a job.

"I did, and for the first year, it was fine. It was great. I like bookkeeping. I'd like to be able to do more—that's why I wanted to go to grad school—but I liked the job, the other people in the department were nice, and I was still living at home, so I was saving a ton of money for school."

"What happened after the first year?"

Violet's eyes darkened and her lids dropped, hiding her gaze. "After the first year, I applied and got into a graduate program in accountancy. I loved it. I went at night and worked full time. I didn't have much of a social life, but I didn't really care."

"And?" I pushed.

"And then things started getting weird."

"What do you mean, weird?" My mind raced through all of the ways work could get weird, particularly for a young woman. I didn't like any of them. The way Violet shifted in her seat, tightening her arms around her raised knees, didn't make me feel any better.

"The owner of the company, my father's friend, started —" Violet paused searching for the right words. "He started taking an interest in me. It was little things at first. Stopping by my desk, emailing to ask me to pop by his office. He said he was just checking on me, that he wanted to reassure my dad that I was doing well. I didn't think much of it."

I was afraid I knew exactly where this was going. "And then?" I prompted.

"And then, he started doing it more. Taking me out to lunch. Other people in the office noticed, commented on it. I was uncomfortable with the attention, but I wasn't sure what to do. It wasn't like I could go to human resources about it. I'd known him since I was a little girl."

"Name?" I asked, trying for casual.

Violet was too smart to fall for that. Shaking her head, she refused to answer. I let it go. For now. I'd find out later. Cooper probably already had the name in her file.

"Did you talk to your father about it?" I asked.

"I did," Violet said. "He told me I should be happy to have the attention. That I shouldn't waste the opportunity." She let out a harsh laugh. "I was so stupid. I had no idea what he was talking about."

"Did you ever confront your employer about it?"

Violet shook her head. "I should have. I was so busy between work and school, I was distracted, and I didn't realize what was going on. Not really. It was an annoyance. Until it wasn't."

I did not like the way that sounded. "What happened?"

Violet laid her cheek on her knees and stared across the room, seeing the past in place of our hotel suite. "I started dodging his lunch invitations and he asked me to dinner. He was subtle, but it was obvious that he wasn't interested in hearing a 'no'. That should have been a red flag. But I went. And like everything else, in the beginning, it was okay. A little weird, but okay. He asked about my family, and school, and how I liked working for his company. But after a while, the conversation started to shift. He wanted to know who I was dating, how many children I wanted to have. Things that were too personal for a family friend to ask about. I thought about finding another job but—"

"School," I finished for her.

"Exactly. I'll give him this, he was very smart. If he'd started the whole game the first year I worked for him, I would have been out the door. At that point, by the time I started really getting uneasy, I'd been at the company for two years and was a year into my master's program. It seemed foolish to walk away over a few dinners and a weird feeling in my stomach when he looked at me."

"But you did leave," I said, baldly, "so something happened."

"Something happened," Violet agreed. She sat up and reached for her empty coffee cup, taking her time refilling it. After she took a long sip, she said, "He maneuvered me into dinner at his house. Like everything else, it seemed so innocent. He wanted to talk about a new account, and then he remembered he'd left a file at his house. Once we were there he confessed he'd ordered dinner in."

"Tell me you walked out, and he fired you."

"Not exactly," Violet said, with a shaky laugh. "Like an idiot—like the naïve, accommodating woman my parents raised me to be—I wasted time trying to figure out a polite way to go home. Before we finished our first glass of wine, he tried to kiss me. And then...and then he wanted more than that."

Chapter Nineteen

Aiden

Violet's eyes were glued to her coffee cup, and I couldn't read her face. My gut twisted as I asked, "Did he—"

Before I could finish the sentence, she cut me off with a sharp shake of her head. "No. He tried. He tore my blouse, but when he tried to pull up my skirt, I kneed him in the balls and punched him. He caught me in the eye with an elbow, but I managed to get out the door. I don't remember how I got home. My car was at the office, and he lived over a mile from my parents' house. I must have walked. He didn't follow."

"He didn't come after you?"

"He didn't have to. He did one better. He called my parents. They were waiting when I walked through the door. My father was disgusted. My mother was confused. She couldn't understand why I didn't just let him do what he wanted to do. He was rich, and connected, and he wanted me. My father explained that they had an arrangement. I was part of it. They had business together. His friend wanted another wife. Someone young. Malleable. My father offered me."

"And they thought you'd just go along with it? If he wanted to marry you, why bother hiring you or sending you to school?"

"That's what I wanted to know," she said. She shook her head again and took another sip of coffee, but her eyes were stormy and sad. "Apparently, he wasn't quite ready to settle down again, but he didn't want me wandering around out there making unsuitable connections and doing God knows what, so he and my father figured giving me a job and sending me to school would keep me occupied. As for going along with it, I honestly don't think it occurred to either of my parents that I would defy them."

"They seriously thought they would just present you with a groom and you'd march right up to the altar? Have they met you?" I couldn't wrap my head around this vision of Violet as an obedient daughter. She was too strong, too single-minded.

Her lips curved up in a hint of a smile. "They did. Except for choosing to major in business, I always did what I was told. My brother was the rebellious one, and they cut him off when they decided he was unsuitable."

"What did he do? Rob a bank?"

"He got a tattoo and a motorcycle. And then he dropped out of college."

"That's it? I guess I could see cutting off the family money if he dropped out of school."

"No, Aiden, they didn't cut him off financially. They cut him out of the family. They excised him like a tumor. Threw him out and never spoke his name again. He had academic scholarships and he worked. He wanted to study computer science instead of economics, and they refused to foot the bill so he paid for everything himself. But he didn't fit what they wanted in a son and that was that. I was forbidden to talk to him, but we were close. We figured out ways to stay in touch. They might have been disappointed in him, but I wasn't. He's the best brother in the world."

"So, if they kicked your brother out of the family for buying a motorcycle and getting a tattoo, what did they do to you?"

"I can see you're getting it," she said. "After days of ranting and raving at me, telling me how ungrateful I was, how I owed them, my father finally laid down the law. Marry his friend or get out. I packed a bag and left in the middle of the night. They'd confiscated my cell phone, purse, and passport. I walked to the nearest gas station and called my brother collect. It was a mess. I didn't have my driver's license, credit cards. Nothing. By the time I got everything figured out, I learned my parents had closed my bank accounts, taking every penny I'd saved for school."

"They stole your money?" I hoped I never had the opportunity to meet Violet's parents. They sounded like a nightmare. First, they'd sold their daughter, then they'd set her up to be raped, and when she didn't go along they stole everything she had? Everything she'd worked for?

Something burned in my chest. Something beyond just anger. I wanted to track them down and make them pay for the way they'd treated her. Right after I found this family friend.

"They didn't see it that way," Violet said. She picked a croissant off one of the plates and nibbled at the corner. "I'd opened the accounts jointly when I was a kid, for birthday checks from relatives, that kind of thing. It never occurred to me to open another one, so they had the authority to close them and transfer the money to their own accounts. I guess they saw it as a repayment for an investment that didn't pan out."

"That investment being you," I said.

I'd lost my parents far too young, but I had almost twenty years of memories. The scent of my mother's perfume when she hugged me. Whiskey and cigars when my father let me sit on his lap at his big desk.

Love.

Unconditional love from two parents who valued their children above all else. I couldn't imagine the kind of family Violet described.

"That investment being me," she agreed. "My mother thought she couldn't have children after my brother. They tried for years. Finally, she went through IVF trying to get pregnant with me. Eventually, it worked, but it was expensive. I wasn't surprised they cleaned me out. Not that they needed the money. It wouldn't have been about the money."

"No, it sounds like it was about spite. Revenge," I said, disgusted.

Violet lifted one shoulder, then dropped it. "That's pretty much my parents. If you don't get your way, go straight for petty revenge. There are no shades of gray for them. You conform to their standards or you don't exist. I had no interest in marrying a man old enough to be my father, a man I didn't even like that much, just to make them happy."

"And that was it? They didn't come after you? Did they check to make sure you were all right?"

"I don't know. I wasn't that hard to find. My brother was living out of state, but he dropped everything to come get me. He gave me a place to live, a job. He's my family, not them. My guess is that they were waiting for me to come crawling back. It probably didn't occur to them that I might leave for good."

"And you haven't seen them since?"

"No. I wouldn't be surprised if I never saw them again. I doubt they want to hear from me, and I don't really want to see them."

"I wouldn't either," I agreed. She didn't need people that toxic in her life. "But that doesn't explain why you never went back to school. It's been a few years, hasn't it?"

"It has. And like I said, at first it was money. My brother said he'd pay for school, but he was already doing enough. I didn't want to be a burden. Then he started a new company, and I got so wrapped up in that, I wasn't worried about school and now...I don't know. I guess it's time to start figuring this stuff out."

Before I thought better of it I said, "Winters, Inc. has a tuition match program."

Violet's eyes flew wide, and she stared at me in shocked surprise for what felt like a full minute before her chest started to shake, and she burst into laughter. Just when I thought she was going to stop, she opened her mouth to say something, caught my eye, and dissolved into giggles again.

Tears streamed down her cheeks before she got herself under control. I didn't have to guess why she was laughing. The parallels were absurd. The only difference was, she'd come to my bed willingly. And I didn't want her as part of some deal with her father. I just wanted Violet. Still, I could see why she was amused.

I wasn't surprised when she finally said, "No way in hell." Wiping the tears from under her eyes, she let out another quick giggle. "Are you nuts? All this situation needs is me tying myself to your company even further. You need to fire me, not pay for my grad school tuition. I thought you were smarter than this."

"I am. Except, apparently, when it comes to you."

Truer words had never been spoken. All my good sense went right out the window where Violet was concerned, and I could not have cared less. Sitting here, sharing breakfast, finally getting inside her head, and learning who she was, I didn't care about being smart.

I was happy.

I'd take happy over smart any day, especially if it was with Violet.

"What do you want to do today?" I asked, hoping she'd go for the obvious change in subject. I didn't want to talk about her family anymore, and I definitely didn't want to talk about her job with Winters, Inc.

She was right, I needed to fire her. I just wasn't ready yet.

"I don't know, I hadn't thought about it. What do you want to do?"

"Are you finished with breakfast?" I asked, taking in the crumbs of her croissant on the otherwise empty plate.

Wiping her hands on a cloth napkin, she looked down at the plate. "I'm done."

That was all I needed to hear. I was out of my chair and scooping her up before she saw me coming. She let out a high-pitched squeak and flung her arms around my shoulders for balance as I carried her across the living room, straight for the bedroom.

When she got her balance she looked up at me, raised one eyebrow and said, "Really? Again?"

I tossed her on the mattress, loving the way her breasts bounced beneath her T-shirt. "Really. Again. And again."

Violet had her clothes off in a blink.

She let me take off the pink lace underwear. If I'd thought things would be different after the rush of first passion, I would have been wrong. In the light of day, now that the edge was off, we took our time. I explored every inch of her body, finding out what made her squirm and what made her scream.

We spent the entire day in that bed. It wasn't a race to orgasm. No one was keeping score. It was fingers and tongues and long, lazy touches. Endless kisses, slow and deep. Violet riding me until ecstasy spread across her face, my hand between her legs, and my mouth on her breast.

Soft murmurs of sweet nothings. Napping and waking to reach for each other again. We finally surfaced when our stomachs rumbled too loudly to ignore. I ran a bath and ordered dinner after Violet told me what she wanted, and we soaked in bubbles and hot water until the waiter knocked on the door.

Violet turned pink with embarrassment when I answered in my robe. Once the waiter was gone, she wrapped herself in her own robe and didn't bother with clothes. We ate, steak for me and pasta for Violet, chocolate tort for dessert. The chocolate tort, we ate in bed.

"Movie?" Violet asked.

"I'm embarrassed to say I don't think I can have sex again for at least an hour," I admitted.

Violet laughed, her breasts jiggling beneath her robe, distracting me. "Only an hour? I think we've had more sex in the last twenty-four hours than I've had in my entire life."

"That's just sad, sweetheart."

"It kind of is."

"We'll have to make up for lost time," I said, "after we take a break. You pick the movie."

It wasn't a test, exactly. More that I was curious to see

what kind of movie Violet would pick. She pulled up the hotel's basic cable channels, but I grabbed the remote and switched her over to pay-per-view. She slid me a sideways glance and said, "I'm not picking porn."

"I wasn't suggesting porn, you perv," I said, though I made myself a liar by immediately imagining watching porn with Violet.

Later. Another time. I wondered if she'd be up for it.

I was so caught up thinking about Violet and porn that I missed the movie she picked. It wasn't until I saw the opening credits that I realized it was a recently released offbeat comedy I'd been meaning to see and hadn't found the time.

"Is this okay?" she asked, handing me the remote.

"It's great," I said, meaning it.

"It was between this or that disaster flick about earthquakes and tsunamis. I want to see that one but this screen is too small."

I completely agreed. "We can watch that one at home. The screen in our theater room is huge."

Violet sent me another one of those sideways looks and murmured, "Of course, it is."

I ignored her and pulled her into my side. Violet rested her head on my shoulder. She dozed off just before the end credits rolled.

I let her sleep all night, but woke her in the morning with my mouth on hers. She turned into me as if we woke together every day, and I knew there was no way I could give her up. I sensed that pushing Violet too hard was the worst possible plan, but I could feel time slipping away.

It was Sunday and the plane was waiting. I could talk to her in the office on Monday. We had to sort this out. She still hadn't come clean about her reasons for taking the job at Winters, Inc. I knew enough for my own peace of mind, but I wanted to hear it from her.

I felt like I could trust her, but I wanted to know that I could.

I had to know that I could.

I needed to know she trusted me enough to be honest. Until we got past that, we couldn't move forward. And I needed to move forward with Violet.

I saw it happen when we got on the plane. Her body, languid and relaxed, stiffened as if she'd braced for the reality of home. I meant to wait until Monday. To confront her on my territory, in my office. I couldn't do it. We'd begun our descent into Atlanta when the words spilled from my mouth.

"When are you going to tell me the truth?" Immediately I wished I could take it back.

Shutters fell over her eyes. Her shoulders straightened and she crossed her legs, lacing her fingers together and resting her hands on her knee. She was perfectly composed. Impenetrable. Fuck.

"The truth about what?"

Her evasion got under my skin and I said, "You know what. I already know and I want to hear it from you. Why did you take the job at Winters, Inc.? What were you after?"

"What do you mean you already know?" she asked, the first hint of emotion thawing her gaze. "What do you think you know?"

"I know what you were up to," I said. I'd been tracking her for weeks. She hadn't made a move that wasn't documented. "But I want you to tell me. I want you to trust me enough to be honest. I'm tired of this game"

"If you're tired of me," she said in a frozen voice, "we can solve that easily enough."

"That's not what I said. I'm not tired of you. I don't think I'm ever going to get tired of you. I'm tired of the game. I'm tired of the lies. Just tell me the truth."

"Then tell me what you think you know," she insisted.

"I know why you took the job. I know what you were doing while you were in the company. I don't care. I don't care about any of it."

I wasn't prepared for the gleam of tears in her eyes. "You know why I was there and you don't care? After everything I told you, you don't care."

I was missing something.

I didn't care that she'd been looking for dirt on me. There wasn't any. She couldn't hurt me with anything she'd found. But I had to be missing something because Violet looked as if I'd just stabbed her in the heart.

"Violet. It's okay. Just tell me who put you up to it and we can just get past it."

"And then what? And then we just keep doing this?" She gestured between us. "We just keep sleeping together? Is sex the only thing that matters?"

"Yes. No. Sex isn't the only thing that matters, and yes we just keep doing this. You and me. I like being with you. I want to get the rest of it out of the way. I want to forget about it."

"And it's just that easy for you, isn't it."

"I don't see why it has to be more complicated than that," I said, carefully. I needed to know who'd sent her to Winters, Inc., but then I'd be happy if we never talked about any of this again.

Violet lifted a finger to wipe underneath her lashes. It

came away wet and my gut clenched tight. What was I missing?

She shook her head slowly, her eyes unbearably sad. "I can't forget about it. I let myself get sidetracked with you and I shouldn't have."

The plane bounced twice as the wheels touched the tarmac. Violet didn't look at me. She wouldn't look at me as we got off the plane. She wouldn't meet my eyes in the car.

I'd fucked up, and I didn't know how.

At least I had Monday. I was going to drag her into my office and we'd start all over again. I was going to figure out what the fuck was going on so I could get it out of my way and concentrate on Violet.

"I'll see you tomorrow. Don't even think about calling in sick," I ordered, hating the angry tone in my voice.

Violet only nodded. She collected her purse and suitcase and disappeared through the doors of her building without looking back.

Chapter Twenty

Violet

Aiden Winters was a world-class asshole. I could not believe I'd fallen for his act.

So romantic.

So sweet.

So appealingly bossy.

I'd forgotten who he was. What he was. And in forgetting, I'd proven that I was still a naïve idiot. I couldn't believe he sat there and told me he knew all about Chase's company and he didn't care.

If he knew I was there trying to save my brother's company, and he knew how much my brother meant to me, how could he say he didn't care?

Unless everything had just been a line to get me into bed. Unless he was playing me the whole time. And I'd given it up so easily, like the sap that I was.

I punched the elevator button harder than necessary and let out an angry breath. I was an idiot but at least I'd gotten good sex out of it. Fresh tears sprang to my eyes as I thought of the way Aiden had woken me that morning. His lips feathering across mine, his hands...

No. I was not thinking about Aiden.

I was not thinking about anything that had happened over the weekend. Or before that.

I was not going to think about Aiden at all.

I let myself into the empty condo, grateful that Chase wasn't home yet. I'd need the rest of the week to lick my wounds and figure out where to go from here. We'd left Las Vegas in the middle of the afternoon, but thanks to the time change it was almost nine in Atlanta.

I wasn't tired.

I was exhausted all the way to my bones.

I left my suitcase on the floor of my bedroom, taking out only my toiletries case, and dropped my clothes on the floor, pulling on a well-worn sleep shirt. Flicking on the TV, I tried to distract myself with reruns of a nineties sitcom I hadn't watched in ages.

It didn't work. I lay there, tossing and turning, as season one melted into season two, and the night unraveled in restless sleep. I finally slipped under as the sun kissed the sky, my cheeks wet and my heart shattered.

My alarm woke me right on time for a job I had no intention of going to. I dragged myself out of bed anyway. I needed a shower. I needed to wash away the weekend and get my head in gear. Before I figured out the rest of my life, I needed coffee. I'd barely cleared my doorway when the sound of a familiar voice cut through the room, scaring me half to death.

"What the fuck is this, Violet?" My brother stood in the kitchen, his blue eyes blazing, waving a piece of paper at me.

"Chase! What are you doing here?"

"I live here. What is this, Violet? What are you up to?"

Crap.

In his hand, Chase held my pay stub from Winters, Inc.

Double crap.

I would never have left it sitting around if I'd thought he'd be home this soon.

Inanely, I said, "You weren't supposed to see that. Why are you home early?"

"The job wrapped up faster than I expected. And no shit I wasn't supposed to see this. The question is, why do you have it? What the hell are you doing working for Winters, Inc.?"

Chase was pissed.

Chase never yelled at me. My big brother could be a son of the bitch to anyone else, but he was a marshmallow where I was concerned. Unfortunately, he was also overprotective. Bracing myself, I headed for the coffee maker and ignored his question.

"Violet," he said in warning.

"Yeah, I get it. I'll explain. Just let me get a cup of coffee. Chill out. I'm fine. Everything's fine."

"If everything's fine, then where the hell were you this weekend?"

Stalling, I asked, "How do you know I wasn't here?"

Chase lifted one blonde eyebrow and stared me down. "Because your suitcase is sitting in the middle of your bedroom floor, and you set the alarm in away mode Friday morning. You didn't deactivate it until last night."

I grunted in the back of my throat. I should have known. Chase was sneaky. Of course, he would have checked the alarm. I poured my coffee, added half-and-half, and leaned back against the kitchen counter, studying my brother.

His golden blond hair was cut short on the sides and a little longer on top, the messy waves falling into his blue,

blue eyes. With the scruff on his cheeks and the hint of a tattoo under his sleeve, he looked like a fallen angel.

He was *my* angel. My big brother was always there for me. When my parents kicked me out he'd dropped everything and driven across two states to get me. He'd given me a home, a job, and more important than any of that, he'd loved me. No matter what.

I knew, no matter how stupid my plan had been, no matter that I hadn't succeeded, Chase would forgive me for kissing the enemy.

Not that I was going to tell him about the kissing part. There were some things my big brother did not need to know.

Biting the bullet, I took a fortifying sip of coffee and laid out my plan for Chase. If I'd been watching from the outside, it would have been funny the way Chase turned pink, then red, gritting his teeth so hard I imagined I could see steam coming from his ears. As the target of his fury, it wasn't that entertaining.

In a tight voice, Chase summed up my story. "So what you're saying is that you got a job there under false pretenses to try to find dirt on Aiden Winters and force him to give us the company back. But they caught you and still let you keep your job. Do you want to explain why?"

"Not exactly," I said, wishing I could force the blush from my cheeks. I wasn't a very good liar, and I'd never been able to lie to Chase, not that I tried that often.

"You didn't find anything on Winters that you could use, right?"

I shook my head. It might have been worth it, worth the ache in my heart, if I'd found dirt on Aiden and forced him to give us the company back. But I hadn't. My plan had been a failure on all fronts.

"Vivi," Chase said gently, using his childhood nickname for me, "what have you gotten yourself into?"

"It's okay," I reassured, "I'm not going back. It's over."

"Do they have evidence against you? Can they press charges?"

"No," I assured him, though I wasn't entirely positive that was true. I didn't think Aiden would press charges against me for hacking his email and files, but he probably could, if he wanted to.

Crap.

"Are you going to tell me where you were this weekend?"

"No, I don't think I am," I said. Chase narrowed those familiar blue eyes on me, and I could practically see his brain recalculating.

"Did you spend the whole time you were at Winters, Inc. working under Carlisle Daniels?"

Relieved at the change in subject, I said, "They aren't making it work without you. Some of it, but the new technology is—"

"That's not what I asked, Vivi. I can guess exactly how they're doing with my tech. What I want to know is if you stayed safely buried in the department they made of my company."

"Not exactly," I admitted. Chase stared me down. "Aiden Winters brought me on as one of his assistants a few weeks ago."

"Fuck!" Chase exploded off his stool and slammed his palm into the granite countertop. I jumped, sloshing coffee down the front of my robe. I opened my mouth to yell at him when he said, "Violet! You do not want to get on the radar of a man like Aiden Winters. What the fuck were you thinking? Do you know what he could do to you?"

"He's not what you think—" I started to protest, and then drew up short.

Hadn't he told me just the day before that he'd been playing me? That he knew exactly what I was doing and he didn't care? He didn't care that he'd stolen my brother's company and gutted it. If he didn't care about that, he couldn't care about me. Which meant Chase was right.

"You spent the weekend with him, didn't you?" Chase asked. He knew me way too well.

I busied myself wiping at the coffee stain on my robe, as if that would do any good, and avoided Chase's eyes.

I could feel him staring at me. Then he said, his voice painfully gentle, "You've been crying. My poor Vivi. What happened? Did he hurt you? I'll fucking kill him if he—"

"He didn't hurt me. Not the way you mean. He was... sweet. Kind of. I liked him. I'm sorry, Chase. I'm sorry. I know he's an asshole and he stole your company and I didn't mean to, but I liked him."

"What. Did. He. Do?" Chase asked, his voice low. Dangerous.

I forced myself to meet his eyes, wincing at the pity I saw there. I *was* pitiful with my puffy face, my tear stained cheeks, and my coffee-stained robe. I felt pitiful.

Letting out a long sigh, I said, "He admitted he was playing me. He admitted he knew why I was there, and he didn't care, he just wanted to keep—"

I didn't need to put that part into words. Not unless I wanted to watch my brother's head explode.

"I'll fucking kill him," Chase said, moving around the end of the island, reaching for his keys.

I set my mug down on the counter with a clatter and dove in front of him. "No! Just let it go. I'm a big girl, and I made a mistake with the wrong guy. I'm not the first woman to do it, and I won't be the last. I learned my lesson and it's over. It's over. Can we just let it go? I'm sorry I couldn't get the company back. I just wanted to fix everything."

Chase pulled me into a rough hug, squeezing tight as he rested his chin on the top of my head. "Vivi, it's not your responsibility. I'm the one who lost the company. I'm the one who didn't double check the contracts."

I soaked up my brother's embrace. "I messed up with Aiden. But it's over. Don't go after him. He may have been an asshole in the end, but he was a gentleman."

Chase gave me a suspicious look. "How can he be an asshole and a gentleman?"

"I don't know, he just is. He was a gentleman right up until he was an asshole, okay? I just want to move on. I need to find a new job."

"You know I can find you something—"

"Chase, I can find a job. Maybe after I do that, I can actually get my own place to live."

"Hell, no," my brother cut in. "I'm not letting you out of my sight until I'm sure you're not going to do anything else that's crazy."

"When do I ever do anything crazy?" Rethinking that, I amended, "Other than this whole thing with Winters, Inc."

"Rarely," Chase admitted. "You're sensible to a fault. But I don't like you getting involved with Aiden Winters. That can't mean good things. I want you where I can keep an eye on you. Keep you safe."

"Chase, he's not going to—"

"Humor me. Have you quit? Officially?"

Belatedly, I remembered Aiden saying he'd see me tomorrow. It was tomorrow and I had no intention of going into work.

"Not officially, but—"

"Do it now." Chase picked up my phone off the counter and handed it to me. "Email your resignation right now, while I'm watching. No loose ends. Just cut your losses and get out. Is there anything you need out of your desk?"

I thought of my stapler and the little cactus and my mug. I shook my head. They weren't worth the humiliation of seeing Aiden again.

With Chase looming over my shoulder, I opened my email app and composed a new draft, addressed to Aiden.

It said only:

Aiden,

This has gone far enough. I quit.

Violet

My heart twisted in my chest as I tapped the icon to send the email. I don't know what I expected from Aiden, but somewhere in that sex-hazed weekend, I'd started to hope for more.

I hadn't been thinking of the end.

But the end was here, and it hurt like hell.

Chapter Twenty-One

Violet

Chase hung around for another few hours, pretending he wasn't keeping an eye on me as I unpacked my suitcase, got dressed in jeans and an old T-shirt, and grabbed my tablet to start cruising the classifieds for a job.

Typical of my brother, he dropped the whole subject of my failed plan to get his company back and my stupidity in getting involved with Aiden Winters. Chase wasn't one to nag. He had his say, and he was done. That didn't mean he wasn't keeping an eye on me. He'd said more than once, it didn't matter how old I got, he'd always be my big brother.

When he was satisfied I planned to stay out of trouble, he changed and headed to the gym in our complex, saying, "After I work out, we can go and get some lunch. Maybe buy groceries."

My stomach was just starting to rumble when a fist pounded on the door. Checking the clock I realized it was about time for Chase to be finished with his workout. He must have forgotten his key. It wouldn't be the first time.

Leaving my tablet on the coffee table, I went to the front

door and swung it open. "I thought you put a key in your gym bag."

"You should check the peephole before you open the door."

Standing in the doorframe, his hands in the pockets of his suit pants, was Aiden Winters. And he did not look happy.

He was right, I should have checked the peephole before I opened the door.

What was he doing here?

Answering my question he pulled his phone from his pocket and shoved it in my face. My email was on the screen. "Would you care to explain this, Violet?"

"It's my resignation letter," I said, slowly. "I thought that was clear."

Pushing past me into the condo, Aiden said, "And I thought I was clear. You don't quit until I fire you. I told you if you tried to run I would find you."

I closed my eyes and tried to summon the ice queen. I needed to straighten my spine, raise my chin, and give him one of my withering looks.

I couldn't do it. I was tired somewhere deep inside that had nothing to do with a lack of sleep.

Since the minute I laid eyes on him, Aiden Winters drew me like a magnet. I'd wanted him, against my better judgment, and every day I worked with him, I wanted him a little bit more. Over the weekend my defenses had cracked too far to repair. He'd wormed his way into my heart, and I couldn't find it in me to shut him out.

Abandoning all pretense, I slumped against the kitchen counter and stared at my brightly polished toes. "What do you want with me, Aiden? I thought we cleared everything up yesterday on the plane."

Aiden shoved his phone back in his pocket and stood in front of me, so close the tips of his shoes touched my toes. He crossed his arms over his chest and glowered down at me.

"Maybe that conversation cleared something up for you," he said, "but I'm confused as hell. Why are you mad at me for saying I don't care that you were spying on me? Shouldn't it be the other way around?"

"How can you not get it?" Copying his posture, I crossed my arms over my chest and glared at him. "Maybe I lied when I got my job, and maybe I was poking around in your company where I shouldn't have been. But you stole from us. I'm not the one who's wrong here. And the fact that you don't even care about what you did? I can't let that go. I'm sick that part of me even wants to."

Aiden was speechless, so thrown by my accusation he took an involuntary step back. "What are you talking about? What did I steal from you? I never laid eyes on you until that day in the elevator."

What was *I* talking about?

What was *he* talking about?

Hadn't he said yesterday that he knew exactly why I was there?

Tired of dancing around the subject I said flatly, "I'm talking about CD4 Analytics. I'm talking about you stealing my brother's company, signing the papers, and then booting him out."

Aiden's eyes narrowed on my face and he shook his head slowly. "Who exactly is your brother? Gage oversaw the CD4 Analytics acquisition, but I thought we bought the company from a guy named Harrison."

"You didn't buy it *from* Harrison, you bought it *with* Harrison. Harrison switched the contracts on Chase, changed some of the language at the last minute, giving him —you—the power to vote Chase out and take his shares. Which you did three days after the contract was signed."

Aiden shook his head again. "Gage knows more details than I do, but if your brother is the founder of CD4 Analytics, we didn't fire him. He bailed on us. We tried to track him down in the beginning, and once we found him, he refused to take our calls."

"No, he didn't," I insisted. "He thought the terms of the agreement had him keeping his position. He wasn't done developing the new tech. You know that because it's a mess. Your team can't figure out how to make it work without him."

Shoving his hands in his pockets, Aiden said wryly, "I'm aware of that. The guy who used to be Carlisle's boss, the guy who originally spearheaded the acquisition, got fired over that. Considering the most appealing part of the company isn't working, we're not exactly getting our money's worth."

"Good, since neither did Chase."

"So you think I screwed your brother out of his company, and you got a job at Winters, Inc. to do what? What was your plan?" he demanded.

"I thought if I could find some dirt on you, I could use it to force you to give Chase his company back," I admitted.

"Violet, that's ridiculous. First of all, there isn't anything to find. And second, I can't give you the company back. I can talk to your brother. We can work something out. We need his help. But Vi, I promise you, we may play rough sometimes, but we have never deliberately screwed someone out of their company. That's not how we operate. CD4 Analytics was a lot more valuable with your brother still on board. Why would Harrison have forced him out before he sold the company to us?"

"You weren't working with Harrison?" I asked, stymied.

"No," he said. "He approached us about the sale months before it happened, and part of the deal was that the lead techs come with the company."

"So, he bought the company from Chase, switched the contracts to seize Chase's stock," I said, putting the pieces together, one by one, "and then sold it to you—"

"—and made a mint off your brother's shares," Aiden finished for me. "Fucking hell. That's underhanded. It's criminal."

"Yeah, except we can't prove it. Chase went after him, but we don't have a case. Chase signed the contracts he didn't realize had been switched. It was stupid, and it lost him his company."

Aiden pinched the bridge of his nose and closed his eyes, thinking. "Would your brother be open to an approach from Gage? We'd be prepared to make him a generous offer to come take over and get the acquisition back on track."

"I don't know," I said. "He's been doing consulting. He just finished up a job, but I don't know what he has on next. I don't know if he'll talk to you. He wasn't happy when he came home and figured out what I'd been doing."

"He didn't know?" Answering his own question Aiden said, "Of course, he didn't know. Did he kick your ass when he found out?"

"How'd you guess?" I asked, both annoyed and amused.

Aiden slanted me a superior look. "Because I have a little sister, and if she came up with such a dumbass plan, I'd kick her ass when I found out."

"Yeah, well, he also found out I spent the weekend with

you, so I wouldn't joke too much about ass kicking. I had to physically stop him from hunting you down this morning."

"I'm not going to hide from your brother, sweetheart. If he wants to come after me for getting involved with his little sister, that's fine. I get it. I'll deal with him, and he'll just have to get used to me."

"I don't know what that means," I confessed.

I couldn't keep up. We'd always assumed Aiden was working with Harrison. The turnover was too fast. One minute Chase was signing the contracts and a few days later Winters, Inc. owned the company. It seemed impossible that Harrison had been working alone.

The real question was, did I believe Aiden? If he was telling the truth, then he hadn't admitted to playing me.

"Yesterday you said you knew what I was doing at the company and you didn't care. Since you didn't know I was Chase's sister, what did you think I was doing there?"

Aiden shrugged one shoulder, looking uncomfortable. "Exactly what you were doing. Looking for dirt on me. Except I didn't think you were doing it for your brother, I figured you had a client. When I asked you for the truth, I just wanted you to tell me who the client was."

"And you didn't care that I was spying on you?" I asked, disbelieving.

He should have cared.

Then again, he should have fired me the second he found out what I was up to.

"Vi, you were under surveillance since the first time you got into my emails. We have every keystroke on file and you've been isolated from anything sensitive since almost the beginning. At first, I kept you close because I was hoping you'd lead me to whoever sent you in the first place. Then I kept you close because I didn't want you to leave."

"Aiden," I said, at a loss for words. "I'm sorry. It was a stupid plan. I just...I was with Chase from the beginning of CD4. He worked so hard, and he loved that company. I couldn't stand watching him lose everything like that. I wanted to fix it, and I didn't think about whether that was fair to you, or anyone else. I just wanted to help my brother."

"You could have landed yourself in a lot of trouble, Vi," Aiden said, stepping closer and squeezing my shoulders in his strong hands. The heat of his body radiated between us, drawing me closer. I wanted to lean forward and fall into him.

"I know," I said. "I'm not usually that reckless. I just, I needed—"

"You needed to help your brother. I get it. I'd do anything for my family, and they've pointed out that I'm not always rational when I think I'm protecting them. But you took too big a risk, sweetheart. Promise me you're not going to do something like that again."

"Get a job with Winters, Inc.?" I asked, trying to keep up with his shift in mood. His hands slid down my arms and pulled me closer. Almost close enough to kiss. The woodsy Aiden scent of him was distracting.

"No, promise me you won't do something that leaves you open to criminal charges."

Dazed by his nearness, I met his dark eyes and promised, "I won't. That was a one-time thing. I swear."

"Then your brother better keep his ass out of trouble, because I won't have you throwing yourself in front of him every time he fucks up."

"Hey," I protested, trying to pull back. His fingers tightened around my arms, not letting me move. "Chase is not a fuck up. Chase is brilliant and he works his ass off. He made one mistake—"

"Fine," Aiden said, cutting me off. "I don't want to fight about your brother. Considering you said he was pissed when he found out what you were up to, I'll give him the benefit of the doubt. For now. But I'm not going to let you put yourself in danger. For anyone."

"First of all, I'm not your problem—"

"You are absolutely my problem, Violet," Aiden said. "Everything about you is my problem. My problem and my business. You can't brush me off with some lame resignation email."

"You can't—"

"Do you want to come back to work?" Aiden asked, interrupting me.

"At Winters, Inc.? No. No way," I said, scrambling to keep up.

"Good. Because you're fired. Have dinner with me tonight."

"What?" I stared up at him, finding myself leaning into him exactly the way I'd wanted to, my breasts brushing his chest, his hands sliding back up my arms to cup my chin.

"Have dinner with me, Vi," he said, lowering his head slowly, closing the distance between his mouth and mine. His breath whispered across my lips. "I woke up without you this morning and I didn't like it. Have dinner with me. And then we'll see."

I parted my lips to say okay, but I didn't get the chance. His mouth was on mine, his fingers cradling the back of my head, angling my face up to his. My arms wrapped around him, and I held on, falling into the kiss, tasting him, opening for him.

I was lost, and he felt so good I couldn't think, couldn't

get my head together, when Chase's voice cut through the room.

"What the fuck is going on? Get your goddamn hands off my sister."

Oops. In the shock of seeing Aiden, I'd completely forgotten that Chase would be home any second.

Aiden stepped back just enough to angle his body in front of me. "I'd say that's up to your sister."

Great, just what this situation needed. Two overprotective males trying to establish dominance over the female. Like I couldn't take care of myself. I rolled my eyes, though neither of them noticed. Before he could stop me, I slid out from behind Aiden and stepped between them, evading Chase when he reached out to grab my hand.

Taking a deep breath, I said, "Aiden, this is my brother Chase. Chase, this is Aiden. I think you two have a lot to talk about. And none of it has to do with me." Catching my brother's eye, I said, "Chase, I think you should hear him out. It didn't happen the way we thought it did."

"And you believe this guy?" Chase asked, sending Aiden a withering look.

"I believe him," I said to my brother. Turning to look at Aiden, I found him staring at Chase like he'd seen a ghost.

Before I could ask him what was wrong, Chase said, "Vivi, no. I know you want to believe him but—" He sent Aiden a sidelong look filled with mistrust.

Aiden, for his part, didn't seem to notice. He was studying Chase like he was a bug under a microscope. His attention made me uneasy. Chase took my hand and tugged me closer, away from Aiden. I vaguely heard Aiden murmur, "Excuse me", before Chase started in on me again.

"You're gorgeous, Vivi, and you're smart. So smart. But you don't have a lot of experience with men. And none with men like this. I'm not surprised he's interested in you. He'd be crazy not to be. But that doesn't mean you can trust him. Or isn't he the reason you cried yourself to sleep last night?"

Like I really wanted Aiden to know about that. I looked over my shoulder, prepared to be embarrassed, but Aiden wasn't there.

Before he could come back, I hissed under my breath, "He was, but it was a mistake. A mix-up. I thought he knew things about what happened with the company. I thought he was just playing with me, but I was wrong. He wasn't working with Harrison, Chase. Harrison must have misrepresented the ownership of CD4, he was trying to get you to sell at the same time he was after Winters, Inc. to buy. That's how it happened so fast. But they didn't know, and they were pissed you didn't come along with the company. The guy in Winters, Inc. who brought the deal to the table ended up getting fired over it."

Chase dropped my hand and took a step back. "You believe him," he said, considering the possibility that he'd been wrong about Harrison and Aiden Winters.

"I do. I do believe him. I looked, and I never found anything on Aiden. On any of them. They may not be saints but they're fair. Aiden's been more than fair with me."

"Yeah, I'm sure," Chase scoffed. "Like he doesn't have an ulterior motive for that."

"Don't be an asshole," I said, poking him in the arm. "He asked me out to dinner."

Chase rolled his eyes to the ceiling as if imploring the heavens for patience. "Vivi. Can't you find another guy? Maybe you'll meet someone when you go back to school."

"I didn't say I was going back to school," I protested. "I'm looking for a job. I just need to build my savings back up a little bit and then I'll go."

"You are going back to school," Chase said, implacable. "Your savings would be fine if I hadn't fucked up and gotten you screwed out of your shares of CD4 Analytics along with my own. If the sale had gone through the way it was supposed to, you would have had more than enough money to go back to school. This is my fault, and I'm paying your tuition."

"Chase, stop blaming yourself. It happened. It's over. You've looked out for me since Mom and Dad kicked me out. You gave me a place to live. You gave me a job. It's not like I didn't get paid every day I worked for CD4, and the company before that. I'm not mooching off you for school, too. I can work."

"This isn't a discussion," Chase said. "I already sent for information from the University of Georgia, Georgia Tech, and Emory. I set up appointments at all three for next week so you can talk to someone in admissions about transferring your credits."

Hands on my hips, I didn't bother to hide the aggravation in my voice when I said, "Chase, stop organizing my life. I can do this on my own."

"I know you can, Vivi. But you're taking too long, so I did it for you." My annoyance didn't ruffle Chase. He just gave me a cool stare, and before I could respond, a hand closed over my shoulder. From behind me, Aiden said, "Not UGA. The commute to Athens is too far. I'll talk to someone at Emory. She won't have any trouble transferring her credits."

"Because a Winters can take care of this with a phone call," Chase said, with a sneer.

"Both of you, shut up," I said. I'd had enough of bossy men for one day. "I don't need either of you fixing everything for me. Just back off." Looking at Chase, I went on,

"Talk to Aiden about the company. I'm going to go brush my hair and then we can get lunch." To Aiden, I said, in a softer voice, "I don't need your help with school. I can do this on my own. What time are you picking me up for dinner?"

Aiden's eyes softened, and he raised one hand to stroke my cheek. "How's seven-thirty? Nothing fancy unless you want to get dressed up."

I shook my head. "Casual is good for me."

"Then I'll see you at seven-thirty." He dropped his head and pressed a light kiss to my lips. I tried not to feel disappointment when he pulled away. Making out in front of my older brother would not smooth the way between the two of them.

I left the room to brush my hair, hoping I wouldn't return to a fist fight in progress. I was only gone a few minutes, but when I came back, Chase was alone.

Before I could ask, he said, "We have a meeting tomorrow afternoon. Aiden, his cousin Gage, and me. He said we'd work things out." Chase shrugged. "We'll see. I don't like you going out with him."

"I know you don't," I said, giving him a quick hug on the way to the front door. "Good thing I'm not asking for permission."

I ignored his big brother glare and slipped out the front door on the way to the car. Considering the way the day had started, things were looking up.

Chapter Twenty-Two

Aiden

Gage answered my call with, "Are you planning on coming back to the office anytime soon? Or am I handling these meetings on my own?"

I ignored his sarcasm and said, "Neither. You're canceling our meetings. I'm headed to the Sinclair Security offices. Meet me there."

The sarcasm fell from Gage's voice. He was all business when he said, "Why? What happened?"

"I don't know," I answered. "Maybe nothing. Maybe everything."

"Cryptic much?" Gage complained.

"I have to call Cooper. I'll explain when I see you."

I thought about the comb in my pocket, carefully wrapped in tissue, and Violet's brother, a carbon copy of my cousin Vance. A little older. But the same blue eyes. The exact same shade of blonde hair. The same build, the same chin, the same nose. He was the right age.

I wasn't ready to hope we'd found what we'd been searching for. I'd considered verifying his identity before telling Gage, but I wouldn't shut Gage out. We were in this together.

Wondering if I was jumping the gun, I called Cooper Sinclair at Sinclair Security. Cooper and his brothers had taken over the company from their father and grown it into the premier security company in the southeast, arguably in the entire country.

We'd grown up together. The Sinclairs were like family. Ever since we'd discovered Gage's mother, my aunt Anna, had given up a child for adoption when she'd been in college, we'd been searching for him. We'd lost enough family already.

My parents were gone, Gage's parents were gone, all four of them killed over a love affair gone wrong. Anna's missing child was the root of it all. My aunt Anna and uncle James had met in college while she was dating James's best friend, William. For reasons none of us had discovered, Anna broke up with William.

She took a semester off, and while she was away she fell in love with James through long letters and brief visits. She'd returned to Atlanta engaged to James. They'd married a short time later and from all reports, and my memory of childhood, had been deeply devoted to one another.

It wasn't until Charlie stumbled upon the adoption records that we'd learned Anna hadn't just broken up with William, she'd had his child and given it up for adoption. William, for his part, played the devoted family friend for years, brushing off Anna's defection as ancient history. All the while he'd been seething with envy and rage.

William had been responsible for James and Anna's murders. He'd stalked my cousin Annalise for years, transferring his obsession with Anna to the daughter who could have been her twin. When my parents discovered the truth, William had killed them rather than face the scandal.

So many lives torn apart over love and jealousy.

Whoever Anna's missing child was, he was walking into a mess. We were desperate to find him, but he might not be happy to learn that while his biological mother was one of the best women I'd ever known, his father was a murderous psychopath.

None of us believed in the sins of the father. We didn't blame Anna and William's child for William's insanity. We just wanted to find him. But Anna had given her newborn son to Maxwell Sinclair to hide. Even back then, she hadn't wanted William to know where their child was.

William had seemed to take her engagement to James in stride, but some instinct had driven Anna to keep the child from his father. Maybe she'd suspected he'd hold the baby over her head or use him to drive James away. Instead, they'd all remained good friends; my parents, uncle James and aunt Anna, William Davis, and Maxwell Sinclair.

We'd never known the tensions simmering beneath the surface of those lifelong relationships. Had William known Maxwell had hidden his child? Had Maxwell suspected William of my parents' deaths? We had no answers.

Anna and James had died because of William. William himself had murdered my parents. And Maxwell Sinclair had disappeared. The official story was a car accident. He'd driven off a bridge into a river, and his body had never been found.

I'd known Maxwell my entire life. He was intelligent and he could be ruthless. His death seemed a little too convenient.

Since we'd discovered William's secret life we'd learned that nothing was as it seemed. Maxwell hadn't been content with running Sinclair Security. He and William had been neck deep in a whole line of criminal enterprises, including arms dealing, money laundering, and a series of private adoptions that involved huge sums of money. Cooper, Knox, Evers, and Axel were still digging into their father's death.

Some days it seemed like every secret we uncovered only exposed more lies.

In the face of so much deceit, it seemed naïve to hope I'd found my missing half-cousin. I was too cynical to plan for good luck, but I couldn't deny Chase Westbrook's uncanny resemblance to my cousins. He wasn't just a mirror image of Vance, I could see Annalise in his high cheekbones in the shape of his eyes, Gage in his build, Tate in the sound of his voice.

Chase fit right in with the rest of Anna's children. I could see nothing of William in him. Maybe there wasn't. Maybe Chase had nothing to do with Anna Winters and William Davis. A DNA test would tell one way or the other.

Sitting at a red light, I pulled out my phone and called Cooper's direct line. It rang through to a beep, then began to ring again.

A familiar voice answered, "You've got Evers."

"Ev, Aiden. Cooper out?"

"He's in DC on a job, won't be back till next week. What's up?"

"I'm headed to you, Gage too. Do you have time?"

"Depends. I have a meeting, but I can push it out. Something wrong?"

"I may have found Anna's missing son," I said, feeling the tug of hesitation as the words left my mouth. Was it wishful thinking? Was I jumping the gun? Maybe, for both. But, I had to know.

"I'll move my meeting," Evers said, immediately.

"Thanks. See you in a few."

A tray of coffee and pastries waited on Evers's desk when I got there. He had the phone to his ear, but he waved me to a seat and held up one finger. Carefully, I pulled the tissue wrapped comb from my pocket and laid it on the desk before pouring myself a cup of coffee. My thoughts were a whirl. If I was right, if Chase Westbrook was Anna's missing son, we'd have to be careful.

As things stood now, he hated us. Stealing a man's company and dismantling it wasn't the best way to bring him into the family. It didn't matter that we hadn't done it on purpose. In the end, Chase had nothing to show for his hard work, and we owned what was left of the company he'd built.

Gage showed up before Evers ended his call and took the seat beside me, helping himself to a cup of coffee. He reached for the tissue wrapped comb on Evers's desk. My hand shot out to stop him.

"What's going on?" he asked in a low voice.

"I went to Violet's."

"Did you fire her?" Gage interrupted.

I slanted him a look. "Yes, I fired her. I also found out what she was doing at Winters, Inc. in the first place. Her brother is the founder of CD4 Analytics. Harrison scammed him out of his company."

"Which explains why we couldn't find him," Gage said, putting the pieces together. "And she was what? Trying to figure out a way to get the company back?"

"Something like that," I said.

"Is the brother open to an offer? We could use his help," Gage said.

I saw him turning the problem over in his head. Before

he could get distracted, I said, "He could be triplets with Vance and Annalise."

Gage gave me a hard stare. I shook my head. "I know what you're thinking and this has nothing to do with Violet. I'm telling you, Chase Westbrook looks so much like Vance, it's scary. He has Anna's eyes, Anna's hair, Anna's face."

"It can't be that easy," Gage said. "Not after looking and finding nothing."

"Sometimes, you get lucky. Anyway, if he is who we're looking for, this isn't easy. He thinks we stole his company. And Violet's parents sound like a nightmare. He may not want anything to do with us."

"The name Chase is familiar, but there wasn't a Westbrook associated with CD4," Gage said.

"The parents disowned him when Violet was in high school. He may be using a different last name."

Across from us, Evers set the phone down. "I caught most of that. You think your Violet's older brother is Anna's missing kid?"

"He looks enough like Anna, like Vance and Annalise, that I think it's worth checking out." Nudging the tissue wrapped comb towards Evers I said, "I stole his comb. How long does it take to do a DNA test?"

Carefully, Evers picked up the comb and unwrapped the tissue. Pulling a pair of glasses with magnifying lenses from the top drawer of his desk, he examined the hairs caught in the comb. "Well, you got the roots of the hair. That makes a difference. People think hair is good for DNA, but it's actually shit unless you get the root."

"How fast can you tell us?" Gage asked.

"We have a local lab on retainer. A rush will cost you."

"I don't care about the cost," I said.

Evers raised an eyebrow. "You really think this guy is Anna's son, don't you?"

"If you'd been there, you'd understand why I'm so sure. It wasn't just his eyes and his hair and his bone structure. It was the way he held himself. The way he moved."

"Find out how fast they can do it," Gage said. "I want to know what we're dealing with before Aiden elopes with his sister."

Evers studied me with sharp eyes. After a lifetime of friendship, I couldn't hide much. "How sure are you that she's not playing a game? She hooks you, serves you her brother up on a platter, they get nice and cozy in the Winters family and before you know it—"

"You're not the only one who thinks something is off with this girl. The brother only makes her more sketchy," Gage agreed.

Evers shuffled through files on his desk before pulling one out and opening it. "I've been looking into Violet Westbrook. Accounting major at University of Tennessee, graduated with honors. Applied to a few master's programs before taking a job at a family friend's accounting firm. Worked there for a little over two years before she was fired under questionable circumstances. Parents, Suzanne and Henry Westbrook. Henry is a financial advisor, Suzanne a homemaker.

"As far as we can tell they haven't had any contact with their daughter since she was fired from the accounting firm. I haven't tracked down her birth certificate yet. Info on the brother is thin. He went by Chase Westbrook until he dropped out of college to found his first company based off a data mining algorithm he developed while he was in school.

"He's gone by Chase Brooks for the last few years, but he didn't formally change his name. Sold the first company for a mint, spent a few years developing the algorithms he'd use as the foundation for CD4 Analytics. And while it looks like the two of you scammed him out of his company, I'm assuming my research missed something, or are you taking the term 'corporate raider' to heart these days?"

"We all got scammed by Harrison, the guy who sold us CD4 Analytics. Violet was at Winters, Inc. trying to figure out a way to get her brother's company back," I said.

Gage shook his head and studied his coffee before raising his eyes to share a sympathetic glance with Evers. They thought Violet was playing me. Thought I was so wrapped up in her body that I couldn't see what was right in front of me.

They were wrong. I knew Violet. She'd done something stupid because she thought she was helping her brother. No one understood dedication to family more than I did.

"What makes you so sure you can trust Violet Westbrook?" Evers asked. "My research so far doesn't raise any warning flags, aside from the situation at her first job, but that doesn't mean she's innocent. This could be a scam."

"I know I can trust her because I know Violet," I said, ignoring the disbelieving glance Gage threw my way. "And I know what happened with the family friend and the accounting firm. It's Violet's story, I'm not telling either of you. She wasn't at fault. That's all you need to know."

"Aiden—" Gage started. I cut him off.

"I get how this looks from where you're sitting, but you need to back off. Violet doesn't have a key to the house. She doesn't have my bank account numbers or my credit card. Violet is not the issue right now. The DNA test is the issue. Let's get that done, and then we can figure out everything else."

Evers held up a finger, then picked up his phone. A

quick conversation later he had us a guarantee for a quick turn on the DNA. I didn't even wince at the cost. I needed to know if my gut was right.

"I'm going to send a guy with the sample. He'll stay until the results are in and personally bring them back. I don't want any leaks. Everything coded by number, not by name."

"How long?" I asked.

"They can't guarantee twenty-four hours, but they're bumping other rush orders to work you in. My guess is by lunch tomorrow you'll know one way or the other. Does your girl have any idea about this?"

"No. Not what I suspect, not that we're looking for Anna's son."

"Good, keep it that way," Evers said. "I'll do some more digging and—"

"Forget about Violet," I said. "Look into her brother. I want to know everything we can about Chase Westbrook. He and Violet are tight. Her parents kicked her out and cut all contact after she refused to marry a man who tried to assault her. Chase drove across two states in the middle of the night to get her. Gave her a home, found her a job—I thought he was going to deck me when he walked in and found us together."

"If he's so protective, what the hell was he doing letting her try to infiltrate Winters, Inc.?" Gage asked.

"Apparently, he was working a consulting job out of town and had no idea what she was up to. Violet said he was furious when he found out."

"Well, that's something," Gage muttered under his breath. Like me, Gage was no stranger to being an overprotective older brother. He might be suspicious of Violet and

Chase, but he could respect Chase looking out for his little sister.

"It wouldn't be a bad idea to keep your distance from the sister until we know what we're dealing with," Evers said.

Gage barked out a laugh and shook his head. "Good luck with that. I've been trying to get this moron to stay away from her for weeks. One whiff of her perfume and all he can think about is—"

"Don't say another fucking word," I said. "I'm taking Violet out for dinner tonight. I am not keeping my distance. You're both wrong about her. I don't care. Violet doesn't have to prove anything to you. The only person she needs to worry about is me."

"Shit, man, does this girl have a golden pussy? I've never seen you so stupid over a woman. You're in deep with her after one weekend in Vegas. I heard all about that from Axel. For what it's worth, he likes her."

I leaned forward and pinned Evers with my eyes. "We've been friends since you were in diapers, and because of that, I'm going to cut you some slack. But if you ever talk about Violet like that again, I will beat you down until you can't walk for a week. Are we clear?"

Evers went still for a long moment as he studied my face. He nodded once and said, "We're clear. And just so you know, if she's fucking with you, if they turn this around on you, none of us will rest until we end them both."

"Fair enough," I agreed. "But that's not going to happen."

Gage interrupted. "Axel liked her?"

"Axel and Dylan both liked her," Evers said shooting me a cautious look. "Axel said she looked a little shy. A little overwhelmed. But all about Aiden."

"She reminds me of Elizabeth," Gage said. "When I get close all I see is ice."

"Maybe that's because every time you've talked to her you've been a complete asshole," I put in.

"Not a complete asshole," Gage murmured.

"Close enough," I said.

Evers shoved his chair back from his desk and stood. "As much fun as it is to watch the two of you bicker, I have a rescheduled meeting to get to. Don't sign the family silver away to your girlfriend or her brother until we get the tests back. The second we have them, I'll call. For now, all you can do is wait."

Twenty-four hours had never seemed so long. By this time tomorrow, we'd know if we'd found Anna's missing child.

We thought we wanted answers.

We thought we needed the truth.

We should have learned by now, when you went digging for the truth, in the end sometimes all you wanted was the comfort of familiar lies.

Chapter Twenty-Three

Violet

Chase was there when Aiden picked me up for our date, lurking by the front door, glaring at both of us. He'd asked—no, demanded—that I call Aiden and cancel. I'd refused.

I wanted to see where this thing with Aiden could go. I'd never truly thought there could be something real between us. Even if I could put aside his stealing Chase's company, my lies held us apart. But Aiden hadn't stolen Chase's company and he understood why I'd lied to get a job with Winters, Inc. Everything keeping us apart was gone, and all I wanted was Aiden.

True to his word, he didn't take me anywhere fancy. He showed up at my door in jeans and an untucked, white button-down with the sleeves rolled up. I'd only seen him dressed casually once, at breakfast in our hotel suite in Vegas, and we hadn't been dressed for very long. Even on the plane home, he wore a suit.

Aiden in jeans—jeans that showed off his ass to perfection—with rolled up sleeves... Yum. I could spend all night just staring at his forearms.

I thought about jeans myself, but for a first date, I just couldn't do it. And this was our first real date. Vegas didn't count. Everything that came before was just a prelude. I didn't have to hide the truth anymore and that changed everything.

I chose a linen wrap dress in cherry red. Simple, stylish, but the color was fun. It didn't hurt that the wrap style emphasized my curves and made my waist look tiny. I paired it with matching red wedges and pulled one side of my hair back with a pin adorned with a red silk poppy. The rest I left down. I'd noticed in Vegas that Aiden liked my hair down.

The only awkward part about our date was getting through the front door under Chase's disapproving glare. I love my big brother. Adore him.

But when his voice chased me down the hall with, "I'll be waiting up," I only rolled my eyes. He could wait up all he wanted. I didn't have a curfew and the only person I answered to was me.

In the elevator, I turned to Aiden and said, "Sorry about that. He's protective."

Aiden pressed a fingertip to my shoulder, trailing it down my bare arm until he reached my hand and tangled his fingers with mine. Tugging me a few steps closer he leaned down and pressed his lips to the top of my head.

"Don't apologize," he said, unsuccessfully hiding a laugh, "I have a baby sister and a younger cousin. Be grateful you've only got the one brother. Both Charlie and Annalise had all of us ganging up on their dates."

"How many of you are there?" I knew his family was big, and I knew parts of their backgrounds.

Anyone who hasn't been living under a rock knows about the Winters family. But I didn't know any of them personally except for Aiden and Gage. After our last confrontation, I'd be happy to go the rest of my life without seeing Gage again.

On the short drive to the restaurant, Aiden filled me in.

"On my side, there's me, the oldest. Then Jacob—he runs his own real estate company. Then Holden, he's a partner in WGC. Winters Gaming Corp. And Charlie—Charlotte—is the baby. On my aunt and uncle's side, Gage is the oldest. Then Vance and Annalise—they're twins. Tate is the youngest. He's the other partner in WGC. Jacob owns Winters House in Buckhead."

"The historic building that has the art gallery and the coffee shop on the first floor?" I'd gotten coffee there once or twice before.

"That's the one. He named it Winters House to mess with me since our family home is also called Winters House. He has the penthouse. He shares it with his fiancée Abigail. Holden and Tate each have half a floor. Tate married his girlfriend Emily on New Year's Eve. She's a game designer and works at WGC with them. Holden is engaged to his girlfriend, Jo, and she lives with him. Vance is married and has a toddler. Rosalie. You know Gage got married to Sophie not long ago, and Annalise and her fiancé Riley get married at the end of the month."

"What about your little sister? Are you two the only Winters who haven't paired off?"

Aiden pulled his car into a tiny parking lot behind a small building that looked like a cottage nestled between high-rise condo complexes much like my own. Amazing scents drifted out the back door. Curry and coconut. My stomach rumbled.

"Are you okay with Indian?" Aiden asked, sliding his arm around me and guiding me through the parking lot.

"I love it. I've seen this place, but I've never eaten here before."

"Their naan is amazing."

"I could eat naan all day," I said, my mouth watering at the thought of the light, fluffy, Indian flatbread I loved. I wasn't kidding. If we got a basket before our meals, Aiden would have to fight me for every bite.

The restaurant was small, filled with artfully arranged booths separated by vibrantly colored silk curtains. The dim lights and flickering candles combined with the privacy of the booths left me feeling as if Aiden and I were the only two people in the restaurant despite the dinner crowd.

When Aiden slid in beside me instead of taking the seat opposite, I didn't complain. The truth was, I'd missed him. I hadn't liked waking up alone either. One weekend away together and already I was used to him. Too used to him.

He didn't answer my question about his sister until we'd ordered drinks and had menus in front of us.

"Charlie?" I asked, curious. He'd mentioned more than once that he was overprotective, and I wanted to know if she'd managed to fall in love despite Aiden scaring away all her potential suitors.

"Charlie fell in love with her husband while we were estranged, which is the only way Lucas Jackson got within fifty feet of her. He was not what I had in mind for my baby sister."

"Why? What's wrong with him?"

Aiden flipped his menu shut and stared at the cover before he answered. "Nothing. There's nothing wrong with Lucas Jackson. He runs a division at Sinclair Security. He's smart as hell, tough as nails, and if anyone so much as looks at Charlie the wrong way he'll beat the hell out of him. But he's also a little rough. Tattoos, motorcycle. He went private after the army and his résumé has a lot of blank spaces. Dangerous blank spaces. The first time he crossed our paths he was working undercover as the president of the Raptors motorcycle club."

"Hmph," I said, "I guess I could see how you might not want the president of a motorcycle club hooking up with your little sister."

"I wasn't thrilled, but Charlie wasn't speaking to me at the time, and she'd moved out of Winters House, so unfortunately—or fortunately, given the way things turned out—I didn't get a say."

"Why wasn't she speaking to you?" Chase and I didn't always get along perfectly. I could imagine all sorts of circumstances that might have Aiden's little sister angry at him, but I wanted to know what had really happened.

I wanted to know even more when he slid me a hesitant look as if he didn't want to admit what had caused their rift. I poked him in the side. "Tell me. What did you do?"

"What makes you think I did something?" he asked, trying to sound offended.

I pressed my lips together to fight a smile. "You look guilty. And I have an overprotective brother of my own. I don't know your sister, but I'm already guessing whatever happened was your fault."

Aiden rolled his head back and stared at the ceiling for a long moment, either trying to find the right words or praying for deliverance. Finally, he said, "I fired her. She was working at Winters, Inc. as a vice president—Gage was still away in the military—and all she did was work. She had no life. She was exhausted, and she hated her job, but she wouldn't admit it. We always thought Gage would take his place at the company. But after my parents died he joined the Army and pretty much never came home. Charlie—"

Aiden's voice faded out, his eyes unfocused as he drifted in memory.

"Charlie wanted to help, didn't she?"

Aiden let out a breath and nodded. "She was so young when our parents died. She doesn't even remember Gage's parents. I practically raised her, and ever since she was a teenager all she talked about was coming to work for Winters, Inc. I knew, even back then, that it wasn't right for her. I encouraged her to try other things, but she was dead set. The company was her legacy. But I couldn't watch her anymore, always stressed, unhappy. I hated seeing her unhappy."

"Couldn't you tell her to slow down?"

Aiden laughed. "I could. I did. Over and over. She refused to listen. If I worked late she worked late. Finally, I fired her. She was pissed. She was beyond pissed. She stole a fifteen thousand dollar bottle of whiskey, got drunk, and ended up kissing her next-door neighbor."

"Lucas Jackson?" I guessed.

"Lucas Jackson," Aiden confirmed. "Eventually, she forgave me. Now she has a business flipping houses, he helps when he's not running his hacker team at Sinclair, and I've never seen her happier."

"Which you think justifies firing her," I concluded.

"Doesn't it?" He raised an eyebrow at me. I shook my head.

"I'm glad she's not still mad at you, but just because you think you know best doesn't mean you get to make decisions for other people. You're just like Chase, setting up admissions interviews at grad schools when I've told him I'm not ready to go back yet."

"You're stalling, Violet. You wouldn't have started your master's in the first place if you hadn't wanted to go. You're treading water when you could be moving forward. Your brother's only trying to help."

I shoved my shoulder into Aiden's arm and scowled. "Arguing with you about this is pointless, isn't it? You're going to be on his side."

"Not exactly. I can personally vouch for Emory's MBA program. I'll make a few phone calls and—"

"No," I said.

"Don't be stubborn, Vi. I can help with this. I'm not promising you'll get in. That depends on your grades and GMATs, but I'm guessing those were both pretty good since you graduated college with honors."

"They are good, but that's not the point, Aiden. You and Chase are just alike. So sure you know what's best. So ready to steamroll everyone else, and you think it's okay because it's for their own good."

"I can't help it if I'm always right," Aiden said. "It's a burden I have to bear."

I might have thought he was serious, his delivery was that good, but I caught the slight raise of his lips and the twinkle in his warm brown eyes.

"You're not always right," I said darkly. "You didn't fire me when you should have. You didn't know I wasn't going to cause serious trouble. Keeping me on was stupid."

"You're here, aren't you? Maybe I wasn't stupid. Maybe I knew you. Maybe I knew I could trust you and you just needed to learn you could trust me."

"Don't be sweet when you're being annoying."

I had more to say, but Aiden stopped me with a kiss, wrapping his long fingers around the back of my neck and moving his lips over mine in a warm, gentle caress that had me leaning into him, wanting more before the scuff of the waiter's shoe reminded me where we were.

That kiss lingered on the edge of my mind all through dinner. The food was delicious. Aiden didn't fight me for the naan, and by the time dinner was over I was stuffed and relaxed.

Being with Aiden was easy. We never ran out of things to talk about. Movies, books, hobbies. Sometimes we agreed, often we didn't, but either way, we had fun. The push and pull of conversation with Aiden was entertaining and a little like foreplay. A lot like foreplay.

Never before had I regretted living with my brother. I already knew I wasn't bringing Aiden home to my place. Not as long as Chase was there. A glaring brother standing over us was as good as a cold shower.

Aiden was signing the check when he looked up and said, "Tell me you're not ready to go home."

"I'm not ready to go home," I said, honestly.

"Do you want to go out somewhere else? Or somewhere quiet?"

"Somewhere else like a bar or club?"

"Something like that, yeah."

I shook my head. "Somewhere quiet."

The smile that spread across Aiden's face lit his dark eyes. I thought in that moment that I would do anything to make him smile like that. He took my hand under the table and squeezed before he said, "Come back to Winters House with me. No one will be there. We can watch a movie. Or I can show you my tie collection."

"Your tie collection? Exactly how many ties do you have?"

"Way too many. And they're all displayed in my closet. Which is right next to my bedroom."

"Mmmm. I've always admired your ties." Not exactly true. Aiden's ties were nice, but I wasn't that into men's accessories. I had, however, always wanted to see his bedroom. Especially after Vegas. A thought occurred to me. "Doesn't your cousin Gage live in Winters House? He won't be happy to see me."

Aiden looked away as he led me out of the restaurant and around to the parking lot. I didn't miss the muscle twitching in the side of his jaw. "Gage and Sophie had plans for dinner and a movie. They won't be home. Lise and Riley were going out with Charlie and Lucas. Even Mrs. W and Abel—our housekeeper and cook—have the night off. The house should be empty."

"That sounds good," I said as I got into the car. I wasn't afraid of Gage. I was cautious. "I don't want to cause trouble with your family. Gage doesn't like me."

"I can handle Gage," Aiden said. "Between my cousin and your brother, we'll figure it out."

Chapter Twenty-Four

Violet

Winters House was a short drive from the Indian restaurant, deep in the heart of Buckhead, the most exclusive residential neighborhood in Atlanta. Driving through the winding wooded streets, you'd never guess you were in the heart of a major metropolitan area.

The beeping cars, the high-rises, the shopping malls and highways all melted away, buffered by trees and hills and the serenity offered by huge houses on huge lots. Winters House was one of the biggest.

Aiden pressed the remote on his visor and a set of black iron gates swung open smoothly and silently. Lined by towering oak trees arching above, the drive wound deeper into the grounds of Winters House until the structure itself came into view.

An enormous Mediterranean-style mansion, built in a square around a central courtyard, the creamy stucco walls and red tile roof were warm and welcoming despite its size.

Directly ahead I saw a second set of gates barring the

entrance to a porte-cochère that led to the inner courtyard. Aiden turned to the left and followed a narrower branch of the drive around the side of the house, arriving in front of a generously sized six-car garage.

I couldn't help but notice that every bay was full. Odd, since Aiden had said no one was home. He was around the front of the car, opening my door before I could open it myself. I'd grown up in a pretty house, but the Winters family garage was nicer than most people's living rooms.

The garage door opened into a mud room that was the same. Every jacket neatly hung, car keys on labeled hooks, custom cabinets for storing outdoor shoes and padded benches so you could sit comfortably while you put on your boots. Distracted by my first glimpse of Winters House, I almost didn't hear the voices a room away.

Under his breath, Aiden said, "Fuck." He turned around, placed his hands on my shoulders and started to urge me back to the garage.

"I wanted to be alone with you," he said. I wanted the same thing.

Aiden had the door half open when a woman's voice called out, "Aiden. When did you get home? And who do you have with you? You didn't say you were going on a date."

Letting out a defeated sigh, Aiden turned, sliding his arm around my shoulder, bringing me with him. In front of us stood a younger, female version of Aiden. Her hair, cut just below her chin, fell in tousled curls more auburn than brown. Avidly curious ocean blue eyes skipped from me to Aiden and back again.

"You must be Violet." She stuck out her hand.

"I am," I said, cringing a little at the stiffness in my

voice. The ice queen always made an appearance when I was shy. Sometimes I didn't know how to turn her off. I didn't want to freeze out Aiden's curious younger sister, but I couldn't seem to warm up my voice when I said, "Charlie? Aiden's told me so much about you."

I shook her hand, trying to relax as Aiden rubbed my back in a long, soothing stroke.

"I thought you all were going out."

Charlie grinned at Aiden. "Obviously. But Gage ended up working too late to catch a movie, so he and Sophie were home, and then Vance and Maggie had a thing, so Riley and Lise said they'd watch Rosie, and we all ended up staying here and ordering pizza. We were about to watch a movie, if you guys want to join us." Her eyes danced as she said, "Or not."

Aiden wrapped his arm around me and gave me a squeeze, murmuring, "We might as well go in, but I'll make our excuses and we'll think of something else."

"It's fine," I said, in that frosty voice, when both of us knew it was anything but fine.

I wanted to meet his family. Eventually. Not tonight. Not yet. I could only imagine what Gage had told them about me. I already knew he detested me. I wasn't ready for a house full of Winters.

Aiden's arm dropped from around me and he took my hand as we walked from the mud room into an expansive family room. An enormous flat-screen hung above a dark stone fireplace. A three-sided sectional, filled with lounging Winters, faced the fireplace and TV.

Behind it, windows looked into the courtyard of Winters House. In the center, a lit fountain glowed through the darkness. I caught a glimpse of a huge white kitchen on the other side of the mud room door, and past the family room, a wide hall continued to the front of the house.

I shifted uncomfortably beside Aiden, fighting the urge to step behind him when Gage's glare landed on me. If he could have struck me dead where I stood, I imagined he might have tried. I forgot about the rest of them and met his furious gaze with one of pure ice.

I understood why Aiden's cousin didn't like me. I understood well enough that I didn't even think he was wrong. If I'd suspected someone of taking advantage of Chase, I would have reacted exactly the same way.

That didn't mean I liked it.

And it didn't mean I was going to back down. If Gage Winters thought I was afraid of him, he would only be more open in his dislike.

Aiden tugged me forward, placed his hands on my shoulders, and said to the room, "Everyone, this is Violet. Violet this is everyone." He went around the room pointing out his family and giving their names.

After his description, it wasn't that hard to figure out who was who. The only one I didn't guess right away was Annalise, one of the twin cousins. There was something about her that tickled the back of my mind. I would have been sure we'd met, except I knew that we hadn't. The shape of her eyes, or the shade of her hair. I didn't know what it was, but I would have sworn I knew her.

I was so distracted staring at Annalise I almost missed it when Gage, who was sitting on the side of the couch closest to us, turned to face Aiden and said, "Is this a good idea? Bringing her here?"

Aiden gave his cousin a look that would have silenced most men, but Gage appeared immune. Even his wife

Sophie, sitting behind him, squeezed his arm when she saw Aiden's face. Gage ignored her.

Before Aiden could say something he might regret, I stepped forward and met Gage's eyes. "Would you prefer I leave? I can call for a ride if you object to my being in your home."

"I do object," Gage said, through gritted teeth, "but Aiden doesn't seem to care."

"I care," Aiden said, his voice coldly furious, "but I generally ignore you when you're being an asshole."

Aiden took a step forward. I said quietly, "Aiden. Don't do this. Why don't you just take me home?"

He looked down at me. "Because I won't be run out of my own fucking house."

Charlie stepped between Aiden and Gage and threaded her arm through mine, pulling me from Aiden's side toward the kitchen. "Let's get a glass of wine," she said. "Or beer. Whatever. Let's get the hell out of here before those two go at it again."

"Go at it?" I asked, my ears trained behind me to catch bits of the continued argument. I heard the word 'liar' in Gage's voice. Then Aiden's, though he was too quiet for me to make out his response.

"Oh yeah," Charlie said, laughing to herself. "Let's just say when Gage came home, his reintroduction to the family was not smooth. Somehow he got it in his head that Aiden was interested in Sophie." With a sidelong glance, she reassured me, "Which he was not, but our aunt Amelia pulled a prank and Gage ended up jumping Aiden at the dinner table. They didn't stop until Mrs. W poured a pitcher of water on them."

"It was funny," Sophie said from the doorway of the kitchen, "but I could do without a repeat."

I stood at the square, marble top kitchen island and watched as Charlie pulled a bottle of white wine from the refrigerator. She held it up, raising an eyebrow in question. After casting a longing glance at the mud room and the door to the garage, I nodded my head and said, "Yes, please."

Charlie poured me a glass of wine, as well as one for Sophie and for herself. She grabbed another glass out of the cabinet when Annalise snuck into the room. Leaning against the counter Annalise smiled and said, "I couldn't decide whether to get out my phone and start recording or get the hell out. I missed the first fistfight. It might be fun to have one on record."

Alarmed, I looked through the open doorway of the kitchen into the family room. Aiden and Gage stood in front of one another, their postures stiff, voices angry, but it didn't look like anyone had thrown a punch.

"Don't worry," Annalise said. "I bailed when I realized they were just going to yell at each other. I've heard enough of those two bickering to last a lifetime." Looking at Charlie she said, "Be grateful you were too young to get stuck with them. They might be close as brothers, but sometimes they fight like an old married couple."

Charlie handed out our glasses of wine and ranged herself in front of me, one eyebrow raised. "So, you're Violet. I'm curious—are you an ice-cold carbon copy of Elizabeth? A scheming liar trying to destroy Winters, Inc. from the inside? Do you have a nefarious plan to brainwash my older brother and run off with the family fortune?"

I absorbed Charlie's questions as I took a careful sip of wine. In my coolest, most unruffled voice I said, "Is that the story Gage is spreading? Creative."

"Maybe," Annalise cut in, "but is any of it true?"

As if to give the impression I was thinking over my

answer, I took another sip of wine and studied the gleaming white coffered ceiling.

"It depends. An ice-cold carbon copy of Elizabeth? I won't deny the ice-cold part, but I'm not a copy of anyone, particularly that harpy."

Charlie laughed and shook her head. "I heard you put her in her place. She's such a bitch."

"And then some," I agreed.

Sophie's low voice interrupted. "And the part about the company?"

"Gage isn't wrong about that. Not entirely," I said, carefully.

"And yet Aiden spent the weekend with you," Annalise said. "He took you out to dinner. He brought you home."

"He did," I said. "I think the real question is, do you trust his judgment? Do you think Aiden is susceptible to the manipulation of a woman? Or anyone for that matter?"

The three Winters women looked at me, nonplussed. I took another sip and set the glass down on the island. From the other room, I heard Gage accuse Aiden of thinking with his dick, and I decided enough was enough.

"I'll make this easy for you. I met Aiden under false pretenses. My intentions were good, but I lied. I thought he'd done something to hurt someone I love, and I was trying to set it right. He knows the truth now and he doesn't care. I'm not interested in Winters, Inc. I'm not interested in the family fortune. The only thing I'm interested in is Aiden. Now, if you'll excuse me, I think it's time I go home."

No one stopped me as I strode from the kitchen. I came up behind Aiden and laid my hand on his back, leaning into him as I rose up on my toes. "Take me home Aiden. Don't fight with your cousin."

Immediately he stopped yelling at Gage and turned to

look down at me. Tucking a strand of hair behind my ear he said quietly, "I won't let him talk about you that way."

"Do you agree with him? Do you think I'm a scheming whore out to take you for everything you have?" I asked, equally quietly.

"Of course, not," Aiden spit out. "Don't be ridiculous."

"No, don't *you* be ridiculous. The only person I care about is you. You're not going to change his mind tonight. And I don't want our lovely evening to end like this. If you really want to fight, why don't you take me home and kiss me in front of my brother? Then we can both watch his head explode before he tries to kill you."

That surprised a laugh out of Aiden. He tugged on a strand of my hair, smiling down at me, the anger drained from his face, his eyes warm.

"Or maybe," he said in a low rumble, "I'll get us a hotel room and we can order up some chocolate cake. Eat it in bed."

"That's the best idea I've heard all day."

Without another word to his gathered family, Aiden took my hand and pulled me to the garage.

As we drove out of Buckhead, Aiden said, "I don't know why I thought it was such a good idea to have the whole family under one roof. I should kick them all out and then I can fuck you in every room of the house."

Heat swept through me at the thought of breaking in Winters House, room by room. It was a huge house. That was a lot of sex. Sex with Aiden. I pressed my knees together and tried not to squirm in my seat.

"I'm sorry about my family. Was Charlie grilling you?"

"She was fine. More curious than anything." I thought about the considering look in Annalise's eyes. Charlie's pointed questions. "They love you. They're just looking out for you."

Aiden grunted in the back of his throat. His aggravation made me smile. "They're annoying. I have no idea where they got the idea that they can tell me what to do."

At that, I burst out laughing. He sounded so disgruntled, like a petulant child. He looked at me from the corner of his eye. "What's so funny?"

"You," I managed through my giggles. "You're so used to being the master of the universe, arranging everyone like pieces on a chess board, and you don't know what to do when they won't obey."

"Hm. I don't think I'm the master of the universe," he argued, spurring another round of giggles.

"Right," I said. "Sure you don't. Didn't you tell me you fired your own sister to keep her from working too much? Is that the only time you've made decisions for them without asking what they want?"

"You make it sound like it's a bad thing," Aiden said. "I'm looking out for them. I'm the head of the family. It's my job."

"I know," I said, reaching across the center console to rest my hand on his arm. He dropped his hand from the steering wheel and closed it over mine. "And now they're looking out for you. They love you," I said again. "They want to protect you."

"From you?" he asked, raising an eyebrow as if I was no threat.

"Well, you did marry Elizabeth," I pointed out. "Maybe they're just putting me through the wringer in self-defense. They don't want to be stuck with Elizabeth 2.0."

"There is that," he agreed. "But you shouldn't have to

deal with Gage's bad attitude, or the rest of them interrogating you."

"Aiden, it's fine. I appreciate you looking out for me. No one really has, you know. I've always only had Chase. It means a lot that you want to protect me from your family, but I don't want you to. I have to win them over on my own."

"You shouldn't have to win them over at all."

"No?" I tugged my hand from his and turned in my seat to face him. "Are we together? Or are we just having sex until we burn out?"

Aiden pulled to a stop in front of the attendant at the Hotel Intercontinental and raised a finger to tell him to wait. His eyes caught mine, dark and deadly serious. "We're together. I've told you, this is more than sex."

"Then you have to give them time, Aiden. You can't make them like me. Either they will, or they won't. And if we're good together and you're happy, they'll see that. In the meantime, I can handle them. Even Gage."

Aiden's eyes warmed, and he leaned in to press his lips to mine.

"I don't deserve you," he said.

"Maybe not, but I'm not letting you go."

"Works for me."

He opened his door, signaling the attendant to open mine, and passed over the keys before we made our way to the front desk. A few minutes later we were cruising up in the elevator to the Ambassador's Suite. Not long after that, the promised slice of chocolate cake arrived.

Aiden brought it straight to bed, though he didn't bother with a fork. While I watched with wide eyes, naked beneath the smooth sheets, Aiden swiped one finger through the thick frosting, painted it across my nipple and sucked it off.

I didn't end up getting much of the cake, but I got my fill of Aiden. And orgasms.

Chocolate, Aiden, and orgasms. I couldn't imagine anything better. His family, my brother—none of it mattered. When I was with Aiden, everything else melted away until it was just us. Just Aiden and me. Exactly the way I wanted it.

Chapter Twenty-Five

Aiden

I had too much work to worry about Evers's phone call. The test would be done when it was done. Staring at the phone wouldn't speed it up. I told myself that more than once, even though my heart jumped every time a call came through. The morning passed. Lunch came and went. I'd cleaned out Violet's desk, and her little cactus sat beside my monitor, reminding me of her.

I needed another coffee. We'd stayed up half the night making use of the wide king bed in our hotel suite. Licking chocolate frosting off her smooth skin was just the beginning. Fucking her in Vegas had been one thing. That was a vacation, a few days away from our real lives.

Last night was real. Despite the friction caused by both of our families, nothing felt better than falling asleep with Violet in my arms. Soon enough I'd bring her home to Winters House and everything would be perfect. Soon enough.

I hated to admit she was right. I couldn't command my family to accept her any more than she could force her brother to like me. They needed time and I'd have to be patient. I didn't mind being patient if it would get me what I wanted in the end, but I didn't like waiting for Violet. I wanted her to be mine. Full stop.

I wasn't going to question it.

Was I moving fast? Absolutely.

Too fast? Hell, no.

Thinking of our suite at the Intercontinental, her promise to meet me there for dinner, our progress felt glacially slow. Once I'd decided Violet was mine, I didn't want to wait. I didn't want to sneak around.

Staying in a hotel to avoid our families left me feeling like a teenager. Fitting, since Violet gave me the refractory period of one. I was topped up on orgasms, but I could use a little more sleep.

I was about to get another cup of coffee when my phone rang. Squelching the leap in my chest at the sound, I picked it up. "Yes?"

"You sitting down?" Evers.

"Just tell me," I said, not in the mood for him to yank my chain.

"We don't have Anna Winters's DNA, or William Davis's. But based on the results from Anna's children it looks like Chase Westbrook is Anna's son."

I let out a long breath. I'd had a feeling. I'd been almost positive. But thinking and knowing were two very different things.

"You there?" Evers said.

"I'm here. Just...thinking."

"It's a lot to work out," Evers said, "but just remember, this doesn't change anything. He's Anna's son, but that doesn't mean you can trust him. Or his sister. Just go slowly—"

"Evers, shut up. I don't know if I can trust Chase, but I

do know I can trust Violet. And you're wrong, this changes everything. For all of us."

"It doesn't have to," Evers argued and then let out a defeated sigh. "But you're going to do what you're going to do. I've known you too long to think differently. I'll send over the paperwork so you and Gage have it. When I'm done I'll send over my report on the Westbrooks."

"Anything interesting I don't know about?" I asked, hating myself for the small niggle of doubt hiding under my question.

"Not yet. The parents are a little weird. Word is they never talk about their children. Cut them off and forgot about them. Cold."

"That was the impression I got from Violet. They had their children's futures planned and when Chase, and then Violet, didn't fall in line they erased them." I changed the subject. I hated thinking about Violet's parents. "Have you figured out how they crossed paths with your father?"

"Not yet. I can't find any trace of paperwork on Chase's adoption. If you can, if things go well, see if he has it, or knows where to find it. Anything in writing would help."

"I'll see what I can do," I promised. "I'll keep you posted. Don't worry about sending the papers over, we'll swing by and grab the report."

I hung up and swiveled in my desk chair, staring out the window of my office. What were the chances Anna's son just happened to own a company we'd acquired? The odds seemed right up there with winning the lottery. The unusual happened every day. This could be a lucky coincidence. Or it might be more.

I wanted to trust Violet. I did trust Violet. At the very least I trusted her motives, if not every decision she'd made, but Chase...he was a wildcard. Picking up my phone I dialed Gage. When he answered I said, "I need you in my office."

"On my way."

Gage had barely cleared my door when he caught the look on my face. "Evers called."

"Just got off the phone with him," I confirmed.

"And it's true? He's ours?"

"He is. Can you take a break? We need to go talk to him."

"He's due here in two hours," Gage said.

"I don't want to do this here. I'll call Violet and see if they're home. Better to do this on their turf, where they're comfortable."

"Where they're comfortable?"

"This is going to come as a shock," I said, thinking of Violet. "After their parents kicked them out, all they've had is each other. Now, all of a sudden, Chase is going to have a whole new family. And Violet still only has Chase. I don't want to throw this at her in my office. I want her to feel safe."

Gage hitched up his shoulder with impatience. "This isn't about your girlfriend."

"It's not only about her," I agreed. "It's about all of us."

"Call her. I'll rearrange my schedule. Meet you at the elevators."

Violet answered her phone with a relaxed, "Hey, how's your day?"

When I asked if we could move our meeting from Gage's office in two hours to their condo now, she agreed but her relaxed tone shifted to cautious curiosity.

We needed to get this out in the open. Chase had a right to know who he was. I still felt like I was holding a grenade and someone had pulled the pin before I was ready to throw.

We stopped by the Sinclair Security offices to grab a copy of the file with the DNA results. Nothing much in the report made sense to me. I was a businessman, not a geneticist, but I understood the summary on the first page. *98% chance subject A is a sibling to sample subjects.*

Violet opened the door when we knocked and immediately looked past me to Gage. I didn't need eyes in the back of my head to know Gage was glaring at her. Again. The moment her eyes met his, her periwinkle gaze shifted to a chilly lavender and her chin went up half an inch.

She led us to the living room where Chase waited on a couch. "Can I get you anything to drink? Coffee? Tea? Arsenic?" This last she directed at Gage. Chase watched the interplay and smirked.

"Nothing for me, thanks," Gage said.

The second he laid eyes on Chase Westbrook, he forgot his animosity toward Violet. He couldn't stop staring at the half-brother he'd never met. Violet looked between Gage and her brother, concern clouding her expression.

"Why did we move the meeting here?" she asked me. "Wouldn't it be easier to talk about CD4 at the office?"

"It would," I agreed, "but this isn't about the company. This is personal."

"I don't understand," Violet said, taking a seat beside Chase. Chase rested his ankle on his knee and looked from me to Gage.

"I do," he said. "When did you figure it out? Before or after you stole my company?" His fingers tapped on the top of his thigh, and he watched us with cool, assessing eyes.

Vance's eyes. Anna's eyes.

I said, "We didn't steal your company," at the same time Gage said, "After."

I shot a quelling look at Gage, and as usual, he ignored me. Leaning forward, he braced his elbows on his knees and said, "We didn't steal your company. I thought Aiden covered that yesterday."

"That's the story he's selling," Chase said.

"It's the truth," Gage shot back. "What I want to know is, how long have you known? Did you know when you relocated to Atlanta?"

"I've known since I was seventeen," Chase said evenly.

Violet swiveled on the couch to face him. "Will someone please tell me what you're talking about? Know what?"

Chase looked at her and his face softened. Reaching out, he closed his fingers over her forearm. "Vivi, it's complicated."

"It's not that complicated," Gage cut in. "My mother got pregnant in college. She gave up the baby for adoption. That baby is your brother. We didn't know until a few months ago and we've been looking for him ever since."

"That's not possible. Chase isn't adopted." Violet scowled at Gage, clearly suspecting he was up to something. Her angry gaze faltered as she looked to me, waiting for me to set him straight. I handed her the file.

With trembling hands, she opened it, her eye skimming the first page. Gently, I said, "Chase is subject A. I stole his comb yesterday and we tested his DNA."

"Yesterday?" Her voice was faint. "But that's too fast. You can't have a DNA test done that quickly. There must be a mistake."

"There's no mistake," Gage said, leaning forward to pull

the file from her hands. "We'll get you a copy of the test results, but there's no question. Chase is my brother."

"Half-brother," Chase shot back, resting his hand on Violet's back.

She shrugged it off. "You knew?" Violet whispered, staring at Chase, her eyes shadowed, wounded. "You never said anything. Why didn't you say anything? Why didn't you tell me?"

"Vivi, it's not a big deal." He tried to take her hand, but she pulled back.

"How can you say that? Of course, it's a big deal. Is that why we moved here?"

Chase shrugged a shoulder and finally started to look uncomfortable. "Maybe. I was curious, okay? And we were done with St. Louis. I never planned to contact them." Looking at us he said again, "I never planned to contact you."

Chapter Twenty-Six

Aiden

"Why not?" Gage demanded. "We're your family."

Chase's laugh was brittle enough to hurt my ears. Even Violet flinched at the sound.

"You're not my family. I don't have a family, except for Vivi."

"You're my half-brother," Gage pressed. "You have a sister." A quick glance at Violet and he clarified, "Another sister. Two more brothers, aside from me, and four cousins."

"I don't have any cousins," Chase said. "And I don't need you. Your mother threw me out like yesterday's trash. She had the perfect life all lined up, and I was in the way, so she got rid of me. Went on to marry your father and raise the perfect little family."

"Chase." Violet pressed her lips together and reached for her brother's hand, squeezing his fingers in hers.

"No, Vivi. I never planned to contact them. We don't need them."

"Then why did you mention Winters, Inc. to Harrison? Back when he first approached, you told him you weren't selling and then somehow Winters, Inc. came up. At the time I thought it was because CD4 would fit with their portfolio, but that wasn't it, was it?"

"It was a stupid idea. Clearly." Chase shot me a furious look. "If I'd never mentioned Winters, Inc. to Harrison, none of this would have happened. I'd still have my company. Vivi wouldn't have met you. One moment of weakness and everything went sideways."

"Fine," Violet said, squeezing her brother's fingers again. "It didn't turn out the way you planned. But they're here now. They wanted to find you. Doesn't that mean something?"

"I don't see why it has to mean anything" Chase shot back. "It's biology. That's all. She wasn't my mother. She got rid of me. Why should I care about her real kids?"

"Chase, she's not here. She made her choices, and she can't explain them. She's gone. But you have a brother sitting right in front of you. Don't throw that away because you're angry at a dead woman."

"Vivi, you don't understand," he started.

Violet interrupted and went on, "I don't. I don't know how you feel right now because I've never been in this situation. But Mom and Dad—" she bit her bottom lip and looked up at the ceiling. I saw with a jolt of alarm the shimmer of tears in her eyes. "Mom and Dad threw you out, threw us both out, because we weren't what they wanted. We weren't what they planned for. It was wrong. And it was cruel. Don't do that. You're better than that. Better than them. I'm not saying you have to love him."

She blinked back her tears and looked at Gage with such icy disdain I wanted to kiss her until she melted. "Personally, I think he's a jerk. But his younger sister seemed very nice and there's two more I haven't met. You should at least give them a chance."

Chase squeezed her hand before he let go. "You're a better person than me, Vivi."

"I'm really not," she muttered under her breath.

Gage muttered back, "Trust me, we're aware of that."

I bit back a laugh as Violet dropped her hand beside her knee, out of her brother's sight, and shot Gage the finger.

Time to get this meeting back on track.

"Look, we're not going to figure this out today. We need to talk about the company. We both got screwed on this deal and if we could sign CD4 Analytics back to you, we'd consider it."

"But you've already torn it apart and absorbed it," Chase finished.

"Basically. That doesn't mean we can't work something out. You still have a meeting scheduled with Gage in an hour. Why don't you come back to the office with us, and you two can sit down and talk over the options."

Through gritted teeth, Chase said, "Fine."

"In the meantime, I need to ask you what you know about your adoption."

"What do you mean?" Chase asked, his familiar blue eyes going guarded, alert. He shifted an inch away from Violet.

"Obviously, you know something, since you knew you were my brother before I told you," Gage said, watching Chase carefully. "We need to know how you found out, and if you have any paperwork, anything in writing."

"Why?" Chase demanded. "You have a DNA test. Why would you need paperwork?"

"It's a long story," I said, not sure how much to tell him. The Sinclair's problems were their own, and until we knew the full scope of their father's misdeeds, we didn't need to spread gossip. I settled for, "Your adoption was the first in a series of private and expensive adoptions that we're not sure were legal. We're trying to track down as many as we can to make sure they were all above board. Any clues as to who might have been involved would be helpful."

Chase crossed his arms over his chest and sat back. "That's not my problem."

"Chase!" Violet said, clearly surprised by her brother's attitude. She swatted him across the chest with the back of her hand and shot him a look I recognized from my own interfering sister.

"Vivi, leave it alone," Chase ordered. "All of this happened a long time ago. Digging it up now won't do anyone any good."

"You don't know that," she said. "If they think some of the adoptions weren't legitimate, there could be parents out there missing their children. If you can help—"

"I can't." Chase surged to his feet and paced into the kitchen. Grabbing a glass and a bottle of bourbon, he poured himself a healthy slug and tossed it back. "I can't help."

"How can you be sure?" Gage pressed. "How did you find out you were adopted?"

Chase poured another finger of bourbon in the class and stared down at it. "I found the file. In the basement. It had her first initial and her last name. It took me a while, but I finally dug up the hospital where she gave birth, figured out who she was."

"If you didn't want to find your family, why go to all that trouble?" I asked, curious.

"I don't know," Chase admitted, and I believed him.

Behind his anger, his determination to shut us out, there was a lost kid, pissed at the world and alone except for his sister. "I just needed to know. And once I did—" He shrugged his shoulder with a jerk and swirled the bourbon in his glass. "It just didn't seem important anymore. She was dead. The last thing you'd want was a bastard your mom got rid of in the first place."

Out of the corner of my eye, I saw Gage grit his teeth and I knew he wanted to stand up for his mother, to insist she hadn't thrown Chase away. Except none of us knew exactly why she'd been so determined to give him up. And not just give him up, but hide him.

Had she known what William was? It seemed hard to imagine since he'd remained friends with our parents for years after their failed romance in college. Had she worried that a child would interfere with her dream of finishing medical school and being a doctor?

Anyone who might have known what she was thinking was dead. I couldn't offer Chase reassurances about his mother. All we had was the family we were now, a family that wanted to know him.

"You don't owe us anything," I said, "but if you have a copy of that file, or you know how we can get one, it would give us a place to start."

"Did you take it with you?" Violet asked, staring across the room at Chase with worried lavender eyes. "If it's still at home—"

"I didn't take it," Chase said, cutting her off. "They probably wouldn't have noticed if I did, but I just copied mine, and left the rest alone."

"The rest?" Violet asked. "What else was there?"

Chase set his glass down with a thud, the blood draining from his face so quickly I wondered if he was about to pass out. In a choked voice he said, "Nothing. There wasn't anything else. Just medical bills."

Violet's eyes narrowed and slowly, she shook her head. "What else did you find, Chase?"

I got a bad feeling in my stomach as I looked between the siblings. Chase couldn't meet Violet's eyes. He sent a longing glance at the bottle of bourbon beside him but didn't pick it up. I knew Violet too well to think she was going to let this go.

I had the absurd urge to grab her arm and drag her from the condo before she badgered the truth out of her brother. If the look on his face was anything to go by, the truth was going to hurt.

"Chase. Just tell me. Was it about you? Me? Something about Mom and Dad?"

She rose to her feet and took a step toward Chase, but at the flash of panic on his face, I stood and grabbed her arm. I tried to pull her close, but she shook me off.

"Chase, just tell me. Whatever it is, it can't be that important if you've been sitting on it all this time."

Not exactly true, I thought. He'd known who his mother was for years, and he'd kept his mouth shut about that. Whatever he didn't want to tell Violet, I knew it wasn't just a big deal, it was catastrophic.

"Vivi," Chase said in a low, soothing tone. "Can't you just trust me? Haven't I always looked out for you?"

"Always," Violet agreed. "But that doesn't mean you can lie to me. It was about me, wasn't it? Whatever you found, it was about me. Why won't you tell me?"

Her last words came out in a hoarse whisper. My chest burned at the sight of a single tear trailing down her cheek.

"She lied about the IVF," Chase said, so low I could barely hear him.

Violet took a step closer and said, "What?"

"She lied about the IVF. She pretended she was getting fertility treatments and we went away. When we came back, she had you."

I saw Violet start to crumple before her knees gave way. I slid my arm around her waist to hold her up, taking her weight. Her face was ashen, her eyes wide with shock.

"Why? Why would she lie? Why would she bother to fake a pregnancy? It doesn't make sense."

Chase's laugh was short and caustic. "You know how they are. Appearances are everything. No one knew I was adopted. When she still couldn't get pregnant, she decided faking was the next best thing. Dad made up a temporary transfer overseas and they told everyone she was pregnant when they left."

Violet shook her head, her shining hair swinging in a wide arc as she stared at the floor and tried to make sense of this new information. I pulled her close, pressing her into my chest and said quietly, "It doesn't matter, sweetheart. She's still your mother. Chase is still your brother."

Violet's hand found mine and she squeezed hard, once. So quietly, only I could hear she said, "I know that. And I don't care if I share blood with them or not." A laugh escaped her chest, high-pitched and almost hysterical. "I think I'd almost rather I didn't."

"Then what?" I said in her ear. She was trembling in my arms, her breath shallow, her pulse racing, her eyes wet with tears. If she didn't care about being adopted, then why was she teetering on the edge of a breakdown?

My Violet didn't fall apart.

My Violet turned to ice. She didn't shatter.

Holding tight to my hand, she turned to look at her brother. "How could you lie to me about something like this?" She choked on the words as they caught in her throat. "All this time and you knew. All this time you've been lying to me."

Chase's voice was anguished. "Vivi, no, it wasn't like that. You were so young when I found out. You were only nine. I couldn't tell you."

"You've had nineteen years," she said as tears flowed down her cheeks. "What about when you picked me up after I left home? We spent days talking about how awful they were, and never in all of that did it occur to you to tell me the truth? I wasn't a child anymore. Not then. Or any day after. And still, you lied to me."

"I didn't lie, I just didn't tell you," Chase said, weakly. I resisted the urge to shake my head. Not a good excuse.

Violet agreed because she shrieked, "Not telling me is lying."

"I thought it was best—"

"That's not for you to decide. You don't get to choose what's best for me. You don't get to hide who I am because you think I can't handle it. That's not your decision."

Violet yanked her arm from mine and scrubbed the tears from her face with the heels of her palms. Chase moved forward, and she threw up a hand. "Stop. Don't touch me. Don't come near me. Just go away." Her voice caught on the last word and she swallowed hard. "I hate you right now," she whispered just before she bolted for the front door.

Chase reeled back. Violet snatched her purse from the table beside the door and shoved her keys in the pocket of her jeans.

Thinking fast, I tossed my own car key in Gage's lap and followed her out, saying to Chase, "Give her time."

I caught up with Violet in the stairwell. Deftly plucking

the keys from her pocket, I took her arm and led her from the stairs to the elevator bank. It was a measure of how miserable she was that she didn't fight me, and when the elevator doors closed she let me pull her into my arms. Pressing her cheek to my chest, she held on to my waist, her body shuddering with sobs.

Chapter Twenty-Seven

Aiden

Violet didn't resist when I opened the passenger door of her blue Volkswagen Beetle and ushered her inside. She buckled her seatbelt, closed the door, and leaned her head against the window, the glass fogging from her breath and the tears still streaming down her cheeks.

I didn't even think about it. I pulled out of her parking garage and pointed her little car straight at Winters House. My chest hurt worse every time her breath hitched. I knew what it was to feel betrayed by your own family. And I knew what it was to be on Chase's side of things, making decisions and keeping secrets to protect the ones you loved.

I couldn't fix what was wrong. That was between Violet and Chase. I knew she'd forgive him, eventually. They were too close, and she loved him too much to hold a grudge forever. On the other hand... I'd seen Violet play the avenging angel. She'd infiltrated my company in the name of justice. If she was mad enough at Chase, I was afraid to guess what she might do.

The garage was empty when we pulled in. Even

Sophie's car was missing. Sophie had originally joined our household as a live-in nurse for our great-aunt Amelia. She was married to Gage now, but she took her job seriously, and she loved Amelia, despite my great aunt's crotchety, troublemaking ways.

When the weather was good, Sophie and Amelia liked to walk at the Arboretum and then go to our friend Annabelle's coffee shop in the Virginia Highlands to have one of Annabelle's sugar-free hot cocoas.

Amelia's diabetes-friendly diet was a source of contention between her and Sophie. Amelia snuck sweets, and Sophie ferreted them out and confiscated them. Annabelle had developed the hot cocoa recipe for Amelia, and Amelia took advantage as often as she could. They would probably be gone for hours.

Mrs. W, our housekeeper since my childhood, and Abel, our cook, might be home, but they were both discreet enough to give us space if they thought we needed it. I rounded the front of the Beetle and opened Violet's door. She sat there, slumped, seatbelt still buckled, staring blindly between her feet.

"Come on sweetheart," I said, leaning over and unfastening her belt. Docile, she allowed me to pull her from the car and slide my arm around her waist. I guided her through the mud room, past the family room and kitchen where she'd had the misfortune to meet my family the night before, past the dining room, to the two-story entry hall. She barely looked around, just wiped under her eyes with the back of her hand and let me lead her up the staircase to the second floor.

The upper level of Winters House was smaller than the main floor. It housed only two bedroom suites, Gage's and mine. Both suites had a sitting room, bedroom, dressing room, and bath. Gage's wasn't small, but mine, as the master suite, was bigger than most homes. Before so much of my family had moved back, it felt cavernous. Now I was grateful for the space and privacy.

Violet didn't truly take in her surroundings until I sat her on the edge of the bed and leaned down to tug off her shoes. Dropping my suit coat over an armchair, I urged her back onto the bed and joined her, pulling her into my arms and tucking her head against my shoulder.

"Sorry," she whispered into my shirt. "I'll stop in a minute."

"You don't have to stop," I said into her hair. "Cry if you want to. I'd be pissed as hell if I were you. And hurt."

"I hate crying," she said, her voice wobbly. "It makes me all snotty." She gave a wet sniffle. I sat up a little and leaned across her to grab a tissue off the bedside table. Violet took care of her runny nose, then settled back against me, her breath still jagged, tears still leaking from her eyes, soaking into my dress shirt.

I rubbed her back and searched for something to say. I came up empty. I didn't have anything comforting to offer. She wouldn't want to hear what I was thinking.

I understood Chase. I'd done plenty of fucked up things in the name of protecting my family. I'd screwed up Annalise's relationship with Riley when she was in college. Screwed it up so badly it took them over a decade to find one another again. She'd forgiven me, partly because it was as much Riley's fault as it was mine, but I'd still fucked up.

And it hadn't been that long ago that Charlie had stopped speaking to me because I'd fired her. Maybe it had been for the best, but it was still an asshole move, and I knew it at the time. It hadn't stopped me then and probably wouldn't stop me now.

I knew all about making hard decisions to protect your family. Chase had known about us all these years and hadn't made a single attempt to get in touch.

He'd looked after his little sister. He'd taken her in when her parents cut her off, gave her a place to live, a job. Loved her. Supported her. Yeah, he'd fucked up not telling her she was adopted. Violet had a right to know.

Still, I knew why he kept his mouth shut. He hadn't wanted to see that look in her eyes the moment she realized that everything she knew about her family was a lie.

Violet's breath evened out and I looked down to see her eyes closed, her pale lashes fanned across her flushed cheeks, spiky with tears. My phone beeped. I pulled it from my pocket to check the screen. Gage.

Where are you?

Tapping with one finger I wrote back, *Home.*

With Violet?

Y

That was a cluster fuck. We rescheduled the meeting for tomorrow. Want you there. She's staying at W H?

Y

No comment from Gage. I wasn't sure Violet would be willing to stay. If she was uncomfortable being at Winters House, I'd check us back into the Intercontinental. Or see if Jacob had an empty unit in his building. I knew she wasn't going back to Chase's condo anytime soon.

Making a decision, I eased away from Violet and got off the bed. She didn't move when I unsnapped her jeans and slid them down her legs. When I reached beneath her T-shirt to unfasten her bra and tugged the straps down her arms, she only sighed and turned into the pillow.

We hadn't gotten much sleep the night before, and she was emotionally exhausted. I pulled the covers over her body, drew the curtains and wrote a short note. Setting it on the pillow beside her, next to her phone, I left the room, shutting the door behind me.

I found Mrs. W in her office by the kitchen, looking down at a notepad and chewing on the end of the pencil. Her hair in a bun, her dark dress without a wrinkle, she was almost identical to the young woman who'd joined our staff at eighteen, not long before my aunt and uncle died. There were a few threads of gray in her dark hair and faint creases in the skin around her eyes and mouth, but otherwise, Helen Williamson defied the passing of the years. With our parents dead, she was the closest thing we had to a mother, and every single one of us adored her.

Except for Aunt Amelia. Those two had been sworn enemies for decades, at least until Amelia's penchant for pulling pranks had crossed the line a few weeks ago. It turns out that when you hide a bullion cube in a shower head, the person who stands beneath smells like chicken soup for a few days afterward.

Mrs. W was not amused. When Abel, who we all suspected was sweet on her, pranked Amelia back, it seemed my great aunt decided to call a truce. The rest of us were relieved, but I wasn't convinced the détente would last.

"When did you come home?" she asked, concern in her dark eyes. I was far more likely to work into the night than to show up in the middle of the day.

"Just a little while ago," I said. "I brought someone with me. The woman I've been seeing, Violet Westbrook. She's had a shock, a family problem with her brother. They live together, and she needed some space. She's sleeping in my room upstairs. I'm going to run to her place and get some of her things."

Anyone else would have pressed for more information, but Mrs. W was the soul of discretion. She'd pull out her own fingernails before she'd ask any of us a personal question. And even without poking at us, she managed to know every detail of our lives. If she was curious about Violet, I knew she'd satisfy that curiosity without upsetting Violet or interrogating me.

All she said in response was, "Do you know how long she'll be staying? Will she be with you, or should I prepare a guest room?"

"She'll stay with me. As for how long she'll be here, that depends."

Mrs. W said nothing, only raised an eyebrow. To her, I said what I wasn't ready to admit yet to Gage, or to Violet. To anyone else for that matter. "If I get my way, she'll stay forever."

Mrs. W pressed her lips together in a tight line and gave a nod. She could be impossible to read. I knew she'd make up her own mind about Violet. If she decided Violet didn't measure up, she'd never say a word. I was sure she'd hated my first wife, Elizabeth. Sure because everyone had hated Elizabeth, and because Mrs. W's response when I told her Elizabeth would be leaving was a simple and quiet, "It's about time."

I wasn't worried. Knowing Mrs. W and Violet, those two would be peas in a pod. Everyone else would be fine, too. Gage was the only Winters living in the house that worried me. The last thing Violet needed was my cousin giving her a hard time.

I headed out in Violet's car and called Gage on his cell.

"Hey," I said when he answered. "Violet's sleeping. I'm going to get her stuff. When are we meeting with Chase?"

"Tomorrow morning. Nine. He was a mess after you left," Gage said. "I feel bad for the guy."

"I'm not admitting it to Vi, but yeah, I hear you."

Gage gave a knowing laugh. "If anyone would be on his side, it's you."

"Don't start with me. Look, I'm calling because Violet feels like hell. I want her to stay with me. If you're going to be an asshole, tell me now and I'll check us into a hotel. I'd rather have her at Winters House, but not if you're going to make her feel unwelcome."

Under his breath I heard Gage swear. "Fuck me." Louder, after an exaggerated sigh, he went on, "Fine. I'll be nice. I'm still not sure about her. But I'll cut her some slack for major family drama. I'd rather have her in Winters House where I can keep an eye on her."

"I'm asking you to be truly nice, not be fake nice and then glare at her behind my back," I clarified.

"I can be nice. What, you're the only one who gets to look out for his family? She didn't exactly have the best beginning—"

"I know. I was there. But we're past that now and I'm asking you to do me a favor and be nice to my girlfriend. Please. I want her to like my family, not think you're all a bunch of jackasses."

"I said I'd be good."

"I'd settle for you keeping your mouth shut and letting Sophie do the talking. She's an angel. You're like the troll under the bridge."

"Fuck off. I'm the one with the gorgeous wife. You're the dumbass hooking up with a potential criminal."

"She's not—" I started to say before Gage cut me off.

"Yeah, yeah, yeah. We'll see. In the meantime, you get her moved in where we can keep an eye on her."

"Somehow," I said dryly, "that's not all that comforting."

"Wasn't meant to be," Gage said, cheerily, before he hung up.

I loved my family. I'd die for anyone of them. But sometimes they were a royal pain in my ass.

The security gate to Chase's underground parking opened as I approached in Violet's car and the card on her key ring gave me access to the elevator. I knocked once on the condo door before I let myself in.

Chase Westbrook was sprawled across the couch, a half-full tumbler of bourbon balanced on his chest. He sat up awkwardly when he saw me, sloshing the liquor on his shirt. With a nearly silent curse, he set his tumbler on the coffee table and lurched to his feet, his eyes searching over my shoulder for his sister.

"Where is she?" he demanded. "What did you do with her?"

"I didn't do anything with her," I said, my voice as close to soothing as I could get. "I took her home—"

"This is her home," Chase interrupted.

"I took her to my home. I tucked her into bed, where she cried herself to sleep. Is that what you wanted to hear? I came to get some of her things."

Chase deflated with a long exhale and sank back to the couch, hanging his head for a moment before he picked up his tumbler of bourbon and drained what was left.

"I should have told her," he said.

"Yeah, you should have," I agreed.

"Are you going to tell me what an asshole I am, too?"

"Nope." I stared down at Violet's brother, Anna's son. Half-brother to my cousins. He wasn't related to me by blood, but that didn't matter. Whether we wanted it or not, this man was family. Even without his connection to

Anna Winters, he belonged to Violet, and Violet belonged to me.

No matter how I looked at it, Chase Westbrook was a part of our lives now. I couldn't leave him alone and miserable. Not like this.

I grabbed the tumbler from the wet bar in the kitchen and helped myself to some of the bourbon he'd left on the counter. Sitting in a chair opposite the couch, I sipped the bourbon and thought about what to say.

Finally, I went with, "I have a little sister, too. And on top of that, I have two younger brothers, and four younger cousins. I've been the head of the family since I was twenty and my parents died. I know all about doing the best you can to keep them safe and happy. And I know all about fucking up in the process. Violet's hurt. She's pissed. But she'll forgive you because she loves you."

Chase shook his head, his blonde hair falling in his eyes, reminding me so much of my cousin Vance I felt for a moment like I'd stepped into an alternate universe. Add a few inches to that hair and slap some more tattoos on him, and Violet's brother turned into my cousin.

At that thought, it occurred to me that we needed to have a family meeting, and despite Violet being angry with Chase, we'd have to orchestrate introductions. There was no way the rest of my family would be willing to wait once they found out Chase existed. It had only been a few months, but it felt like we'd been looking for Anna's missing son forever.

He was the last piece in the puzzle of their deaths. Finding Chase, bringing him into the family, would let us finally put the past to rest.

"You seem pretty sure about that," Chase said, turning his empty tumbler in his fingers.

"I am. She just needs time."

"I wanted to tell her for so long. After they kicked me out, I wanted to tell her, but she was still living at home, going to school, and I didn't want to do anything to fuck that up for her. And then they tried to force her to marry Walters and she was just fucking destroyed." Chase raised his head and his blue eyes were wide with outraged fury. "They tried to fucking sell her to a man old enough to be her father and when she had the nerve to object they booted her out. Haven't spoken to her since. She called me collect from a gas station in the middle of the night. I was two states away. Do you have any idea how helpless I felt?"

"I can imagine," I said quietly. I could. I would have been sick to be that far away if one of my family had needed me. All I had to do was imagine Charlie or Annalise on a payphone at a gas station in the middle of the night. Yeah. I understood.

"I never should have left her with them. I had the money by then. I could have put her through school, but she wanted to prove something. That she could do it herself. That she could be the daughter they wanted. It was bullshit. She shouldn't have had to be anybody but herself. And they never really saw her. They never saw either of us."

"They didn't try to find her? They never called? Sent a letter?" I couldn't imagine it. I couldn't fathom that they let their daughter walk out the door in the dark of night and never bothered to find out what had happened to her.

Chase got up and carried his glass to the bottle of bourbon where he refilled it. "Not as far as I know. They didn't really want children. They wanted, I don't know, pets, or robots. They wanted to be able to tell us what to think and who to be and what to do. What they got were two human beings with thoughts and feelings they couldn't control. Once they realized what being parents was about, they lost interest. I was done trying to win their approval long before I found those files in the basement, but Vivi never gave up. Not until fucking Walters almost raped her and she found out her own father had set it up. That was enough to break anyone's heart, even one as stubborn as Vivi's."

I gritted my teeth at the way he laid it out. If I couldn't understand her parents tossing her out the door and letting her go without a second thought, I sure as hell couldn't make sense of her father whoring her out to his friend. It didn't make a fucking bit of difference that he'd intended for the friend to marry her.

He'd treated her like a piece of property. Sent her to that man's house knowing his friend expected to fuck her, and not only did he not warn her, he'd punished her for resisting. The more I thought about it, the more I wanted to hunt down the people who'd raised Violet and make them pay for what they'd done.

I tossed back the rest of my bourbon and stood. "I'm going to get some of Vi's things. Gage says we have a meeting tomorrow?"

Chase nodded. "I'll be there." He held his half-full glass in the air in a wry salute. "I'll even be sober."

He didn't say a word as I went down the hall to find Violet's bedroom. I located a suitcase under her bed and filled it with everything I thought she might want or need for an extended stay at Winters House. I did my best with her makeup and toiletries. If I missed anything she could always come back while Chase was at Winters, Inc. for our meeting.

Chase's glass had been topped up in the short time I was in Violet's room. He was going to feel like hell when the liquor wore off. Not my concern. Violet was my concern. Chase would have to take care of himself.

On my way to the door, Violet's suitcase in hand, I stopped and turned. "I'll see you tomorrow."

Chase's eyes were a little unfocused when they met mine. "Take care of her. Promise me you'll take care of her."

When I said, "I will," it felt like more than a promise. It felt like a vow. A vow I planned to keep.

Chapter Twenty-Eight

Aiden

The house was still empty when I returned. I carried Violet's suitcase into my suite to find her curled up on the bed in an old flannel robe she must have dug out of the back of my closet. A gift from some forgotten ex-girlfriend, I doubted I'd ever worn it. I wasn't a robe kind of guy.

Spotting the suitcase, she said, "I got your note. You didn't have to do that, but I appreciate it. Thank you."

"Not a problem. I doubt it helps, but your brother is miserable."

Her eyes went stormy and she shook her head. "You're right, it doesn't help. And he should be miserable." Under her breath she said, "Jackass."

"I know from experience, older brothers can often be jackasses."

A ghost of a smile curved her lips. "I bet you do." Standing up and straightening the robe she said, "I don't want to stay with Chase right now, but I can't impose on you. I'll change, and then I'll see about finding something."

"I'd prefer you stayed with me."

"I appreciate the offer. I really do. But I don't want to make your family uncomfortable, and I don't want to take advantage of your hospitality."

"You won't make my family uncomfortable. Gage already promised to behave. And you can't be taking advantage of my hospitality when I'm offering it freely."

"It's too soon. This is all going so fast, and it's too soon."

I rolled her suitcase to the door of the walk-in closet, taking a quick detour to set the tote bag with her toiletries and makeup on the bathroom counter. Violet watched, slowly shaking her head at the way I was ignoring her, until I came to stand directly in front of her and pulled her into my arms.

She smelled like my soap, woodsy with a hint of spice. The masculine scent shouldn't have been so appealing, but as it rose from her skin I knew I'd never shower again without thinking of Violet. Of the way she fit in my arms, of how beautiful she was just like this, her face bare of makeup, her hair wet, her body warm.

"I know it's fast. But I know what I want, and I want you. If you need to slow this down, I can do that. But I don't want to. I want you here, with me. I want you in my bed. I want you at my breakfast table."

Violet's mouth dropped open in surprise. I had to stop myself from kissing her. Those pink lips, her wide lavender eyes. She rarely looked so unguarded. So open.

"I don't know what to say. I—"

"Say you'll stay with me."

The absent shake of her head belied the words that came from her mouth. "Just for a few days. Then we'll see."

It wasn't a wholehearted agreement, but I'd take it.

Assuming Gage didn't run her off, all I needed was a few days to convince Violet she belonged by my side.

Giving into my impulse, I lowered my head and took her mouth. I wasn't ready for her response. She melted into me, her full breasts pillowing against my chest, her tongue reaching for mine, driving me straight from arousal to desperate need.

I tugged at the belt of her robe as her busy fingers pulled at my tie. A button popped and rolled to the carpet. I don't remember stepping out of my shoes and pants. Just Violet pulling back, then pushing on my shoulder, nudging me to the bed. I tried to take her with me and she ordered, "Sit."

I wasn't going to argue. I stripped off my socks and leaned back against the headboard, taking my hard cock in hand and stroking, watching her loosen the belt of my plaid flannel robe and slowly peel open the lapels. She was naked beneath, and she dropped the robe back off her shoulders, letting it fall to the floor at her feet.

I gripped my cock hard, struggling to stay where I was. I wanted to touch. I wanted my hands all over her body. I wanted to spread her legs and fuck her hard. To fill her with me. To own her.

My head wanted to court her.

My body wanted to claim her.

Her eyes moved from my hand on my cock to my face and back again, her bare pink mouth curving into a knowing smile as old as female desire. She knew—or thought she knew—exactly how much I wanted her.

If she could see inside my head, if she knew the ferocity of my need, she'd probably run screaming.

Instead, she strolled to the bed, hips swaying, and climbed on, straddling my lap and putting her perfect round breasts right in my face. I released my cock to cup them in my hands, rubbing her hard nipples with my thumbs.

She spread her knees, dropping her hips until the heat between her legs grazed the head of my cock. I sucked in a harsh breath. Her pussy already slick with arousal, she stroked over me, spreading her desire, teasing us both.

She swayed forward, letting the head of my cock dip the tiniest bit inside her, clasping me with sweet, tight, wet heat before she swayed back to stroke me over her clit. Then it was her turn to gasp.

I gave myself over to her sweet torture, distracting myself from my cock's demands by pulling first one nipple, then the other, between my lips, nipping and sucking until Violet couldn't take anymore and sank all the way down my length.

Her head dropped forward as she watched my mouth on her breasts. Eyes half closed, she rose and fell on my cock, grinding her swollen clit into the base on every down stroke with a little moan of pleasure.

I sank my fingers into her ass, holding her down as I surged up, dragging the orgasm from her, throwing my head back as her pussy clenched and released around me, almost pulling me over the edge along with her.

I wouldn't last much longer.

Couldn't last much longer.

Flipping her to her back, I pressed her knees to her shoulders and braced my weight on my elbows, hands on her arms, holding us both motionless as the echoes of her climax faded. Her eyes were dark, almost midnight blue and dazed with pleasure, her mouth open, bottom lip so plump and pink I had to sink my teeth in for a taste.

I kissed her until she squirmed beneath me, rocking her hips up the little bit she could move. I kept her there, knees high and spread wide, arms pinned, and took her mouth with mine until she gave a frustrated, keening cry and bucked up hard.

I let go of everything. Her arms. My restraint. Her legs wrapped around my hips, hanging on as I plunged into her, losing myself in her body, in her pussy, her mouth, the scent of her hair, and the silk of her skin.

Losing myself in everything that was Violet.

Imprinting myself on her.

Absorbing her into me.

Making her mine.

The orgasm surged up my spine, exploding from my cock, detonating in my brain as I spilled myself inside her.

It wasn't until I rolled to my back, taking Violet with me, my cock sliding from her pussy, that I realized our mistake. For the first time in my entire adult life, I had completely forgotten a condom.

Not wanting to freak her out I said, quietly, "We didn't use protection."

Laying half on top of me, Violet went stiff. Before she could pull away, I wrapped my arm around her and held her close. "I had a physical six weeks ago. I've been tested, so you don't have to worry about that."

"I get the birth control shot," she said in a thin, anxious voice. "I won't get pregnant, but what about since your physical?"

She went rock solid at the chuckle that tumbled from my lips. I knew laughing was the wrong move but I couldn't help it. "My physical was the day before we shared the elevator. Since I saw you, I haven't even looked at another woman, much less fucked one."

The tension eased from her body and she rolled to her side, raising her eyes to mine. "Really?"

The open disbelief made me laugh again. "Really," I confirmed. "I never settle for less than exactly what I want. The second I laid eyes on you, I wanted you. Only you."

"Now you've had me," she said teasingly, a thread of uncertainty running through her words.

I craned my neck to brush my lips over her cheekbone. "Yes, I have. But not enough. Never enough."

"Do you want to skip the condoms then?"

"If you're okay with it. I can show you my test results if you want," I offered.

She pressed her lips to my collarbone. "No, I trust you."

I wanted to thank her. To tell her how much it meant to know I had her trust. Words jumbled in my head, stilted and wrong.

I settled for holding her close, feeling her heart beat against mine before urging her up and into the shower with me. She started to complain, but her hair was still wet from her own shower and once I stroked slick, soapy hands down her back, she let out a contented sigh and relaxed.

It wasn't hard to talk her into coming downstairs and joining me on the terrace behind the house. The day was unseasonably cool for June in Atlanta, in the low seventies, perfect for enjoying the garden before summer kicked in.

Violet twisted her damp hair into a knot at the nape of her neck, pulled on a pink linen sundress I'd packed for her and did something with her face before she pronounced herself ready to leave the room.

She followed me down to the main level, waiting a moment while I grabbed my laptop and some papers from my home office. I'd taken the rest of the day off, but there were still a few things I had to check on. When I came back, she held her tablet in one hand.

The terrace was deep and ran most of the width of the house. I led Violet to a small table beside a chaise lounge.

"Do you mind if I get some work done?"

"Hmm?" Violet stared out over the gardens, distracted. I understood. The gardens of Winters House were stunning, and early summer was their best season. Suiting the house, the gardens were formal, the beds arranged with precision, separated by stone walkways, a riot of color and beauty.

"How is it that you don't sit out here all day?" she asked. "It's gorgeous."

"I guess I'm used to it." Mr. Henried, the gardener, designed and maintained the landscaping at his discretion. I'm sorry to say I mostly just stayed out of his way. As long as things looked well maintained and attractive, I didn't care what he did. "Do you know anything about gardening?" I asked.

"Not really," Violet, murmured, settling onto the chaise. "I don't think I could ever get used to this. There's so much to look at. Can I wander later?"

"You can do anything you want. I packed you a bathing suit." I nodded my head in the direction of the sparkling water of the pool.

"I noticed. My smallest bikini. I've only worn it once. I don't suppose you could have packed the one piece?"

"Not likely." Though now that I thought about it, I wasn't sure I wanted Violet in that bikini in front of Gage and Riley. Was it too late to go back and get the one piece? Or maybe one of those full-skirted bathing suits women wore in the last century.

The terrace doors swung open and Mrs. W joined us. "Excuse the interruption. I wanted to see if you'd like a tea tray."

At the sound of her voice, Violet set down her tablet and stood.

With a flash of nerves at introducing the two women, I said, "Violet, this is Mrs. W. She runs the house and keeps us all in line. Mrs. W, this is Violet."

Violet approached Mrs. W and held out her hand. "It's lovely to meet you. I apologize for springing a last-minute guest on the household. If there's anything I can do to ease the imposition, please let me know."

Mrs. W graced Violet with an unexpectedly warm smile and took her hand in a firm shake.

"Nonsense. It's a pleasure to have any guest of Aiden's. Don't worry about a thing, just make yourself comfortable." Then, shocking the hell out of me, in a low voice that was almost conspiratorial, she went on, "It's nice to see this one relaxing instead of working all hours."

Violet looked at the papers spread before me. "Well, he's still working."

"True, but he's doing it out here in the sunshine, enjoying the gardens, instead of closed up in his office."

"I suppose that is an improvement," Violet agreed. "I've told him more than once that he works too hard."

"If you can get him to spend a little less time in the office and a little more time enjoying life, I know we'd all be grateful." At that, Mrs. W winked at me and turned to leave. Before she disappeared back into the house, she said, "I'll bring a tray so you have something to snack on."

When she was gone, Violet said, "She adores you."

"I adore her back. I knew she'd like you." I hadn't known, but I'd suspected. Still, I wasn't quite prepared for my satisfaction at seeing the two women hit it off. I trusted my own judgment, but I trusted Mrs. W's almost as much. I hadn't paid attention with Elizabeth, but I was paying attention now.

"She was only being polite," Violet demurred.

"Trust me," I said with a low laugh, "for Mrs. W, a smile and personal talk about the family is as good as a hug."

Violet smiled distractedly and settled back into the chaise, only looking up to thank Mrs. W when she brought the tray of tea, tiny sandwiches and cookies.

Afternoon tea was a tradition when we were children, one both of our mothers, then just my mother, shared with the Winters children. A small way to spend some time connecting as a family over a snack and some sweets. After my mother was gone, Mrs. W kept the tradition alive, in memory of the women we'd lost.

Violet joined me at the table and poured us both tea, admiring the delicate china service my mother had so loved, placing shortbread and crustless cucumber sandwiches on a plate for me before helping herself. I watched her stare absently into her steaming cup, not touching the food she'd taken for herself.

"What's wrong?"

"Nothing. Everything's fine. Just thinking."

"About?" I pressed.

Violet let out a sigh. She picked up a sandwich but didn't take a bite. "I need to go see my parents."

I didn't have to look hard to see her reluctance. I could guess why she was so determined. My gut reaction was to bar her from ever seeing those people again, but it wasn't like I could stop her.

"You want to see the files," I guessed.

Her chin was set in mulish determination. "Chase should have copied both of them. Those files are about us. I have a right to know where I came from. And if it can help your friends, help other people find answers, I need to do something."

"We'll go tomorrow."

"Thank you," Violet said, with a look of such relief I felt like I'd slain a dragon for her.

She should have known there was no way I'd let her go anywhere near her parents on her own.

They'd hurt her enough.

If I had my way, no one would ever hurt her again.

Chapter Twenty-Nine

Violet

The drive from Atlanta to Chattanooga was an easy two and a half hours. Aiden's Aston Martin ate up the road, hurtling us down I-75 toward my parents and the confrontation I was dreading. It didn't matter that they weren't my biological parents.

Finding out that I'd been adopted changed everything. And nothing.

Whoever was responsible for my DNA, they were strangers. They had nothing to do with my childhood. Nothing to do with Suzanne and Henry Westbrook. Nothing to do with their expectations and my failures.

I stared through the window for most of the drive, marshaling my resources. I would show them nothing. No pain. No fear. All they would get from me was ice. I didn't want to renew our relationship or mend fences. I wanted to get my hands on those files. That was all.

We pulled up in front of the house I'd grown up in at exactly five-thirty. The brick colonial looked just as it had the last time I'd seen it, right down to the tidy landscaping and artfully arranged flower pots on the front steps.

Unless their schedule had changed, my father would have arrived home from work fifteen minutes before and would be in the parlor with my mother enjoying a pre-dinner drink.

I wasn't ready, and I was out of time.

I'd dressed in the only suit Aiden had packed, the ice blue linen he'd liked so much when I'd worn it in Las Vegas. I was glad. I was tired of hiding myself in boxy, drab suits. They could take me as I was.

I almost wished I'd snapped a picture of my mother's expression when she saw us in her doorway. For just a second her face went slack, jaw dropped, eyes wide and disbelieving.

Her frosted blonde hair, so like Chase's and my own, was arranged in the same sleek bob she'd had for years. Like me, she wore linen, though her calf-length skirt was topped with a light Cashmere twin set. My mother did love her twin sets. The delicate pearl buttons matched the string around her neck and the studs in her ears. Her blue eyes were cool when she regained her composure.

"Violet. What brings you here unannounced?" she asked, neither stepping back from the door to invite us in or bothering to say hello.

Aiden's squeeze of my fingers gave me strength. I lifted my chin and looked down my nose at the woman who'd raised me, then thrown me out without a moment of pity.

"I won't take much of your time. I have a few questions, and if you'll answer them, I'll leave."

"And who is this?" she asked, raking Aiden with a gaze like a blade, ready to carve him to pieces. I knew her too well. When she heard his last name, she'd shift gears fast enough. My parents were predictable, and they were dyed in the wool snobs.

Taking control, Aiden held out his hand for hers. "Aiden Winters. Of the Atlanta Winters. If you don't mind, as Violet said, we won't take much of your time."

At the sound of his name, my mother warmed to wealth and position as she never had to her children. She took Aiden's hand in both of hers as if he were a long-lost relative.

"Of course, of course. I'm sorry, I was just so surprised to see Violet. We haven't heard from her in so long, you see. Come in. Come in."

Finally, she stepped back and held the door wide, inviting us inside. "Henry and I were just having a drink. What can I get you?"

We followed her in, Aiden and I sharing a glance behind her back. He rolled his eyes at her ridiculous shift in manner, his expression almost startling a giggle from me.

It wouldn't do to laugh: that would put her on edge and I needed her relaxed. I bit my lip to keep the sound inside and shook my head at him.

My father's face when he saw me was almost enough to startle the laugh right back out of me. He went white, then red, and shot my mother a furious glare. She stepped into the breach with a flutter of one hand towards Aiden. "Darling, Violet has stopped by for a short visit and brought Aiden Winters with her."

The look she sent him was so heavy with expectation I had to bite my lip again. Did she know how obvious she was? My father's eyes flew wide before he regained his composure and came to his feet, thrusting his hand toward Aiden.

Not only did he not speak to me, he didn't even look at me. As much as the sight of his face made my stomach turn, his disinterest in his only daughter was a stab to my heart.

He shook Aiden's hand heartily, embarrassingly enthusiastic. "So good of you both to visit. What can I get you to drink?"

Aiden said politely, "Whatever you're having."

No one acknowledged my quiet, "Nothing for me, thank you."

My father fixed drinks and we sat. I found myself perched on the edge of the loveseat beside Aiden. Chase and I were never allowed in this room unless we were in trouble. Then, at my mother's direction, I always sat here, back straight and eyes level as I listened to her castigate me for whatever it was I'd done wrong.

My mother handed me a glass of wine I hadn't asked for and said, "Violet, you look well."

"Thank you."

"So, how do you know our Violet," my father asked Aiden. "I can't imagine how you might have crossed paths."

"You'd be surprised," Aiden said. "Violet has made a place for herself in Atlanta. My family and I are very fond of her."

I resisted the urge to poke Aiden in the side. If Gage was fond of me, I'd hate to see his reaction to someone he disliked.

"How did you meet?" My mother asked, her eyes flitting between us.

Already tired of this conversation, I set the glass of wine on the coffee table untouched and leaned forward. "I spoke with Chase yesterday."

My father's voice was a slap. "Do not speak his name in our home."

"He's your son and my brother. I will speak his name. He's doing very well, not that you care."

"Your brother," my father said weightily, "chose to turn his back on this family."

"He dropped out of college, got a tattoo, and bought a motorcycle. He didn't kill someone. He just didn't fall in line with your plans. He didn't turn his back on you, you turned your back on him."

My mother pursed her lips in disapproval and avoided my gaze, making a tiny sound of distress in the back of her throat. I realized I'd raised my voice. Seeing them again, being here, reminded me of all the reasons I'd walked out the front door and never returned.

Focus, I lectured myself. *You're not here to fight with them. You're here to get those files.*

Aiden's palm flattened on the small of my back just under the edge of my suit jacket, his hand warm through the thin silk of my blouse. The simple touch soothed, and I leaned into him just a little. "Chase said that we were adopted. Why did you never tell me?"

Both of my parents froze, faces blank. My mother recovered first. "He's a liar. Violet, you know that. We had no choice but to cut him off after his behavior became unacceptable. You can't believe a thing he says."

"So it's not true?" I asked, fully aware who the real liars were.

My father blustered, "Of course, it's not true. Look at you. You're the image of your mother."

Except that I wasn't. Our hair color was the same, but hers was helped by a bottle. I was taller, and curvier, and though her eyes were similar to Chase's, no one in the family had the same odd bluish-purple of my own.

I'd seen a picture of Aiden's cousin Vance at Winters House. He was right, Chase and Vance were almost identical.

I ignored my father's comment. "Then you're denying it."

"Of course, we're denying it," my mother said, tugging at the strand of pearls around her neck as if it were a tightening noose. "It's ridiculous. It's just your brother trying to cause trouble again."

Sensing that we were wasting our time, Aiden leaned into me and said quietly, though loud enough for them to hear, "Sweetheart, we don't need to talk about this. We've had a long drive, why don't you go freshen up while I get to know your parents."

I manufactured the most saccharine smile I could come up with and aimed it straight at Aiden. "Of course. I'll be right back." To my parents, I said, "Excuse me."

As I left the parlor and walked down the hall to the kitchen I heard my father say, "That's how you have to handle her. She needs guidance. Direction. If you don't keep her in line, she gets out of hand."

I resisted the urge to eavesdrop and picked up my pace. Bypassing the small powder room off the kitchen, I headed straight for the basement door.

I was too angry at Chase to talk to him yet, but I didn't need to ask where he'd found the files. Like the rest of the house, the basement was ruthlessly organized. There were only two file cabinets in the storage closet beneath the stairs, each of them with three drawers, and none were locked. It probably hadn't occurred to my parents we'd ever bother to look inside.

My heart raced and sweat coated my palms as I opened a drawer and scanned the neatly labeled folders. I trusted Aiden to keep my parents occupied, but I'd feel better once I found what I needed. The first drawer was filled with tax information, a folder for each year going back well over two decades.

The second drawer held receipts, titles to their vehicles, and, weirdly, every report card either Chase or myself had ever brought home. I couldn't imagine why my parents would have saved them. Especially since they'd thrown us both out of the house. But there they were, organized by year. I skipped past them and dug further.

Chapter Thirty

Violet

In the very back of the middle drawer of the second cabinet, buried behind years of medical bills, I found a thin, unmarked, manila folder. Hands shaking, I pulled it from the drawer and unwound the string holding the flap closed. The stack of papers slid out in a neat pile.

There wasn't much. A contract with my parent's names. Two birth certificates. There was no name on the first, but the birthdate was Chase's. Chase Westbrook was identified on the second certificate, with the same birthdate. Several pages below I found a second contract and a second set of birth certificates with my own birthdate.

Carefully sliding the pages back into the envelope, I closed the flap, winding the string to secure it, and stuck them in the waistband at the back of my skirt, beneath my blouse, settling my suit jacket into place. Conscious of time passing, I checked the rest of the drawers for anything else. There was nothing. Time to get moving.

I made my way back upstairs silently and came to an abrupt halt in the hall when I heard my father say, "I'm sure you don't need my advice, son, but I would keep her away from her brother. He's a troubled man, has been since he was a teenager."

"I wasn't aware," Aiden said smoothly with just the right note of concern. "Troubled how?"

"Violent outbursts, lying. He's delusional."

My mother added, "For years I suspected he was doing drugs."

"You'll need a firm hand with Violet," my father said. "She's stubborn. Digs her heels in when she should do what she's told. Talks back."

"When she was younger, she was such a sweet girl," my mother said, her voice weighted by nostalgia and regret. "We should never have allowed her to go away to college."

"It wasn't college so much as allowing her to live in the dorms," my father said. "She became positively unruly after that. Disobedient, with a smart mouth."

"But you look like just the kind of man to bring out the best in her, doesn't he, Henry?" I didn't have to see my mother to picture the inquiring tilt of her head or the ingratiating smile on her face.

"He does, he does," my father agreed.

Did they not realize how rude it was to talk about Aiden in the third person when he was sitting right in front of them?

Reminding myself that eavesdroppers rarely heard anything flattering, I continued down the hall, allowing my heels to echo on the hardwood, announcing my presence. I took my seat beside Aiden and picked up my glass of wine, taking the tiniest sip.

"Have you all been getting to know each other?" I asked.

Aiden's eyes met mine, and he knew immediately that I'd been successful. I was uncomfortably aware of the envelope tucked against my lower back beneath my clothes. Just a few more minutes and I'd make our excuses.

My mother smiled in Aiden's direction. "We have. But you haven't told us how long you two have been seeing each other."

I opened my mouth to answer, but Aiden got there first. "Just about a month."

"Oh, not very long then." My mother sounded disappointed. "Then I suppose it's too soon to expect any announcements."

I hadn't spoken to these people in years, so why was my mother's behavior so impossibly embarrassing? Heat rose to my cheeks as I hissed, "Mother!"

I was about to apologize to Aiden for her presumption when she smoothed her skirt over her knees and gave me a pointed look. "Gordon Walters got married last year."

I took a deliberate sip of my wine before I said, "How unfortunate for his new bride."

My father set his tumbler of whiskey on the side table with a rattle of glass on wood. "That's enough of that. You're lucky we stopped you before your lies could damage his reputation. When I think of what he could have done for this family, and what you ruined—"

My mother reached out a hand and patted my father's knee, murmuring, "Henry, now is not the time. Perhaps we ought to give Violet the opportunity to redeem herself." This was followed by another pointed look at me and a quick glance at Aiden.

For someone who put so much stock in good manners, my mother could be oblivious. Did she think Aiden was an idiot?

Aiden's jaw clenched. I'd never told him the name of the man who'd assaulted, then fired me. Now I didn't have to. Aiden was far from an idiot and he'd figured out exactly who my parents were talking about.

Fury radiated from him. I couldn't imagine how my parents didn't notice. It was there in his tight mouth, the lines around his eyes, the coiled tension in his legs and arms.

When he spoke, his voice was level and implacable. "I'm sorry to cut this visit short. Violet and I have an engagement elsewhere in the city, and we need to go."

He rose to his feet, bringing me with him. We walked to the door, trailed by my parents. My mother said, "It was lovely to meet you. I hope Henry and I will see you again soon."

Aiden turned and met her eyes. His face expressionless, he said, "I doubt that," and swept me out of the house, leaving them gaping after him in astonishment.

I didn't let out a breath until I fastened my seatbelt and Aiden pulled away from the curb. As soon as we were moving, I leaned forward, untucked the back of my blouse beneath my jacket and pulled free the papers I'd stolen. Aiden looked over to see the manila envelope in my lap.

"You found the files?"

"It's not much, but yes."

"Good, because we're never going back there again."

"Fine with me," I agreed. I'd been on edge every second we were in that house. Now that I'd escaped, my goal accomplished, the adrenaline faded, and I was left with a sick, sad ache in my chest.

It was fine with me. Better than fine. There was nothing for me in that house. Nothing for me with those people. My eyes dropped to the envelope in my lap. I opened it and withdrew the stack of papers, scanning the contract on top.

Based on the dates, it was Chase's. A quick look told me

there wasn't much useful information. Maybe a professional investigator could find more. Or maybe I was just distracted. My eyes blurred with tears and I looked out the window.

Finding out that I was adopted should have been a relief. It could have been an explanation for my parents' coldness, their disinterest in me once it became clear I wouldn't serve their purposes. It wasn't. Biology had nothing to do with their miserable parenting.

I knew their treatment would have been the same if I'd been born of my mother's body. They lacked the capacity for love. For compassion. For anything other than enduring self-interest. It was who they were. They were incapable of nurturing, of devotion, of everything that made a parent into a parent.

Love wasn't about blood, it was in the heart.

Neither of them had one.

I let out a gusty sigh as I blinked away the moisture in my eyes. Aiden took my hand, lacing his fingers through mine.

"You can out-ice queen your mother any day, sweetheart."

"Hmph. She taught me everything I know."

He lifted my fingers to his mouth and kissed my knuckles, eyes flashing to my face before they returned to the road ahead. "She's a poor imitation of you."

"Thank you for coming with me. I'm sorry they were so horrible"

Aiden surprised me with a laugh. "You're not responsible for them. Believe me, they're not the worst I've met. Dropping a name like mine rarely brings out the best in people."

I thought about that, what it meant in his life for his

very name to draw greed and grasping hands from the people he met. "You deserve better than that."

"Some people would say I deserve far worse," he said, stroking his thumb along the back of my hand.

"They'd be wrong. Don't forget, I spent weeks trying to dig up your worst transgressions and came up blank."

"I work too much to have any juicy transgressions," Aiden said, the side of his mouth curling up in a wry smile. "My life is a lot fewer strippers and a lot more spreadsheets than people think."

I had a sudden flash of a stripper pole installed in Aiden's office and laughed out loud. "How about no strippers and fewer spreadsheets?"

Aiden pulled his eyes from the road just long enough to scan me with a hot glance. "How about you strip for me every night I come home on time?"

Heat pooled between my legs. My voice was husky when I said, "That might get predictable. How about you get a reward of my choosing every night you don't work late?"

"I'll tell the executive team to adjust my schedule," he said, and I couldn't tell if he was kidding or not.

I hoped he wasn't. I liked this thing we had going. I liked being with him. Unless he was playing me, Aiden seemed to intend for this to go on. But if it did, I wanted us to be together. Not me rattling around his big house by myself while he worked all hours of the day and night.

I wanted him, had feelings for him, feelings that went way beyond attraction and sex, but I wanted a relationship. Not crumbs of his time. I wasn't sure he could give me that. I thought he wanted to. Intended to. But wants and intentions didn't always translate to action. I'd just have to wait and see.

I flipped through the papers on my lap again, pulling up the contract dated a few weeks after my birth. The names typed beneath the scrawled signatures meant nothing to me. Before the thought fully formed in my head, the words left my mouth. "I want to find them."

"Who?" Glancing down at the papers on my lap Aiden said, "Your biological parents? Are you sure? You don't know the can of worms you'd be opening."

"No, but they can't be worse than Suzanne and Henry." I was half joking, but Aiden's response was deadly serious.

"You're wrong. Is there a number on that contract?"

I knew what he meant and scanned for a dollar amount. When I found it I swallowed hard. "Holy shit," I said, under my breath.

"How much?"

"Chase's doesn't say. Mine says seven hundred and fifty thousand dollars."

Aiden gave a low whistle. "People will do a lot of things for that kind of money, Vi. We can look for them. I'll put the Sinclairs on it. They're going to go through that paperwork with a fine-tooth comb trying to track down what Maxwell was up to. They'll want to talk to the parties to those contracts anyway. But don't forget, this wasn't an agency adoption. It was private, and a lot of money changed hands. There are a lot of ways that doesn't add up to a pretty picture."

"You don't know that," I said quietly. The look Aiden gave me was soft, gentle.

"I don't," he agreed. "I'm just saying that most cases end up with a reputable agency. I don't know why your parents didn't go that route. Having met them, and knowing you and your brother, I'd guess they were more interested in special ordering their children. The hair and eye color for both of you is too close to your mother. That's not a coincidence."

"That's my guess, too," I agreed.

"That much money with those kinds of requirements leave the door open for a much more unsavory arrangement than a normal, above-board adoption. You need to be on guard. People willing to sell their child for close to a million dollars may not have the kind of motivation you're looking for."

"I still want to find them. I want to know."

"Then we'll find them. I promise."

Chapter Thirty-One

Violet

I shut the door to Aiden's suite behind me, my feet dragging on the carpet. It had been a long day, and dinner with Aiden's family had worn me out. There was only so much of Gage I could take. Keeping my cool when I wanted to throw my wine glass in his face took way too much energy. I'd spent my day going to two interviews and swimming laps in the pool, but I felt as if I'd run a marathon.

If I'd been more awake, I might have seen it before I was almost on top of it. On the other hand, if I'd been more awake I probably would have screamed loud enough to alert the entire house.

I slapped my hand over my mouth to hold in my shriek. I couldn't stop my feet from stumbling back, tangling and almost spilling me to the floor in my haste to get away from the long black snake curled in a circle on the crisp, white sheets of the bed, half hidden beneath my pillow.

My heart thumped in my ears, drowning out the sound of my harsh breathing, panicked whimpers leaking from behind my hand.

Run, I ordered myself. *Run, run, run!*

I sagged against the window frame, mere feet from the side of the bed, knees like jelly, feet rooted to the carpet. That was a big snake. Big, and black, and...not moving.

Reason slowly invaded my panic-stricken brain. The snake wasn't moving. And how the heck had a snake that belonged in the woods made its way to the master suite on the second floor of Winters House?

I'd only been there a week, but a few hours was enough to tell me that Mrs. W ran a tight ship. I wasn't sure a field mouse would have the nerve to breach the walls of Winters House, much less an enormous rat snake.

I don't know how long I stood there waiting out what I was increasingly sure was a rubber snake. I'd have to touch it to verify my hunch, and I couldn't quite bring myself to move yet.

Maybe it was sleeping. Were snakes light sleepers? I had no clue. I was a suburban girl. I'd never been camping. I didn't hike. My experience with snakes was limited to a quick trip through the reptile house at the zoo.

I'd like to say I kicked the ice queen into gear, strode to the bed, and picked up the snake. The woman I wanted to grow up to be might do that. I wasn't there yet. Instead, knees still shaking, I sprinted to the dressing room and grabbed shoes at random, snatching sandals, heels, and sneakers from the closet shelves. Armed with footwear, I crept back to the bed, stopping a few feet away, watching the snake warily.

It hadn't moved.

I was absolutely, positively, almost sure it hadn't moved.

For a second, I thought about yelling for Mrs. W. I had a feeling she could rout an invading army. One rat snake under my pillow would be no match for her.

Only one thing stopped me. If the snake wasn't real, if it was, in fact, a rubber snake, then I knew exactly who'd slipped it beneath my pillow, and why.

Aiden's great aunt Amelia was known as a prankster. And she didn't like me. She didn't dislike me, either. Aunt Amelia didn't pull her punches. She'd said straight out the day before, "I can't quite figure you out, girl. You remind me a little too much of his first wife. I'm keeping an eye on you."

I'd given her a cool look and said, "Fair enough. I'm not sure about you either."

Sophie, Gage's wife, who I'd learned was sweet and endlessly patient, had given me a kind smile at my answer. I was pretty sure Sophie liked me. Then again, Sophie was nice to everyone, so it was hard to tell.

Annalise and Riley were polite, but not particularly warm. Gage was the same, and I could tell being civil cost him. Every day I debated leaving Winters House. Every night I told myself, just one more day. Aiden had asked me to stay. He'd asked me to give this a chance, give his family a chance, and I'd promised I would.

In Aiden's favor was the fact that I didn't, at the moment, have anywhere to go. I didn't want to blow my savings on a hotel and finding an apartment would take time. It made sense, both in terms of finance and my potential commute, to find a job first. I was working on it, but that too took time. My only sensible option, other than Winters House, was my room in Chase's condo.

If I wanted to go home, I had to forgive him first. I wasn't ready. Not yet. I was close, but as much as I loved my brother, I was still pissed.

I forced myself to inch closer to the side of the bed. The head of the rubber snake stuck out from beneath the white pillowcase, just a little more exposed than the coils of black scales tucked mostly beneath the pillow. The snake had a dull sheen to it. If it were real, wouldn't the scales be shiny?

I shifted my weight to the balls of my feet, ready to run screaming bloody murder if the creature beneath my pillow moved. I tossed a sneaker at the pillow, letting out a barely audible squeak and jumping back even as it struck the snake and tumbled harmlessly to the floor.

The snake didn't move.

I threw a sandal. The sneaker had knocked the pillow awry and the sandal landed square in the middle of the snake's coiled body.

The snake still didn't move.

It's rubber, you idiot. Just go pick it up.

That would be sensible. But, just in case, I tossed a nude pump, a spike-heeled sandal, a pink wedge, a ballet flat, and a flip-flop. The snake looked less terrifying and more silly covered in my shoes.

And I was absolutely, positively, mostly, really, sure that it was fake.

I still approached the side of the bed with my eyes squeezed half shut. I reached out, fingers trembling, and grasped the heavy, cool, rubber length of the fake reptile.

At the confirmation that there was not a giant snake in my bed, I sank on the side of the mattress in relief.

I thought about calling Aiden, and just as quickly rejected the idea. He was in Houston overnight. It was the first time he'd traveled for business since we'd officially been together, and the trip was so quick he hadn't invited me to join him. I didn't mind being left out. Twelve hours of meetings didn't sound like my idea of fun.

If I told Aiden about the snake, he'd rush to my defense. And if I wanted to make a place for myself with his family, I couldn't hide behind him every time they tested me. I wasn't afraid of Amelia Winters. I'd heard about her pranks.

I pulled the heavy rubber snake onto my lap and stared down at it, considering. She'd probably been expecting me to scream. Maybe to come running out of Aiden's rooms, terrified and hysterical.

Aunt Amelia didn't know me very well. I didn't do terrified and hysterical. At least, not in public. The shoe throwing episode, my pounding heart, and my wobbly knees were between me and the rubber snake. If Amelia was expecting me to entertain her, she'd be disappointed.

I'd learned that when people wanted to get a rise out of you, the most satisfying response was to give them absolutely nothing. It was guaranteed to drive the other person crazy.

Smiling to myself, I picked up the shoes I'd thrown, silently apologizing for the abuse, and replaced them in the closet. I hid the snake in there along with them.

I had plans for that snake.

Aiden didn't call that night. I got a quick text close to midnight that said only, *Miss you. Been a long day. Be home for dinner tomorrow.*

His bed was too big without him. I'd gotten used to falling asleep beside him, used to waking up with him. Used to the feel of his lips on my skin, his hands on my body. It was a little scary, how easily I'd fit into life at Winters House. To life as part of a couple. I'd never had anything like this with a man.

I thought I understood the pattern of relationships. Dating, sex, maybe moving in together. What I had with Aiden was different. We fit. We could talk all night or sit in silence. I knew what he was thinking by the way he raised an eyebrow, and when no one else saw beneath my cool mask, Aiden could read my mind.

He was everything good and honest, and when he smiled at me, my heart beamed. This was way too fast to fall in love. I didn't seem to be able to stop myself. I wasn't sure I wanted to.

I tossed and turned for hours before I found sleep. When Aiden was beside me, I could bury my worries. His presence overwhelmed me, distracting me with the physical, giving me a rock to lean on while I sorted out everything else. Without him there, I was adrift.

I'd feel better once things were settled. Once I was talking to Chase again. Once I had a job and a place to live. Once we'd found the people who'd sold me to my parents.

I hadn't called Chase. Hadn't texted him. Hadn't told him I'd stolen our files from our parents and handed them over to Sinclair Security. I knew from Aiden and Gage that Chase had taken a temporary position with Winters, Inc. working in the department they'd created from his company.

When Gage mentioned him, it was with admiration and even a hint of affection. They must have been getting along. I was happy for Chase. For both of them.

It wasn't that I was upset about being adopted. I'd been estranged from my parents for so long this additional wedge of separation didn't mean much. And Chase was my brother, blood or not.

But he'd lied to me. Lied about something fundamental to who I was, for years. He'd had chance after chance to come clean. Every time I thought about sending him a text or dialing his number I got angry all over again. I loved him, but I wasn't ready to forgive him.

I'd sent out my résumé and applied for a few jobs that

looked promising, even gone on a handful of interviews, but so far, I hadn't found anything that felt like a good fit. I hadn't had a job offer or a second interview. Even in a good market, finding the right job didn't happen overnight.

I'd only been looking a week, but on top of everything else not having a steady paycheck left me anxious. I had money saved, but that was for school. Not money to burn while I lounged around Winters House, unemployed.

Ditto for the apartment. I'd looked at a few places, but everything I liked was over my budget. Until I found a job it didn't make sense to sign a lease.

All the un-woven threads of my life kept me up, circling in my head, questions without answers, until I finally dropped off to sleep.

I woke in time for breakfast, still tired, but without circles under my eyes to show it. Perfect. Evidence of a sleepless night wasn't part of my plan.

I had another interview later in the morning, and I dressed for it before breakfast in a pale gray sheath dress with matching jacket. My plum heels brought out the hint of lavender in the gray fabric and matched the filmy, patterned scarf I wound around my neck. I braided sections of my hair, smoothed other sections until they shone, and twisted all of it into a chignon at the nape of my neck.

I reached for a pair of pearl earrings, stopped, and let my hand fall to my side. They went with the dress—professional, appropriate, and pretty. And they reminded me of my mother. I had nothing against pearls. I loved pearls. But not today. I chose a pair of simple sterling knots and put them on. Dressed in my armor of choice, I was ready to face the enemy.

Chapter Thirty-Two

Violet

It took everything I had to keep my face smooth and distantly polite when I saw the bright, eager look in Aunt Amelia's eyes as I strode into the dining room. If I'd had any doubt as to who was behind the rubber snake in my bed, they were razed as Amelia took in my composure and her face fell.

Her disappointment was palpable. It was hard not to laugh. Harder when Sophie smirked at Amelia and shot me a wink. I'd only been in Winters House a week, but I was learning that Sophie didn't miss much. Like Mrs. W, she was quiet, well mannered, and sharp as a tack. She'd have to be to keep up with Amelia.

"Did you sleep well?" Amelia asked, probing for a reaction, her dark blue eyes avidly searching my face, deep wrinkles furrowed in the thin, papery skin of her forehead.

"Like a baby," I said, "and you?"

"Amelia always sleeps like a baby. Or the dead," Annalise said from behind me, entering the dining room and taking a seat beside me. Her fiancé Riley lived with her in Winters House, but he rarely joined us for breakfast. A vice president with Sinclair Security, he left early on workdays to ensure he'd be home every night for dinner.

"Good to know," I said to Annalise, sliding a sly glance at Amelia. Her eyes flashed wide for a split-second. Good. Let her wonder what I might get up to while she slept.

Annalise spotted the byplay and to distract her I said, "How are the wedding plans going?"

"They're going," she said, rolling her eyes. "I don't know why a small wedding involves so many details."

"Told you so," Sophie said.

"It doesn't help that we're only mostly sure the house will be done in time," Annalise said, serving herself eggs and a biscuit from the platters on the table.

She and Riley were living in Winters House for the moment, only until the renovations on her parents' home were complete. Anna and James Winters had lived in an arts and crafts style cottage on the grounds of Winters House, less than a quarter mile away through the woods.

I didn't have the full story, and I wasn't comfortable asking, but somehow the house had caught fire a few weeks earlier and needed to be repaired before Annalise and Riley could move in. They wanted the wedding to take place in the great room of the house she'd grown up in and apparently the renovations to the kitchen were holding up the project. For reasons I didn't understand, it seemed vitally important to the family that the house in the woods be put to rights before Annalise and Riley's wedding.

Everyone knew the basics of the Winters family legend—two double murders, grieving children inheriting enormous wealth and a multinational corporation that made them all billionaires when Aiden was still in college.

I didn't know the details, and I wasn't about to ask. What Aiden and I had was too new to weigh down with memories of his past, and my family had provided more than enough drama for the last few weeks. If I'd known Annalise better I might have probed, but I didn't, and I hadn't.

"Do you need help?" I asked. "I have an interview this morning, and there are some jobs I want to look into when I get back, but otherwise I'm available if you need an extra set of hands."

"You don't mind?" Annalise asked.

"You'd better watch out," Sophie warned, "she's a demon with her lists."

"I'm not afraid of lists. I like lists. And she can't be as bad as Aiden."

"I forgot you worked as his assistant for a while," Annalise said.

"One of them," I agreed.

"I thought you were just there spying on him," Amelia said, still trying to get a rise out of me. I wasn't sure exactly what she wanted. For me to lose my temper? She'd have a long wait if that was her goal.

"In part, I was."

"Find anything interesting?" Amelia asked.

"Sadly, no. He told me he works too much to have any compromising stories hidden away."

Amelia snorted. "That's for damn sure. It's a waste of a healthy young man if you ask me."

"Agreed," I said. "But when I wasn't spying on him, I actually was working as his assistant. I wouldn't have lasted more than a day if I was afraid of lists."

"Well, if you really don't mind helping, there are some things I could use a hand with. This afternoon?"

"This afternoon is perfect," I said.

Something settled inside me at Annalise's acceptance of

my offer to help. I didn't like feeling like a freeloader, moving into Aiden's house, however temporarily, and acting like I belonged here. There wasn't much I could do to contribute.

Aiden didn't need my help covering the bills or the groceries, and Mrs. W and her day staff kept the house neat as a pin and running like clockwork. Abel fed everyone, and Mr. Henried and his gardening staff kept the grounds landscaped to perfection. None of them needed me, but Annalise did, and I needed something to do aside from stewing over my brother, my still-unknown biological parents, and my lack of a job or a home.

I finished my breakfast and excused myself, going back to Aiden's room to review my notes for the interview. I wasn't sure how interested I was in the job—bookkeeping for a medical supply parts company didn't sound terribly interesting—but I wasn't in a position to be picky.

The interview went well enough, but I wasn't hoping to be asked back. There wasn't much opportunity for promotion and the company was a long commute from the north side of Atlanta where I thought I'd prefer to live. Close to Aiden.

Was it stupid to assume we'd be together long enough that his location should factor into my job search? Maybe. I wanted to hope we'd be together, hope we had something real. If we did, I didn't want to take a job that would leave me sitting on I-85 for two hours a day getting to and from the office.

I got home, changed out of my suit and hunted up Annalise. She invited me out to lunch, and we ate cheeseburgers and fries surrounded by notebooks and a binder filled with clippings of things she'd already chosen for the wedding.

Annalise never mentioned Chase, and I tried not to think about it, but now that I knew she was his half-sister, I couldn't stop seeing the similarities. Their eyes were the same blue, their mother's blue, their hair the same shade of golden blond. Something in the curve of her lips, the rise of her cheekbone, mirrored my brother's face. It made me both ill at ease and weirdly comfortable with her, as if we were already friends.

Finally, in the middle of lunch, I blurted out, "Have you and Vance met Chase yet? Has your younger brother?"

Guilt crossed her face. "Yeah. Aiden said you were still angry with him. He asked us not to bring it up."

So like Aiden to look after me, and so selfish of me not to think about what Annalise and her siblings might be going through. Her eyes, so like Chase's, studied me with concerned apprehension, and I rushed to set her at ease.

"It's okay," I reassured her. "I'll get over it. I'm just mad, that's all. Do you mind talking about it? Meeting him?"

"No. I don't mind. We all went by the office the other day, had lunch together."

"Was it weird?"

Annalise hovered on the edge of uncertainty before she appeared to make a decision and shook her head, laughing a little under her breath. "It was hella weird. Vance is my twin brother, but when you put him side-by-side with Chase—" She shook her head again. "It's eerie."

"You should have seen Aiden's face the first time he saw my brother. Chase was ready to beat the shit out of him for daring to touch his baby sister and Aiden just stared. I didn't get it until I saw a picture of Vance. It is eerie. If Chase grew his hair out and got a few more tattoos, they could really mess with people."

Annalise burst out laughing. When she got herself

under control she said, "Yeah, you're going to fit in just fine."

My chest warmed at her easy acceptance, and I asked the thing I most wanted to know. "Is he doing okay? Could you tell?"

"He was a little stiff. Kind of standoffish at first. But he warmed up by the end of lunch. We're going to do it again in a day or two. Vance invited him over for dinner."

"That's good. That's good. I was worried."

"We're a lot to have dumped in your lap all at once," Annalise said, and I was reminded exactly why I hadn't spoken to my brother in over a week.

"Except it's not all at once," I said, bitterness sharpening my tone. "He's known about you for almost twenty years."

"And you still don't know where you came from, do you?" Annalise asked, gently.

I picked up a French fry, swiping it back and forth through a mound of ketchup. "Aiden said the Sinclairs are still trying to track down the attorney who brokered the adoption."

"Maybe if you knew, you wouldn't be so mad at Chase."

"Maybe," I said. "I'm curious. I want to know who they are, but they'll never be my parents. We may not be on good terms, but my parents are the ones who raised me, not whoever cashed that big check they wrote. I'm not mad at Chase because I don't know where I came from. I'm mad because he lied."

"I get that," Annalise said, munching on her own fries. "Believe me, I get that. Riley..." She trailed off.

"Riley what?" I probed, curious. I'd only seen them together over the last week, but the two of them were tight. Reading each other's minds, finishing each other's sentences tight. Like they'd been together for decades.

"It's a crazy story, but—"

It *was* a crazy story. Totally insane, involving a stalker, first love, lies, betrayals, attempted murder, and an eleven-year separation that finally ended in Annalise almost dying, and then getting engaged to Riley.

Wilder than any nighttime soap opera, I would have been entertained if the person telling the story had been a stranger and not a woman I hoped would become a friend. When she finished with her happy ending Annalise looked away, suddenly hesitant.

"What? What is it?"

"I don't think anyone's told him yet," Annalise said slowly, not meeting my eyes, "but William Davis, the man who was stalking me, the man who killed my aunt and uncle and almost killed me—he's Chase's father. He dated my mother in college before she met my father."

I stared at her, utterly speechless. "And no one's told Chase?"

"Not as far as I know. We've only met the one time, and it didn't feel like the kind of thing you throw in a conversation. Hey, it's great to meet you, so glad you're part of the family, and by the way, your sperm donor was a psychopath who died a few weeks ago while he was trying to kill me."

"I could see how that would be awkward," I said, dryly. I thought about the mess we were all in—the tangled past and the lies to cover it up. "Gage works with him every day now, right? Will you ask him to tell Chase? He needs to know, and the longer he doesn't the worse it will be when he finds out. And if he thinks all of you know and you're not telling him, making a fool of him—"

"Shit, I hadn't thought of it that way. I'll talk to Gage tonight."

"Thanks." I was angry at Chase, but that didn't mean I

wanted to see him hurt. The sooner he knew the truth about William Davis, the better for everyone.

"You're in pretty good shape for someone who almost got burned to death a few weeks ago," I said.

"True love heals all wounds." A private, secret smile spread across Annalise's lips. I could only hope she was right.

After lunch we drove around town taking care of errands on the wedding list—checking on the cake, the flowers, stopping by the caterer. I almost didn't make it home in time to set my plan in motion.

Chapter Thirty-Three

Violet

Annalise and I parted ways outside the kitchen, her to work on prepping more of her photographs for an upcoming gallery show and me to find out exactly where Sophie and Aunt Amelia were.

It didn't take me long to locate Sophie hiding from the heat of the afternoon in the cool, dark library, reading a book. Amelia lay stretched out on the sofa napping. I didn't interrupt, just eased back out of the room and jogged up the stairs to Aiden's suite as silently as I could.

Grabbing the rubber snake from the dressing room, I tucked it under my arm and made my way back down to the first level just as quietly, ducking into the dining room and shutting the door behind me.

Out of nowhere, I heard, "Do you need something?"

I jerked, startled, and almost dropped the snake. Mrs. W stood across the room in the doorway leading to the butler's pantry and the kitchen. Knowing she would understand, I held up the rubber snake and said, "I found this under my pillow last night."

Mrs. W nodded, knowingly. "I was wondering what her

mood was about this morning. She should have known you wouldn't scare that easily."

I was absurdly pleased at the compliment. "Does she always sit in that chair?" I asked, gesturing, snake in hand, at the seat Amelia had occupied since I'd been at Winters House.

"Always," Mrs. W confirmed, a sly smile ghosting across her lips.

"I'm just going to leave her a gift," I said, rounding the table and pulling out Amelia's chair.

Mrs. W made a show of not looking at me. "I've forgotten the napkins. I'll be back in a few minutes to set the table."

I grinned to myself and carefully positioned the snake where Amelia wouldn't see it until she pulled out her chair. Payback was a bitch. If this didn't do the trick, I'd figure out something else.

I was early to dinner. I had no intention of missing the show. Amelia must have gotten used to easy prey, or the indulgence of her family, because she was not at all prepared for the fat rat snake curled up on her chair when she drew it back from the table.

Her piercing scream brought feet pounding down the hallways. She raised one arm and pointed at me shrieking, "You! You did this!"

I stood with my hand on the back of my chair, serene, and said, "I'm afraid I have no idea what you're talking about. Did what?"

"This! This thing in my chair!"

Aiden and Gage entered the dining room at the same time, Aiden still carrying his briefcase, his jacket over his arm. I hadn't seen him in twenty-four hours. My heart eased to have him so close. I was in deep if I missed him that much after barely a day apart. I didn't have time to dwell on that thought.

Amelia threw her arm out, pointing it to me and accused, "She put a snake in my chair!"

"Excuse me? Where would I get a snake?"

Amelia crossed her arms over her chest and narrowed her eyes at me. "You know exactly where you got the snake," she snapped.

Seeing his great aunt was in no real distress, Aiden came up beside me, sliding his arm around my waist. He dropped his head to place a kiss on my cheek and whispered, "Missed you."

Revenge on Amelia suddenly seemed unimportant. I went up on my toes and pressed a kiss to his lips, murmuring against them, "Missed you, too."

From across the room, Amelia barked, "Don't you ignore me."

I didn't know which of us she was talking to, and I didn't care. Gage rounded the table to see the rubber snake on the chair, shook his head, and with a laugh said to his great aunt, "What did you do?"

"What did *I* do? She—she—"

"Are you saying Violet put the snake on your chair?" Aiden asked, his eyes twinkling but his face deadly serious. "Violet? Did you do this?"

I pulled away from Aiden and strode around the table to stand beside Gage. Pretending to study the snake on Amelia's chair I said consideringly, "You know, it does look an awful lot like the snake I found under my pillow last night when I went up to bed. Except, I put that snake in the closet. I have no idea how it could have gotten down here. Curious."

Gage scooped up the snake and tossed it across the table

to Aiden, who reached up to pluck it out of the air. He gave it a good look, turning it over in his hands. "Realistic. And heavy." To Amelia, he said, "That's twice. First the short-bread and now Violet got you with your own prop. I think it's a sign."

"A sign I need to step up my game," Amelia muttered under her breath.

"It was pretty good, actually," I said. "You almost had me there for a minute."

"You didn't scream," Amelia said, clearly disappointed.

I shrugged a shoulder and smiled in genuine amusement. "Maybe next time."

"There's not going to be a next time," Aiden pronounced. "Right, Amelia? We're not trying to run Violet out of the house."

"Is that the same snake you used on Mrs. W? The one you put in with the root vegetables in the cellar?" Gage asked.

"No, that one is long gone," Aiden said.

I thought I heard Amelia say something like, "I know where to get another one," but I wasn't going to call her out. The whole snake under the pillow thing might have been funny if it hadn't been my pillow.

I stepped away, about to cross the room to Aiden when Gage's hand closed around my arm. In a low voice meant for my ears alone, he said, "I talked to Annalise this afternoon. I'll tell him. Tomorrow."

I nodded once. "Thank you."

Gage let go of my arm and I walked away, wondering if he was warming up to me. He hadn't had to set my mind at ease, and it was nice of him to bother. Still, it wasn't like he'd welcomed me with open arms. The night before at dinner, he'd poked at me the entire meal, staying just on the right side of good manners, but pushing me nonetheless. If he was treating Chase well, I'd let it go.

After the snake incident, the denizens of Winters House seemed to accept me as one of their own. Amelia, rather than trying another prank, sidled up to me one afternoon when I was using Aiden's desk in his office and showed me a catalog of fake insects. They were alarmingly realistic. Apparently, my pranking her back had convinced Aunt Amelia she had a fellow troublemaker in the house.

I might have suggested something about cockroaches in Gage's sock drawer. I'd definitely told Amelia if she put a single bug in Mrs. W's kitchen I'd rat her out in a heartbeat. Amelia had admitted she was banned from pranking Mrs. W.

Aiden loved his great aunt, but he also loved Mrs. W. The bullion in the shower incident had been a step too far, even for his indulgence.

I'd been at Winters House a full two weeks, no closer to making up with my brother or finding a job. I'd gone on another two interviews, neither of which had been promising. One asked me back for a second interview but offered a salary too low for my experience. The other hadn't been a good fit, the job more limited than what I wanted and the benefits minimal.

I was in the library with Annalise going over ideas for flower placement during the ceremony when Aiden came in brandishing a piece of cream linen resumé paper.

Shoving the page in my face, Aiden demanded, "Violet, why did I find your résumé on my printer?"

I took the paper from him and scanned it before setting it down beside me. "Thank you. The printer was taking too long to warm up. I was going to go back for it later."

"That doesn't answer my question. Why are you printing out your résumé?"

Giving him a long look, I said slowly, "Because I'm looking for a job. I always email it in with my application, but it's good form to bring a copy with me to the interview."

"Don't be a smart ass," he said. "I can find you a job."

I gave in to the urge to roll my eyes but resisted the smile that wanted to crack across my face at Annalise's laugh. Patiently, I said, "I'm aware of that. I don't want you to get me a job, Aiden. I can get my own job."

"It would be easier if you'd just let me take care of it," he said.

I took a deep breath, pushing back the sarcastic comment that wanted to jump from my mouth. "Has it ever occurred to you that your life would be a lot more relaxing if you stopped trying to take care of everything for everyone?"

Annalise snorted a laugh and said under her breath, "That'll be the day."

Aiden gave her a disgruntled look and said, "Stay out of this. You're a pain in my ass, and you're Riley's problem now."

"I'll always be your problem," Annalise said affectionately. "But I'll get out of your way." With a sympathetic glance in my direction, she left the library, closing the door behind her.

When we were alone, Aiden said, "This isn't necessary, Violet. I thought you were going back to school. I told you I'd set up an appointment with the graduate admissions counselor—"

"And I told you," I said, standing and crossing my arms over my chest, "that I didn't want you to do that. I haven't decided about school yet. I'm still thinking about it."

"You've been thinking about it for the last few years,"

Aiden countered. "It won't take much to get you enrolled in the MBA program at Emory. If you want a job, I'll find something you can do part-time."

"You're not listening to me. I don't want an MBA. I'm looking at the accountancy program at UGA. They have one of the best programs in the country, and their rate of graduates who pass the CPA exam the first time is excellent. Plus, they have a concentration in data analysis that's really interesting—"

"Athens is too far away," Aiden argued.

"It's a little over an hour. And MARTA has a bus. I haven't checked the times, I don't know if it would line up with my class schedule, but I probably wouldn't even have to drive."

"You are not taking public transportation."

"Then I guess it's a good thing I'm not asking your permission," I said, my voice perfectly calm when what I really wanted to do was ball my résumé up and throw it in his face.

"Violet, you're being unreasonable. An MBA with an accounting concentration is more versatile and—"

"Aiden. Stop."

His look of surprise was almost comical. Not many people told Aiden Winters 'No' when he was giving orders. Before he could get going again, I tried to explain.

"I'm not being unreasonable, and you're still not listening. I know you're used to organizing everyone's life, but I don't want you to organize mine."

"I'm not trying to organize your life, I just want things to be easier for you."

"Aiden, I need you to understand. I've spent most of my life doing what I was told because someone else thought it was best for me. Doing what was best for me left me standing in a gas station in the middle of the night calling Chase for help because I was jobless, homeless, and one of our father's friends almost raped me. And do you know what I learned from that? I learned that I can't trust anyone to know what's best for me. *I'm* the only one who knows what's best for me."

"Was playing corporate spy and getting caught your idea of what's best for you? Because if—"

"No, of course, not. I made a mistake. I'm going to make mistakes. But they'll be my mistakes. And when I get a job, or finish school, that will be mine too. Mine, because I earned it, not because someone smoothed the way for me."

"There's nothing wrong with asking for help, Violet."

"I don't need any help," I said in a near shout.

"Really? From where I'm standing, you're still unemployed and homeless."

That struck me right in the gut. The blood drained from my cheeks leaving me abruptly cold. Nausea rolled, and I stepped back, looking for escape.

"That's not fair." Even to me the words sounded childish.

"Life isn't fair, Violet."

"I'm aware of that," I said, suddenly exhausted. I was very aware how unfair life was. Sometimes it threw you bounty you hadn't earned. And sometimes you worked your ass off and got served shit.

Life wasn't fair, but was it too much to expect Aiden to be?

He pressed harder. "There's nothing wrong with using what advantage you have to make things easier."

I was beating him over the head and he still didn't get it. "I'm not arguing against asking for help. But you're not waiting for me to ask. You're just telling me what to do."

"Because I'm right, and you don't know what you want. I'm trying to give you direction."

I'd heard those words before. Hearing my father's criticism coming from Aiden was too much.

"Did you decide to take my father's advice? Are you trying to give me a firm hand? Some guidance? You can go to hell."

It was Aiden's turn to go pale. His cheeks went grey under his tan. His eyes were stricken when he said, "Violet, that's not what I meant."

"That's what it sounded like," I said, quietly, too drained to raise my voice. "And I'm done with that. If you just want me to be an extension of you, to do what I'm told and let you make all the decisions, then this isn't going to work. I don't want to live like that."

I didn't want to hear any more excuses. I needed some air.

A minute alone.

A break.

Pushing past Aiden, I stalked from the library, blinking against a sudden rush of tears. The last thing I wanted was to be caught crying in the middle of the hall. A hand closed around my elbow, pulling me backward into a dark room.

The light flicked on and I saw floor to ceiling racks of wine behind glass doors, discrete gold locks built into the handles. A square island in the center of the room with a black granite top. And Aiden, turning the bolt of the heavy wooden door, locking us in.

Chapter Thirty-Four

Violet

"What are you doing?" I asked, momentarily struck dumb. I'd been trying to get away from him. How had we ended up locked in a tiny room together?

The determination on his face answered that question. Because Aiden wasn't done talking, that's how.

"There's no privacy in this house. Unlike the rest of them, I'm smart enough to remember to lock the door."

"Let me go. I don't want to talk to you right now."

"Not until you hear me out."

"I think I've heard enough of what you have to say."

"No, you haven't."

"Aiden—"

"I'm sorry."

"What?"

"I'm sorry. You're right. I wasn't listening. I was treating you like a problem to solve. I don't want you to be an extension of me. I want you to be you."

"You have to let me make my own decisions," I said quietly. "I need to figure this stuff out for myself."

"I know." Aiden took a step forward, backing me into the island, his hips pinning me in place. He ran his hands down my arms and dropped his forehead to mine. At the contact, he let out a long breath, just standing there, holding me, saying nothing. After a long moment, he stepped back.

"You have to understand. I've been taking care of my family since I was twenty. My parents were gone. My aunt and uncle had been dead since I was a kid. It was all on me. The company, the kids. I was trying to convince the board I could take over for my father and helping Annalise and Vance with their college applications. Taking Tate to get braces. Sitting up all night getting puked on when Charlie had the flu. I was scared out of my mind, and the only way I got through it was to convince everyone I knew exactly what I was doing. Especially myself. I couldn't stop to doubt or I'd lose my nerve. Eventually, I guess I convinced myself I really did know everything."

"Oh, Aiden." I reached for him, my heart breaking at the thought of him carrying so much on his own.

Aiden raised a hand to ward me off. "I don't want you to feel sorry for me. That's not it. I'm trying to tell you, I don't know how to do this. I've never done it before."

"Done what?"

"This." He gestured with his hand between us.

"A relationship? You were married."

"She was never a partner, Violet. She was happy to let me set the agenda as long as I signed the checks."

"I don't want you to take care of me, Aiden." I reached for him again, catching his hand in mine. He let me pull him closer. "I just want to be with you."

"I want to be with you too," he said.

"I don't want to be just another thing for you to take

care of, Aiden. I don't want to be a line item on your to-do list."

"I don't know how to sit back and let you struggle when I can make it easier for you," he admitted.

I let go of his hand and hooked my fingers in his belt, tugging him close enough to wrap my arms around his waist.

Resting my cheek against his chest, feeling the thump of his heartbeat through his dress shirt, I let out a deep sigh.

"I need you to try," I said. "The way you take care of your family, of the people who matter to you, is one of the things I love about you, Aiden. It means everything to know that if I need you, all I have to do is ask. But that doesn't mean I don't need to do this on my own."

He rested his cheek on the top of my head, his arms around my shoulders, the tension draining from his body.

"I can try. I promise I'll try."

"That's all I ask. If it helps, I've never done this before either."

Aiden raised his head and leaned back, holding me against him, studying my face. "I know I'm not the first man you've been involved with."

"No, you're not the first. But it's never been like this before. No one's ever mattered like this before."

He traced the curve of my lower lip with his fingertip. "Scared?"

"Terrified." I tasted his skin against my mouth.

Dropping his hands, he gathered the fabric of my skirt and hiked it above my hips. Cool air slid over my skin as he lifted me and set me on the island, making space for himself between my spread legs.

"So am I," he admitted. "I'm in love with you. I think I fell in love with you that day in my office when I hired you as my assistant. You were so cool, like ice, but underneath I could tell you wanted to tell me to go to hell. I'd never wanted a woman like I wanted you. I figured I'd fuck you and then fire you."

The abrupt vulgarity startled a laugh out of me. "Lovely," I said. "But I figured that part out in the interview."

He tucked a strand of hair behind my ear, his dark eyes hot and a little hesitant. "I knew that too. And I never saw it coming. We were playing a game, playing each other, and then you were the last thing I thought about at night and the only person I wanted to see first thing in the morning. You're sharp as hell, and sarcastic, and funny, and a stone-cold bitch when you need to be. You're so fucking gorgeous I can have you all night and still not want to let you out of bed in the morning. And I'm scared to death I'm going to fuck this up and lose you."

"Aiden, I love you, too. You're not going to lose me."

"You don't know what it's like. Not yet. My family is huge and nosy. If they aren't poking around in my business, it's the media looking for dirt. I work too much. I'm overbearing, and I'm used to getting my way."

"I know all that, and I'm still here. I love you. You, Aiden. Not your family, or your name, or your money. I love you. I love the way you kiss and I love watching movies with you. I love dancing with you and talking to you, and when I make you smile I feel like I've touched the sun. I just need you to let me be a partner. I don't want to be one more burden. You carry too much already."

"You could never be a burden, Violet. I love you. I love you until it makes me crazy. You can trust me."

"I don't think there's anyone I trust as much as I trust you," I said, hearing the tremor in my voice. It was true, and I think that scared me as much as loving him. The only other person I'd ever trusted this much was my brother. Thinking about him didn't exactly build my confidence.

Aiden's lips brushed the hinge of my jaw, hovering over the tender skin before he lightly bit the side of my neck, sending shivers all the way to my toes. He ran his hands down my sides and I knew what he wanted. Bracing myself on my elbows, I raised my hips off the granite countertop, letting him push up my skirt and slide the scrap of lace beneath down my legs. The stone was cold against my heated skin.

My arms holding me up, my legs spread wide to Aiden's hungry gaze, all I could do was lay there and watch him. He moved slowly, so slowly it was torture waiting for him to touch me. One by one, he slid the pearl buttons of my blouse open, the thin silk falling away to reveal pale gray lace that matched the thong he'd shoved in his pocket.

A guttural groan rumbled in his throat. His fingers shook as he hooked them in the cups of my bra and yanked the lace beneath my breasts. They were heavy enough, full enough, to hold it there, my flesh spilling out into his hands. I felt like a virgin sacrifice, body on offer, ready and willing to be taken.

Ready, willing, and eager. But Aiden wanted to make me wait. His hands molded my breasts, his mouth dropped to mine. His tongue thrust inside and I wished it was his cock. Fingers pinched my nipples, sparks shooting straight to my clit. I rolled my hips into his, drowning in his kiss, desperate to get him to move, to get naked, to fuck me.

Then he was nudging my entrance, pressing inside, breaking our kiss to take my breast in his mouth as he filled my pussy with his thick cock. He started slowly, sliding deep, grinding the base of his cock into my clit before easing almost all the way free of my clasping pussy, then doing it all over again. And again.

His mouth fed at my breasts, sucking, nipping, devouring me whole, his cock keeping up the same steady pace. Thrust, grind, slide. I was losing my mind, the slow build pushing me higher and higher, not quite enough to shove me over the edge.

Aiden owned me. My heart. My body. Everything.

I was blind with need, deaf to everything but the rasp of my breath, the slick sounds of our bodies moving together, the growls of possession rumbling from Aiden's chest. I barely registered the rattle of the door handle, the sound of muted voices through the heavy wooden door.

Aiden ignored it. I whimpered into the quiet room, falling back, the cold granite firing off the nerves in my damp skin. Arms splayed, I arched my back, pressing my breast deeper into Aiden's mouth.

More.

Faster.

Harder.

I didn't know what I was saying, what I was begging for. I wrapped my legs around his waist, hooking my feet for leverage and thrusting into him, holding him there so he couldn't slide out.

"Please. I need it, Aiden."

His eyes went black with lust, his grin feral with possession. Hand on my thighs, Aiden spread my legs, pushing my knees wide and flat to the counter, pinning me in place. I tried to squirm, to take more of him, to get him to move. I managed no more than an inch before his grip stilled my restless body.

"Tell me what you want," he ordered in words so low and rough I had to struggle to make sense of them.

When I did, I had only one answer. "You. I want you."

"You want this?" Aiden drew back until the head of his cock was barely past the gate of my pussy. He slammed inside, the sudden pressure on my clit driving a burst of pleasure straight to the base of my skull, exploding in my brain.

"Yes. God, yes. Please. Yes." I wasn't making sense. It didn't matter. Aiden knew what I wanted. He always did.

He leaned over me, covering me with his body, sucking and biting at my shoulders, my neck, my breasts as he fucked me in hard, deep strokes that got more and more uneven, ragged, harder and rougher as we climbed the peak together.

I went first, my pussy seizing around his cock, sucking and clenching so hard I couldn't breathe. His control shattered, his teeth sinking into the side of my neck, his groan torn from him as he came, filling me with him, sending me flying.

It wasn't until later, when I had my breath back, that I remembered the noise at the door.

"Oh, my god."

"I know." I could feel him grinning into my neck, licking the spot he'd bitten. I shivered, my still tender pussy pulsing around his softening cock.

"Not that. Did someone almost come in?"

Aiden chuckled, the shaking of his body sending more aftershocks through me. "They tried."

"I should be embarrassed,"

"Are you?"

I thought about it. "Maybe later. I feel too good right now to be embarrassed about anything."

Aiden braced himself on his elbows and looked down at me. A frown creased his forehead. Shifting his weight, he lifted a hand and stroked the side of my neck where his mouth had been, tracing a tender spot there before sliding to my shoulder and from there to the side of my breast.

"What?" I asked, alarmed at the dark expression in his eyes.

"I marked you. I'm too rough with you."

Wiggling my arm from my side, I caught his fingers and brought them to my lips. I kissed them once, then again, then turned my face into his palm and rested my lips there. Tasting the salt of his skin, I said, "I liked it. I love that you lose control with me."

"I never want to hurt you." The remorse in his voice burned a path straight to my soul.

"And if I asked you to stop? If I looked like I was in pain?" I took his face in my hands and brought his mouth to mine. "You'd never hurt me, Aiden."

"I couldn't," he swore against my lips.

"No, you couldn't. You'd never hurt someone you loved."

"Never," he agreed, between kisses, "Never you, Violet. I love you."

His mouth moved to my neck, my shoulders, passing over my skin in reverent, gentle touches so filled with love my heart sighed. "I love you." He kissed and made promises, his cock hardening inside me, rocking into me, as sweet and gentle as the first time had been rough and claiming. I came beneath him, clutching his arms and sobbing out my orgasm, overwhelmed with pleasure and raw emotion.

Aiden followed me, breathing into my ear, "Mine. You're mine, Violet. Always."

At the time, his words filled my heart with joy. I wanted that. Wanted to be his.

I should have stopped and thought about what that meant. Thought about what he was saying.

By the time I realized, it was too late.

I was too lost in him, in the promise of us, to protect myself from the inevitable.

And when the crash came, it tore me apart.

CHAPTER THIRTY-FIVE

VIOLET

A few days after the scene in the wine room, Gage got the bright idea to have a family dinner, complete with the newest member of the Winters family, my brother. I wasn't sure if he was trying to bring Chase further into the Winters fold or aggravate me.

Knowing Gage, he was multitasking. He tossed the idea out in the middle of dinner, fully aware that everyone would love the idea, making me look like a churlish bitch if I objected.

The truth was, I was nursing a grudge. It was long past time to forgive Chase. He'd screwed up. Fine. But he'd done it because he loved me. I could cut him some slack in the face of decades of being the best big brother on earth.

Unable to stop himself from poking at me, Gage said point blank, "He won't come unless you invite him."

I resisted the urge to roll my eyes. The only thing worse than Gage getting under my skin was letting him know how deeply he annoyed me. I buried the need to scowl or make a sarcastic remark and gave him my best ice queen.

"I'll call him tonight. Find out when everyone is free and I'll make sure he's here."

Gage only inclined his head in agreement, mischief sparking in his eyes. He knew he drove me nuts. My hand itched to wing my dinner roll at his head, ice queen be damned. Instead, I raised my chin and turned my eyes to Aiden, dismissing Gage. If a low chuckle drifted over from his side of the table, I ignored it.

Chase being Chase, he didn't make me work for it. I called, he apologized for lying, and I said I was sorry for taking so long to get over it. Just like when we were kids, that was all it took. I could hold a grudge like a champion, but not against Chase.

"I'll come to dinner if you'll think about coming home," Chase said.

I sighed, half in exasperation and half in affection, looking up to make sure the door to Aiden's office was firmly closed.

"I'll think about it."

"It's too soon, Vivi. You barely know this guy."

I let out an exasperated breath. "I've known him for more than six weeks."

"Do you hear yourself? Six weeks. That's nothing. You go away with him for the weekend, and now you're living with him?"

"I'm not living with him. I'm looking for a job, and as soon as I find one I'm getting my own place."

"You don't need your own place. You have a place. Here."

"Chase, I can't live with you forever."

"I didn't say you had to. But it doesn't make sense for you to move out and pay rent on your own apartment when I have plenty of room here."

I raised my eyes to the ceiling, praying someone in the heavens would deliver me from overbearing men. "Can we talk about this later? On the list of things I have to figure out about my life, where I'm living is somewhere in the middle. First I need to find a new job."

"I'm sure your boyfriend would—"

"Shut. Up. I've already had this argument with him, I don't need to hear it from you. I can find my own job."

"Okay, okay. Shutting up."

More than ready to change the subject I said, "So, did you hear about our little raid on Mom and Dad's file cabinet?"

"Gage got me a copy of the papers you gave the Sinclairs," Chase said, carefully.

"Aiden said they're trying to track down the attorney who brokered the adoption."

"Are you trying to find them? Your biological parents?"

"Of course. Why wouldn't I?"

"I can think of a lot of reasons why," Chase snapped. "Starting with the fact that there are all sorts of things fucked up about that adoption. Not just how much they paid. You're poking a hornet's nest."

"Is this why you didn't tell me? Because you didn't think I should go looking for them?"

Chase was silent for so long I checked the screen of my phone to make sure we hadn't been disconnected.

Finally, gently, he said, "I'm afraid of what you're going to find, Vivi. I've read that contract. More than once. That was not a standard adoption. This wasn't some kid who got pregnant by accident and decided to have the baby and give it to a good family. Mom and Dad paid three quarters of a million dollars for you. That kind of money? It does not point to good things."

"I don't know what that means, Chase," I said.

He sighed, and when he spoke again he sounded sad. "I don't know either, Vivi. Not exactly. But I talked to Gage about it, talked to Cooper Sinclair. After their father died they found out he was involved in some shady business. Yours was not the only high-priced adoption they've come across. They're digging, and they don't have anything solid, but people paying that much money for babies...I'm scared for you. I wish you'd just let it go."

"I can't." The words felt pulled out of me, breaking as I spoke. "I need to know."

"Vivi, if you think you're going to find someone to make up for what happened with Mom and Dad, I don't—"

"That's not it. I'm not looking for another family, or a mother to love me. I just want to know. I want to know the whole story so I can put it behind me. They lied to us, and you lied to me. I want to know the truth."

I couldn't explain it any better than that. It nagged at me, not knowing where I came from. I kept thinking that if I just had answers I could close it all up like a book and put it on the shelf. Make it part of my history and leave my parents and that contract behind.

"Okay. I'm not going to try to stop you. But I'm here. Always. You know that, right? Forget about all this stuff with the Winters family. You're my family. You're my sister, my Vivi, and nothing's ever going to change that."

"I know that, Chase. I love you, and I'm sorry I was such a bitch about the whole thing, you just hurt my feelings." A tear ran down my cheek, taking me by surprise.

"Yeah, well, sometimes I'm an asshole."

I giggled, the sound watery, but it was enough to reassure Chase.

"See you at dinner?"

"Don't be late," I warned.

"It's not me you have to worry about," Chase said before he hung up.

He hadn't been at Winters, Inc. for long, but he'd heard plenty about Aiden's reputation for working late. His comment might have been a stab in the dark, but it turned out to be wholly accurate. The night Chase was supposed to join the family for dinner, my phone vibrated with a text.

Running late. Be there for dessert.

Was he kidding me? The first time I was here with his entire family and he was bailing on me? Not going to happen.

"What is it?" Annalise asked seeing my expression as I stared at my phone.

"Aiden's going to be late."

"How late?" she asked, grimly.

"Not late at all if he values his life," I said under my breath. Headlights flashed through the front windows. A car pulling into the courtyard. "Excuse me."

I went down the hall to Aiden's office and pulled up his number, pacing the carpet in front of his desk. He answered with a rushed, "Violet, I can't talk now."

"Tell me what's going on."

"Later, sweetheart. I'll try to make dessert, I promise." To someone else he said, "Put that over there and then get me copies of the file I emailed. Close the door behind you."

"Aiden!" I shouted.

Silence. Then, vaguely annoyed, "Violet."

"What's going on that's more important than dinner?"

"There's an opportunity, a deal we lost opened back up. We need to reevaluate our initial offer and see what we can do to—"

"Stop," I interrupted. "Stop and think about what I

asked, Aiden. What's going on that's more important than dinner with your family? Everyone is here. And do you know who isn't here? You."

"I know, Violet, but they won't miss me, and I have to get this—"

"Aiden, no. They will miss you. You're crazy if you think they won't. Tell me why you work so hard."

"Vi, you can't run a company like this without working hard. It's part of the deal."

"But you don't have to. What do you need? More money? Another house? Another plane? Why do you do it?" I knew the answer, I just wanted to make him say it out loud, to force him to really hear the words.

"Violet, my father left me this company. This is my heritage. This company belongs to my family. I'm working for them. For all of them. For Vance's little girl, for the kids I'm going to have one day."

"I know," I said quietly. "And what do you think your family would rather have? More money or you at the dinner table?"

"Violet—"

"No, be honest. If I asked them. If I asked Charlie right now what she'd rather have, higher stock prices or her brother here for a family dinner, what do you think she'd say?"

"Vi—"

"Or Gage? If I dragged him in here right now and asked, what do you think he'd say? Tell me the truth."

"He'd tell me to put the offer together tomorrow and get my ass home," Aiden said, slowly.

"I know that things are going to come up that you can't avoid. I know that you love what you do, that Winters, Inc. is a part of who you are. But this can wait until tomorrow, can't it? I'll come in and help if you need an extra hand. You've given so much of your life to that company, so much of your life to your family. They're here, happy and healthy, celebrating being together, and you're missing it. You worked so hard to get them here and you're missing it. Come home."

Aiden went quiet. I heard a tapping in the background, his pen against his desk as he thought about his options. Finally, he said, "I'll be there in twenty."

I was still saying, "See you soon," when he hung up.

"Thank you."

I jumped at the unexpected voice and turned, almost dropping my phone. I bobbled it, the smooth plastic case slipping through my fingers before I managed to get a grip on the edges.

Charlie stood there, her tousled auburn curls pulled back on one side with a sparkly bobby pin in the shape of a dragonfly. A smile curved her lips and her eyes were soft on my face.

"Thank you," she said again. Embarrassed by her warmth, I rubbed the screen of my phone against my hip and slid it in my pocket.

"He works too much," I said, trying for distantly cool and instead sounding awkward. It killed me to admit that I cared what anyone thought of me, but I wanted Charlie to like me. She was Aiden's baby sister, the sister he'd practically raised, and at our first meeting, she hadn't seemed thrilled I was with her brother.

"I know. He fired me for being a workaholic, but does he slow down? No."

"Well, you know it's not the same," I said, dryly. "Aiden is the King of the Universe. Mortal rules don't apply."

"Ha! He'd like to think so. You'll have fun curing him of

the idea. I already heard about the résumé fight. And the locked wine room."

"Oh, God." I sank into one of the armchairs opposite Aiden's desk, smacking my cool hands over my suddenly fiery cheeks. "I thought I heard someone try to come in."

Charlie smirked. "That's the downside of this family—no privacy. We know everything, and what we don't know, we eventually badger out of you."

"Privacy is overrated. Privacy is what you get when your family doesn't care about you." I could taste the bitterness in my words, and I didn't like it.

I wanted to shrug it off as if it didn't matter that my parents didn't love me. I couldn't forget my father not bothering to greet me when we'd visited. He hadn't asked how I was. Where I was living. If I was alright.

I had all the privacy I wanted from them, and I would have traded it in a second to know they cared what happened to me. They weren't built like that. I knew it, I'd had a lifetime of experience as a teacher. And still, I held on to a grain of hope.

The sympathy in Charlie's ocean blue eyes burned. I didn't want her to feel sorry for me. How could she not? She'd lost her own parents, but from all accounts, they'd loved their children with everything they had.

Aiden had been young, but he'd stepped into the breach to hold the foundation strong. They were loud, and interfering, and nosy, but this family knew how to love. I couldn't help but envy Chase a little for having a claim to a portion of that love.

I was adrift, tethered only to Chase and he'd found himself a whole new family.

I shoved my self-pity aside, bolstered a little when Charlie said, "Mrs. W likes you. Aunt Amelia says you have starch. And you got Aiden to unchain himself from his desk and come home for dinner. I guess you can stay." Her quirky smile pulled a faint grin from me.

"I definitely won't dump a bucket of water on your head," she added, the smile flashing into mischief, making her look a decade younger. I'd bet Aiden had had his hands full with Charlie when she was a teenager.

"You dumped a bucket of water on Elizabeth's head?"

"From the landing. They were on their way to a black tie dinner. She was wearing chiffon and her hair was in these huge curls."

I smacked a hand over my mouth, my shoulders shaking with laughter as I imagined Elizabeth's cool, blond beauty drenched with water, her mascara running, hair flattened, chiffon dress turned to sodden rags.

When I got my breath back I said, "Please tell me someone has a picture of that."

"I wish. Aiden was furious. I was grounded for a month. Totally worth it."

"I bet. The last time we met I was tempted to throw my champagne in her face. If she comes near Aiden again, I might."

"I'll keep my phone handy, just in case."

The family dinner went better than I expected. Annalise had spread the word about Aiden's attempt to bail and my dragging him home. We all marveled at how much Chase and Vance looked alike, which was only a little weird. Chase sat across from me, both of us flanking Aiden at the head of the table, and watched us with sharp eyes all through the meal. If he was looking for fault in Aiden, he didn't find it. We were all on our best behavior.

Gage didn't poke at me, Aiden didn't provoke Chase, Aunt Amelia didn't hide any plastic insects in the salad.

All in all, things were good. I should have been sleeping like a baby. Instead, I lay awake beside Aiden, staring at the ceiling, unable to settle my mind. When I slept my dreams were uneasy, and when I woke in the dark with a jerk, I had only memories of shadowy hallways. Of wandering in the dark. Of being lost.

I didn't need a psychology degree or a shrink to tell me the loose ends in my life were plaguing my sleep. I knew once things were settled—once I found a job, an apartment, got a name from the Sinclairs—I'd feel less adrift.

Telling myself that I was doing my best didn't help. Every day I sent out résumés, made phone calls. I went on interviews and got turned down for a job I really wanted. This time it turned out I wasn't qualified enough, reminding me that if I didn't get a job, I'd never save enough for tuition, and I'd never finish school.

Every day I asked Aiden if he'd heard from Cooper, if they'd found the attorney or a name. Every day he said they hadn't. With each day that passed, my uncertainty grew.

Maybe they wouldn't find anyone. Maybe the contract was just a dead end and I'd never know. Maybe I wouldn't find a job I liked, wouldn't be able to save enough for school. Wouldn't get in when I applied. My grades had been good, my GMAT scores were strong, but the program was competitive.

Aiden's words ate at me. I was still jobless and homeless.

Five years after my parents had thrown me out, and I had nothing to show for myself. I'd spent most of that time helping Chase build a company that no longer existed, and I'd lost a chunk of my savings when Harrison had changed the contracts and stolen it out from under us. I was back at square one. Again.

I lay beside Aiden in bed, still and quiet so I didn't wake him, my thoughts going in circles. I didn't want him to know about any of it—the bad dreams, that I wasn't sleeping.

He wouldn't be able to stop himself from trying to fix everything. He'd never understand that if he fixed it for me, I'd only feel worse. I just needed to hang in there and keep trying. Eventually, I'd find the right job, find a place to live, find the people behind that contract. I knew everything would work out.

But in the dark of night, my worries keeping me from sleep, I didn't quite believe it.

Chapter Thirty-Six

Violet

A few days before Annalise and Riley's wedding I sat at Aiden's desk putting together an application for a job opening I'd found in the paper. From the brief description, it sounded perfect. A bookkeeping position, full time, but with flexible hours and the opportunity to do some of the work from home.

If I got it, the flexible hours would let me go back to school part-time. The company was only accepting applications through the mail, and while I had cream linen envelopes to match my résumé paper, I didn't have a stamp.

Aiden's desk drawers were as organized as I would have expected, each one partitioned with wood inserts to hold pens, paper clips, envelopes—anything and everything he might need.

Except for stamps.

I was about to go hunt down Mrs. W—if there was a stamp somewhere in this massive house, she would know—when I spotted the border of an American flag sticking out from beneath the wooden tray in the center desk drawer.

I nudged the tray to the side and pulled at the flag, hoping it was a sheet of stamps. It was, and in my relief at finally finding what I needed, I didn't realize the paperclip around the sheet of stamps had snagged on a stapled set of documents Aiden had shoved beneath the tray.

I peeled a stamp from the sheet and stuck it to my envelope, setting the envelope aside. I was preparing to replace the stamps when I spotted a date in Aiden's handwriting scrawled on the border of the pages I'd dislodged from beneath the tray.

My birthdate—and a phone number that was not my phone number. My palms damp, my heart pounding a little too hard, I teased the papers from beneath the tray. It was a copy of the contract for my adoption.

Why would this be in Aiden's desk? And what was that phone number? It didn't have an Atlanta exchange. It couldn't be Sinclair Security. My hands trembling, my stomach a little queasy, I opened my laptop and pulled up the reverse lookup form on the White Pages website. I typed in the number and hit enter.

It only took a second to return a result. A residential number in Huntsville, Alabama. The webpage obscured the name and address connected to the phone number. For an additional fee, I could have that and more.

I tried to tell myself I was chasing a dead end. This couldn't be anything important, or Aiden would have told me. He'd said, repeatedly, that they hadn't found anything. A little lightheaded, I pushed back from Aiden's desk and ran upstairs to get my purse.

All it took was a credit card number and I had what I'd been looking for. A name. LeAnne Gates. An address outside of Huntsville where, according to the background check I'd acquired for a mere $12.99, LeAnne Gates had lived for the past fifteen years.

Prior to that, she lived in a suburb of Chattanooga, not far from where I'd grown up. She'd been married and divorced, was an only child, had no criminal record, but a tidy collection of traffic violations. She'd declared bankruptcy in her early twenties, after her divorce, but had purchased a house a few years after. No record of a mortgage, and a quick Internet search showed that the property had cost over half a million dollars. It had been purchased exactly 28 years before, a month after my birthdate.

Bile rose in the back of my throat, caustic and sour. I swallowed hard and kept looking. She'd moved again five years later, this time to a house twice as big and twice as expensive. Again, no record of a mortgage.

The background report didn't give me her employment history. I couldn't tell what kind of car she drove. I could be way off base.

But LeAnne Gates's phone number in Aiden's handwriting was scrawled across the contract for my adoption. A contract that paid seven hundred and fifty thousand dollars a month before she'd purchased a new home for cash.

I stared down at the angular spikes of Aiden's handwriting.

Aiden.

He'd said they'd found nothing.

Promised me they were still looking.

And here was what I'd wanted, right in front of me, hidden in his desk drawer.

My stomach heaved, and I swallowed hard, again. I clicked the icon of the printer, the whir and clank of the ink cartridge deafening in the silent room. Three pages slid into the tray, one by one. I folded them and slipped them into my purse, then sank back into Aiden's chair, holding my purse on my lap, unable to tear my eyes from the slash of Aiden's writing on white paper.

He'd lied to me.

I heard myself tell him that he was the only one I could trust.

What a fucking idiot. I was so stupid. Sinclair Security was the best. Maybe they'd been hamstrung without any evidence, but now they had contracts. They had the name of an attorney. Of course, they'd been able to find what I was looking for.

How long had Aiden known? How long had he been sitting on her name? Her address?

My lungs were tight, squeezing my breath. My head throbbed. This was so much worse than interfering in my job search or trying to get me into graduate school.

Every day I'd asked, and every day he'd lied.

He knew how important it was to me, and he lied.

I couldn't stop hearing it echo in my head. *I don't think I trust anyone as much as I trust you.*

Had he laughed to himself when I told him I wanted us to be partners?

It all seemed like a joke now. I felt painfully naïve.

Falling in love with Aiden Winters and thinking he would ever consider me an equal. Thinking we could make this work. When in reality, Aiden Winters did what he wanted, when he wanted, and he steamrolled over anyone who got in his way. Including me.

"Here you are. Do you want a glass of wine before dinner?"

I jolted at the sound of Aiden's voice, my eyes flashing

to the clock in the corner of my laptop screen. Five thirty-five. I'd been sitting, staring into space for almost forty-five minutes.

"Violet? What's wrong?"

The gentle concern in his voice was too much. I picked up the contract, damned by his handwriting and that phone number, and shoved it in his direction. "What is this?" Even to my numb ears, my voice was flat. Dead.

Aiden didn't take the contract. His eyes moved from the papers in my hand to my face and back. His words still gentle, placating, he said, "Violet—"

"LeAnne Gates," I interrupted. "Is she the one? I know you know." I shoved to my feet and closed my laptop, grabbing my bag and jamming it in.

"Violet, we're still looking into it, it's not—"

"Just tell me." My shriek hurt my ears. Aiden winced and reached out. Clutching my laptop bag in one hand and my purse in the other I danced back out of reach.

"Violet, just calm down."

"Don't tell me to calm down," I shouted, sliding into full-on hysteria.

Didn't he know that telling someone who was freaking out to calm down was like throwing gasoline on a fire?

If the situation called for calm, I'd be fucking calm. This was not the time for calm. "Just tell me. Is that her? Is that her phone number?"

Aiden circled his desk, slowly closing in on me, holding his hands up, palms out. "Violet. Let's sit down. We'll have a drink, and I'll explain."

With every word my fury grew. Where did he get off trying to handle me? I wasn't the liar. I wasn't the one hiding information and keeping secrets.

It wasn't even his business. It was my life.

"I don't want a drink."

Aiden's heavy crystal tumblers sat beside a matching decanter on the side table, sparkling at me. Mocking me. Everything in Aiden's life was so perfect. Arranged exactly as he liked it.

Just like he was trying to arrange me.

If he had to lie a little, to keep things from me, if that was what was best for me then it was okay, right?

I didn't plan it. My purse fell from my fingers. My hand whipped out, grabbed one of those tumblers, and I let it fly. It exploded against the wall behind Aiden's head in a shower of glittering shards.

The destruction soothed the rage inside me, and I snatched another, pitching it as hard as I could. I wasn't aiming for Aiden. I didn't have it in me to hurt him like that.

I was cold, but I wasn't cruel.

The third tumbler exploded in a crash as loud as the others. I threw the last, only regretting that there weren't any more.

"Violet! Stop." Aiden lunged for me. I swung my laptop case into his arm, driving him back and stepping around the desk out of reach.

Through gritted teeth, I said, "Just tell me the truth."

Aiden let out a long breath. "Fine. Yes. That's her."

"How long have you known?"

"Vi—"

"How long?" I demanded, hearing myself shriek again. I didn't care. I didn't care about hiding my emotions, I didn't care about protecting myself. How could I? I'd let Aiden in so far past my shell, so far past the ice queen, and the whole time it hadn't meant anything.

"Since the day after we visited your parents," he admitted.

My anger fell away, replaced by empty, gray, nothing. My eyes were dry. The words I spoke sounded like they came from someone else. "You said I could trust you. You said you loved me. Why? Why bother if it was all a lie?"

"It wasn't a lie. I wasn't lying. I love you."

My ears were ringing. He sounded like he was so far away. I shook my head, trying to make sense of his excuses.

"No. I don't think you do love me. Or if you do, it's not the kind of love I want. It's not enough if you don't respect me. It's not enough if I can't trust you."

Aiden reached for me again. I moved away, leaning down to scoop my purse off of the carpet.

"Don't," I said.

"You at least owe me the courtesy of letting me explain," he said, stiffly.

I shook my head. "I don't think I do."

"Violet, she's not what you think—I was going to tell you we found her, but then I talked to her and—"

"You called her? That's why you wrote the number down. You called her and talked to her. You had no right."

The emptiness was gone. My voice cracked on the pain of his betrayal. LeAnne Gates had nothing to do with Aiden. And everything to do with me.

"I had every right. I love you. I'm trying to protect you. I didn't want...she wasn't..." He took in the expression on my face and fumbled.

"You had no right," I whispered, unable to force more breath into my words. I walked past him, dodging when he tried to grab my arm.

From behind me I heard him say, "You need to calm down. We can talk about this later."

I only nodded, the click of my heels on the stairs light and precise, a counter to the weight on my heart. I reached Aiden's rooms and locked the door behind me. It was his house. He had a key, but the lock between us made me feel better. I couldn't look at him, couldn't stand the concern in those warm brown eyes I'd come to know so well.

Dumping my purse and laptop case on the bed, I sank down, slumped, staring at the carpet between my feet. I don't know how long I sat there, motionless. I didn't cry. I didn't pace, or rage, or throw anything else. I might have sat there all night, but the rattle of the door handle pushed me to action.

"Go away, Aiden."

"Just talk to me. Be reasonable."

I didn't answer. I had nothing to say. I thought we'd had this out already. I thought he understood. Instead, he'd only been humoring me, saying what I wanted to hear while he did what suited him. What I wanted didn't matter.

Numb, working methodically and quickly, I pulled my suitcase from the closet and packed. I left nothing. Not a hairpin, a sock, or a tube of lip gloss. Nothing except the lingerie Aiden bought me in Las Vegas. I left that in the drawer, untouched.

He was nowhere in sight when I unlocked the door and carried my things downstairs. I almost made it all the way to my car.

Aiden was waiting for me in the kitchen, my silver key ring dangling from one finger. "Don't even think about it. You can't just leave."

"If you won't give me my keys, I'll call for a ride," I said.

He'd asked me to calm down. I was calm. I wasn't hiding my feelings under a shell of composure. I was blank. Empty of everything. And all I wanted was to go home.

"Don't be ridiculous," Aiden said, impatient. "Put your things down, and we'll go talk. If you just let me explain, I can make you understand."

"Understand why you lied to me? Is that what you want me to understand? How when I told you I trusted you more than anyone else you were lying to me? No, I don't think I want you to explain that. What I want is for you to give me my keys and get out of my way."

"What's going on here?" Mrs. W stepped between us, holding up a hand to keep Aiden back. Her voice was grave when she said, "Aiden, give me Violet's keys."

"No." He sounded like a sulky teenager. In any other situation, I might have laughed.

"I will not allow you to keep her here if she wants to leave. Give me Violet's keys."

Aiden didn't move. Mrs. W snatched the keys from his hand and physically shoved him out of the way. He was too surprised to stop her.

I took the opportunity to rush past them both, taking the keys Mrs. W held out as I went. I threw my things in the tiny hatchback of my Beetle, started the car, and fled Winters House.

My phone started ringing before I cleared the driveway. I turned it off. There was only one person I wanted to talk to, and I'd see him soon enough.

Chase was watching a rerun of an old World Cup game when I walked in. One look at my face—at my suitcase—and he turned off the television.

"Vivi, what happened? What did he do?"

At the familiar sound of his voice, my cracked heart split open. I dropped my purse, my suitcase, everything in my hands. My keys clattered as they bounced off my shoe and skidded across the floor. My eyes were wet, tears clogging my nose. I sucked in a breath, tried to speak, and choked.

Chase was there, pulling me into his arms, stroking his hand over my hair the same way he had when I was a child woken from a nightmare. He rocked me, murmuring, "Shhh, Vivi. I've got you. It's okay. I've got you."

Chapter Thirty-Seven

Violet

"Are you going to throw something at me if I tell you I think this is a bad idea?" Chase's eyes slid off the road and touched on my set face.

I'd made the mistake of telling him about the crystal tumblers. I didn't lose my temper often but when I did, well, the mess in Aiden's office attested to the result.

"Maybe. If I were you, I wouldn't take the risk," I warned. "I told you I could do this by myself. You insisted on coming with me. I appreciate the support, but if you're going to be an ass about it, you can let me out and I'll call for a ride."

Proving I was serious, I unlocked my phone and tapped the icon of the ride share app.

Chase snorted in disgust and rolled his eyes. "Put that away, Vivi. There's no way in hell I'm letting you do this on your own. I just want it on record that I think it's a mistake."

"So noted. I'm not stupid. I'm fully aware that this is probably a terrible idea. Can you understand why I still have to know?"

Chase didn't answer, just tapped his index finger on the

steering wheel. Finally, he said, "You do remember me moving us to Atlanta and not telling you why, right? So, yeah, I get it. That's why I'm driving all the way to Huntsville, why I called and made a fake appointment to award LeAnne Gates a cruise she didn't win."

"Thanks. What did Gage say when you told him you were taking the day off?" It was the closest I would come to asking about Aiden.

"You don't want to know."

I took in the set of his chin, the hard line of his jaw. "Yeah, I guess I probably don't."

I was trying not to think about him. Aiden. Just the sound of his name in my head came with a spike of agony. Aiden. I never wanted to see him again. Never wanted to see any of them again. And my brother was tied to them for the rest of his life.

I closed the thought out of my mind. I could grieve, and wallow, and sulk over Aiden Winters later. First, I had to get through the morning.

"Looks like this is it," Chase said, slowing in front of a gatehouse manned by a security guard. Chase gave the fake name he'd used when he made the appointment and we were waved through. Easy as that.

We followed the GPS directions through a maze of streets filled with identical, oversized McMansions. The landscaping was pristine and consistent. There were no toys on the lawns, no cars parked on the street, no basketball hoops in the driveways or trampolines in the yards. Everything around us was carefully monitored perfection. I'd bet the neighborhood association would form a lynch mob if a blade of grass grew a millimeter too long. I had the sudden urge to tell Chase to turn around, to forget the whole thing.

Then it was too late, and we were there, coming to a

stop in front of number fifty-seven Arcadia Drive. I stepped from the car and pulled on the ice queen like an old cardigan. My hair was back in a sleek twist, my makeup in shades of charcoal, my lips a deep, perfectly lined rose. I wore the gray linen sheath with plum heels, pearls at my ears and around my neck.

Perversely, I wanted my mother here with me in spirit as she never would be in person. She'd made her mistakes as a parent. I was the first to point that out. But she'd taught me how to be strong. How to keep my weaknesses to myself, how to fight even if I used chilly politeness instead of my fists.

I was ice, from the inside out. Whatever happened inside that house, I would put it behind me and move on. I would put all of this behind me and move on.

I thought I was ready. When the door swung open and LeAnne Gates laid eyes on Chase, she smiled the smile of an older woman appreciating an attractive younger man.

I needed a moment to compose myself before she spotted me. It was like looking in a mirror. Lavender eyes the exact shade of my own in an oval face crowned by thick, shiny hair in the same strands of gold and platinum I'd brushed that morning.

Unlike my classic sheath dress and designer heels, she wore a hot pink tank top with a plunging neckline over a bra that pushed her breasts high and together, the skin between wrinkling in protest.

Her leopard print capris were skintight, showing the line of her thong across her hip, the black lace peeking up in the back. Her feet, with toenails the same hot pink as her tank top, were jammed into a pair of clear plastic slides with heels that had to be at least 4 inches.

Her hair was teased into a style I hadn't seen since

reruns of eighties soap operas and her mascara was so thick it looked like caterpillars lay across her eyelids.

Those black-rimmed eyes lit on me and she froze. She knew. She went stiff, started to swing the door shut. Chase's hand flew up to block her. He wedged his foot in the door, easing her back, pulling me inside along with him.

"You can't just come in here," she said. "I'll call security." Her voice grated against my ears, shrill with a twang that wasn't Alabama, wasn't Tennessee.

"We'll only take a few minutes of your time. I can promise you, this will be less complicated if you talk to us now. You don't want us to come back."

She went still at the vague threat, her eyes locked on my face, wide and afraid.

"You're not supposed to be here. How did you find me? No one is supposed to know. That's how it works."

"Why don't you tell us how it works, Ms. Gates," Chase said, easily. "Let's just sit down and have a chat. Then we'll get out of your hair and you'll never see us again."

Chase didn't bother to be harmless or charming very often, and it always threw me. When he flashed that smile and twinkled those blue eyes at a woman, young or old, they melted.

Suckers.

Usually, I had to resist the urge to snicker. Today I was grateful as LeAnne Gates relaxed and led us into her parlor.

The room was decorated in rose and avocado, the velvet couch a shade of gold that would have been all the rage in the seventies. Every piece of furniture was covered with plastic. It crackled as I sat, sticking to the backs of my legs before I smoothed my skirt down.

Our unwilling hostess crossed the room to the drink cart

and poured herself a generous serving of vodka. She didn't bother to offer a drink to either of us.

"I don't know what the two of you are doing here," she began. "I told the other one I wasn't talking."

"Other one?" Chase probed.

"Maxwell's boy, and the one who came with him. Snotty assholes. Maxwell was a gentleman. Gentlemen enough, if you know what I mean." She leered at Chase and took an impatient swig of her drink. A cigarette appeared out of nowhere. She popped it between her lips and lit it, taking a long drag.

She must have seen something she didn't like in my face, because she stabbed the cigarette in the air in my direction and said, "Never drank or smoked while I was working. Having my fun now."

"While you were working? In what capacity were you working for Maxwell Sinclair?"

"You playing a game? I told the other one. You want me to talk, you get out your wallet. I don't do nothing for free."

"How much?" I cut in. "How much to answer our questions?"

There was a hint of fear beneath her sneer. She looked me up and down. "More than you have."

Chase leaned forward, bracing his elbows on his knees, and sent her an affable smile that belied the words that came out of his mouth. "We have a copy of the contract you signed with Marshall Pitt. We're not sure how legal it was and we're considering asking some friends in law enforcement for their opinion. If you don't want to talk, we won't waste any more of your time. I'm sure they'd be happy to help."

She fell for his bluff hook, line, and sinker. "That sumbitch was never supposed to turn over my name. None of y'all should be here." She stabbed the cigarette in the air towards us again before taking a long drag and exhaling in Chase's face.

He sat back and started to stand, holding his hand out to me. "Let's go. I'll call Detective–"

"Wait! Wait. Ten thousand and I'll tell you anything you want to know. Cash."

Chase dropped his hand to his side and looked down at her. "Five and not a penny more."

"Chase!" I hissed. What was he doing?

"Done. But I ain't saying nothin' until I see the money. This bank don't take checks."

"Agreed. But you don't get the money until I'm satisfied with your answers."

She got to her feet and tottered on her slides across the thick carpet to the drink cart, splashing more vodka in her glass.

I watched in fascination as she stubbed the cigarette out in an overflowing ashtray and lit another from the pack I now saw she had concealed in the hip pocket of her capris. A diamond studded gold lighter flashed and she blew a cloud of smoke in my direction.

"Well? No money, no talking."

Chase turned to me, handing me the keys to the car. "There's a briefcase in the backseat. Go get it please."

"Chase," I said, again, under my breath.

Before I could articulate my protest, Chase pulled me to my feet and leaned in, whispering in my ear, "You want to do this, we're going to do it. I figured it would go this way, and I came prepared. Go get the briefcase, Vivi."

A little shocked, I took the keys and did as he asked. I wanted to tell him to get it himself, but I knew he wouldn't leave me alone with LeAnne Gates. I wasn't sure I wanted him to, so I did as I was told.

I came back to find her halfway through her second cigarette and second tumbler of vodka. A haze of smoke hung in the parlor. I had no idea what had been said while I was gone, but Chase was gritting his teeth and looking at our hostess as if she were a cockroach under his shoe.

I handed him the briefcase and sat beside him pretending I expected to see the neatly wrapped stack of hundred dollar bills he removed and set on the coffee table. I guess it was a good thing I'd brought him with me. I'd been so focused on finding this woman, it hadn't occurred to me to arrive prepared for bribery.

LeAnne Gates picked up the stack of cash and ran her thumb across the top, riffling the bills. She waved the money under her nose and inhaled, rolling her eyes to the ceiling. "I just love the smell of money. If they made it into a perfume, I'd wear it every day."

"What work did you do for Maxwell Sinclair?" I asked, tired of her stalling.

Chapter Thirty-Eight
Violet

"You look smarter than that, girl. You know what I did for Maxwell. That's why you're here."

"He paid you to get pregnant and deliver a healthy baby," Chase said, answering my question.

She tapped her index finger on her nose then pointed it at Chase. "You got it in one. I can tell you're the brains of this operation."

"How did it work?" Chase asked. "Did he have a client before or after you got pregnant?"

"Before, of course. He'd get an order, find the right man, put us together, and most of the time I popped out exactly what the client wanted. That's how you get the big payday. Clean bill of health, right hair color, right eye color."

She pointed the cigarette at me and shook her head. "You were a problem. Those eyes. Only one with my eyes. It's a—whad'ya call it?"

"Recessive gene?" Chase offered.

"That's it. Recessive. Shouldn't a come out. Lost me a quarter million. I was lucky they took you, but they said it was close enough and they didn't want to wait."

"How many times?" Chase asked. On the way here, I'd imagined asking so many questions. Now that I was confronted with this woman who'd given birth to me and sold me as easily as she might a litter of puppies, my mind was blank.

"Nine. I tried for ten, but the last one wouldn't catch. Lost two in a row, Maxwell said I was done."

"Profitable venture," Chase commented.

She winked at him and tossed back the rest of her vodka. "Profitable and easy. Only thing my mama ever gave me was a clean health history and a body that was good at having babies. All I had to do was eat right, avoid smokin' and drinkin' and keep my fingers crossed I had a boy when the client wanted a boy and a girl when they wanted a girl."

"What did you do if they wanted a boy and you had a girl?" I asked, horrified by the potential answers. Her response didn't make me feel any better.

She shrugged a shoulder and I got the feeling she truly could not have cared less when she said, "It depends. Sometimes I tried again, sometimes they took what they got."

"And if you tried again? What happened to the baby they didn't want?"

"Who knows? My job was to hand over healthy babies and cash my check." She flexed her toes, slapping the sole of her plastic slides against her heel. Her eyes narrowed on me, she said, "Don't you get any ideas. You're nothing to me. You were a payday and that money's been spent. Once you walk out of here, I don't want to see you again, you understand me, girl?"

She dismissed me. Pulling another cigarette from the pack at her hip, she lit it, looking at Chase with a heavy-lidded gaze. "Now, if you want to come back, you'd be more than welcome as long as you keep your questions to yourself."

I repressed the urge to shudder in revulsion. The thought of Chase and this woman...ugh. So much gross I didn't know where to start.

"So you don't know—" I didn't know how to ask. I couldn't bring myself to call the man who'd impregnated her my father. For better or worse Henry Westbrook was my father. I didn't have to articulate the question. She knew what I wanted to know.

"Don't know. Don't care. Maxwell delivered him, I fucked him until I got pregnant, then he disappeared. He cashed his check, I cashed mine. Mine was a hell of a lot bigger on account of all the work I had to do." Her laugh was a cackle that made my skin crawl.

"When was the last time you saw Maxwell Sinclair?" Chase asked.

"More'n five years ago, which is what I told the other one and his partner."

"You didn't know he was dead," Chase pressed. Surprise flashed across her face.

"Dead? He's not dead."

"What makes you say that?"

"Because I get my check every month, right on schedule, signed by Maxwell himself."

"Check for what?" I asked.

"Check for keepin' my mouth shut."

I gave her a blank stare, then looked at the stack of money on the couch beside her. She rolled her eyes and tried to share a sympathetic glance with Chase. "She always this naïve?"

Chase ignored her question. "Did you tell this to Maxwell's son?"

"Nah. They pissed me off. Telling me to keep my mouth shut, like I was going to go around town blabbing. Told me to keep away from any of the babies I had, like I'd want to look for them. If I'd wanted my own, I would'a had one. Little parasites."

Tilting her head to the side, she gave me a speculative look. The light dawned, and her eyes widened before they narrowed again. "The brown-eyed one with the stick up his ass was yours, wasn't he? Looked rich. You listen good. You get him hooked on that pussy, make him pay 'fore you start saggin'. You fuck him good, you'll get yourself set up before he trades you in." Another jab of the cigarette in my direction. "There. Good advice. Don't say I never gave you nothing." She cackled again, exhaling smoke in my face. My stomach turned over.

Chase looked at me, clearly at the end of his patience. "Are we done?"

I let out a long breath. There wasn't a question in my mind of my answer when I said, "We're done."

I lowered my window when I got in the car, hoping the fresh air would clean the stench of smoke from my clothes and hair. Neither of us said anything as we followed the GPS directions out of the maze of streets and through the security gate.

We were speeding down the highway when Chase said, over the rush of wind through my open window, "I never thought I'd say this, but that woman made Suzanne look like fucking Donna Reed."

Trust Chase to make me laugh. Our mother always hated it when he called her Suzanne. And he was right, Suzanne wouldn't win mother of the year, but compared to LeAnne Gates, she'd been a pretty good deal.

She hadn't hugged or tucked me in at night. She'd tried

to sell me in marriage to a man old enough to be my father and kicked me out of the house when I refused to let that same man rape me. And still, she was a better mother than LeAnne Gates.

I snickered. "You sure you don't want to go back and take her up on her offer? She really seemed to like you."

"Let's never mention that part again."

"Deal. And I'll pay you back. I didn't think—"

"No, you won't."

"Chase—"

"Violet. Shut. The. Fuck. Up. Just shut up."

I crossed my arms over my chest and blew out a breath. "Fine. Throw your money away."

"It was a cheap price to pay if we can consider this whole thing over and done." He took his eyes from the road and looked at me until I raised my gaze to meet his. "Is it? Over and done?"

"For me? Yeah. Yeah, it's over. It's depressing and kind of gross. But it's over. Someone's going to have to tell one of the Sinclairs what she said, though. About their father."

Chase sighed. "What a bitch. Not telling them their father might be alive. I'll make sure they know."

"You're all in the loop over there now, aren't you? Working with Gage, getting to know the Sinclairs..."

"Vivi, it's not like that—"

I waved my hand in the air and shook my head at him. "Ignore me. I'm just having a shitty day in a shitty week. I'm glad things worked out for you. With the company, and the Winters. I'm just—"

I felt my eyes get wet, and I swallowed. I'd cried enough yesterday. I wasn't doing it again.

I'd said all I wanted was to find the name on the

contract so I could close the book on my past and move forward.

Now it was done.

It was time to look to the future. Find a job. Get an apartment. Save up enough money to go back to school.

Get over my broken heart and settle in to a life without men. Maybe I'd get a couple dozen cats. Take up knitting and drink lots of tea. Wasn't that what spinsters did?

Chase cleared his throat, interrupting my thoughts. "Don't hate me, but I get why he did it. Honestly? That woman was the reason I never told you. I didn't know what we were going to find, but I was afraid of something like that. Aiden met her. He loves you. He was trying to protect you from her."

"I know he was. But he lied. Every day I asked and he lied. Do you understand why I can't live like that? Knowing that it doesn't matter what I want, what's important to me. That if he thinks I'm wrong, he'll just tell me whatever I want to hear to keep me in line."

"Not to keep you in line, Vivi. To protect you. To keep you from being hurt."

"But that's not his choice." My voice cracked on a sob. I bit my lip, pushing it back. When I thought I could talk again I said, "It's not his choice. Sometimes life hurts. And if I want to risk it, that should be up to me. I don't want to be kept on a shelf, protected from everything. I want to live my life. I want to take chances. And I want to be able to trust the man I love with all my heart. I want to trust that he believes in me, that he has my back, not that he's going behind it."

"Yeah, I get it. I do. I'm just saying, you might want to cut him some slack."

"I don't think I can. Not on this."

"Annalise invited me to the wedding. Why don't you come with me?"

My mouth fell open and I stared across the front seat at him, incredulous. I felt rotten enough that I wouldn't see the wedding I'd helped put together. Sad that I'd miss seeing my new friend get married. Sick at the thought of ever seeing any of them again.

"Not a chance," I said.

Chase sighed but didn't argue. I turned on the radio, cranking the volume to discourage further conversation. I knew he meant well, but it was no shock that my brother saw Aiden's side of things.

Chase loved me, but he and Aiden were cut from the same cloth. Bossy, overbearing, and convinced they knew what was right, all the time, every time. Just like Aiden, if Chase could have wrapped me up and put me on a shelf, protecting me from all of life's ills, he would have.

If that was the life I'd wanted, I would have let our parents marry me off to Gordon Walters and spent the rest of my life trading freedom for safety.

Gage was waiting at our front door when we stepped off the elevator. He and Chase exchanged chin lifts. To Chase, Gage said, "How'd it go?"

Chase just shook his head and unlocked the door of the condo. Gage followed us inside. Chase headed for the kitchen, saying over his shoulder, "Anyone want a beer? I need a beer."

"Not for me," Gage said. "Violet? Can I have a minute?"

It was the most polite Gage had ever been. I wasn't in the mood to spar with him, but the sooner I found out what he wanted, the sooner he would leave.

Raising an eyebrow I said, "How can I help you?"

"I want you to get your things and come back to Winters House with me."

If he'd asked me to marry him I couldn't have been more shocked. All I managed was a stunned, "What?"

He shoved his hands in his pockets and, for just a second, despite his dark hair, he looked so much like Chase I had to blink.

"Look, Aiden fucked up. He knows it, you know it, I know it, everybody knows it. He fucked up and he's sorry. He's miserable. He's a mess. I swear if you give him another chance, this won't happen again. He's not perfect, but he never makes the same mistake twice."

"You hate me," I said, struggling to catch up.

"I don't hate you. I didn't trust you. For good reason."

I inclined my head in his direction, acknowledging his point, but saying nothing.

"You're good for him. You make him happy. He deserves to be happy."

"And what about me? What about what I deserve?" I was grateful my voice stayed even. My chest ached, but I wasn't sure I believed Gage's claim not to hate me. I would not let him see me cry.

"No one will ever love you like he will," Gage said. "When Aiden loves he does it with everything he has. He will never give up on you. He will never fail you. He'll never cheat on you. He'll spend the rest of his life doing anything he can to make you happy, because that's the way he's built. That's the kind of man he is."

"But will he tell me the truth? Will he respect my decisions when he doesn't agree with me? Or will he go behind my back and arrange things the way he wants them because it's for my own good?"

Gage had the grace to sigh and look away rather than argue.

"That's what I thought," I said. "Go home, Gage."

"Just talk to him, Violet. At least answer your phone."

I looked to Chase, standing in the kitchen, a beer in his hand, his eyes thoughtful. I knew what he would say if I asked.

Why was everyone on Aiden's side?

"You can all just go to hell. I'm going to take a bath."

I turned and stalked out of the room. From behind me I heard my brother say with a laugh, "That went well."

I raised my middle finger over my shoulder just before I turned the corner, ignoring Chase's answering chuckle. I was taking a bath. With lots of bubbles. And then I was going to consider moving somewhere far, far away where there were no men. Right now, that felt like the answer to all my problems.

Chapter Thirty-Nine

Aiden

Sunlight speared through the curtains, stabbing my retinas. I threw my arm over my eyes, reaching for Violet with my other hand and finding only cool, bare sheets. Fuck. The reek of sweat and stale whiskey reached my nose. My temples throbbed and my mouth tasted sour. Fuck.

For the first time since I was a teenager, I'd gotten drunk enough to pass out. I had a vague memory of Gage and Riley dragging me upstairs and dumping me in my bed. Of Gage telling me that if I puked I'd have to clean it up myself before they'd rolled me to my stomach and left.

At first, when she walked out, I held it together. I was so fucking arrogant. So sure she'd be back. So sure she'd answer her phone, listen to my messages and realize that I was right. Realize that I loved her and understand that was enough.

But she hadn't.

She hadn't answered the phone.

She hadn't come back.

Finally, Chase had called. "Back off, man. She needs a

little space. I can't believe you fucked up this bad. You're the one she went running to when she found out I lied to her. What the fuck did you think would happen when she caught you?"

He hung up on me, leaving his question rattling in my head.

The answer was, I hadn't thought she'd catch me. I'd thought I'd bury LeAnne Gates so deep, Violet would never find her and eventually she'd stop wondering. That paper had been in my desk less than a day and she'd found it. Rotten fucking luck.

I'd been so sure.

So fucking arrogant.

And now she was gone.

I cracked an eyelid and peered at the clock on my bedside table. 10 AM. I couldn't remember the last time I'd slept this late. It was Annalise and Riley's wedding day and I was a hungover, miserable, bastard. I couldn't fix the miserable part, or erase the hangover, but I could get my ass out of bed and take a shower.

In the bathroom, I filled a glass with water from the tap and drained it. Swallowing two aspirin, I drank a second glass of water before stepping into a steaming hot shower. Between the water, the aspirin, and the shower, I was feeling a little more human when I finally made my way downstairs in search of food.

The dining room doors were open, conversation filtering out, but I bypassed the room and headed down the hall to my office, closing the door behind me.

I sent a quick text to Mrs. W.

In my office. Coffee and breakfast.

Back in the day, the house had been equipped with pull cords for summoning the help, and later an intercom system. Now, with the full-time staff reduced to Mrs. W, Abel, and Mr. Henried, we relied on text message. I saw the notice pop up that my text had been received, but there was no answer.

I attempted to read the paper while I waited, but I couldn't focus on anything. I kept seeing Violet's face as she pitched the crystal tumblers at my head, the explosion of shards around me. I always knew she had a temper. I could see that fire inside her from the beginning.

I'd never expected it to be aimed at me. Not like that. I hadn't been afraid when she'd been angry. She could throw whatever she wanted. She could rage, she could yell. I didn't get scared until she went blank and quiet. I could take her fire. As long as she didn't lock me out.

That's where I was now. Firmly locked out. She wouldn't take my calls. She wouldn't see me. I knew from Gage that she and Chase had gone to see LeAnne Gates. I'd wanted to spare her that. To spare her that woman and her cruel laugh, the way she dismissed Violet as just another job, had complained that Violet's eyes, those unforgettable twilight eyes, had cost her so much money.

LeAnne Gates was crass and greedy and nothing about her had anything to do with Violet. They might have looked alike, but that meant nothing.

Violet was good, and clean, and honest. She hid so much, worked so hard to protect herself, but I knew what was in her heart. I'd wanted her the second I saw her. Then she intrigued me, so coolly contained, so daring.

When I realized what she'd done for her brother, saw the way she loved, so fierce and so strong, I'd wanted her to love me like that. I wanted all that fiery determination, that loyalty, that devotion. And for such a short time, I'd had it. Then I'd fucked it all up.

Knuckles rapped on my office door. It opened to reveal Mrs. W, carrying a tray. She set it down on my desk and left without sparing me a word. She hadn't spoken to me since she'd confiscated Violet's keys and helped her escape Winters House.

I looked at the tray and sighed. Cold coffee and even colder oatmeal. Not a biscuit or slice of bacon in sight. This wasn't the first time I'd been treated to the cold shoulder à la Mrs. W. I'd be eating cold oatmeal until I fixed things with Violet.

I lifted my spoon and dug into my penance. I hated oatmeal, but I needed food if I was going to muscle past this hangover. I'd worked my way through half the bowl when the door opened again. Charlie peeked her head in, then shoved the door open with her shoulder.

"This didn't come from me," she said, lifting a travel mug of steaming coffee and a linen-covered basket that smelled like yeast and butter and country ham. Annalise followed her in, still holding her coffee. Charlie set the travel mug and basket in front of me, and both of them made themselves comfortable in the armchairs opposite my desk.

Annalise took a sip of coffee, swallowed, and said, "You look like hell. We're sticking you in the back of the wedding pictures."

"I'll be fine," I said, knowing I wouldn't.

"Hmph," was her response. She took another slug of coffee and sent Charlie a pointed look.

"Aren't you going to go fix this?" Charlie demanded.

"She isn't speaking to me," I said, avoiding Charlie's eyes. I pulled the napkin off the basket in front of me to reveal a scrambled egg, ham, and cheese biscuit sandwich. With a grateful sigh, I picked it up and took a bite. Charlie's annoyed voice broke through the first decent moment I'd had in the last two days.

"Seriously? The great Aiden Winters is going to give up because Violet won't answer her phone? If that's all you've got, you don't deserve her."

"I never thought I'd say this, but I'm not sure he does," Annalise cut in.

I swallowed, washing down the biscuit with a gulp of scalding coffee. "Thanks for the loyalty."

"You know, it's not easy being female in this family," Annalise said. "Charlie and I know how Violet feels. I would have thought you'd learned your lesson."

"Gage always says you don't make the same mistake twice, but you keep making this one over and over." Charlie eyed the silver tray that usually held my whiskey service, now bare except for the empty decanter. "Does she know she smashed over ten thousand dollars worth of crystal?"

"Ha!" Annalise almost spit out her coffee. "I'm not telling her. She'll freak. And he deserves it."

"Maybe we shouldn't have forgiven him so easily," Charlie commented. "Maybe it just made him think he can keep getting away with it."

Annalise gave me a speculative look before turning to Charlie. "You might be right."

"I know I messed up," I said.

"Do you? Do you really? Are you sorry you lied to her? Or are you sorry you got caught?" Charlie's eyes were narrowed and her cheeks flushed. Charlie in a temper could be awe-inspiring.

I thought about my answer and then settled for the truth. Given the mess I was in, the truth seemed safest, even if it pissed her off.

"Both, okay? I'm sorry I got caught, but I'm more sorry I lied."

"Do you know where you really fucked up?" Charlie asked, watching me with a speculative look. "You let her face one of the most important moments in her life without you. You had to set the terms, you tried to keep her away, and instead, she went without you, knowing the man she loves wasn't at her side. That's where you fucked up."

My appetite gone, I set the rest of my breakfast back in the basket. Sick realization washed over me. I'd tried so hard to maneuver her where I wanted her and instead, I'd forced her to face that woman alone. It didn't matter that Chase had been with her, or that he was the only man I trusted to watch out for her the way I would.

All that mattered was that I'd driven her away when she'd needed me.

"She's not going to let you control her." Annalise's voice was gentle. "You know that, don't you? Don't even bother going after her if you think you can just sweep this under the rug and do it again the next time she has plans you don't like. Trust me. I've learned the hard way. Lying doesn't work, even when you think it's for the other person's good. Even when you think you're keeping them safe. Lies aren't the answer."

I stared into my steaming coffee, absorbing Annalise's words. If anyone knew about lies and love and doing the wrong thing for the right reasons, it was Annalise.

She and Riley had lost over a decade because they'd both lied, each thinking they were protecting the other. I'd been there in the middle, lying to both of them for the same reason.

It was a miracle they'd found one another again, but falling in love for the second time—that had nothing to do with luck. Annalise and Riley made it work because they'd refused to let go. Watching them, I'd learned love on its own wasn't enough. You had to be willing to dig deep, to do the hard work, to take risks. I should have known, and instead, I'd still messed up with Violet.

"You have to figure this out, Aiden. What about when you have kids?" Charlie pushed. "They're going to fall down. They're going to make mistakes. They're going to fail, and get their hearts broken. You won't be able to protect them from that any more than you could protect us from the same thing."

"You don't know what it's like," I said. "You don't know how helpless it makes you feel, to see someone you love struggling, hurting, and not be able to help."

"Not the way you mean," she agreed. "But I know it was hard getting all of us dumped on you when you were only twenty. Going from being a college student to a parent when you were still grieving Mom and Dad. I don't know how you did it. And I don't want to think about what it would have been like for me, for any of us, if you hadn't stepped up the way you did. You were always there. Always. But you need to let go a little. You can't control everything. And if you try to control her, you'll lose her forever."

Annalise stood and tapped Charlie on the back of the shoulder. At the signal, Charlie got to her feet. "I love you, Aid. Go fix this."

Annalise grabbed the basket and napkin. "Don't want to leave the evidence," she said. "I'm not getting on Mrs. W's bad side, even if it is my wedding day." She leaned over my desk and kissed my cheek. "Go get Violet and bring her home. And be back in time for the wedding or I'll kill you."

Chapter Forty

Aiden

Chase answered the door to my knock. With a quick look over his shoulder, he said under his breath, "What took you so long?"

"I'm an idiot."

"And an asshole," he added.

"That too," I agreed.

"I'm going to hit the gym. If I come back and she's not good? I will fucking end you. Do you get me?"

Menace radiated from every pore on Chase's body. I had no doubt that if I didn't make Violet blissfully happy her brother would be thrilled to grind me into a pulp.

If I didn't figure out how to make her blissfully happy, I'd let him. First, I had to get her to talk to me. Chase disappeared down the hall. He was back a minute later dressed in gym shorts and a T-shirt with the sleeves cut off.

Just before he opened the door, he called, "Vivi? Can you come out here?" He waited for her answering, "Just a sec," before he said, "Good luck," and left.

Violet looked better than me, but not by much. I was guessing she'd skipped the hangover, but the purple smudges under her eyes told me she was sleeping about as well as I was.

She was still in her pajamas, a faded T-shirt embroidered with a sheep jumping over the moon and a pair of paper-thin, cotton, striped pajama pants in the same dusky lavender as her eyes. Her long hair was bundled into a knot, loose strands spilling everywhere.

Her eyes were bruised. Not the smudges beneath, but deeper. How could I have hurt her so badly? The person I wanted to protect the most and instead I'd broken something precious.

"Where's Chase?"

"He went to the gym. Can I talk to you for a minute?"

"If you have to." Her eyes were bruised, but her voice was coldly polite. Distant. "I'm going to get a cup of coffee. Would you like one?"

Her good manners were a slap.

That was my girl. Hurt and angry, but she wouldn't give an inch.

I could play that game. "I'll take a cup."

Her nod of acknowledgment was my only answer. I followed her to the kitchen and leaned against the counter, watching her take down two matching mugs, measure beans, prepare the coffee. She pressed the button on the coffee maker and turned around, leaning on the counter opposite me and crossing her arms over her chest. She lifted her chin, and in her unique Violet way, managed to look down her nose at me despite the difference in our heights.

"If you have something to say, you might as well just say it."

"I have a lot of things to say. Starting with this. I know where I went wrong. It wasn't in trying to protect you." Her mouth opened, and I held up a hand to stop her. Her lips pressed together in a tight line, holding back her words. Her glare told me I didn't have much time before she lost patience.

"I'll always try to protect you, Violet. That's who I am. I'm never going to be comfortable with you walking into a situation that might hurt you. And if you try to tell me you don't feel the same way, I'll call you a liar. But I know where I went wrong."

"And?"

"You went anyway. I hid that woman from you because she was cruel. She was greedy, and nasty, and the kind of woman who would have seen everything you are and only tried to tear it apart. I won't apologize for wanting to shield you from that. But I should have known that you'd go anyway. And I should have realized that by lying to you, I forced you to do it alone."

"I wasn't alone. Chase was with me."

I shook my head. "It's not the same. I should have been there. Not to control you, not to tell you what to say or what to do, but to be there. At your side. At your back. I should have been with you because I love you, and I never want you to face anything on your own. When I lied to you, I might as well have just walked away. I'm sorry. I'm so fucking sorry."

I couldn't read her face. Her eyes were a wall of ice, everything else about her completely, utterly neutral. Abruptly, she turned to face the coffee maker. When she picked up the pot, her hand shook. The glass of the carafe rattled against the coffee mug, and she set it on the counter without pouring a drop, without turning around.

I couldn't do it anymore, couldn't stand the distance between us. I crossed the kitchen and came up behind her, taking her shoulders in my hands and turning her to face me. Her eyes were glued to the center of my chest, her expression a mask except for the almost imperceptible tremble of her lower lip.

Fucking hell, if she cried I was going to lose it. Angry tears were one thing. This, this lost, shattered Violet was more than I could take.

"I told you," I said, "I don't know how to do this. I'm so used to being the one in charge of everything. I don't know how to share the weight, but I want to learn. I can't promise you I'll never fuck up again. I'm pretty sure I will. But I'll never lie to you again. I swear it."

A single tear gathered on her lashes and rolled down her cheek, gutting me. In a tiny voice, she said, "I don't know if I can trust you. And I don't know how we can do this if I can't trust you."

I pressed a kiss to the top of her head, breathing in the sweet pea scent of her shampoo and beneath that, Violet, warm and familiar and mine.

"I can promise you that I'll never lie again. I can promise that I love you, that I respect you, that I'll listen to you, that I won't go behind your back ever again. And I do. I promise all of that. But promises are just words. If you give me another shot at this, I swear you won't regret it."

Her forehead hit my chest, the wet of her cheek soaking through my shirt. Tentatively, I wrapped my arms around her, holding her as a sob hitched her chest. "I love you so much. And when I saw that paper and I realized...you don't know how much that hurt. Everyone was lying to me. My parents, Chase, and I thought you were the one person—" Her words choked off.

My voice hoarse, I managed to say, "I am. I made a mistake, Vi. And it was a bad one. But I am the one person who won't lie to you. Never again. I swear. About anything."

Her arms crept around me, her fingers curling into the fabric of my shirt, holding on with desperate strength. "I don't want to be alone. I was fine with it before. And then I had you and it was so good. It was everything. You were everything. Please don't do that to me again."

"Never," I vowed, relief washing through me in a giddy wave. "I'll put it in our wedding vows. We'll take out the part about obeying—"

A quick laugh jerked her shoulders. "Like I'm going to promise to obey."

"I know better than to ask. I don't want that. I want to be a partner, Vi. I don't want to do this on my own anymore. I don't want to spend my life working late and missing everything that really matters. I need you. I need you to call me on my bullshit and put me in my place. I need you to remind me what's important. I want to share my life with you. You're the only woman I'll ever love. Come home with me."

Fear stabbed my heart when she shook her head, rolling her forehead against my chest, still hiding her face from me.

"Violet, do you want me to beg? Tell me what you want, and I'll do it."

Her hands uncurled from my shirt, and she stepped back, forcing distance between us. The heat of her body was gone, leaving me cold. I rubbed at the wet cotton of my shirt where her tears had soaked through the fabric.

Using the back of her hands, she wiped beneath her eyes, looking everywhere but at me. I kept my mouth shut and waited, every second that ticked by lasting a million years. She poured the coffee I didn't want, splashing in half-and-half and stirring, exactly the way I liked it.

I took the mug she handed me and sipped, tasting nothing. Waiting. My head was on the executioner's block and Violet held the axe. She drank her own coffee and when her eyes finally met mine they were hesitant. Careful.

"I'm not coming home with you," she said. "We did this all backwards. We've only been on one date, and then I was living with you. Chase was right. It was too fast."

"You want to date?"

"I think so, yes." At the incredulous look on my face, she said again, "Yes. I want to date. It's too soon for me to live with you, and it's way too soon to talk about wedding vows."

She was wrong, but I wasn't going to push my luck. I didn't need to date Violet to know that she was the only woman I'd ever love, but if she needed time, I'd give it to her.

"And while we're dating, will you be dating anyone else?" If she didn't give the right answer, my patience would be at an end. I could give her time, but I wouldn't share.

A ghost of a smile curved her lips. "Don't be absurd. Why would I waste my time with anyone else if I can have you? I never settle for less than the best."

"Damn straight. So Vegas doesn't count as a date?"

Violet sipped her coffee, then shook her head, the shadows finally sliding from her eyes. "Vegas was a serious lapse in judgment."

"Not on my part."

"Definitely on mine. I almost wish you'd seen Chase's face when he realized where I'd been and who I'd been with. I thought his head was going to explode."

"A lot's changed."

"Everything's changed," she said.

"Will you come with me to Annalise's wedding?"

"I'd love to."

Taking her coffee from her hand, I set both our mugs on the counter and pulled her into my arms again, resting my cheek against her temple, just holding her there, exactly where she belonged.

"Thank God. If I came back without you, Annalise and Charlie would have killed me. Mrs. W hasn't spoken to me since you walked out."

Violet's giggle was the sun sliding from behind the clouds, a shimmering golden light chasing away the dark.

"You think it's funny? I woke up this morning with the first hangover I've had in nearly twenty years and she gave me cold oatmeal and even colder coffee for breakfast."

"Poor baby." She patted my chest, but I wasn't buying it.

"Don't pretend you feel sorry for me."

"Not even a little bit," she agreed. "Are you hungry? We don't have much but I can probably scramble some eggs."

"I don't want food, sweetheart. I just want you."

Acutely aware that Chase would only be at the gym for so long, I scooped Violet into my arms. She yelped in surprise, throwing an arm around my shoulders and hanging on as I carried her to her bedroom and kicked the door shut behind us.

Since my hands were full I said, "Lock it." I shifted so she could reach.

"Bossy," she commented.

"I said I'd never lie to you. I didn't say anything about bossing you around."

"Good thing I like you bossy."

It was because that was one thing that would never change.

I was done with talking. We'd been apart for two days, and it felt like a year. I needed Violet, needed her skin against mine, needed to be inside her, to feel her, and hear her, and smell her, to be a part of her the way she was a part of me.

I lay Violet out across the bed, stripping her clothes, looking down at her body. All I could think was, *mine.*

Mine.

She'd given me a second chance, and I wasn't going to waste it. This time, it wasn't going to be fast and rough and out of control. I wanted it to last forever, to be inside her forever.

I was out of my own clothes and beside her, pulling the covers over us and her body into mine. Rolling to my side, I hooked her leg over my hip, my hands roaming everywhere I could reach.

Her skin was so soft, her rounded curves filling my hands, molding to me. I took my time, memorizing her shape with my fingertips, stroking, kissing, tasting every inch of her, imprinting myself on her body.

When she was ready, I slid inside and held her there, filled with me. Perfect.

"I could stay like this for the rest of my life," I said against her mouth.

Her answer was a kiss, a graze of her lips, a taste of her tongue. Sweet, and languid, she kissed me like we had all the time in the world. And we did.

After, I carried her to the shower, unwilling to let her out of my sight for even a few minutes. Not yet.

She was pinning up her hair, wearing a strapless black lace bra, matching panties, and a pair of silver spike-heeled sandals when a fist pounded on her bedroom door. Her brother's voice shouted, "Better get moving. Riley and Lise will kill you if you're late."

Violet rolled her eyes in the mirror. She was almost ready. I only had to change when we got to Winters House.

Plenty of time. I stared at the curve of her ass, barely covered by sheer black lace, and reminded myself that there was plenty of time, but not that much. Not enough to peel the lace down her legs and... Later.

Later.

"Stay with me tonight."

"Just tonight," she agreed.

"For now. Just tonight. We'll see about the rest tomorrow."

Wisely, Violet ignored me and finished getting dressed, though she did throw a few things in a small bag to bring with us. I'd take my victories where I could get them.

She wanted time. I'd give her time.

I'd court her and woo her and show her that I could be the man she wanted. The man she deserved. And when she believed, when she really trusted me again, I'd make her mine forever.

Epilogue
Violet

It turns out, Aiden and I had different definitions of dating. I thought we'd go out to dinner. Go to the movies. And sex. I assumed there'd be sex.

Sex was about the only common element between my idea of dating and Aiden's. My version of dating included Aiden picking me up at my door, taking me somewhere suitable, and dropping me off at the end of the evening. Simple. Classic.

Aiden's version varied widely, but it was rarely simple, and it almost always involved my spending the night. In Winters House. In a hotel room. Sometimes that hotel room was in Paris. Or London. Once, it was in Tokyo. Tokyo. Who goes to Tokyo on a date? Apparently, Aiden Winters does. Before Aiden, I'd only used my passport once, on a short trip to Canada with my mother.

I tried to stay firm on my resolve not to move into Winters House. At first, I compromised with both Aiden and my brother and agreed to stay in Chase's condo. Chase wanted me there because he had the ridiculous idea that I shouldn't live alone in the big city.

Cue my eye roll.

Aiden, because he didn't want me to sign a lease he was sure he could convince me to break. I was too smart to bet against Aiden, and I didn't really want to move twice, so I'd stayed put.

Night by night, date by date, more of my things had made their way into Aiden's suite in Winters House. The first time Mrs. W consulted with me on the grocery list Aunt Amelia had snickered and said, "You might as well just pack your things and move in, Violet. If Aiden doesn't talk you into it, Helen will."

Aunt Amelia was the only one who called Mrs. W by her first name, Helen, and it was a mystery how she got away with it when the two of them didn't quite get along.

That was just one of the mysteries of the Winters family. They were a lot to get used to, especially after growing up in such a different household. In the Westbrook home, quiet obedience was prized. Not at Winters House. They were loud and argumentative and nosy. And fun. Almost always, they were fun.

Aiden got his way by the end of the summer, but not because I agreed to move out of Chase's condo. I was tricked into it. In a way. Chase and Lucas had hit it off. Maybe it was because they were both outsiders. Lucas and Riley were already tight, partly because they worked together at Sinclair Security, and Chase fit right in.

He started hanging around Lucas and Charlie's renovations after work and on weekends, helping out here and there. He'd always loved learning new things. I think after spending all day in front of a computer terminal, Chase liked the chance to work with his hands.

He liked it so much, he ended up falling head over heels for a run-down cottage they'd bought after it went into foreclosure. The place was a mess, but it was within walking distance of the shops and restaurants on Highland Avenue, was on a decent sized lot, and had an oversized detached garage that could double as a guest house or home office.

Lucas and Charlie planned to have it ready to move into by early fall. Everything was going right on schedule until Chase's condo sold faster than we'd expected and there was a delay on materials for the new house. Suddenly, Chase and I were homeless.

We moved into Winters House temporarily. Well, temporarily for Chase. By the time his new place was done, we'd been living in Winters House for over a month. All of my things were there. For the first time in years, I felt like I was home.

Even Chase told me to stay put. He'd been showing me around the new house when he'd stopped in the kitchen and said, "You're not coming, right? You're going to stay with Winters?"

Relieved that he wasn't going to argue about it, I said, "I think so. I want to. Why? Do you think I should? Or are you just trying to get rid of me so you can be alone with your new girlfriend?"

He'd scowled before rolling his eyes. "She's not my girlfriend. Yet."

He was having a hard time convincing the object of his affection to give him a chance. She was gun shy, but Chase was persistent. My money was on him. No woman could resist my brother for long. He'd win her over. Eventually.

He poked me in the arm. "I don't need to get rid of you to get the girl. Any woman who wants to ditch my baby sister isn't the right one for me." Then, more seriously, "You know I always have a place for you. Always. But Winters loves you. He's going to ask you to marry him. I don't know why he hasn't yet. And I know you don't want to move out. Just make it easy and stay where you are."

So I did.

Aiden and I were slowly working out a rhythm. He was who he was. I called him the king of the universe as a joke, but I wasn't far off. When I really thought about the number of people who depended on him for their livelihood —not just the employees of Winters, Inc., who numbered in the tens of thousands, but the businesses that relied on his company through complex agreements and contracts—the amount of responsibility was mind-boggling.

It was my mission in life to force him to put his crown aside and just be a man.

That didn't mean we didn't argue. Constantly. He tried. He really tried. And he was learning to compromise. In one of the biggest ironies of my life, I'd landed my dream job and it ended up being with WGC, Winters Gaming Corp., the gaming and technology company run by Aiden's youngest brother Holden and youngest cousin Tate.

Who would have guessed that a tech company would require a snail mail application? In fact, it was the very application that had led me to the contract hidden in Aiden's desk and LeAnne Gates. After that disaster, I'd completely forgotten about the stamped envelope I'd left sitting on Aiden's desk. Mrs. W had mailed it and I'd been called in for an interview.

It turned out WGC had issues with corporate espionage. Their flagship game was a huge seller and competitors would do almost anything to find out what was coming up. Even for a position like bookkeeper they did their hiring off-site and through an intermediary. I didn't know who the job offer came from until I'd signed an ironclad nondisclosure agreement.

When I found out, I'd assumed Aiden was behind it and I'd been furious. He'd been as surprised as me. Holden and Tate were the only ones who had any idea I'd applied for the job, and they knew exactly who I was when they offered it to me.

I hadn't been sure about taking it. On one hand, the salary and benefits were good, and the flexible hours would let me go back to school part-time. On the other hand, I wasn't comfortable accepting favors in the form of employment. Holden and Tate swore I was the best qualified applicant, but I wasn't sure I believed them.

In the end, I took the job. I'd been there five months and it was everything I hoped it would be. WGC was laid back, the employees dedicated and passionate, with a sense of humor. Half the time they acted like work was play and it made every day in the office entertaining.

Two days a week I commuted to Athens, an hour away, and attended classes towards my Master's Degree in Accountancy at the University of Georgia. My compromise was the car and driver Aiden sent with me. I'd insisted I could take the bus. In fact, we'd had a knockdown, drag-out fight about it.

Providing me with a car and driver was a ridiculous waste of money, in my opinion. I could drive myself, but the bus gave me two hours a day to study. Aiden pointed out that I could do that far more comfortably in the spacious backseat of his Bentley.

It was Charlie, the master of fighting with Aiden, who tipped the balance. We'd been arguing—again—our disagreement getting more heated as the fall semester grew closer, until she pulled me aside and said, using the nickname she'd picked up from Chase, "Vivi, choose your battles. Don't waste your energy on the car thing. Let him have his way and fight him on something really worthwhile. Trust me. It works better if you save your disagreements until you really need them. Do you want to take the bus that badly?"

"But it's a waste of money," I'd protested.

It was one thing when Aiden was with me. Then I didn't question the private plane or the hotel suites. But this was different. This was just me. I was perfectly fine taking the bus.

Charlie just poked me in the shoulder and laughed. "Seriously? Not to Aiden. First of all, he's not even going to blink at what a car and driver costs two days a week. Second, he'd spend any amount of money to make sure that you're safe and comfortable. Let him. It's just money. He's got enough of it."

So I gave in. Charlie was right. Aiden didn't love me because I was a pushover. He loved me because I stood up to him, but there was nothing wrong with choosing my battles wisely. And I had to admit, if only to myself, that the Bentley was a whole lot more comfortable than the bus.

Really, after six months, we only had one ongoing issue. We couldn't settle on a plan for our wedding.

Not that Aiden had asked. Not formally. There was no ring and no date. I wasn't fishing for one. In my opinion it made more sense to wait at least a full year. Wasn't that the conventional wisdom? You should be with someone for all four seasons before you commit for life?

I couldn't help being cautious. I think Aiden worried that I still didn't trust him, but that wasn't it.

I struggled to put it into words. My whole life had changed. Before I met Aiden, I was adrift, tethered only to Chase, mostly alone in the world. And then there was Aiden and his big, messy, affectionate family. My life had been quiet and a little lonely. Overnight, it seemed, it was full, bursting with friends and love, so much so it felt like a dream.

A tiny part of me was afraid I'd wake up one morning and it would all be gone. Moving into Winters House, marrying Aiden—those things were so big. So permanent. So final. Deep in my heart, I feared taking that kind of step would break the spell and I'd wake up alone.

I hemmed and hawed on wedding ideas. Aiden's brother Jacob and his fiancée Abigail were in the final stages of planning the wedding to end all weddings. I knew I didn't want something like that.

I didn't know what I wanted. A small destination wedding? Something at Winters House? Winters House had seen its share of weddings in the last few years; Tate and Emily, Charlie and Lucas, Gage and Sophie, and most recently Annalise and Riley, though they'd married at their house in the woods and not in the main house.

I wanted something different. Not a big splashy society event—just the idea of that gave me the shudders—and not something at home.

Something different. I just couldn't figure out what that was.

I even had a dress. Crazy, I know. Who buys a dress before a proposal? Me, it turns out. I didn't mean to. Buying a wedding dress was the last thing on my mind when I joined Abigail, Charlie, Maggie, Sophie, Emily, Jo, and Annalise at the bridal shop to pick out bridesmaids dresses.

Abigail wanted her future sisters and cousins-in-law to make up her wedding party. The lot of us were quite a crowd. The shop was closed just for us, and there'd been champagne. A lot of champagne.

I blamed it on the discount. When the wedding dress of

my dreams was sixty percent off because of an almost invisible tear in the silk—it was like a sign from the heavens. I couldn't say no.

Annalise talked me into trying it on, and once I saw myself in the three-way mirror I knew this was my dress. Strapless white corded lace with a low back, the bodice sparkled with a spray of hand sewn beads. And the skirt... the skirt was a confection. Yards and yards of that delicate corded lace, it bloomed from the tight basque waistline, the train flowing behind me.

The dress was fit for a queen. Romantic and elegant, it made a statement. With my summer tan and my hair pinned up, I looked regal. Timeless. For the first time, looking at myself in the mirror, wearing that dress, I felt like I could be Aiden's bride.

The rest of the girls agreed, and I ended up with a wedding dress hidden in the back of Charlie's closet. She said she didn't trust Aiden not to peek and ruin the surprise. I'd agreed.

Time marched on, and still, we were in limbo. Just before Christmas, Aiden talked me into a long weekend in Las Vegas. He had some details to wrap up for his project with Dylan Kane, and we both wanted to get away for a few days. This time I skipped the meeting with Dylan, opting to give myself an early Christmas gift of a spa day.

While Aiden went over reports and toured the site, I got a massage, some kind of seaweed mud wrap thing, a facial and a mani-pedi. By the time I wandered back to our suite in my robe I was relaxed and glowing.

Aiden was waiting for me, along with a chilled bottle of champagne and that same Harry Connick Jr song we'd danced to all those months ago. Before I could think about changing out of my robe, he took my hand and pulled me into his arms.

That was Aiden. He still worked too much, though he was getting better, but he never forgot to take the time for romance. We danced, my cheek against his chest, his arms holding me close. The song ended too soon. I expected another, but the room fell silent.

Aiden dropped to his knee. My heart went crazy in my chest, pounding so hard the rush of it filled my ears. I'd been waiting forever, and still some part of me hadn't believed this moment would come.

Reaching into his pocket, he pulled out a small black velvet box. His fingers wrapped around mine, pulling them to his lips for a kiss.

"Say yes."

A smile curled my lips. Typical Aiden.

"Not until you ask," I countered.

"Be mine, Violet. I want to spend every day of my life making you as happy as you make me. Say yes."

He still hadn't asked, but I could let it slide. Usually, I was more than happy to bust his chops, but not now. Not for this.

Aiden didn't have to ask. I was already his. There was no man I'd ever love the way I loved Aiden. I thought about teasing him a little longer, but the emotion, the longing in his eyes, filled my soul, and I said the only word in my heart.

"Yes."

He rose to his feet, flipping the lid on the velvet box. Still holding my fingers in his hand, he worked the ring free and tossed the box on a nearby table. My mouth went dry when I got a good look at the ring.

I hadn't thought about the ring. Not really. The dress,

absolutely. But not the ring. If I had, I wouldn't have imagined this. A brilliant round center stone surrounded by a geometric bezel frame on a micropavé band, every bit of the ring sparkled.

The frame and band were set with small glittering diamonds and the center stone was...let's just say it was big. Really big. The round stone and the angles of the surrounding frame had an art deco look, as if the ring was from the twenties.

Aiden slid it on the ring finger of my left hand. "It was my mother's, and my grandmother's before her. Now it's yours."

"What about..." I didn't want to say her name, not in the middle of Aiden's proposal, but he *had* been married before.

He shook his head. "I never even thought of it. I should have known it was a mistake when I never considered giving her this ring. And with you, I never thought of anything else. I imagined you wearing this ring the last time we were in this room."

"You didn't," I murmured, transfixed by the sight of all those diamonds on my finger. This was more than a ring. It was his legacy. His history. Our future.

"I did. You were trying to figure out how to get away from me, and I was already planning to keep you."

I laughed a little, dizzy with love, happiness fizzing in my veins like champagne. Aiden hit a button on his phone to restart the music and pulled me close. His lips grazing my temple, we swayed together.

"If you want, we can do it here. Tomorrow."

Startled, I leaned back. He was serious. "But the family and..."

"They're here. Charlie has your dress."

I just stared at him, completely at a loss for words. They were here? Charlie had my dress? How long had he been planning this? Before I could get my thoughts together, Aiden explained.

"If this isn't what you want, we'll figure out something else. Anything. But if you want to get married now, Dylan reserved the garden chapel. I checked it out this afternoon. It's beautiful—stained glass and flowers. I took pictures for you."

"What if this isn't what I want? What if I want to wait?"

Aiden pressed his mouth to mine in a slow, sweet kiss. "Then we'll wait. We'll make a party of this weekend and take our time deciding exactly what you want for your wedding."

"But you want this?" Everything was moving so fast, I couldn't quite catch up.

"I want you to be my wife. That's it. I'd prefer to do it sooner rather than later, but I can wait if that's what you need. I would have married you months ago if I hadn't thought the idea would scare you away."

A laugh bubbled up. "It might have." I looked at the sparkle of the ring on my finger, brilliant against Aiden's dark suit coat. Then I looked into his warm, brown eyes, so full of love.

I didn't want to wait either. And I didn't want a big wedding. I just wanted Aiden and our family. And I wanted it now. This weekend. Here.

"Yes," I said, the laugh still caught in my voice. "Yes. Let's do it now. Everyone's really here?"

"They got here this afternoon. I had to charter an extra plane, but we managed to get everyone. My family, Chase, Annabelle, the Sinclairs."

"Perfect. That's perfect." I didn't need to see pictures of the chapel. I trusted Aiden. And this was exactly right. We didn't need a fuss, we just needed our family and each other.

"Where are they now?" I asked, looking around, half expecting the whole crew to jump out and surprise me.

"I don't know, and I don't care." Aiden swept me up into his arms, just as he had that first night in this room, and he carried me off to bed. "Tomorrow you can celebrate with our families. Tonight, you're all mine."

And I was. That night, the next, and every night that came after.

Thank you for reading Aiden & Violet's story!

But what about Chase?

If you want to read The Counterfeit Billionaire, turn the page!

SNEAK PEEK

THE COUNTERFEIT BILLIONAIRE

CHAPTER ONE

Chase

"We have a problem."

We have a problem. Those were the last words I wanted to hear from Charlie Winters.

I didn't need a problem. I already had enough of those as it was.

I leaned back in my chair, crossing my arms over my chest. "What kind of problem?"

I didn't have to ask. There were only a few possibilities.

It could be about the family. This was the least likely. Charlie is my half-siblings' cousin, and while that made us sort-of related, Charlie was never the chosen emissary of family news. She left that to her older brother Aiden.

It could have to do with my sister, Violet, who was dating Aiden and, if my guess was right, would be his fiancée any day now.

I know what you're thinking, but my sister dating my half-siblings' cousin isn't as weird as it sounds.

Okay, it *is* as weird as it sounds.

Maybe I should explain.

Here's the short version: Violet and I grew up not knowing we'd been adopted. The Winters grew up not knowing one of their own had been given up for adoption as an infant.

I'd discovered the truth at eighteen, but I told no one, not even Violet.

You're probably thinking that's weird, too. Why didn't I go straight to the Winters and claim my birthright? They're disgustingly rich, obscenely powerful, and a piece of that should have been mine.

I didn't want it.

I have my reasons. And I've made my way pretty damn well without their influence.

But now, because I'd been careless, the Winters had discovered me and Violet had fallen in love with the head of the entire clan, Aiden Winters.

So here I was, smack in the middle of the family I'd been avoiding since I'd discovered they existed. And now Charlie Winters had a problem.

I fought the urge to sigh.

Charlie is a spitfire. Younger than me, she's the princess of the Winters clan, a workaholic vice president at Winters, Inc. until Aiden fired her.

Once she'd gotten past her anger, she'd realized she hated working for the company and had gone into business renovating houses with her husband Lucas.

Which brought us to option number three. The problem was my house. I did not want the problem to be my house.

I hadn't meant to buy a house.

I definitely hadn't meant to buy a ramshackle pseudo-

Victorian cottage in the Virginia Highlands neighborhood of Atlanta. I had a perfectly nice condo in Midtown, thank you very much.

But I liked to hang out with Charlie's husband Lucas, who worked with her on their renovations when he wasn't running his division of scary hackers at Sinclair Security.

I'd taken to stopping by their latest project and chipping in when I was tired of staring at a computer screen. I'm a coder and a serial start-up addict. I can fall into my laptop for hours on end, but when I surface, I like to get my hands dirty.

Lucas and Charlie were always glad for the help. One afternoon in early July I'd gone along with Lucas to see a foreclosure.

Mistake.

I never thought the first time I fell in love it would be with a house. I'd wanted it. I'd needed it. It was made for me. Well, except for the part where it was falling down around our ears.

But I'd loved the tiny lot, walking distance to Highland Avenue and shaded with old growth trees. I'd loved the peaked gables of the roof and the detached garage with a studio above that would make the perfect home office.

I'd been instantly at home in the wide-open kitchen, bathed from the light streaming in through the tall windows.

The idea of owning it had gone straight to my head. Before I knew it, I was buying the place, hiring Charlie and Lucas to fix it up, and putting my condo on the market.

I did not have time for a problem. The condo was in a hot location and I'd sold it for above my asking price after an insane bidding war. We closed in two weeks.

The plumbing fixtures were supposed to be installed in

the studio today, and Violet and I planned to camp out there until the woodwork and other finish carpentry was done in the main house.

Our bags were packed, stacks of boxes waiting for the moving van. A problem was not on the schedule.

Charlie tucked one of her auburn curls behind her ear and gave me the same grin she used on Aiden when she wanted to get out of trouble. I didn't envy him raising this one.

I liked Charlie. She was fun, a smart-ass, and one of my favorite Winters. According to her brothers, she'd also been a handful as a teenager.

At least my Vivi had been a sweetheart. She didn't start giving me older brother heart attacks until...well, right about the time she met Aiden Winters.

"Don't try the cute grin on me, Charlie. Just don't tell me it's the house."

Charlie's grin dissolved, and she adjusted the papers on her clipboard, rearranging them and tapping them neatly on the edge before re-fastening them in place, avoiding my eyes.

"Well, see, the thing is... Remember that quarter-sawn oak that we special ordered for the living room and the entry?"

I nodded. When she'd shown me the difference in the grains between regular and quarter-sawn oak I'd had to have the quarter-sawn, though I'd balked a little at the difference in cost. I could guess what Charlie was getting at.

"There's a delay."

"There was a mix-up with the shipments and the one that was supposed to go to us ended up going to another project. It's going to be at least three to four weeks."

Before I could say anything, Charlie held up a finger.

"Unfortunately, that's not the only problem. We had a delay on the appliances for your kitchen, and the fixtures for the bathroom in the studio. I know you and Violet were planning on staying there while the woodwork was finished, but we're not going to be able to get a C.O. by the time you close on the condo."

"And we can't live there without the Certificate of Occupancy? Even if we don't tell anyone?"

"Chase, you won't want to. There's no bathroom. Maybe you're okay peeing in the yard, but do you think Vivi's going to like that?"

She wasn't wrong. My sister was tough, but she liked her creature comforts. She would not be happy with a sleeping bag on an unfinished floor and no bathroom.

"Charlie, you're killing me here. Violet and I are all packed up. We've got to be out of the condo by the beginning of next week," I said, trying to work out the logistics in my head while I glared at Charlie, who managed to look sheepish.

"I can't believe the first time a job really goes sideways and it's yours," Charlie said, shaking her head.

A suspicion tugged at me, and I couldn't stop myself from asking, "Does Aiden have anything to do with this?"

Charlie burst out laughing, the sound light and irreverent.

"I wouldn't put it past him. You know how he's been scheming to get Violet to move in with him, but I swear this is ordinary bad luck. I'm really sorry. At least you have a place to go. There's plenty of room at Winters House for both of you. You can stay there until your place is ready. I promise it won't be that long."

I wasn't sure I believed her about Aiden. I'd learned he was honest to a fault, but he was also determined to talk

Vivi into living with him. She was equally determined to take things slow.

Heads of state folded in the face of Aiden Winters' hard glare, but my Vivi put her hands on her hips and glared right back.

Usually, I'd be on her side. I was, mostly. But I also knew she loved Aiden to the depths of her heart. She belonged with him. She was just scared.

All she needed was a nudge. Maybe this was it.

Still, I hated the idea of moving into Winters House. My relationship with the Winters family was a hell of a lot more complicated than my sister's, and the idea of packing up my suitcases and installing myself in one of their lavish guest suites didn't sit right.

Ever since they'd discovered Anna Winters had given up her child at birth, they'd been looking for me. The Winters children had lost too much family in their short lives.

First Anna and James Winters in what the police had called a murder/suicide. Then Hugh and Olivia Winters had died in a nearly identical crime years later.

So much loss. So much death.

The remaining Winters were eager to hold on to any scrap of family they could find. Even the bastard son who'd been tossed aside the moment he'd been born.

They'd been looking for me, but I hadn't wanted anything to do with them.

I'll admit, I might have been wrong about that.

I'd imagined Anna as a desperate social climber who'd gotten rid of me so I wouldn't interfere with her pursuit of James Winters and the wealth he could give her.

In my mind, my half-siblings and their cousins had been

spoiled, entitled brats who would sneer at the idea I had any claim on such a lofty family.

Instead, they weren't that different than anyone else. Private jet and mansion aside, they were honest, loyal, and not the least bit superficial.

They'd suffered the worst losses imaginable at a young age, and every one of them knew what was important in life.

Love and family.

Not money.

Not power.

Love. Family.

They were good people. I was glad as hell my sister had found a man like Aiden to watch out for her, glad she'd been welcomed into the family with open arms.

I just wasn't sure I wanted to be welcomed along with her.

They all wanted to pretend the past was as simple as Anna giving me up and them finding me years later. Everyone wanted to talk about my mother. About Anna.

No one wanted to talk about my father. Anna might have been beloved, but the man whose seed created me had destroyed all of their lives.

Evil.

There was no other word for William Davis. He'd been responsible for Anna and James' deaths. He'd killed Hugh and Olivia himself. And he'd come so close to killing my half-sister, Annalise, it was a miracle she'd survived.

That man, that monster, was my biological father.

The Winters family thought we could brush that aside.

I knew they were wrong.

Now I'd have to move in with them, to pretend we were the fucking Brady Bunch when we all knew my father was a lot less Mike Brady and a lot more Hannibal Lecter.

It wasn't my worst nightmare, but it was close.

If I didn't think it would hurt my sister's feelings, I'd get a hotel. Charlie must have seen what I was thinking because she said quietly, "Chase, it'll be okay. I know it's weird, but it's only for a few weeks. I swear. And if you hate it, you can come crash at our place."

She and Lucas lived in an arts and crafts house Charlie had restored. It was only a few blocks from my new place and I'd hung out there more than a few times.

I didn't answer, just shook my head. Still, in that quiet, soothing tone, Charlie ventured, "Maybe this is a good thing. I know you see Gage at the office, but that's work. We've all noticed you dodging the family. And I get it. I do. But there's no harm in getting to know us better, is there?"

Talk about loaded questions. Whether I liked it or not, Charlie's aunt was my mother. Her cousins were my half-siblings. There was nothing I could do to change that, so I might as well embrace it and take advantage of the opportunity to hang out with my family.

The logical side of my mind laid all that out while the rest of me wanted to take off running and never look back. Our history was complicated and dark and ugly.

Maybe they wanted to forget the past, but I didn't see how we could.

Also by Ivy Layne

Don't Miss Out on New Releases, Exclusive Giveaways, and More!!

Join Ivy's Readers Group @ ivylayne.com/readers

THE HEARTS OF SAWYERS BEND

Stolen Heart

Sweet Heart

Scheming Heart

Rebel Heart

Wicked Heart

THE UNTANGLED SERIES

Unraveled

Undone

Uncovered

The Winters Saga

The Billionaire's Secret Heart (Novella)

The Billionaire's Secret Love (Novella)

The Billionaire's Pet

The Billionaire's Promise

The Rebel Billionaire

The Billionaire's Secret Kiss (Novella)

The Billionaire's Angel

Engaging the Billionaire

Compromising the Billionaire

The Counterfeit Billionaire

The Billionaire Club

The Wedding Rescue

The Courtship Maneuver

The Temptation Trap

ABOUT IVY LAYNE

Ivy Layne has had her nose stuck in a book since she first learned to decipher the English language. Sometime in her early teens, she stumbled across her first Romance, and the die was cast. Though she pretended to pay attention to her creative writing professors, she dreamed of writing steamy romance instead of literary fiction. These days, she's neck deep in alpha heroes and the smart, sexy women who love them.

Married to her very own alpha hero (who rubs her back after a long day of typing, but also leaves his socks on the floor). Ivy lives in the mountains of North Carolina where she and her other half are having a blast raising two energetic little boys. Aside from her family, Ivy's greatest loves are coffee and chocolate, preferably together.

VISIT IVY

Facebook.com/AuthorIvyLayne
Instagram.com/authorivylayne/
www.ivylayne.com
books@ivylayne.com

Made in United States
Orlando, FL
24 August 2023